GONE FOR GOOD

Books by Harlan Coben

GONE FOR GOOD

A NOVEL BY

HARLAN COBEN

ORION

First published in Great Britain in 2002 by Orion Books
an imprint of The Orion Publishing Group
Orion House, 5 Upper St Martin's Lane, London WC2H 9EA

A CIP catalogue record for this book is available
from the British Library

ISBN (hardback) 0 75284 604 3
ISBN (trade paperback) 0 75284 605 1

Printed and bound in Great Britain by
Clays Ltd, St Ives plc

For Anne
A ma vie de coeur entier

GONE FOR GOOD

1

Three days before her death, my mother told me—these weren't her last words, but they were pretty close—that my brother was still alive.

That was all she said. She didn't elaborate. She said it only once. And she wasn't doing very well. Morphine had already applied its endgame heart squeeze. Her skin was in that cusp between jaundice and fading summer tan. Her eyes had sunken deep into her skull. She slept most of the time. She would, in fact, have only one more lucid moment—if indeed this had been a lucid moment, which I very much doubted—and that would be a chance for me to tell her that she had been a wonderful mother, that I loved her very much, and good-bye. We never said anything about my brother. That didn't mean we weren't thinking about him as though he were sitting bedside too.

"He's alive."

Those were her exact words. And if they were true, I didn't know if it would be a good thing or bad.

We buried my mother four days later.

When we returned to the house to sit shivah, my father stormed through the semi-shag in the living room. His face was red with rage. I was there, of course. My sister, Melissa, had flown in from Seattle with her husband, Ralph. Aunt Selma and Uncle Murray paced. Sheila, my soul mate, sat next to me and held my hand.

That was pretty much the sum total.

There was only one flower arrangement, a wonderful monster of a thing. Sheila smiled and squeezed my hand when she saw the card. No words, no message, just the drawing

Dad kept glancing out the bay windows—the same windows that had been shot out with a BB gun twice in the past eleven years—and muttered under his breath, "Sons of bitches." He'd turn around and think of someone else who hadn't shown. "For God's sake, you'd think the Bergmans would have at least made a goddamn appearance." Then he'd close his eyes and look away. The anger would consume him anew, blending with the grief into something I didn't have the strength to face.

One more betrayal in a decade filled with them.

I needed air.

I got to my feet. Sheila looked up at me with concern. "I'm going to take a walk," I said softly.

"You want company?"

"I don't think so."

Sheila nodded. We had been together nearly a year. I've never had a partner so in sync with my rather odd vibes. She gave my hand another I-love-you squeeze, and the warmth spread through me.

Our front-door welcome mat was harsh faux grass, like something stolen from a driving range, with a plastic daisy in the upper left-hand corner. I stepped over it and strolled up Downing Place. The street was lined with numbingly ordinary aluminum-sided split-levels, circa 1962. I still wore my dark gray suit. It itched in the heat. The savage sun beat down like a drum, and a perverse part of me thought that it was a wonderful day to decay. An image of my mother's light-the-world smile—the one before it all happened—flashed in front of my eyes. I shoved it away.

I knew where I was headed, though I doubt if I would have admitted it to myself. I was drawn there, pulled by some unseen force. Some would call it masochistic. Others would note that maybe it had something to do with closure. I thought it was probably neither.

I just wanted to look at the spot where it all ended.

The sights and sounds of summer suburbia assaulted me. Kids

squealed by on their bicycles. Mr. Cirino, who owned the Ford/ Mercury dealership on Route 10, mowed his lawn. The Steins— they'd built up a chain of appliance stores that were swallowed up by a bigger chain—were taking a stroll hand in hand. There was a touch football game going on at the Levines' house, though I didn't know any of the participants. Barbecue smoke took flight from the Kaufmans' backyard.

I passed by the Glassmans' old place. Mark "the Doof" Glassman had jumped through the sliding glass doors when he was six. He was playing Superman. I remembered the scream and the blood. He needed over forty stitches. The Doof grew up and became some kind of IPO-start-up zillionaire. I don't think they call him the Doof anymore, but you never know.

The Marianos' house, still that horrid shade of phlegm yellow with a plastic deer guarding the front walk, was on the bend. Angela Mariano, our local bad girl, was two years older than us and like some superior, awe-inducing species. Watching Angela sunning in her backyard in a gravity-defying ribbed halter top, I had felt the first painful thrusts of deep hormonal longing. My mouth would actually water. Angela used to fight with her parents and sneak smokes in the toolshed behind her house. Her boyfriend drove a motorcycle. I ran into her last year on Madison Avenue in midtown. I expected her to look awful—that was what you always hear happens to that first lust-crush—but Angela looked great and seemed happy.

A lawn sprinkler did the slow wave in front of Eric Frankel's house at 23 Downing Place. Eric had a space-travel-themed bar mitzvah at the Chanticleer in Short Hills when we were both in seventh grade. The ceiling was done up planetarium style—a black sky with star constellations. My seating card told me that I was sitting at "Table Apollo 14." The centerpiece was an ornate model rocket on a green fauna launching pad. The waiters, adorned in realistic space suits, were each supposed to be one of the Mercury 7. "John Glenn" served us. Cindi Shapiro and I had sneaked into the chapel room and made out for over an hour. It was my first time. I didn't know what I was doing. Cindi did. I remember it was glorious, the way her tongue caressed and jolted me in unexpected ways. But I also remember my initial wonderment evolving after twenty minutes or so into, well, boredom—a confused "what next?" along with a naïve "is that all there is?"

When Cindi and I stealthily returned to Cape Kennedy's Table Apollo 14, ruffled and in fine post-smooch form (the Herbie Zane

Band serenading the crowd with "Fly Me to the Moon"), my brother, Ken, pulled me to the side and demanded details. I, of course, too gladly gave them. He awarded me with that smile and slapped me five. That night, as we lay on the bunk beds, Ken on the top, me on the bottom, the stereo playing Blue Oyster Cult's "Don't Fear the Reaper" (Ken's favorite), my older brother explained to me the facts of life as seen by a ninth-grader. I'd later learn he was mostly wrong (a little too much emphasis on the breast), but when I think back to that night, I always smile.

"He's alive. . . ."

I shook my head and turned right at Coddington Terrace by the Holders' old house. This was the same route Ken and I had taken to get to Burnet Hill Elementary School. There used to be a paved path between two houses to make the trip shorter. I wondered if it was still there. My mother—everyone, even kids, had called her Sunny—used to follow us to school quasi-surreptitiously. Ken and I would roll our eyes as she ducked behind trees. I smiled, thinking about her overprotectiveness now. It used to embarrass me, but Ken would simply shrug. My brother was securely cool enough to let it slide. I wasn't.

I felt a pang and moved on.

Maybe it was just my imagination, but people began to stare. The bicycles, the dribbling basketballs, the sprinklers and lawn mowers, the cries of touch footballers—they all seemed to hush as I passed. Some stared out of curiosity because a strange man strolling in a dark gray suit on a summer evening was something of an oddity. But most, or again so it seemed, looked on in horror because they recognized me and couldn't believe that I would dare tread upon this sacred soil.

I approached the house at 47 Coddington Terrace without hesitation. My tie was loosened. I jammed my hands in my pockets. I toed the spot where curb met pavement. Why was I here? I saw a curtain move in the den. Mrs. Miller's face appeared at the window, gaunt and ghostlike. She glared at me. I didn't move or look away. She glared some more—and then to my surprise, her face softened. It was as though our mutual agony had made some sort of connection. Mrs. Miller nodded at me. I nodded back and felt the tears begin to well up.

———

4

You may have seen the story on *20/20* or *PrimeTime Live* or some other television equivalent of fish wrap. For those who haven't, here's the official account: On October 17 eleven years ago, in the township of Livingston, New Jersey, my brother, Ken Klein, then twenty-four, brutally raped and strangled our neighbor Julie Miller.

In her basement. At 47 Coddington Terrace.

That was where her body was found. The evidence wasn't conclusive as to if she'd actually been murdered in that poorly finished subdwelling or if she'd been dumped postmortem behind the water-stained zebra-striped couch. Most assume the former. My brother escaped capture and ran off to parts unknown—at least, again, according to the official account.

Over the past eleven years, Ken has eluded an international dragnet. There have however been "sightings."

The first came about a year after the murder from a small fishing village in northern Sweden. Interpol swooped in, but somehow my brother evaded their grasp. Supposedly he was tipped off. I can't imagine how or by whom.

The next sighting occurred four years later in Barcelona. Ken had rented—to quote the newspaper accounts—"an oceanview hacienda" (Barcelona is not on an ocean) with—again I will quote—"a lithe, dark-haired woman, perhaps a flamenco dancer." A vacationing Livingston resident, no less, reported seeing Ken and his Castilian paramour dining beachside. My brother was described as tan and fit and wore a white shirt opened at the collar and loafers without socks. The Livingstonite, one Rick Horowitz, had been a classmate of mine in Mr. Hunt's fourth-grade class. During a three-month period, Rick entertained us by eating caterpillars during recess.

Barcelona Ken yet again slipped through the law's fingers.

The last time my brother was purportedly spotted he was skiing down the expert hills in the French Alps (interestingly enough, Ken never skied before the murder). Nothing came of it, except a story on *48 Hours.* Over the years, my brother's fugitive status had become the criminal version of a VH1 *Where Are They Now?*, popping up whenever any sort of rumor skimmed the surface or, more likely, when one of the network's fish wraps was low on material.

I naturally hated television's "team coverage" of "suburbia gone wrong" or whatever similar cute moniker they came up with. Their "special reports" (just once, I'd like to see them call it a "normal report, everyone has done this story") always featured the same photographs of Ken in his tennis whites—he was a nationally ranked player at one time—looking his most pompous. I can't imagine where they got them. In them Ken looked handsome in that way people hate right away. Haughty, Kennedy hair, suntan bold against the whites, toothy grin, Photograph Ken looked like one of those people of privilege (he was not) who coasted through life on his charm (a little) and trust account (he had none).

I had appeared on one of those magazine shows. A producer reached me—this was pretty early on in the coverage—and claimed that he wanted to present "both sides fairly." They had plenty of people ready to lynch my brother, he noted. What they truly needed for the sake of "balance" was someone who could describe the "real Ken" to the folks back home.

I fell for it.

A frosted-blond anchorwoman with a sympathetic manner interviewed me for over an hour. I enjoyed the process actually. It was therapeutic. She thanked me and ushered me out and when the episode aired, they used only one snippet, removing her question ("But surely, you're not going to tell us that your brother was perfect, are you? You're not trying to tell us he was a saint, right?") and editing my line so that I appeared in nose-pore-enhancing extreme close-up with dramatic music as my cue, saying, "Ken was no saint, Diane."

Anyway, that was the official account of what happened.

I've never believed it. I'm not saying it's not possible. But I believe a much more likely scenario is that my brother is dead—that he has been dead for the past eleven years.

More to the point, my mother always believed that Ken was dead. She believed it firmly. Without reservation. Her son was not a murderer. Her son was a victim.

"He's alive. . . .He didn't do it."

The front door of the Miller house opened. Mr. Miller stepped through it. He pushed his glasses up his nose. His fists rested on his hips in a pitiful Superman stance.

"Get the hell out of here, Will," Mr. Miller said to me.

And I did.

The next big shock occurred an hour later.

Sheila and I were up in my parents' bedroom. The same furniture, a sturdy, faded swirling gray with blue trim, had adorned this room for as long as I could remember. We sat on the king-size bed with the weak-springed mattress. My mother's most personal items—the stuff she kept in her bloated nightstand drawers—were scattered over the duvet. My father was still downstairs by the bay windows, staring out defiantly.

I don't know why I wanted to sift through the things my mother found valuable enough to preserve and keep near her. It would hurt. I knew that. There is an interesting correlation between intentional pain infliction and comfort, a sort of playing-with-fire approach to grieving. I needed to do that, I guess.

I looked at Sheila's lovely face—tilted to the left, eyes down and focused—and I felt my heart soar. This is going to sound a little weird, but I could stare at Sheila for hours. It was not just her beauty—hers was not what one would call classical anyway, her features a bit off center from either genetics or, more likely, her murky past—but there was an animation there, an inquisitiveness, a delicacy too, as if one more blow would shatter her irreparably. Sheila made me want to—bear with me here—be brave for her.

Without looking up, Sheila gave a half-smile and said, "Cut it out."

"I'm not doing anything."

She finally looked up and saw the expression on my face. "What?" she asked.

I shrugged. "You're my world," I said simply.

"You're pretty hot stuff yourself."

"Yeah," I said. "Yeah, that's true."

She feigned a slap in my direction. "I love you, you know."

"What's not to love?"

She rolled her eyes. Then her gaze fell back onto the side of my mother's bed. Her face quieted.

"What are you thinking about?" I asked.

"Your mother." Sheila smiled. "I really liked her."

"I wish you had known her before."

"Me too."

We started going through the laminated yellow clippings. Birth announcements—Melissa's, Ken's, mine. There were articles on Ken's tennis exploits. His trophies, all those bronze men in miniature in mid-serve, still swarmed his old bedroom. There were photographs, mostly old ones from before the murder. Sunny. It had been my mother's nickname since childhood. It suited her. I found a photo of her as PTA president. I don't know what she was doing, but she was onstage and wearing a goofy hat and all the other mothers were cracking up. There was another one of her running the school fair. She was dressed in a clown suit. Sunny was the favorite grown-up among my friends. They liked when she drove the carpool. They wanted the class picnic at our house. Sunny was parental cool without being cloying, just "off" enough, a little crazy perhaps, so that you never knew exactly what she would do next. There had always been an excitement—a crackle if you will—around my mother.

We kept it up for more than two hours. Sheila took her time, looking thoughtfully at every picture. When she stopped at one in particular, her eyes narrowed. "Who's that?"

She handed me the photograph. On the left was my mother in a semi-obscene yellow bikini, I'd say, 1972ish, looking very curvy. She had her arm around a short man with a dark mustache and happy smile.

"King Hussein," I said.

"Pardon me?"

I nodded.

"As in the kingdom of Jordan?"

"Yep. Mom and Dad saw him at the Fontainebleau in Miami."

"And?"

"Mom asked him if he'd pose for a picture."

"You're kidding."

"There's the proof."

"Didn't he have guards or something?"

"I guess she didn't look armed."

Sheila laughed. I remember Mom telling me about the incident. Her posing with King Hussein, Dad's camera not working, his muttering under his breath, his trying to fix it, her glaring at him to hurry, the king standing patiently, his chief of security checking the camera, finding the problem, fixing it, handing it back to Dad.

My mom, Sunny.

"She was so lovely," Sheila said.

It's an awful cliché to say that a part of her died when they found Julie Miller's body, but the thing about clichés is that they're often dead-on. My mother's crackle quieted, smothered. After hearing about the murder, she never threw a tantrum or cried hysterically. I often wish she had. My volatile mother became frighteningly

8

even. Her whole manner became flat, monotone—*passionless* would be the best way to describe it—which in someone like her was more agonizing to witness than the most bizarre histrionics.

The front doorbell rang. I looked out the bedroom window and saw the Eppes-Essen deli delivery van. Sloppy joes for the, uh, mourners. Dad had optimistically ordered too many platters. Delusional to the end. He stayed in this house like the captain of the *Titanic*. I remember the first time the windows had been shot out with the BB gun not long after the murder—the way he shook his fist with defiance. Mom, I think, wanted to move. Dad would not. Moving would be a surrender in his eyes. Moving would be admitting their son's guilt. Moving would be a betrayal.

Dumb.

Sheila had her eyes on me. Her warmth was almost palpable, more sunbeam on my face, and for a moment I just let myself bathe in it. We'd met at work about a year before. I'm the senior director of Covenant House on 41st Street in New York City. We're a charitable foundation that helps young runaways survive the streets. Sheila had come in as a volunteer. She was from a small town in Idaho, though she seemed to have very little small-town girl left in her. She told me that many years ago, she too had been a runaway. That was all she would tell me about her past.

"I love you," I said.

"What's not to love?" she countered.

I did not roll my eyes. Sheila had been good to my mother toward the end. She'd take the Community Bus Line from Port Authority to Northfield Avenue and walk over to the St. Barnabas Medical Center. Before her illness, the last time my mom had stayed at St. Barnabas was when she delivered me. There was probably something poignantly life-cycling about that, but I couldn't see it just then.

I had however seen Sheila with my mother. And it made me wonder. I took a risk.

"You should call your parents," I said softly.

Sheila looked at me as though I'd just slapped her across the face. She slid off the bed.

"Sheila?"

"This isn't the time, Will."

I picked up a picture frame that held a photo of my tanned parents on vacation. "Seems as good as any."

"You don't know anything about my parents."

"I'd like to," I said.

She turned her back to me. "You've worked with runaways," she said.

"So?"

"You know how bad it can be."

I did. I thought again about her slightly off-center features—the nose, for example, with the telltale bump—and wondered. "I also know it's worse if you don't talk about it."

"I've talked about it, Will."

"Not with me."

"You're not my therapist."

"I'm the man you love."

"Yes." She turned to me. "But not now, okay? Please."

I had no response to that one, but perhaps she was right. My fingers were absently toying with the picture frame. And that was when it happened.

The photograph in the frame slid a little.

I looked down. Another photograph started peeking out from underneath. I moved the top one a little farther. A hand appeared in the bottom photograph. I tried pushing it some more, but it wouldn't go. My finger found the clips on back. I slid them to the side and let the back of the frame drop to the bed. Two photographs floated down behind it.

One—the top one—was of my parents on a cruise, looking happy and healthy and relaxed in a way I barely remember them ever being. But it was the second photograph, the hidden one, that caught my eye.

The red-stamped date on the bottom was from less than two years ago. The picture was taken atop a field or hill or something. I saw no houses in the background, just snowcapped mountains like something from the opening scene of *The Sound of Music*. The man in the picture wore shorts and a backpack and sunglasses and scuffed hiking boots. His smile was familiar. So was his face, though it was more lined now. His hair was longer. His beard had gray in it. But there was no mistake.

The man in the picture was my brother, Ken.

2

My father was alone on the back patio. Night had fallen. He sat very still and stared out at the black. As I came up behind him, a jarring memory rocked me.

About four months after Julie's murder, I found my father in the basement with his back to me just like this. He thought that the house was empty. Resting in his right palm was his Ruger, a .22 caliber gun. He cradled the weapon tenderly, as though it were a small animal, and I never felt so frightened in my entire life. I stood there, frozen. He kept his eyes on the gun. After a few long minutes, I quickly tiptoed to the top of the stairs and faked like I'd just come in. By the time I trudged down the steps, the weapon was gone.

I didn't leave his side for a week.

I slipped now through the sliding glass door. "Hey," I said to him.

He spun around, his face already breaking into a wide smile. He always had one for me. "Hey, Will," he said, the gravel voice turning tender. Dad was always happy to see his children. Before all this happened, my father was a fairly popular man. People liked him. He was friendly and dependable, if not a little gruff, which just made him seem all the more dependable. But while my father might smile at you, he didn't care a lick. His world was his family. No one else mattered to him. The suffering of strangers and even friends never really reached him—a sort of family-centeredness.

I sat in the lounge chair next to him, not sure how to raise the subject. I took a few deep breaths and listened to him do the same. I felt wonderfully safe with him. He might be older and more withered, and by now I was the taller, stronger man—but I knew that if trouble surfaced, he'd still step up and take the hit for me.

And that I'd still slip back and let him.

"Have to cut that branch back," he said, pointing into the dark.

I couldn't see it. "Yeah," I said.

The light from the sliding glass doors hit his profile. The anger had dissolved now, and the shattered look had returned. Sometimes I think that he had indeed tried to step up and take the hit when Julie died, but it had knocked him on his ass. His eyes still had that burst-from-within look, that look of someone who had unexpectedly been punched in the gut and didn't know why.

"You okay?" he asked me. His standard opening refrain.

"I'm fine. I mean, not fine but . . ."

Dad waved his hand. "Yeah, dumb question," he said.

We fell back into silence. He lit a cigarette. Dad never smoked at home. His children's health and all that. He took a drag and then, as if suddenly remembering, he looked at me and stamped it out.

"It's all right," I said.

"Your mother and I agreed that I would never smoke at home."

I didn't argue with him. I folded my hands and put them on my lap. Then I dived in. "Mom told me something before she died."

His eyes slid toward me.

"She said that Ken was still alive."

Dad stiffened, but only for a second. A sad smile came to his face. "It was the drugs, Will."

"That's what I thought," I said. "At first."

"And now?"

I looked at his face, searching for some sign of deception. There had been rumors, of course. Ken wasn't wealthy. Many wondered how my brother could have afforded to live in hiding for so long. My answer, of course, was that he hadn't—that he died that night too. Others, maybe most people, believed that my parents somehow sneaked him money.

I shrugged. "I wonder why after all these years she would say that."

"The drugs," he repeated. "And she was dying, Will."

12

The second part of that answer seemed to encompass so much. I let it hang a moment. Then I asked, "Do you think Ken's alive?"

"No," he said. And then he looked away.

"Did Mom say anything to you?"

"About your brother?"

"Yes."

"Pretty much what she told you," he said.

"That Ken was alive?"

"Yes."

"Anything else?"

Dad shrugged. "She said he didn't kill Julie. She said he'd be back by now except he had to do something first."

"Do what?"

"She wasn't making sense, Will."

"Did you ask her?"

"Of course. But she was just ranting. She couldn't hear me anymore. I shushed her. I told her it'd be okay."

He looked away again. I thought about showing him the photograph of Ken but decided against it. I wanted to think it through before I started us down that path.

"I told her it'd be okay," he repeated.

Through the sliding glass door, I could see one of those photo cubes, the old color images sun-faded into a blur of yellow-green. There were no recent pictures in the room. Our house was trapped in a time warp, frozen solid eleven years ago, like in that old song where the grandfather clock stops when the old man dies.

"I'll be right back," Dad said.

I watched him stand and walk until he thought he was out of sight. But I could see his outline in the dark. I saw him lower his head. His shoulders started to shake. I don't think that I had ever seen my father cry. I didn't want to start now.

I turned away and remembered the other photograph, the one still upstairs of my parents on the cruise looking tan and happy, and I wondered if maybe he was thinking about that too.

When I woke late that night, Sheila wasn't in bed.

I sat up and listened. Nothing. At least, not in the apartment. I could hear the normal late-night street hum drifting up from three

13

floors below. I looked over toward the bathroom. The light was out. All lights, in fact, were out.

I thought about calling out to her, but there was something fragile about the quiet, something bubblelike. I slipped out of bed. My feet touched down on the wall-to-wall carpet, the kind apartment buildings make you use so as to stifle noise from below or above.

The apartment wasn't big, just one bedroom. I padded toward the living room and peeked in. Sheila was there. She sat on the windowsill and looked down toward the street. I stared at her back, the swan neck, the wonderful shoulders, the way her hair flowed down the white skin, and again I felt the stir. Our relationship was still on the border of the early throes, the gee-it's-great-to-be-alive love where you can't get enough of each other, that wonderful run-across-the-park-to-see-her stomach-flutter that you know, *know*, would soon darken into something richer and deeper.

I'd been in love only once before. And that was a very long time ago.

"Hey," I said.

She turned just a little, but it was enough. There were tears on her cheeks. I could see them sliding down in the moonlight. She didn't make a sound—no cries or sobs or hitching chest. Just the tears. I stayed in the doorway and wondered what I should do.

"Sheila?"

On our second date, Sheila performed a card trick. It involved my picking two cards, putting them in the middle of the deck while she turned her head, and her throwing the entire deck save my two cards onto the floor. She smiled widely after performing this feat, holding up the two cards for my inspection. I smiled back. It was—how to put this?—goofy. Sheila was indeed goofy. She liked card tricks and cherry Kool-Aid and boy bands. She sang opera and read voraciously and cried at Hallmark commercials. She could do a mean imitation of Homer Simpson and Mr. Burns, though her Smithers and Apu were on the weak side. And most of all, Sheila loved to dance. She loved to close her eyes and put her head on my shoulder and fade away.

"I'm sorry, Will," Sheila said without turning around.

"For what?" I said.

She kept her eyes on the view. "Go back to bed. I'll be there in a few minutes."

I wanted to stay or offer up words of comfort. I didn't. She wasn't reachable right now. Something had pulled her away. Words or action would be either superfluous or harmful. At least, that was what I told myself. So I made a huge mistake. I went back to bed and waited.

But Sheila never came back.

3

Morty Meyer was in bed, dead asleep on his back, when he felt the gun muzzle against his forehead.

"Wake up," a voice said.

Morty's eyes went wide. The bedroom was dark. He tried to raise his head, but the gun held him down. His gaze slid toward the illuminated clock-radio on the night table. But there was no clock there. He hadn't owned one in years, now that he thought about it. Not since Leah died. Not since he'd sold the four-bedroom colonial.

"Hey, I'm good for it," Morty said. "You guys know that."

"Get up."

The man moved the gun away. Morty lifted his head. With his eyes adjusting, he could make out a scarf over the man's face. Morty remembered the radio program *The Shadow* from his childhood. "What do you want?"

"I need your help, Morty."

"We know each other?"

"Get up."

Morty obeyed. He swung his legs out of bed. When he stood, his head reeled in protest. He staggered, caught in that place where the drunk-buzz is winding down and the hangover is gathering strength like an oncoming storm.

"Where's your medical bag?" the man asked.

Relief flooded Morty's veins. So that was what this was about. Morty looked for a wound, but it was too dark. "You?" he asked.

"No. She's in the basement."

She?

Morty reached under the bed and pulled out his leather medical bag. It was old and worn. His initials, once shiny in gold leaf, were gone now. The zipper didn't close all the way. Leah had bought it when he'd graduated from Columbia University's medical school more than forty years before. He'd been an internist in Great Neck for the three decades following that. He and Leah had raised three boys. Now here he was, approaching seventy, living in a one-bedroom dump and owing money and favors to pretty much everyone.

Gambling. That'd been Morty's addiction of choice. For years, he'd been something of a functioning gambleholic, fraternizing with those particular inner demons yet keeping them on the fringe. Eventually, however, the demons caught up to him. They always do. Some had claimed that Leah had been a facilitator. Maybe that was true. But once she died, there was no reason to fight anymore. He let the demons claw in and do their worst.

Morty had lost everything, including his medical license. He moved out west to this shithole. He gambled pretty much every night. His boys—all grown and with families—didn't call him anymore. They blamed him for their mother's death. They said that he'd aged Leah before her time. They were probably right.

"Hurry," the man said.

"Right."

They started down the basement stairs. Morty could see the light was on. This building, his crappy new abode, used to be a funeral home. Morty rented a bedroom on the ground floor. That gave him use of the basement—where the bodies used to be stored and embalmed.

In the basement's back corner, a rusted playground slide ran down from the back parking lot. That was how they used to bring the bodies down—park-'n-slide. The walls were blanketed with tiles, though many were crumbling from years of neglect. You had to use a pair of pliers to get the water running. Most of the cabinet doors were gone. The death stench still hovered, an old ghost refusing to leave.

The injured woman was lying on a steel table. Morty could see right away that this didn't look good. He turned back to the Shadow.

"Help her," he said.

17

Morty didn't like the timbre of the man's voice. There was anger there, yes, but the overriding emotion was naked desperation, his voice more a plea than anything else. "She doesn't look good," Morty said.

The man pressed the gun against Morty's chest. "If she dies, you die."

Morty swallowed. Clear enough. He moved toward her. Over the years, he'd treated plenty of men down here—but this would be the first woman. That was how Morty made his quasi-living. Stitch and run. If you go to an emergency room with a bullet or stab wound, the doctor on duty had a legal obligation to report it. So they came instead to Morty's makeshift hospital.

He flashed back to the triage lessons of medical school. The ABCs, if you will. Airway, Breathing, Circulation. Her breaths were raspy and filled with spittle.

"You did this to her?"

The man did not reply.

Morty worked on her the best he could. Patchwork really. Get her stabilized, he thought. Stabilized and out of here.

When he was done, the man lifted her gently. "If you say any-thing—"

"I've been threatened by worse."

The man hurried out with the woman. Morty stayed in the basement. His nerves felt frayed from the surprise wake-up. He sighed and decided to head back to bed. But before he went up the stairs, Morty Meyer made a crucial error.

He looked out the back window.

The man carried the woman to the car. He carefully, almost tenderly, laid her down in the back. Morty watched the scene. And then he saw movement.

He squinted. And that was when he felt the shudder rip through him.

Another passenger.

There was a passenger in the back of the car. A passenger who very much did not belong. Morty automatically reached for the phone, but before he even picked up the receiver, he stopped. Who would he call? What would he say?

Morty closed his eyes, fought it off. He trudged back up the steps. He crawled back into bed and pulled the covers up over him. He stared at the ceiling and tried to forget.

4

The note Sheila left me was short and sweet:

Love you always.

S

She hadn't come back to bed. I assume that she'd spent the entire evening staring out the window. There'd been silence until I heard her slip out at around five in the morning. The time wasn't that odd. Sheila was an early riser, the sort who reminded me of that old army commercial about doing more before nine than most people did all day. You know the type: She makes you feel like a slacker, and you love her for it.

Sheila had told me once—and only once—that she was used to getting up early because of her years working on the farm. When I pressed her for details, she quickly clammed up. The past was the line in the sand. Cross it at your own peril.

I was more confused by her behavior than worried.

I showered and dressed. The photograph of my brother was in my desk drawer. I took it out and studied it for a long time. There was a hollow sensation in my chest. My mind whirled and danced, but coming through all that was one pretty basic thought:

Ken had pulled it off.

———

You may have been wondering what'd convinced me that he'd been dead all these years. Part of it, I confess, was old-fashioned intuition mixed with blind hope. I loved my brother. And I knew him. Ken was not perfect. Ken was quick to anger and thrived on confrontation. Ken was mixed up in something bad. But Ken was not a murderer. I was sure of that.

But there was more to the Klein family theory than this bizarre faith. First off, how could Ken have survived on the run like this? He'd only had eight hundred dollars in the bank. Where did he get the resources to elude this international manhunt? And what possible motive could there have been for killing Julie? How come he never contacted us during the past eleven years? Why was he so on edge when he came home for that final visit? Why did he tell me that he was in danger? And why, looking back on it, didn't I push him to tell me more?

But most damaging—or encouraging, depending on your viewpoint—was the blood found at the scene. Some of it belonged to Ken. A large splotch of his blood was in the basement, and small drips made a trail up the stairs and out the door. And then another splotch was found on a shrub in the Millers' backyard. The Klein family theory was that the real murderer had killed Julie and seriously wounded (and eventually killed) my brother. The police's theory was simpler: Julie had fought back.

There was one more thing that backed the family theory—something directly attributable to me, which was why, I guess, no one took it seriously.

That is, I saw a man lurking near the Miller house that night.

Like I said, the authorities and press have pretty much dismissed this—I am, after all, interested in clearing my brother—but it is important in understanding why we believe what we believe. In the end, my family had a choice. We could accept that my brother murdered a lovely young woman for no reason, that he then lived without any visible income in hiding for eleven years (this—don't forget—despite extensive media coverage and a major police search)—or we could believe that he had consensual sex with Julie Miller (ergo much of the physical evidence), and that whatever mess he had gotten himself into, whoever had terrified Ken so, maybe whoever I saw outside the house on Coddington Terrace that night had somehow set him up for a murder and made sure his body would never be found.

20

I'm not saying it was a perfect fit. But we knew Ken. He didn't do what they said. So what was the alternative?

Some people did give credence to our family's theory, but most were conspiracy nuts, the kind who think Elvis and Jimi Hendrix are jamming on some island off Fiji. The TV stories gave it lip service that was so tongue-in-cheek you'd expect your television to smirk at you. As time went by, I grew quieter in my defense of Ken. Selfish as this might sound, I wanted a life. I wanted a career. I didn't want to be the brother of a famous murderer on the run.

Covenant House, I'm sure, had reservations about hiring me. Who would blame them? Even though I'm a senior director, my name is kept off the letterhead. I never appear at fund-raising functions. My job is strictly behind-the-scenes. And most of the time, that's okay with me.

I looked again at the picture of a man so familiar yet totally unknown to me.

Had my mother been lying from the beginning?

Had she been helping Ken while telling my father and me she thought he was dead? When I think back on it now, it was my mother who had been the strongest proponent of the Ken-dead theory. Had she been sneaking him money the whole time? Had Sunny known where he was from the start?

Questions to ponder.

I wrested my eyes away and opened a kitchen cabinet. I'd already decided that I wouldn't go out to Livingston this morning—the thought of sitting in that coffin of a house for another day made me want to scream—and I really needed to go to work. My mother, I was sure, would not only understand but encourage. So I poured myself a bowl of Golden Grahams cereal and dialed Sheila's work voice mail. I told her I loved her and I asked her to call me.

My apartment—well, it's *our* apartment now—is on 24th Street and Ninth Avenue, not far from the Chelsea Hotel. I usually walk the seventeen blocks north to Covenant House, which was on 41st Street, not far from the West Side Highway. This used to be a great location for a runaway shelter in the days before the cleanup of 42nd Street, when this stretch of stench was a bastion of in-your-face degradation. Forty-second Street had been a sort of Hell's Gate, a place for the grotesquely amative intermingling of species. Commuters and tourists would walk past prostitutes and dealers and pimps and head shops and porno palaces and movie theaters, and when they'd reach the end, they'd either be titillated or they'd want to take a shower and get a shot of penicillin. In my view, the perversion was so dirty, so depressing, it had to weigh you down. I am a man. I have lusts and urges like most guys I know. But I never understood how anyone could confuse the filth of toothless crack-heads for eroticism.

The city's cleanup, in a sense, made our jobs harder. The Covenant House rescue van had known where to cruise. The runaways were out in the open, more obvious. Now our task wasn't as clear-cut. And worse, the city itself wasn't really cleaner—just cleaner to look at. The so-called decent folk, those commuters and tourists I mentioned before, were no longer subjected to blacked-out windows reading ADULTS ONLY or crumbling marquees announcing pun-porn titles like SHAVING RYAN'S PRIVATES or BONFIRE OF THE PANTIES. But sleaze like this never really dies. Sleaze is a cockroach. It survives. It burrows and it hides. I don't think you can kill it.

And there are negatives to hiding the sleaze. When sleaze is obvious, you can scoff and feel superior. People need that. It's an outlet for some. Another advantage to in-the-open sleaze: Which would you rather face—an obvious frontal assault or a snakelike danger gliding through the high grass? Finally—and maybe I'm looking at this too closely—you can't have a front without a back, you can't have an up without a down, and I'm not sure you can have light without dark, purity without sleaze, good without evil.

The first honk didn't make me turn around. I live in New York City. Avoiding honks while strolling the avenues was tantamount to avoiding water while swimming. So it was not until I heard the familiar voice yell "Hey, asshole" that I turned around. The Covenant House van screeched alongside me. Squares was the driver and sole occupant. He lowered the window and whipped off his sunglasses.

"Get in," he said.

I opened the door and hopped up. The outreach van smelled of cigarettes and sweat and faintly of bologna from the sandwiches we hand out every night. There were stains of every size and stripe on the carpeting. The glove compartment was just an empty cavern. The springs in the seats were shot.

Squares kept his eyes on the road. "What the hell are you doing?"

"Going to work."

"Why?"

"Therapy," I said.

Squares nodded. He'd been up all night driving the van—an avenging angel searching for kids to rescue. He didn't look worse for wear, but then again, he hadn't started out too sparkly anyway. His hair was eighties Aerosmith-long, parted in the middle and on the greasy side. I don't think I'd ever seen him clean-shaven, but I'd never seen him with a full beard or even a nifty-neat *Miami Vice* growth either. The patches of skin that were visible were pock-marked. His work boots were scuffed to a near whiteness. His jeans looked like they'd been trampled in a prairie by buffalo, and the waist was too big, giving him that ever-desirable repairman-butt-plunge look. A pack of Camels was rolled up in his sleeve. His teeth were tobacco-stained the yellow of a Ticonderoga pencil.

"You look like shit," he said.

"That means something," I said, "coming from you."

He liked that one. We called him Squares, short for Four Squares, because of the tattoo on his forehead. It was, well, four squares, two by two, so that it looked exactly like a four squares court you still see on playgrounds. Now that Squares was a big-time yoga instructor with videos and a chain of schools, most people assumed that the tattoo was some sort of significant Hindu symbol. Not so.

At one time, it had been a tattoo of a swastika. He'd just added four lines. Closed it up.

It was hard for me to imagine this. Squares is probably the least judgmental person I've ever known. He's probably also my closest friend. When he first told me the origins of the squares, I was appalled and shocked. He never explained or apologized, and like Sheila, he never talked about his past. Others have filled in pieces. I understand better now.

"Thanks for sending the flowers," I said.

Squares didn't reply.

"And for showing up," I added. He had brought a group of Covenant House friends in the van. They'd pretty much made up the entire nonfamily funeral brigade.

"Sunny was great people," he said.

"Yeah."

A moment of silence. Then Squares said, "But what a shitty turnout."

"Thanks for pointing that out."

23

"I mean, Jesus, how many people were there?"

"You're quite the comfort, Squares. Thanks, man."

"You want comfort? Know this: People are assholes."

"Let me get out a pen and write that down."

Silence. Squares stopped for a red light and sneaked a glance at me. His eyes were red. He unrolled the cigarette pack from his sleeve. "You want to tell me what's wrong?"

"Uh, well, see, the other day? My mother died."

"Fine," he said, "don't tell me."

The light turned green. The van started up again. The image of my brother in that photograph flashed across my eyes. "Squares?"

"I'm listening."

"I think," I said, "that my brother is still alive."

Squares didn't say anything right away. He withdrew a cigarette from the pack and put it in his mouth.

"Quite the epiphany," he said.

"Epiphany," I repeated with a nod.

"Been taking night courses," he said. "So why the sudden change of heart?"

He pulled into the small Covenant House lot. We used to park out on the street, but people would break in and sleep there. We did not call the cops, of course, but the expense of the broken windows and stripped locks became cumbersome. After a while, we kept the van doors unlocked so the inhabitants could just go inside. In the morning, whoever was first to arrive at the center would knock against the van. The night's tenants would get the message and scurry away.

We had to stop that too, though. The van became—not to get too graphic here—too disgusting for use. The homeless are not always pretty. They vomit. They soil themselves. They often cannot find rest-room facilities. Enough said.

Still sitting in the van, I wondered how to approach this. "Let me ask you a question."

He waited.

"You've never given me your take on what happened to my brother," I said.

"That a question?"

"More an observation. Here's the question: How come?"

"How come I never gave you my take on your brother?"

"Yes."

24

Squares shrugged. "You never asked."

"We talked about it a lot."

Squares shrugged again.

"Okay, I'm asking now," I said. "Did you think he's alive?"

"Always."

Just like that. "So all those talks we had, all those times I made convincing arguments to the contrary . . ."

"I wondered who you were trying to convince, me or you."

"You never bought my arguments?"

"Nope," Squares said. "Never."

"But you never argued with me either."

Squares took a deep drag on the cigarette. "Your delusion seemed harmless."

"Ignorance is bliss, eh?"

"Most of the time, yeah."

"But I made some valid points," I said.

"You say so."

"You don't think so?"

"I don't think so," Squares said. "You thought your bro didn't have the resources to hide, but you don't need resources. Look at the runaways we meet every day. If one of them really wanted to disappear, presto, they'd be gone."

"There isn't an international manhunt for any of them."

"International manhunt," Squares said with something close to disgust. "You think every cop in the world wakes up wondering about your brother?"

He had a point—especially now that I realized he may have gotten financial help from my mother. "He wouldn't kill anyone."

"Bullshit," Squares said.

"You don't know him."

"We're friends, right?"

"Right."

"You believe that one day I used to burn crosses and shout 'Heil Hitler'?"

"That's different."

"No, it's not." We stepped out of the van. "You asked me once why I didn't get rid of the tattoo altogether, remember?"

I nodded. "And you told me to fuck off."

"Right. But the fact is, I could have removed it by laser or done a more elaborate cover-up. But I keep it because it reminds me."

25

"Of what? The past?"

Squares flashed the yellows. "Of potential," he said.

"I don't know what that means."

"Because you're hopeless."

"My brother would never rape and murder an innocent woman."

"Some yoga schools teach mantras," Squares said. "But repeating something over and over does not make it true."

"You're pretty deep today," I said.

"And you're acting like an asshole." He stubbed out the cigarette. "You going to tell me why you've had this change of heart?"

We were near the entrance.

"In my office," I said.

We hushed as we entered the shelter. People expect a dump, but our shelter is anything but. Our philosophy is that this should be a place you'd want your own kids to stay if they were in trouble. That comment stuns donors at first—like most charities, this one seems very removed from them—but it also strikes them where they live.

Squares and I were silent now, because when we are in our house, all our focus, all our concentration, is aimed at the kids. They deserve nothing less. For once in their often sad lives, they are what matters most. Always. We greet each kid like—and pardon the way I phrase this—a long-lost brother. We listen. We never hurry. We shake hands and hug. We look them in the eye. We never look over their shoulder. We stop and face them full. If you try to fake it, these kids will pick it up in a second. They have excellent bullshit-o-meters. We love them hard in here, totally and without conditions. Every day we do that. Or we just go home. It doesn't mean that we are always successful. Or even successful most of the time. We lose a lot more than we save. They get sucked back down into the streets. But while here, in our house, they will stay in comfort. While here, they will be loved.

When we entered my office, two people—one woman, one man—were waiting for us. Squares stopped short. He lifted his nostrils and sniffed the air, hound-dog style.

"Cops," he said to me.

The woman smiled and stepped forward. The man stayed behind her, casually leaning again the wall. "Will Klein?"

"Yes?" I said.

She unfurled her ID with a flourish. The man did the same thing. "My name is Claudia Fisher. This is Darryl Wilcox. We're both special agents for the Federal Bureau of Investigation."

"The feds," Squares said to me, thumbs up, like he was impressed I ranked such attention. He squinted at the ID, then at Claudia Fisher. "Hey, how come you cut your hair?"

Claudia Fisher snapped the ID closed. She arched an eyebrow at Squares. "And you are?"

"Easily aroused," he said.

She frowned and slid her eyes back to me. "We'd like a few words with you." Then she added, "Alone."

Claudia Fisher was short and semi-perky, the dedicated student/athlete from high school who was a little too tightly wound—the type who had fun but never spontaneously. Her hair was indeed short and feathered back, a bit too late-seventies but it fit. She had small hoop earrings and a strong bird nose.

We are naturally suspicious of law enforcement here. I have no desire to protect criminals, but I do not want to be a tool in their apprehension either. This place has to be a safe haven. Cooperating with law enforcement would cripple our street cred—and really, our street cred is everything. I like to think of us as neutral. Switzerland for the runaways. And of course, my personal history—the way the feds have handled my brother's situation—does little to endear me to them either.

"I'd rather he stayed," I said.

"This has nothing to do with him."

"Think of him as my attorney."

Claudia Fisher took Squares in—the jeans, the hair, the tattoo. He pulled on imaginary lapels and wriggled his eyebrows.

I moved to my desk. Squares flopped into the chair in front of it and threw his work boots onto the desktop. They landed with a dusty thud. Fisher and Wilcox remained standing.

I spread my hands. "What can I do for you, Agent Fisher?"

"We're looking for one Sheila Rogers."

That had not been what I expected.

"Can you tell us where we might find her?"

"Why are you looking for her?" I asked.

Claudia Fisher gave me a patronizing smile. "Would you mind just telling us where she is?"

"Is she in trouble?"

"Right now"—she paused a beat and changed the smile—"we'd just like to ask her some questions."

"What about?"

"Are you refusing to cooperate with us?"

"I'm not refusing anything."

"Then please tell us where we might locate Sheila Rogers."

"I'd like to know why."

She looked at Wilcox. Wilcox gave her a very small nod. She turned back to me. "Earlier today, Special Agent Wilcox and I visited Sheila Rogers's place of employment on 18th Street. She was not present. We inquired as to where we might locate her. Her employer informed us that she had called in sick. We checked her last known place of residence. The landlord informed us that she moved out several months ago. Her current residence was listed as yours, Mr. Klein, on 378 West 24th Street. We visited there. Sheila Rogers was not present."

Squares pointed at her. "You talk real purdy."

She ignored him. "We don't want trouble, Mr. Klein."

"Trouble?" I said.

"We need to question Sheila Rogers. We need to question her right away. We can do it the easy way. Or, if you choose not to cooperate, we can travel an alternate, though less pleasant, avenue."

Squares rubbed his hands together. "Ooo, a threat."

"What's it going to be, Mr. Klein?"

"I'd like you to leave," I said.

"How much do you know about Sheila Rogers?"

This was turning weird. My head started aching. Wilcox reached into his jacket pocket and took out a sheet of paper. He handed it to Claudia Fisher. "Are you aware," Fisher said, "of Ms. Rogers's criminal record?"

I tried to keep a straight face, but even Squares reacted to that one.

Fisher started reading from the sheet of paper. "Shoplifting. Prostitution. Possession with intent to sell."

Squares made a scoffing noise. "Amateur hour."

"Armed robbery."

"Better," Squares said with a nod. He looked up at Fisher. "No conviction on that one, right?"

"That's correct."

"So maybe she didn't do it."

Fisher frowned again.

I plucked at my lower lip.

"Mr. Klein?"

"Can't help you," I said.

"Can't or won't."

I still plucked. "Semantics."

"This must all seem a little déjà-vu, Mr. Klein."

"What the hell is that supposed to mean?"

"Covering up. First for your brother. Now your lover."

"Go to hell," I said.

Squares made a face at me, clearly disappointed with my admittedly lame retort.

Fisher didn't back off. "You're not thinking this through," she said.

"How's that?"

"The repercussions," she went on. "For example: How do you think the Covenant House donors would take it if you were arrested for, say, aiding and abetting?"

Squares took that one. "You know who you should ask?"

Claudia Fisher crinkled her nose at him, as if he were something she'd just scraped off her shoe.

"Joey Pistillo," Squares said. "I bet Joey would know."

Now it was Fisher and Wilcox's turn to rock back on their heels.

"You got a cell phone?" Squares asked. "We can ask him right now."

Fisher looked at Wilcox, then at Squares. "Are you telling us that you know Assistant Director in Charge Joseph Pistillo?" she asked.

"Call him," Squares said. Then: "Oh, wait, you probably don't know his private line." Squares stretched out his hand and wiggled his finger in a give-me gesture. "You mind?"

She handed him the phone. Squares pressed the number pad and put the phone to his ear. He leaned all the way back, his feet still on the desk; if he'd been wearing a cowboy hat, it'd be pulled down over his eyes for a little siesta.

"Joey? Hey, man, how are you?" Squares listened for a minute and then he burst out laughing. He schmoozed a bit and I watched Fisher and Wilcox turn white. Normally I'd enjoy this power play—

between his checkered past and current celebrity status, Squares was one degree of separation from almost everyone—but my mind was reeling.

After a few minutes, Squares handed Agent Fisher the cell phone. "Joey wants to talk to you."

Fisher and Wilcox stepped out in the corridor and closed the door.

"Dude, the feds," Squares said, thumbs up again, still impressed.

"Yeah, I'm pretty thrilled," I said.

"That's something, huh. I mean, about Sheila having a record. Who'd have guessed?"

Not me.

When Fisher and Wilcox returned, the color had returned to their faces. Fisher handed the phone to Squares with too courteous a smile.

Squares put it to his ear and said, "What's up, Joey?" He listened for a while. Then he said, "Okay," and hung up.

"What?" I said.

"That was Joey Pistillo. Top gun for the FBI on the East Coast."

"And?"

"He wants to see you in person," Squares said. He looked off.

"What?"

"I don't think we're going to like what he has to say."

5

Assistant Director in Charge Joseph Pistillo not only wanted to see me in person, but alone.

"I understand your mother passed away," he said.

"How do you understand?"

"Pardon?"

"Did you read the obituary in the paper?" I asked. "Did a friend tell you? How did you come to understand that she passed away?"

We looked at each other. Pistillo was a burly man, bald except for a close-cropped fringe of gray, shoulders like bowling balls, gnarled hands folded on his desk.

"Or," I went on, feeling the old anger creep in, "did you have an agent watching us. Watching her. At the hospital. On her deathbed. At her funeral. Was one of your agents the new orderly the nurses whispered about? Was one of your agents the limousine driver who forgot the funeral director's name?"

Neither one of us broke eye contact.

"I'm sorry for your loss," Pistillo said.

"Thank you."

He leaned back. "Why won't you tell us where Sheila Rogers is?"

"Why won't you tell me why you're looking for her?"

"When did you see her last?"

"Are you married, Agent Pistillo?"

He didn't break stride. "Twenty-six years. We have three kids."

"You love your wife?"

"Yes."

"So if I came to you and made demands and threats involving her, what would you do?"

Pistillo nodded slowly. "If you worked for the Federal Bureau of Investigation, I'd tell her to cooperate."

"Just like that?"

"Well"—he raised his index finger—"with one caveat."

"What's that?"

"That she was innocent. If she's innocent, I'd have no fears."

"So you wouldn't wonder what it was all about?"

"Wonder? Sure. Demand to know . . ." He let his voice trail off. "Let me ask you a hypothetical now."

He paused. I sat up.

"I know that you think your brother is dead."

Another pause. I stayed quiet.

"But suppose you found out that he's alive and hiding—and suppose on top of that, you found out he killed Julie Miller." He sat back. "Hypothetically, of course. This is all just a hypothetical."

"Go on," I said.

"Well, what would you do? Would you turn him in? Would you tell him he's on his own? Or would you help him?"

More silence.

I said, "You didn't bring me here to play hypotheticals."

"No," he said, "I didn't."

There was a computer monitor on the right side of his desk. He turned the screen so that I could see it. Then he pressed some buttons. A color image came up, and something inside me clenched.

An ordinary-looking room. Tall lamp in the corner overturned. Beige carpet. Coffee table on its side. A mess. Like a tornado aftermath or something. But in the center of the room, a man lay in a puddle of what I assumed was blood. The blood was dark, beyond crimson, beyond rust, almost black. The man lay faceup, his arms and legs splayed in such way that he looked like he'd been dropped from a great height.

As I looked at the image on the monitor, I could feel Pistillo's eyes on me, gauging my reaction. My eyes flicked to his and then back at the screen.

He pressed the keyboard. Another image replaced the blood-soaked one. The same room. The lamp was out of sight now. Blood

32

still stained the carpet—but there was another body now, this one curled up in the fetal position. The first man wore a black T-shirt and black pants. This one wore a flannel shirt and blue jeans.

Pistillo hit another key. Now the photograph was wide framed. Both bodies now. The first in the center of the room. The second, closer to the door. I could see only one face—from this angle it was not a familiar one—but the other was blocked from view.

Panic rose up in me. Ken, I thought. Could one of them be . . . ?

But then I remembered their questions. This wasn't about Ken.

"These pictures were taken in Albuquerque, New Mexico, over the weekend," Pistillo said.

I frowned. "I don't understand."

"The crime scene was something of a mess, but we still found some hairs and fibers." He smiled at me. "I'm not great on the technical aspects of our work. They have tests nowadays that you simply can't believe. But sometimes it's still the classics that get you through the day."

"Am I supposed to know what you're talking about?"

"Someone had wiped the place pretty good, but the crime-scene people still lifted a set of fingerprints—one clean set that didn't belong to either of the victims. We ran them through the computer and got a hit early this morning." He leaned forward and the smile was gone now. "You want to make a guess?"

I saw Sheila, my beautiful Sheila, staring out the window.

"I'm sorry, Will."

"They belong to your girlfriend, Mr. Klein. The same one with a criminal record. The same one we're suddenly having a lot of trouble finding."

33

6

Elizabeth, New Jersey

They were near the cemetery now.

Philip McGuane sat in the back of his handcrafted Mercedes limousine—a stretch model equipped with armor-reinforced sides and bulletproof one-way windows at a cost of four hundred thou—and stared out at the blur of fast-food restaurants, tacky stores, and aged strip malls. A scotch and soda, freshly mixed in the limo's wet bar, was cupped in his right hand. He looked down at the amber liquor. Steady. That surprised him.

"You okay, Mr. McGuane?"

McGuane turned to his companion. Fred Tanner was huge, the approximate size and consistency of a city brownstone. His hands were manhole covers with sausagelike fingers. His gaze was one of supreme confidence. Old school, Tanner was—still with his shellac-shiny suit and the ostentatious pinky ring. Tanner always wore the ring, a garish, oversize gold thing, twisting and toying with it whenever he spoke.

"I'm fine," McGuane lied.

The limousine exited Route 22 at Parker Avenue. Tanner kept fiddling with the pinky ring. He was fifty, a decade and a half older than his boss. His face was a weathered monument of harsh planes and right angles. His hair was meticulously mowed into a severe crew cut. McGuane knew that Tanner was very good—a cold, disciplined and lethal son of a bitch for whom mercy was about as relevant a concept as feng shui. Tanner was adept at using those huge hands or a potpourri of firearms. He had gone up against some of the cruelest and had always come out on top.

But this, McGuane knew, was taking it to a whole new level.

"Who is this guy anyway?" Tanner asked.

McGuane shook his head. His own suit was a hand-tailored Joseph Abboud. He rented three floors on Manhattan's lower west side. In another era, McGuane might have been called a consigliore or capo or some such nonsense. But that was then, this is now. Gone (long gone, despite what Hollywood might want you to believe) were the days of backroom hangouts and velour sweats—days Tanner undoubtedly still longed for. Now you had offices and a secretary and a computer-generated payroll. You paid taxes. You owned legit businesses.

But you were no better.

"And why we driving way out here anyway?" Tanner went on. "He should come to you, no?"

McGuane didn't reply. Tanner wouldn't understand.

If the Ghost wants to meet, you meet.

Didn't matter who you were. To refuse would mean that the Ghost would come to you. McGuane had excellent security. He had good people. But the Ghost was better. He had patience. He would study you. He would wait for an opening. And then he would find you. Alone. You knew that.

No, better to get it over with. Better to go to him.

A block away from the cemetery, the limousine pulled to a stop.

"You understand what I want," McGuane said.

"I got a man in place already. It's taken care of."

"Don't take him out unless you see my signal."

"Right, yeah. We've gone over this."

"Don't underestimate him."

Tanner gripped the door handle. Sunlight glistened off the pinky ring. "No offense, Mr. McGuane, but he's just some guy, right? Bleeds red like the rest of us?"

McGuane was not so sure.

Tanner stepped out, moving gracefully for a man carrying such bulk. McGuane sat back and downed a long swig of scotch. He was one of the most powerful men in New York. You don't get there—

you don't reach that pinnacle—without being a cunning and ruthless bastard. You show weakness, you're dead. You limp, you die. Simple as that.

And most of all, you never back down.

McGuane knew all that—knew it as well as anyone—but right now, more than anything, he wanted to run away. Just pack what he could and simply disappear.

Like his old friend Ken.

McGuane met the driver's eyes in the rearview mirror. He took a deep breath and nodded. The car started moving again. They turned left and slid past the gates of Wellington Cemetery. Tires crunched loose gravel. McGuane told the driver to stop. The driver obeyed. McGuane stepped out and moved to the front of the car.

"I'll call you when I need you."

The driver nodded and pulled out.

McGuane was alone.

He pulled up his collar. His gaze swept over the graveyard. No movement. He wondered where Tanner and his man had hidden themselves. Probably closer to the meet site. In a tree or behind a shrub. If they were doing it right, McGuane would never see them.

The sky was clear. The wind whipped him like a reaper's scythe. He hunched his shoulders. The traffic sounds from Route 22 spilled up over sound barriers and serenaded the dead. The smell of something freshly baked wafted in the still air and for a moment McGuane thought of cremation.

No sign of anyone.

McGuane found the path and headed east. As he passed the stones and markers, his eyes unconsciously checked birth and death dates. He calculated ages and wondered about what fate had befallen the young ones. He hesitated when he saw a familiar name. Daniel Skinner. Dead at age thirteen. A smiling angel had been sculpted into the tombstone. McGuane chuckled softly at the image. Skinner, a vicious bully, had been repeatedly tormenting a fourth-grader. But on that day—May 11, according to the tombstone—that rather unique fourth-grader had brought a kitchen knife for protection. His first and only thrust punctured Skinner's heart.

Bye, bye, Angel.

McGuane tried to shrug it off.

Had it all started here?

He moved on. Up ahead, he made a left and slowed his pace. Not far now. His eyes scanned the surroundings. Still no movement. It was quieter back here—peaceful and green. Not that the inhabitants seemed to care. He hesitated, veered left again, and moved down the row until he arrived at the right grave.

McGuane stopped. He read the name and the date. His mind traveled back. He wondered what he felt and realized that the answer was, not much. He didn't bother looking around anymore. The Ghost was here somewhere. He could feel him.

"You should have brought flowers, Philip."

The voice, soft and silky with a hint of a lisp, chilled his blood. McGuane slowly turned to look behind him. John Asselta approached, flowers in his hand. McGuane stepped away. Asselta's eyes met his, and McGuane could feel a steel claw reach into his chest.

"It's been a long time," the Ghost said.

Asselta, the man McGuane knew as the Ghost, moved toward the tombstone. McGuane stayed perfectly still. The temperature seemed to drop thirty degrees when the Ghost walked past.

McGuane held his breath.

The Ghost knelt and gently placed the flowers on the ground. He stayed down there for a moment, his eyes closed. Then he stood, reached out with the tapered fingers of a pianist, and caressed the tombstone with too much intimacy.

McGuane tried not to watch.

The Ghost had skin like cataracts, milky and marshlike. Blue veins ran down his almost-pretty face like dyed tear tracks. His eyes were shale, almost colorless. His head, too big for his narrow shoulders, was shaped like a lightbulb. The sides of his skull were freshly shaved, a sprout of mud-brown hairs sticking up from the middle and cascading out like a fountain. There was something delicate, even feminine, in his features—a nightmare version of a Dresden doll.

McGuane took another step back.

Sometimes you meet a person whose innate goodness bursts at you with an almost blinding light. And then sometimes, you meet the direct opposite—someone whose very presence smothers you in a heavy cloak of decay and blood.

"What do you want?" McGuane asked.

The Ghost lowered his head. "Have you heard the expression that there are no atheists in foxholes?"

"Yes."

"It's a lie, you know," the Ghost said. "In fact, just the opposite is true. When you are in a foxhole, when you are face-to-face with death—that is when you know for sure that there is no God. It's why you fight to survive, to draw one more breath. It's why you call out to any and every entity—because you don't want to die. Because in your heart of hearts, you know that death is the endgame. No hereafter. No paradise. No God. Just nothingness."

The Ghost looked up at him. McGuane stayed still.

"I've missed you, Philip."

"What do you want, John?"

"I think you know."

McGuane did, but he said nothing.

"I understand," the Ghost continued, "that you are in something of a bind."

"What have you heard?"

"Just rumors." The Ghost smiled. His mouth was a thin razor slice, and the sight of it nearly made McGuane scream. "It's why I'm back."

"It's my problem."

"If only that were true, Philip."

"What do you want, John?"

"The two men you sent to New Mexico. They failed, correct?"

"Yes."

The Ghost whispered, "I won't."

"I still don't understand what you want."

"You would agree, would you not, that I have something of a stake in this too?"

The Ghost waited. McGuane finally nodded. "I guess you do."

"You have sources, Philip. Access to information I don't." The Ghost looked at the tombstone, and for a moment McGuane thought he saw something almost human there. "Are you sure he's back?"

"Fairly sure," McGuane said.

"How do you know?"

"Someone with the FBI. The men we sent to Albuquerque were supposed to confirm it."

"They underestimated their foe."

"Apparently."

"Do you know where he ran to?"

"We're working on it."

"But not very hard."

McGuane said nothing.

"You'd prefer that he vanish again. Am I right?"

"It'd make things easier."

The Ghost shook his head. "Not this time."

There was silence.

"So who would know where he is?" the Ghost asked.

"His brother perhaps. The FBI picked Will up an hour ago. For questioning."

That got the Ghost's attention. His head popped up. "Questioning about what?"

"We don't know yet."

"Then," the Ghost said softly, "that might be a good place for me to start."

McGuane managed a nod. And that was when the Ghost stepped toward him. He put out his hand. McGuane shuddered, couldn't move.

"Afraid to shake an old friend's hand, Philip?"

He was. The Ghost took another step closer. McGuane's breathing was shallow. He thought about signaling Tanner.

One bullet. One bullet could end this.

"Shake my hand, Philip."

It was a command, and McGuane obeyed it. Almost against his will, his hand rose from his side and slowly reached out. The Ghost, he knew, killed people. Lots of them. With ease. He was Death. Not just a killer. But Death itself—as though the Ghost's very touch could prick your skin, enter your bloodstream, send out a poison that would puncture your heart like the kitchen knife the Ghost had used so long ago.

McGuane averted his eyes.

The Ghost quickly closed the gap between them and clasped McGuane's hand in his own. McGuane bit back a scream. He tried to pull away from the clammy trap. The Ghost held on.

Then McGuane felt something—something cold and sharp digging into his palm.

The grip tightened. McGuane gasped in pain. Whatever the

Ghost had in his hand speared into a nerve bundle like a bayonet. The grip tightened a little more. McGuane dropped to one knee.

The Ghost waited until McGuane looked up. The two men's eyes met, and McGuane was sure that his lungs would stop, that his organs would simply shut down one by one. The Ghost loosened his grip. He slipped the sharp something into McGuane's hand and folded his fingers over it. Then, finally, the Ghost let go and stepped back.

"It could be a lonely ride back, Philip."

McGuane found his voice. "What the hell is that supposed to mean?"

But the Ghost turned and walked away. McGuane looked down and opened his fist.

There in his hand, twinkling in the sunlight, was Tanner's gold pinky ring.

7

After my meeting with Assistant Director Pistillo, Squares and I hopped in the van. "Your apartment?" he asked me.

I nodded.

"I'm listening," he said.

I recounted my conversation with Pistillo.

Squares shook his head. "Albuquerque. Hate that place, man. You ever been?"

"No."

"You're in the Southwest yet everything feels pseudo-Southwest. Like the whole place is a Disney facsimile."

"I'll keep that in mind, Squares, thanks."

"So when did Sheila go?"

"I don't know," I said.

"Think. Where were you last weekend?"

"I was at my folks'."

"And Sheila?"

"She was supposed to be in the city."

"You called her?"

I thought about it. "No, she called me."

"Caller ID?"

"The number was blocked."

"Anybody who can confirm she was in the city?"

"I don't think so."

"So she could have been in Albuquerque," Squares said.

I considered that. "There are other explanations," I said.

"Like?"

"The fingerprints could be old."

Squares frowned, kept his eyes on the road.

"Maybe," I went on, "she went out to Albuquerque last month or hell, last year. How long do fingerprints last anyway?"

"Awhile, I think."

"So maybe that's what happened," I said. "Or maybe her prints were on, say, a piece of furniture—a chair maybe—and maybe the chair was in New York and then it was shipped out to New Mexico."

Squares adjusted his sunglasses. "Reaching."

"But possible."

"Yeah, sure. And hey, maybe someone borrowed her fingers. You know. Took them to Albuquerque for the weekend."

A taxi cut us off. We made a right turn, nearly clipping a group of people standing three feet off the curb. Manhattanites always do that. No one ever waits for the light on the actual sidewalk. They step into the fold, risk their lives to gain yet another imaginary edge.

"You know Sheila," I said.

"I do."

It was hard to utter the words, but there it was: "Do you really think she could be a killer?"

Squares was quiet a moment. A light turned red. He pulled the van to a stop and looked at me. "Starting to sound like your brother all over again."

"All I'm saying, Squares, is that there are other possibilities."

"And all I'm saying, Will, is that your head is up your sphincter."

"Meaning?"

"A chair, for chrissake? Are you for real? Last night Sheila cried and told you she was sorry—and in the morning, poof, she's gone. Now the feds tell us her fingerprints were found at a murder scene. And what do you come up with? Friggin' shipped chairs and old visits."

"It doesn't mean she killed anyone."

"It means," Squares said, "that she's involved."

I let that one sink in. I sat back and looked out the window and saw nothing.

"You have a thought, Squares?"

"Not a one."

We drove some more.

"I love her, you know."

"I know," Squares said.

"Best-case scenario, she lied to me."

He shrugged. "Worse things."

I wondered. I remembered our first full night together, lying in bed, Sheila's head on my chest, her arm draped over me. There was such contentment there, such a feeling of peace, of the world being so right. We just stayed there. I don't know how long anymore. "No past," she said softly, almost to herself. I asked her what she meant. She kept her head on my chest, her eyes away from me. And she said nothing more.

"I have to find her," I said.

"Yeah, I know."

"You want to help?"

Squares shrugged. "You won't be able to do it without me."

"There's that," I said. "So what should we do first?"

"To quote an old proverb," Squares said, "before we go forward, we have to look back."

"You just make that up?"

"Yeah."

"Guess it makes sense, though."

"Will?"

"Yeah?"

"Not to state the obvious or anything, but if we look back, you may not like what we see."

"Almost assuredly," I agreed.

Squares dropped me by the door and drove back to Covenant House. I entered the apartment and tossed my keys on the table. I would have called out Sheila's name—just to make sure she hadn't come home—but the apartment felt so empty, so drained of energy, I didn't bother. The place I'd called home for the past four years seemed somehow different to me, foreign. There was a stale feel to it, as though it'd been empty for a long time.

So now what?

Search the place, I guess. Look for clues, whatever that meant. But what struck me immediately was how spartan Sheila had been. She took pleasure in the simple, even seemingly mundane, and taught me how to do the same. She had very few possessions. When she'd moved in, she'd only brought one suitcase. She wasn't poor— I'd seen her bank statements and she'd paid for more than her share here—but she'd always been one of those people who lived by that "possessions own you, not the other way around" philosophy. Now I wondered about that, about the fact that possessions don't so much own you as bind you down, give you roots.

My XXL Amherst College sweatshirt lay over a chair in the bedroom. I picked it up, feeling a pang in my chest. We spent homecoming weekend at my alma mater last fall. There's a hill on Amherst's campus, a steep slope that starts a-high on a classic New England quad and slides toward a vast expanse of athletic fields. Most students, in a fit of originality, call this hill "the Hill."

Late one night Sheila and I walked the campus, hand in hand. We lay on the Hill's soft grass, stared at the pure fall sky, and talked for hours. I remember thinking that I had never known such a sense of peace, of calm and comfort and, yes, joy. Still on our backs, Sheila put her palm on my stomach and then, eyes on the stars, she slipped her hand under the waistband of my pants. I turned just a little and watched her face. When her fingers hit, uh, pay dirt, I saw her wicked grin.

"That's giving it the old college try," she'd said.

And okay, maybe I was turned on as all get-out, but it was at that very moment, on that hill, her hand in my pants, when I first realized, really realized with an almost supernatural certainty, that she was the one, that we would always be together, that the shadow of my first love, my only love before Sheila, the one that haunted me and drove away the others, had finally been banished.

I looked at the sweatshirt and for a moment, I could smell the honeysuckle and foliage all over again. I pressed it against me and wondered for the umpteenth time since I'd spoken to Pistillo: Was it all a lie?

No.

You don't fake that. Squares might be right about people's capacity to do violence. But you can't fake a connection like ours.

The note was still on the counter.

Love you always.

S

I had to believe that. I owed Sheila that much. Her past was her past. I had no claim to it. Whatever had happened, Sheila must have had her reasons. She loved me. I knew that. My task now was to find her, to help her, to figure a way back to . . . I don't know . . . us.

I would not doubt her.

I checked the drawers. Sheila had one bank account and one credit card—at least, that I knew of. But there were no papers any-where—no old statements, no receipts, no bankbooks, nothing. They'd all been thrown away, I guess.

The computer screen saver, the ever-popular bouncing lines, disappeared when I moved the mouse. I signed on, switched over to Sheila's screen name, clicked Old Mail. Nothing. Not one. Odd. Sheila didn't use the Net often—very rarely in fact—but to not have one old email?

I clicked Filing Cabinet. Empty too. I checked under Book-marked Web sites. More nothing. I checked the history. *Nada.*

I sat back and stared at the screen. A thought floated to the sur-face. I considered it for a moment, wondering if such an act would be a betrayal. No matter. Squares had been right about looking back in order to figure out where to go next. And he was right that I might not like what I find.

I logged on to switchboard.com, a massive online telephone di-rectory. Under Name I typed Rogers. The state was Idaho. The city was Mason. I knew that from the form she'd filled out when she vol-unteered at Covenant House.

There was only one listing. On a slip of scrap paper, I jotted down the phone number. Yes, I was going to call Sheila's parents. If we were going to go back, we might as well go all the way.

Before I could reach for the receiver, the phone rang. I picked it up, and my sister, Melissa, said, "What are you doing?"

I thought about how to put it and settled for: "I have something of a situation here."

"Will," she said, and I could hear the older-sister tone, "we're mourning our mother here."

I closed my eyes.

"Dad's been asking about you. You have to come."

I looked around the stale, foreign apartment. No reason to hang here. And I thought about the picture still in my pocket—the image of my brother on the mountain.

"I'm on my way," I said.

Melissa greeted me at the door and asked, "Where's Sheila?"

I mumbled something about a previous commitment and ducked inside.

We actually had a real-life nonfamily visitor today—an old friend of my father's named Lou Farley. I don't think they'd seen each other in ten years. Lou Farley and my father traded stories with too much gusto and from too long ago. Something about an old softball team, and I had a vague recollection of my father suiting up in a maroon uniform of heavy polyester knit, a Friendly's Ice Cream logo emblazoned across the chest. I could still hear the scrape of his cleats on the driveway, feel the weight of his hand on my shoulder. So long ago. He and Lou Farley laughed. I hadn't heard my father laugh like that in years. His eyes were wet and far away. My mother would sometimes go to the games too. I can see her sitting in the bleachers with her sleeveless shirt and tanned, toned arms.

I glanced out the window, still hoping Sheila might show up, that this could still all somehow be one big misunderstanding. Part of me—a big part of me—blocked. While my mother's death had long been expected—Sunny's cancer, as was often the case, had been a slow, steady death march with a sudden downhill plunge at the end—I was still too raw to accept all that was happening.

Sheila.

I had loved and lost once before. When it comes to affairs of the heart, I confess to a streak of dated thinking. I believe in a soul mate. We all have that first love. When mine left me, she blew a hole straight through my heart. For a long time, I thought I'd never recover. There were reasons for that. Our ending felt incomplete, for one. But no matter. After she dumped me—at the end of the day, that's what she did—I was convinced that I was doomed to either settle for someone . . . lesser . . . or be forever alone.

And then I met Sheila.

I thought about the way Sheila's green eyes bore into me. I thought about the silky feel of her red hair. I thought about how the initial physical attraction—and it was immense, overwhelming—had segued and spread to all corners of my being. I thought about her all the time. I had flutters in my stomach. I could feel my heart do a little two-step whenever I first laid eyes on that face. I'd be in the van with Squares and all of a sudden he'd punch my shoulder because my mind had floated away, floated to a place Squares jokingly called Sheila Land, leaving a dorky smile behind. I felt heady. We cuddled and watched old movies on video, stroking each other, teasing, seeing how long we could hold out, warm comfort and hot arousal doing battle until, well, that was why VCRs have a pause button.

We held hands. We took long walks. We sat in the park and whispered snide comments about strangers to each other. At parties, I'd love to stand on the other side of the room and look at her from afar, watch her walk and move and talk to others and then, when our eyes would meet, there'd be a jolt, a knowing glance, a lascivious smile.

Sheila once asked me to fill out some stupid survey she found in a magazine. One of the questions was: What is your lover's biggest weakness? I thought about it and wrote, "Often forgets her umbrella in restaurants." She loved that, though she pressed for more. I reminded her that she listened to boy bands and old ABBA records. She nodded solemnly and promised that she would try to change.

We talked about everything but the past. I see that a lot in my line of work. It didn't trouble me much. Now, in hindsight, I wondered, but back then it had added, I don't know, an air of mystery maybe. And more than that—bear with me again—it was as though there were no life before us. No love, no partners, no past, born the day we met.

Yeah, I know.

Melissa sat next to my father. I saw them both in profile. The resemblance was strong. I favored my mother. Melissa's husband, Ralph, circled the buffet table. He was middle-manager America, a man of shortsleeve dress shirts over wife-beater T's, a good ol' boy with a firm handshake, shined shoes, slicked hair, limited intelligence. He never loosened his tie, not exactly uptight but comfortable only when things are in their proper place.

I have nothing in common with Ralph, but to be fair, I really don't know him very well. They live in Seattle and almost never come back. Still, I can't help but remember when Melissa was going through her wild stage, sneaking around with local bad boy Jimmy McCarthy. What a gleam in her eye there had been back then. How spontaneous and outrageously, even inappropriately, funny she could be. I don't know what happened, what changed her, what had scared her so. People claim that it was just maturity. I don't think that's the full story. I think there was something more.

Melissa—we'd always called her Mel—signaled me with her eyes. We slid into the den. I reached into my pocket and touched the photograph of Ken.

"Ralph and I are leaving in the morning," she told me.

"Fast," I said.

"What's that supposed to mean?"

I shook my head.

"We have children. Ralph has work."

"Right," I said. "Nice of you to show up at all."

Her eyes went wide. "That's a horrible thing to say."

It was. I looked behind me. Ralph sat with Dad and Lou Farley, downing a particularly messy sloppy joe, the cole slaw nestling in the corner of his lips. I wanted to tell her that I was sorry. But I couldn't. Mel was the oldest of us, three years older than Ken, five years my senior. When Julie was found dead, she ran away. That was the only way to put it. She upped with her new husband and baby and moved across the country. Most of the time I understood, but I still felt the anger of what I perceived as abandonment.

I thought again about the picture of Ken in my pocket and made a sudden decision. "I want to show you something."

I thought I saw Melissa wince, as if bracing for a blow, but that might have been projection. Her hair was pure Suzy Homemaker, what with the suburban-blond frost and bouncy shoulder-length— probably just the way Ralph liked it. It looked wrong to me, out of place on her.

We moved a little farther away until we were near the door leading to the garage. I looked back. I could still see my father and Ralph and Lou Farley.

I opened the door. Mel looked at me curiously but she followed. We stepped onto the cement of the chilly garage. The place was done up in Early American Fire Hazard. Rusted paint cans, moldy cardboard boxes, baseball bats, old wicker, treadless tires—all strewn about as though there'd been an explosion. There were oil stains on the floor, and the dust made it all drab and faded gray and hard to breathe. A rope still hung from the ceiling. I remembered when my father had cleared out some space, attached a tennis ball to that rope so I could practice my baseball swing. I couldn't believe it was still there.

Melissa kept her eyes on me.

I wasn't sure how to do this.

"Sheila and I were going through Mom's things yesterday," I began.

Her eyes narrowed a little. I was about to start explaining, how we had sifted through her drawers and looked at the laminated birth announcements and that old program from when Mom played Mame in the Little Livingston production and how Sheila and I bathed ourselves in the old pictures—remember the one with King Hussein, Mel?—but none of that passed my lips.

Without saying another word, I reached into my pocket, plucked out the photograph, and held it up in front of her face.

It didn't take long. Melissa turned away as if the photo could scald her. She gulped a few deep breaths and stepped back. I moved toward her, but she held up a hand, halting me. When she looked up again, her face was a total blank. No surprise anymore. No anguish or joy either. Nothing.

I held it up again. This time she didn't blink.

"It's Ken," I said stupidly.

"I can see that, Will."

"That's the sum total of your reaction?"

"How would you like me to react?"

"He's alive. Mom knew it. She had this picture."

Silence.

"Mel?"

"He's alive," she said. "I heard you."

Her response—or lack thereof—left me speechless.

"Is there anything else?" Melissa asked.

"What . . . that's all you have to say?"

"What else is there to say, Will?"

"Oh, right, I forgot. You have to get back to Seattle."

"Yes."

She stepped away from me.

The anger resurfaced. "Tell me something, Mel. Did running away help?"

"I didn't run away."

"Bullshit," I said.

"Ralph got a job out there."

"Right."

"How dare you judge me?"

I flashed back to when the three of us played Marco Polo for hours in the motel pool near Cape Cod. I flashed back to the time Tony Bonoza spread rumors about Mel, how Ken's face had turned red when he'd heard, how he'd taken Bonoza on, even though he'd given up two years and twenty pounds.

"Ken is alive," I said again.

Her voice was a plea. "And what do you want me to do about it?"

"You act like it doesn't matter."

"I'm not sure it does."

"What the hell is that supposed to mean?"

"Ken's not a part of our lives anymore."

"Speak for yourself."

"Fine, Will. He's not a part of my life anymore."

"He's your brother."

"Ken made his choices."

"And now—what?—he's dead to you?"

"Wouldn't it be better if he were?" She shook her head and closed her eyes. I waited. "Maybe I did run away, Will. But so did you. We had a choice. Our brother was either dead or a brutal killer. Either way, yes, he's dead to me."

I held up the picture again. "He doesn't have to be guilty, you know."

Melissa looked at me, and suddenly she was the older sister again. "Come on, Will. You know better."

"He defended us. When we were kids. He looked out for us. He loved us."

"And I loved him. But I also saw him for what he was. He was drawn to violence, Will. You know that. Yes, he stuck up for us. But don't you think part of that was because he enjoyed it? You know he was mixed up in something bad when he died."

"That doesn't make him a killer."

Melissa closed her eyes again. I could see her mining for some inner strength. "For crying out loud, Will, what was he doing that night?"

Our eyes met and held. I said nothing. A sudden chill blew across my heart.

"Forget the murder, okay? What was Ken doing having sex with Julie Miller?"

Her words penetrated me, blossomed in my chest, big and cold. I couldn't breathe. My voice, when I finally found it, was tinny, far-away. "We'd been broken up for over a year."

"You telling me you were over her?"

"I . . . she was free. He was free. There was no reason—"

"He betrayed you, Will. Face it already. At the very least, he slept with the woman you loved. What kind of brother does that?"

"We broke up," I said, floundering. "I held no claim to her."

"You loved her."

"That has nothing to do with it."

She wouldn't take her eyes off mine. "Now who's running away?"

I stumbled back and half collapsed onto the cement stairs. My face dropped into my hands. I put myself together a piece at a time. It took a while. "He's still our brother."

"So what do you want to do? Find him? Hand him over to the police? Help him keep hiding? What?"

I had no answer.

Melissa stepped over me and opened the door to head back into the den. "Will?"

I looked up at her.

"This isn't my life anymore. I'm sorry."

I saw her then as a teenager, lying on her bed, jabbering away, her hair overteased, the smell of bubble gum in the air. Ken and I would sit on the floor of her room and roll our eyes. I remembered her body language. If Mel was lying on her belly, her feet kicking in the air, she was talking about boys and parties and that nonsense. But when she lay on her back and stared at the ceiling, well, that was for dreams. I thought about her dreams. I thought about how none of them had come true.

"I love you," I said.

And, as though she could see into my thoughts, Melissa started to cry.

We never forget our first love. Mine ended up being murdered.

Julie Miller and I met when her family moved onto Coddington Terrace during my freshman year at Livingston High. We started dating two years later. We went to the junior and senior proms. We were voted class couple. We were pretty much inseparable.

Our breakup was surprising only in its outright predictability. We went off to separate colleges, sure our commitment could stand the time and distance. It couldn't, though it hung on for longer than most. During our junior year, Julie called me on the phone and said that she wanted to see other people, that she'd already started dating a senior named—I'm not kidding here—Buck.

I should have gotten over it. I was young and this was hardly an unusual rite of passage. And I probably would have. Eventually. I mean, I dated. It was taking time, but I was starting to accept reality. Time and distance helped with that.

But then Julie died, and it seemed as though a part of my heart would never break free of her grip from the grave.

Until Sheila.

I didn't show the picture to my father.

I got back to my apartment at ten o'clock at night. Still empty, still stale, still foreign. No messages on the machine. If this was life without Sheila, I wanted no part of it.

The scrap of paper with her parents' Idaho phone number was still on the desk. What was the time difference in Idaho? One hour? Maybe two? I didn't remember. But that made it either eight or nine o'clock at night.

Not too late to call.

I collapsed into the chair and stared at the phone as if it'd tell me what to do. It didn't. I picked up the scrap of paper. When I'd told Sheila to call her parents, her face had lost all color. That had been yesterday. Just yesterday. I wondered what I should do and my first thought, my very first, was that I should ask my mother, that she would know the right answer.

A fresh wave of sadness pulled me under.

In the end, I knew that I had to act. I had to do something. And this, calling Sheila's parents, was all I could come up with.

A woman answered on the third ring. "Hello?"

I cleared my throat. "Mrs. Rogers?"

There was a pause. "Yes?"

"My name is Will Klein."

I waited, seeing if the name meant anything to her. If it did, she wasn't letting me know.

"I'm a friend of your daughter's."

"Which daughter?"

"Sheila," I said.

"I see," the woman said. "I understand she's been in New York."

"Yes," I said.

"Is that where you're calling from?"

"Yes."

"What can I do for you, Mr. Klein?"

That was a good question. I didn't really know myself, so I started with the obvious. "Do you have any idea where she is?"

"No."

"You haven't seen or spoken to her?"

In a tired voice, she said, "I haven't seen or spoken to Sheila in years."

I opened my mouth, closed it, tried to see a route to take, kept running into roadblocks. "Are you aware that she's missing?"

"The authorities have been in touch with us, yes."

I switched hands and brought the receiver up to my other ear. "Could you tell them anything useful?"

"Useful?"

"Do you have any idea where she might have gone? Where she'd run away to? A friend or a relative who might help?"

"Mr. Klein?"

"Yes."

"Sheila has not been a part of our life for a long time."

"Why not?"

I just blurted that out. I imagined a rebuke, of course, a big, fat none-of-your-business. But again she fell into silence. I tried to wait her out, but she was better at that than I.

"It's just that"—I could hear myself begin to stammer—"she's a wonderful person."

"You're more than a friend, aren't you, Mr. Klein?"

"Yes."

"The authorities. They mentioned that Sheila was living with a man. I assume they were talking about you?"

"We've been together about a year," I said.

53

"You sound as though you're worried about her."

"I am."

"You love her, then?"

"Very much."

"But she's never told you about her past."

I wasn't sure how to respond to that one, though the answer was obvious. "I'm trying to understand," I said.

"It's not like that," she said. "I don't even understand."

My neighbor picked now to blast his new stereo with quadraphonic speakers. The bass shook the wall. I was on the portable phone, so I moved toward the far end of the apartment.

"I want to help her," I said.

"Let me ask you something, Mr. Klein."

Her tone made my grip on the receiver tighten.

"The federal agent who came by," she went on. "He said they don't know anything about it."

"About what?" I asked.

"About Carly," Mrs. Rogers said. "About where she is."

I was confused. "Who's Carly?"

There was another long pause. "May I give you a word of advice, Mr. Klein?"

"Who's Carly?" I asked again.

"Get on with your life. Forget you ever knew my daughter."

And then she hung up.

8

I grabbed a Brooklyn Lager from the fridge and slid open the glass door. I stepped out onto what my Realtor had optimistically dubbed a "veranda." It was the approximate size of a baby crib. One person, perhaps two, if they stood very still, could stand on it at one time. There were, of course, no chairs, and being on the third floor, not much of a view. But it was air and night and I still liked it.

At night, New York is well lit and unreal, filled with a blue-black glow. This may be the city that never sleeps, but if my street was an indication, it could sneak in a serious nap. Parked cars sat crammed along the curb, bumper grinding bumper, seemingly jockeying for position long after their owners had abandoned them. Night sounds throbbed and hummed. I heard music. I heard clatter from the pizza place across the street. I heard the steady whooshing from the West Side Highway, gentle now, Manhattan's lullaby.

My brain slipped into numb. I didn't know what was happening. I didn't know what to do next. My call to Sheila's mother raised more questions than it answered. Melissa's words still stung, but she'd raised an interesting point: Now that I knew Ken was alive, what was I prepared to do about it?

I wanted to find him, of course.

I wanted to find him very badly. But so what? Forget the fact that I wasn't a detective or up to the task. If Ken wanted to be found, he'd come to me. Searching him out could only lead to disaster.

And maybe I had another priority.

First my brother had run off. Now my lover vanishes into thin air. I frowned. It was a good thing I didn't have a dog.

I was raising the bottle to my lip when I noticed him.

He stood on the corner, maybe fifty yards from my building. He wore a trench coat and what might have been a fedora, his hands in his pockets. His face from this distance looked like a white orb shining against a dark backdrop, featureless and too round. I couldn't see his eyes, but I knew he was looking at me. I could feel it, the weight of his stare. It was palpable.

The man didn't move.

There weren't many pedestrians on the street, but the ones who were there, they, well, they *moved*. That was what New Yorkers did. They moved. They walked. They walked with purpose. Even when they stood for a light or passing car, they bounced, always at the ready. New Yorkers moved. There was no still in them.

But this man stood like stone. Staring at me. I blinked hard. He was still there. I turned away and then looked back. He was still there, unmoving. And one more thing.

Something about him was familiar.

I didn't want to take that too far. We were at a pretty good distance and it was nighttime and my vision is not the best, especially in streetlight. But the hair on the back of my neck rose like on an animal sensing terrible danger.

I decided to stare back, see how he reacted. He didn't move. I don't know how long we stood there like that. I could feel the blood leaving my fingertips. Cold settled in near the edges, but something at my center gathered strength. I didn't look away. And neither did the featureless face.

The phone rang.

I wrested my vision away. My watch said it was nearly eleven P.M. Late for a call. Without a backward glance, I stepped back inside and picked up the receiver.

Squares said, "Sleepy?"

"No."

"Want to take a ride?"

He was taking out the van tonight. "You learn something?"

"Meet me at the studio. Half an hour."

He hung up. I walked back to the terrace and looked down. The man was gone.

The yoga school was simply called Squares. I made fun of it, of course. Squares had become one word, like Cher or Fabio. The school, studio, whatever you want to call it, was located in a six-story walk-up on University Place off Union Square. The beginnings had been humble. The school had toiled in happy obscurity. Then a certain celebrity, a major pop star you know too well, "discovered" Squares. She told her friends. A few months later, *Cosmo* picked it up. Then *Elle*. Somewhere along the line, a big infomercial company asked Squares to do a video. Squares, a firm believer in selling out, delivered the goods. The Yoga Squared Workout—the name is copyrighted—took off. Hey, Squares even shaved on the day they taped.

The rest was history.

Suddenly, no Manhattan or Hamptons social event could deem itself "a happening" without everyone's favorite fitness guru. Squares turned down most invitations, but he quickly learned how to network. He rarely had time to teach anymore. If you want to take any of the classes, even ones taught by his most junior students, the waitlist is at least two months. He charges twenty-five dollars per class. He has four studios. The smallest holds fifty students. The largest close to two hundred. He has twenty-four teachers who rotate in and out. As I approached the school now, it was eleven-thirty at night and three classes were still in session.

Do the math.

In the elevator I started hearing the painful strains of sitar music blending with the lapping of cascading waterfalls, a mingling of sounds I find about as soothing as a cat hit with a stun gun. The gift shop greets you first, filled with incense and books and lotions and tapes and videos and CD-ROMs and DVDs and crystals and beads and ponchos and tie-dye. Behind the counter were two anorexic twentysomething-year-olds dressed in black, their entire personas reeking of granola. Forever young. Just wait. One male, one female, though it wasn't easy to tell which was which. Their voices were even and just this side of patronizing—maître d's at a trendy new restaurant. Their body piercings—and there were lots of them—were filled with silver and turquoise.

"Hi," I said.

"Please remove your shoes," Probably Male said.

"Right."

I slipped them off.

57

"And you are?" Probably Female asked.

"Here to see Squares. I'm Will Klein."

The name meant nothing to them. Must be new. "Do you have an appointment with Yogi Squares?"

"Yogi Squares?" I repeated.

They stared at me.

"Tell me," I said. "Is Yogi Squares smarter than the average Squares?"

No laughter from the kiddies. Big surprise. She typed something into the computer terminal. They both frowned at the monitor. He picked up the phone and dialed. The sitar music blared. I felt a whopper headache brewing.

"Will?"

A wonderfully leotard-clad Wanda swept into the room, head high, clavicle prominent, eyes taking in everything. She was Squares's lead teacher and lover. They'd been together for three years now. Said leotard was lavender and oh-so-right. Wanda was a bold vision—tall, long-limbed, and lithe, achingly beautiful, and black. Yes, black. The irony did not escape those of us who knew Squares's—pardon the pun—checkered past.

She wrapped her arms around me, her embrace as warm as wood smoke. I wished it would last forever.

"How are you, Will?" she said softly.

"Better."

She pulled back, those eyes searching for the lie. She'd been to my mother's funeral. She and Squares had no secrets. Squares and I had no secrets. Like an algebra proof using the communicative property, you could thus deduce that she and I had no secrets.

"He's finishing up a class," she said. "Pranayama breathing."

I nodded.

She tilted her head as though she'd just thought of something. "Do you have a second before you go?" Her voice aimed for casual but couldn't quite get there.

"Sure," I said.

She padded—Wanda was too graceful to merely walk—down the corridor. I followed, my eyes level with her swanlike neck. We passed a fountain so large and ornate I wanted to toss a penny in it. I peeked in one of the studios. Total silence, save heavy breathing. It looked like a movie set. Gorgeous people—I don't know how Squares found so many gorgeous people—packed side by side in

58

warrior pose, faces serenely blank, legs spread, hands out, front knees at a ninety-degree angle.

The office Wanda shared with Squares was on the right. She lowered herself onto a chair as though it were made of Styrofoam and crossed her legs into a lotus. I sat across from her in a more conventional style. She didn't speak for a few moments. Her eyes closed and I could see her willing herself to relax. I waited.

"I didn't tell you this," she said.

"Okay."

"I'm pregnant."

"Hey, that's great." I started to rise to offer up a congratulatory hug.

"Squares isn't handling it well."

I stopped. "What do you mean?"

"He's freaking out."

"How?"

"You didn't know, right?"

"Right."

"He tells you everything, Will. He's known for a week." I saw her point.

"He probably didn't want to say anything," I said, "what with my mother and all."

She looked at me hard and said, "Don't do that."

"Yeah, sorry."

Her eyes skittered away from mine. The cool facade. There were cracks there now. "I expected him to be happy."

"He wasn't?"

"I think he wants me to"—she seemed out of words—"end it."

That knocked me back a step. "He said that?"

"He hasn't said anything. He's working the van extra nights. He's taking on more classes."

"He's avoiding you."

"Yes."

The office door opened without knocking. Squares leaned his unshaven mug into the doorway. He gave Wanda a cursory smile. She turned away. Squares gave me the thumb. "Let's rock and roll."

We didn't speak until we were safely ensconced in the van.

Squares said, "She told you."

59

It was a statement, not a question, so I didn't bother confirming or denying.

He put the key in the ignition. "We're not talking about it," he said.

Another statement that required no response.

The Covenant House van heads straight into the bowels. Many of our kids come to our doors. Many others are rescued in this van. The job of outreach is to connect with the community's seedy underbelly—meet the runaway kids, the street urchins, the ones too often referred to as the "throwaways." A kid living on the street is a bit like—and please pardon the analogy here—a weed. The longer he's on the street, the harder it is to pull him out by the root.

We lose a lot of these kids. More than we save. And forget the weed analogy. It's stupid because it implies that we're getting rid of something bad and preserving something good. In fact, it's just the opposite. Try this instead: The street is more like a cancer. Early screening and preventive treatment is the key to long-term survival.

Not much better, but you get the gist.

"The feds exaggerated," Squares said.

"How so?"

"Sheila's record."

"Go on."

"The arrests. They were all a long time ago. You want to hear this?"

"Yes."

We started driving deep into the gloom. The city's hooker hangouts are fluid. Often you'll find them near the Lincoln Tunnel or Javits Center, but lately the cops have been cracking down. More cleanup. So the hookers flowed south to the meat-packing district on 18th Street and the far west side. Tonight the hookers were out in force.

Squares gestured with his head. "Sheila could have been any one of them."

"She worked the street?"

"A runaway from the Midwest. Got off the bus and straight into the life."

I'd seen it too many times to shock me. But this wasn't a stranger or street kid at the end of her rope. This was the most amazing woman I had ever known.

"A long time ago," Squares said as though reading my thoughts. "Her first arrest was age sixteen."

"Prostitution?"

He nodded. "Three more like that in the next eighteen months, working, according to her file, for a pimp named Louis Castman. Last time she was carrying two ounces and a knife. They tried to bust her for both dealing and armed robbery, but it got kicked."

I looked out the window. The night had turned gray, washed out. You see so much bad on these streets. We work hard to stop some of it. I know we succeed. I know we turn lives around. But I know that what happens here, in the vibrant cesspool of night, never leaves them. The damage is done. You may work around it. You may go on. But the damage is permanent.

"What are you afraid of?" I asked him.

"We're not talking about it."

"You love her. She loves you."

"And she's black."

I turned to him and waited. I know that he didn't mean the obvious by this. He was not being racist. But it's like I told you. The damage is permanent. I had seen the tension between them. It wasn't nearly as powerful as the love, but it was there.

"You love her," I repeated.

He kept driving.

"Maybe that was part of the initial attraction," I said. "But she's not your redemption anymore. You're in love with her."

"Will?"

"Yeah?"

"Enough."

Squares suddenly veered the van to the right. Headlights splashed over the children of the night. They didn't scatter like rats under the onslaught. They, in fact, stared mutely, barely blinking. Squares narrowed his eyes, spotted his prey, and pulled to a stop.

We got out in silence. The children looked at us with dead eyes. I remembered a line of Fantine's in *Les Misérables*—the musical version, I don't know if it's in the book: "Don't they know they're making love to what's already dead?"

There were girls and boys and cross-dressers and transsexuals. I have seen every known perversion out here, though—and I'm sure I'll get accused of sexism here—I don't think I've ever seen a female

61

customer. I'm not saying that women never buy sex. I'm sure they do. But they don't seem to cruise the streets to do it. The street customers, the johns, are always men. They may want a buxom woman or a skinny one, young, old, straight, kinky to unfathomable levels, big men, little boys, animals, whatever. Some may even have a woman with them, dragging a girlfriend or wife into the fray. But the customers trolling these byways are men.

Despite all the talk about unfathomable kink, these men for the most part come here to purchase a certain . . . act, if you will. Something performed on them, one that can easily take place in a parked car. It makes sense for both, when you think about it. Convenience, for one thing. You don't need the expense and time of finding a room. Your concern about sexually transmitted diseases, while still there, is lessened. Pregnancy is not an issue. You don't need to fully undress. . . .

I'll spare you further details.

The street veterans—by veterans, I mean anyone over the age of eighteen—greeted Squares warmly. They knew him. They liked him. They were a bit wary of my presence. It had been a while since I'd been in the trenches. Still, some of the old-timers recognized me and in a bizarre way, I was glad to see them.

Squares approached a hooker named Candi, though I deduced that Candi was probably not her real name. No flies on me. She pointed with her chin at two shivering girls huddled in a doorway. I looked at them, no more than sixteen years old, their faces painted like two little girls who'd found Mommy's makeup case, and my heart sank. They were dressed in shorter-than-short shorts, high boots with stiletto heels, fake fur. I often wondered where they find these outfits, if the pimps had special hooker stores or what.

"Fresh meat," Candi said.

Squares frowned, nodded. Many of our best leads come from the veterans. There are two reasons for this. One—the cynical reasoning—is that taking the newbies out of circulation eliminates competition. If you live out in the streets, you get ugly in a hurry. Candi was, quite frankly, hideous. This life ages you faster than any black hole. The new girls, though forced to stay huddled in doorways until they earn turf, are going to get noticed.

But that view is, I think, uncharitable. Reason two, the bigger reason, was that—and please don't think me naïve here—they want to help. They see themselves. They see the fork in the road and while they might not readily admit they took the wrong prong, they know that it's too late for them. They can't go back. I used to argue with the Candis of the world. I used to insist that it was never too late, that there was still time. I was wrong. Here again is why we need to reach them quickly. There is a certain point that once passed, you cannot save them. The destruction is irreversible. The street consumes them. They fade away. They become part of the night, one single dark entity. They are lost to us. They will probably die here or end up in jail or insane.

"Where's Raquel?" Squares said.

"Working a car job," Candi said.

"She coming back here?"

"Yeah."

Squares nodded and turned to the two new girls. One was already leaning into a Buick Regal. You cannot imagine the frustration. You want to step in and stop it. You want to pull the girl away and reach your hand down the john's throat and rip out his lungs. You want to at least chase him away or take a photograph or . . . or something. But you do none of that. If you do any of that, you lose the trust. You lose the trust, you're useless.

It was hard to do nothing. Fortunately I'm not particularly brave or confrontational. Maybe that makes it easier.

I watched the passenger door open. The Buick Regal seemed to devour the child. She disappeared slowly, sinking into the dark. I watched and I don't think I ever felt so helpless. I looked at Squares. His eyes were focused on the car. The Buick pulled away. The girl was gone as though she'd never existed. If the car chooses not to return, it would forever be that way.

Squares approached the remaining new girl. I followed, staying a few steps behind him. The girl's lower lip quivered as though holding back tears, but her eyes blazed with defiance. I wanted to pull her into the van, by force if necessary. So much of this task is restraint. It was why Squares was the master. He stopped about a yard away, careful not to invade her space.

"Hi," he said.

She looked him over and muttered, "Hey."

"I was hoping you could help me out." Squares took another step and pulled a photograph out of his pocket. "I'm wondering if you've seen her."

The girl did not look at the picture. "I haven't seen anyone."

"Please," Squares said with a smile damn near celestial. "I'm not a cop."

She tried to look tough. "Figured that," she said. "You talking to Candi and all."

Squares moved a little closer. "We, that is, my friend here and I"—I waved on cue, smiled—"we're trying to save this girl."

Curious now, she narrowed her eyes. "Save her how?"

"Some bad people are after her."

"Who?"

"Her pimp. See, we work for Covenant House. You heard of that?"

She shrugged.

"It's a place to hang out," Squares said, trying to downplay it. "No big deal. You can stop in and have a hot meal, a warm bed to sleep in, use the phone, get some clothes, whatever. Anyway, this girl"—he held up the photograph, a school portrait of a white girl in braces—"her name is Angie." Always give a name. It personalizes it. "She's been staying with us. Taking a couple of courses. She's a really funny kid. And she got a job too. Turning her life around, you know?"

The girl said nothing.

Squares held out his hand. "Everyone calls me Squares," he said.

The girl sighed, took the hand. "I'm Jeri."

"Nice to meet you."

"Yeah. But I haven't seen this Angie. And I'm kinda busy here."

Here was where you had to read. If you push too hard, you lose them forever. They burrow back into their hole and never come out. All you want to do now—all you can do now—is plant the seed. You let her know that there is a haven for her, a safe place, where she can get a meal and find shelter. You give her a way off the street for just one night. Once she gets there, you show the unconditional love. But not now. Now it scares them. Now it chases them away.

As much as it ripped you apart inside, you could not do any more.

Very few people could do Squares's job for very long. And the ones who lasted, the ones who were particularly good at it, they were just . . . slightly off center. You had to be.

Squares hesitated. He has used this "missing girl" gig as an icebreaker for as long as I've known him. The girl in the picture, the real Angie, died fifteen years ago, out on the street, from exposure. Squares found her behind a Dumpster. At the funeral, Angie's mother gave him that photograph. I don't think I've ever seen him without it.

"Okay, thanks." Squares took out a card and handed it to her. "If you do see her, will you let me know? You can call anytime. Any reason."

She took the card, fingered it. "Yeah, maybe."

Another hesitation. Then Squares said, "See you around."

"Yeah."

We then did the most unnatural thing in the world. We walked away.

Raquel's real name was Roscoe. At least that was what he or she told us. I never know if I should address Raquel as a he or a she. I should probably ask him/her.

Squares and I found the car parked in front of a sealed-off delivery entrance. A common place for street work. The car windows were fogged up, but we kept our distance anyway. Whatever was going on in there—and we had a pretty good idea what—was not something we cared to witness.

The door opened a minute later. Raquel came out. As you may have guessed by now, Raquel was a cross-dresser, hence the gender confusion. With transsexuals, okay, you refer to them as "she." Cross-dressing is a bit trickier. Sometimes the "she" applies. Sometimes it's just a tad too politically correct.

That was probably the case with Raquel.

Raquel rolled out of the car, reached into his purse, and took out the Binaca spray. Three blasts, a pause, a thought, then three more blasts. The car pulled away. Raquel turned toward us.

Many transvestites are beautiful. Raquel was not. He was black, six-six, and comfortably on the north side of three hundred pounds. He had biceps like giant hogs wrestling in sausage casing, and his six-o'clock shadow reminded me of Homer Simpson's. He had a voice so high pitched it made Michael Jackson sound like a teamster boss—Betty Boop sucking helium.

Raquel claimed to be twenty-nine years old, but he'd been saying that for the six years I'd known him. He worked five nights a week, rain or shine, and had a rather devoted following. He could get off the streets if he wanted. He could find a place to work out of, set up appointments, that kind of thing. But Raquel liked it out here. That was one of the things people did not get. The street may be dark and dangerous, but it was also intoxicating. The night had an energy, an electricity. You felt wired out on the street. For some of our kids, the choice may be a menial job at Mickey D's versus the thrill of the night—and that, when you have no future, was no choice at all.

Raquel spotted us and started tottering in our direction on stiletto heels. Men's shoes size fourteen. No easy task, I assure you. Raquel stopped under a streetlamp. His face was worn like a rock battered by centuries of storms. I didn't know his back story. He lies a lot. One legend had him as an all-American football player who blew out a knee. Another time I'd heard him say that he'd gotten a college scholarship based on high SAT scores. Still another pegged him as a Gulf War veteran. Choose one of those or create your own.

Raquel greeted Squares with a hug and peck on the cheek. He then turned his attention to me.

"You looking so good, Sweet Willy," Raquel said.

"Gee thanks, Raquel," I said.

"Tasty enough to eat."

"I've been working out," I said. "Makes me extra yummy."

Raquel threw an arm around my shoulder. "I could fall in love with a man like you."

"I'm flattered, Raquel."

"Man like you, he could take me away from all this."

"Ah, but think of all the broken hearts you'd leave in these sewers."

Raquel giggled. "Got that right."

I showed Raquel a photograph of Sheila, the only one I had. Weird when I think back on it now. Neither one of us were picture-takers, but to have only one photograph?

"You recognize her?" I asked him.

Raquel studied the picture. "This your woman," he said. "I seen her at the shelter once."

"Right. You know her from anyplace else?"

"Nope. Why?"

There was no reason to lie. "She's run off. I'm looking for her."

Raquel studied the picture some more. "Can I keep this?"

I'd made some color copies at the office, so I handed it to him.

"I'll ask around," Raquel said.

"Thanks."

He nodded.

"Raquel?" It was Squares. Raquel turned to him. "You remember a pimp named Louis Castman?"

Raquel's face went slack. He started looking around.

"Raquel?"

"I gotta get back to work, Squares. Bidness, you know."

I stepped in his way. He looked down at me as if I were dandruff flakes he might flick off his shoulder.

"She used to work the streets," I said to him.

"Your girl?"

"Yes."

"And she worked for Castman?"

"Yes."

Raquel crossed himself. "A bad man, Sweet Willy. Castman was the worst."

"How so?"

He licked his lips. "Girls out here. They just a commodity, you know what I'm saying. Merchandise. It bidness with most folk out here. They make money, they stay. They don't make money, well, you know."

I did.

"But Castman"—Raquel whispered his name the way some people whispered the word *cancer*—"he was different."

"How?"

"He'd damage his own merchandise. Sometimes just for fun."

Squares said, "You keep referring to him in the past tense."

"That's 'cause he ain't been around in, oh, three years."

"He alive?"

Raquel became very quiet. He looked off. Squares and I exchanged a glance, waited.

"He still alive," Raquel said. "I guess."

"What does that mean?"

Raquel just shook his head.

"We need to speak with him," I said. "Do you know where we can find him?"

"I just heard rumors."

"What kind of rumors?"

Raquel shook his head again. "Check out a place on the corner

67

of Wright Street and Avenue D in the South Bronx. Heard he might be there."

Raquel walked away then, steadier on the stiletto heels. A car drove up, stopped, and again I watched a human being disappear into the night.

9

Most neighborhoods, you'd hesitate about waking someone at one in the morning. This wasn't one of them. The windows were all boarded up. The door was a hunk of plywood. I'd tell you the paint was peeling, but it would probably be more apt to say it was shedding.

Squares knocked on the plywood door and immediately a woman shouted, "What do you want?"

Squares did the talking. "We're looking for Louis Castman."

"Go away."

"We need to speak with him."

"You got a warrant?"

"We're not with the police."

"Who are you?" the woman asked.

"We work for Covenant House."

"No runaways here," she shouted, nearly hysterical. "Go away."

"You have a choice," Squares said. "We talk to Castman ourselves right now, or we come back with a bunch of nosy cops."

"I didn't do nothing."

"I can always make something up," Squares said. "Open the door."

The woman made a fast decision. We heard a bolt slide, then another, then a chain. The door opened a crack. I started toward it, but Squares blocked me with his arm. Wait until the door opened all the way.

"Hurry," the woman said with a witchlike cackle. "Get inside. Don't want nobody seeing."

Squares gave the door a shove. It opened all the way. We stepped through the frame, and the woman closed the door. Two things hit me at the same time. First, the dark. The only light was a low-watt lamp in the far right-hand corner. I saw a threadbare reading chair, a coffee table, and that was about it. Second, the smell. Take your most vivid remembrance of fresh air and the great outdoors and then imagine the polar opposite. The stuffiness made me afraid to inhale. Part hospital, part something I couldn't quite place. I wondered when the last time a window had been opened, and the room seemed to whisper, *Never*.

Squares turned to the woman. She'd shrunk back into a corner. We could see only a silhouette in the darkness. "They call me Squares," he said.

"I know who you are."

"Have we met?"

"That's not important."

"Where is he?" Squares asked.

"There's only one other room in here," she said, raising her hand in a slow point. "He might be asleep."

Our eyes started to adjust. I stepped toward her. She didn't back away. I got closer. When she lifted her head, I almost gasped. I mumbled an apology and started backing away.

"No," she said. "I want you to see."

She crossed the room, stopped in front of the lamp, and faced us full. To our credit, neither Squares nor I flinched. But it wasn't easy. Whoever had disfigured her had done it with great care. She'd probably been a looker at one time, but it was as though she'd gone through some anti-plastic-surgery regimen. A perhaps once-well-shaped nose had been squelched like a beetle under a heavy boot. Once-smooth skin had been split and ripped. The corners of her mouth had been torn to the point where it was hard to tell where it ended. Dozens of raised angry purple scars crisscrossed her face, like the work of a three-year-old given free rein with a Crayola. Her left eye wandered off to the side, dead in its socket. The other stared at us unblinking.

Squares said, "You used to be on the street."

70

She nodded.

"What's your name?"

Moving her mouth seemed to take great effort. "Tanya."

"Who did that to you?"

"Who do you think?"

We did not bother replying.

"He's through that door," she said. "I take care of him. I never hurt him. You understand? I never raise a hand to him."

We both nodded. I didn't know what to make of that. I don't think Squares did either. We moved to the door. Not a sound. Perhaps he was asleep. I didn't really care. He'd wake up. Squares put his hand on the knob and looked back at me. I let him know that I'd be fine. He opened the door.

Lights were on in there. Full blast, in fact. I had to shade my eyes. I heard a beeping noise and saw some sort of medical machine near the bed. But that wasn't what first drew my eye.

The walls.

That was what you noticed first. The walls were corked—I could see a little of the brown—but more than that, they were blanketed with photographs. Hundreds of photographs. Some blown up to poster size, some your classic three-by-fives, most somewhere in between—all hung on the cork by clear pushpins.

And they were all pictures of Tanya.

At least, that was what I guessed. The pictures were all pre-disfiguration. And I had been right. Tanya had been beautiful once. The photos, mostly glamour shots from what appeared to be a model's portfolio, were inescapable. I looked up. More photographs, a ceiling fresco from hell.

"Help me. Please."

The small voice came from the bed. Squares and I moved toward it. Tanya came in behind us and cleared her voice. We turned. In the harsh light, her scars seemed almost alive, squirming across her face like dozens of worms. The nose was not just flattened, but misshapen, claylike. The old photographs seemed to glow, swarming her in a perverse before-and-after aura.

The man in the bed groaned.

We waited. Tanya turned the good eye first toward me, then toward Squares. The eye seemed to dare us to forget, to etch this image into our brains, to remember what she'd once been and what he'd done to her.

71

"A straight razor," she said. "A rusted one. It took him over an hour to do this. And he didn't just slice up my face."

Without another word, Tanya moved out of the room. She closed the door behind her.

We stood in silence for a moment. Then Squares said, "Are you Louis Castman?"

"You cops?"

"Are you Castman?"

"Yes. And I did it. Christ, whatever you want me to confess to, I did it. Just get me out of here. For the love of God."

"We're not cops," Squares said.

Castman lay flat on his back. There was some kind of tube connected to his chest. The machine kept beeping and something kept rising and falling accordionlike. He was a white guy, newly shaven, fresh-scrubbed. His hair was clean. His bed had rails and controls. I saw a bedpan in the corner and a sink. Other than that, the room was empty. No drawers, no dressers, no TV, no radio, no clock, no books, no newspapers, no magazines. The window shades were pulled down.

I had a sick feeling in the pit of my stomach.

"What's wrong with you?" I asked.

Castman's eyes—and only his eyes—turned toward me. "I'm paralyzed," he said. "A fucking quadriplegic. Below the neck"—he stopped, closed his eyes—"nothing."

I was not sure how to begin. Neither, it seemed, was Squares.

"Please," Castman said. "You gotta get me out of here. Before . . ."

"Before what?"

He closed his eyes, opened them again. "I got shot, what, three, four years ago maybe? I don't know anymore. I don't know what day or month or even year it is. The light's always on, so I don't know if it's day or night. I don't know who's president." He swallowed, not without some effort. "She's crazy, man. I try screaming for help, it don't do no good. She got the place lined with cork. I just lay here, all day, looking at these walls."

I found it hard to find my voice. Squares, however, was unfazed. "We're not here for your life story," he said. "We want to ask you about one of your girls."

"You got the wrong guy," he said. "I haven't worked the streets in a long time."

"That's okay. She hasn't worked in a long time either."

"Who?"

"Sheila Rogers."

"Ah." Castman smiled at the name. "What do you want to know?"

"Everything."

"And if I refuse to tell you?"

Squares touched my shoulder. "We're leaving," he said to me.

Castman's voice was pure panic. "What?"

Squares looked down at him. "You don't want to cooperate, Mr. Castman, that's fine. We won't bother you further."

"Wait!" he shouted. "Okay, look, you know how many visitors I've had since I been here?"

"Don't care," Squares said.

"Six. A grand total of six. And none in, I don't know, has to be a year at least. And all six were my old girls. They came here to laugh at me. Watch me shit myself. And you want to hear something sick? I looked forward to it. Anything to break up the monotony, you know what I mean?"

Squares looked impatient. "Sheila Rogers."

The tube made a wet, sucking noise. Castman opened his mouth. A bubble formed. He closed his mouth and tried again. "I met her—God, I'm trying to think—ten, fifteen years ago. I was working the Port Authority. She came off a bus from Iowa or Idaho, some shithole like that."

Working the Port Authority. I knew the routine well. Pimps wait at the terminal. They look for kids fresh off the bus—the desperate, the runaways, the raw meat, coming to the Big Apple to be models or actresses or start anew or flee from boredom or escape abuse. The pimps watch like the predators that they are. And then they swoop in, take them down, gnaw on the carcass.

"I had a good rap," Castman said. "First off, I'm a white guy. The Midwest meat. It's almost all white breast. They're afraid of the strutting brothers. But me, I was different. I'd wear a nice business suit. I'd carry a briefcase. I'd be a little more patient. So anyway, that day I was waiting by Gate 127. It was a favorite of mine. Got a good view of maybe six different arrivals. Sheila came off the bus and man, she was smoking hot. Maybe sixteen years old and prime-time. A virgin too, though I couldn't tell that right off. I'd learn all about that later."

I felt my muscles tighten. Squares slowly slid his body between the bed and me.

"So I started sweet-talking her. Sling her my best bits, you know?"

We knew.

"So I give her the line about making her a big-time model. But smooth. Not like the other assholes. I'm like silk. But Sheila, she was smarter than most. Cautious. I could tell she wasn't buying it all the way, but that was okay. See, I don't press. I act legit. End of the day, they want to believe, right? They all hear stories about some supermodel being discovered at the Dairy Queen or some such shit, and hey, that's why they come in the first place."

The machine stopped beeping. I heard it gurgle. Then it started beeping again.

"So Sheila sort of crosses her arms, right. She tells me straight up that she never parties or any of that. I tell her hey, no problem, I'm not into that either. I'm a businessman, I say. A professional photographer and talent scout. We'll take some pictures. That's all. Get a portfolio going. Straight up—no partying, no drugs, no nudity, nothing she isn't totally comfortable with. And I'm a pretty good photographer, you know. I got an eye for it. See these walls? These shots of Tanya—I took them."

I looked at the photographs of the once-beautiful Tanya, and the chill struck me deep in my heart. When I looked back at the bed, Castman was staring at me.

"You," he said.

"What about me?"

"Sheila." He smiled. "She means something to you, am I right?"

I didn't reply.

"You *love* her."

He stretched out the word *love*. Mocking me. I kept still.

"Hey, I don't blame you, man. That was some quality tang. And, man, she could suck the—"

I started toward him. Castman laughed. Squares stepped in the way. He looked me straight in the eye and shook his head. I backed off. He was right.

Castman stopped laughing, but his eyes stayed on me. "You want to know how I turned your girl out, lover boy?"

I said nothing.

"Same way as I did Tanya out there. See, I went for the prime

74

cuts, the ones the brothers couldn't get their hooks into. A high-end operation. So I gave Sheila the rap, and eventually I got her into my studio for a shoot. That was it. All I need to do. Put a fork in her, she's done."

"How?" I asked.

"You really want to hear this?"

"How?"

Castman closed his eyes, the smile still there, savoring the memory. "I took a bunch of photos of her. All nice and legit. And when we were done, I put a knife to her throat. Then I cuffed her to a bed in a room that was"—he chuckled, let his eyes open and roll—"corked. I drugged her up. I filmed her when she was half out of it, made it all look very consensual. That, by the way, was how your Sheila lost her virginity. On video. With yours truly. Magical, am I right?"

The rage flared again, started boiling over, consuming me. I didn't know how much longer I could keep from wringing his neck. But that, I reminded myself, was what he wanted.

"Where was I? Oh, right, I cuffed her and shot her up for maybe a week. Prime stuff too. Expensive. But hey, it's a business expense. All businesses got their training regimens, right? Eventually Sheila got hooked, and let me tell you, you can't put that genie back in the bottle. By the time I uncuffed her, that girl would lick out my toe jam for a hit, you know what I mean?"

He stopped as though waiting for applause. It felt as if something were shredding my insides.

Squares kept his voice flat. "So after this, you put her on the street?"

"Yup. Taught her some tricks too. How to get a guy off fast. How to take on more than one guy at a time. All that, I was her teacher."

I thought that I might throw up.

"Go on," Squares said.

"No," he said. "Not until—"

"Then we'll bid you good-bye."

"Tanya," he said.

"What about her?"

Castman licked his lips. "Can you give me some water?"

"No. What about Tanya?"

"The bitch keeps me here, man. It ain't right. Yeah, I hurt her.

75

But I had my reason. She wanted to leave, marry this john from Garden City. She thought they were in love. I mean, come on, this look like *Pretty Woman* to you? She was going to take some of my best girls with her. They could live out in Garden City with her and this john, get cleaned up, some such shit. I couldn't stand for that."

"So," Squares said, "you taught her a lesson."

"Yeah, sure. It's how it is."

"You messed up her face with a razor."

"Not just her face—guy might be into putting a bag over the head, you know what I mean? But yeah, you get the gist. It was a lesson to the other girls too. But see—and here's the funny part—her boyfriend, the john, he didn't know what I'd done. So he comes down from his big house in Garden City, all set up to rescue Tanya, right? The dumbass has a twenty-two. I laugh at him. And he shoots me. This dipwad accountant from Garden City. He shoots me under the armpit with a twenty-two and bam, the bullet goes into my spine. I'm left like this. You believe that? And then, oh, this is precious, after he shoots me, Mr. Garden City sees what I did to Tanya and you know what he does, this great love of hers?"

He waited. We figured it was rhetorical and kept still.

"He freaks out and dumps her. Get it? He sees my handiwork on Tanya, and he just runs out on her. Her great love. Wants nothing to do with her. They never see each other again."

Castman started laughing again. I tried to stay still and breathe.

"So I'm in the hospital," he continued, "totally out of it. Tanya's got nothing. So she signs me out. She brings me here. And now she takes care of me. You understand what I'm saying? She's prolonging my life. I refuse to eat, she sticks a tube down my throat. Look, I'll tell you what you want to know. But you got to do something for me."

"What?" Squares said.

"Kill me."

"No can do."

"Tell the police, then. Let them arrest me. I'll confess to everything."

Squares said, "What happened to Sheila Rogers?"

"Promise me."

Squares looked at me. "We got enough here. Let's go."

"Okay, okay, I'll tell you. Just . . . just think about it, okay?"

He shifted his eyes from Squares to me then back to Squares

again. Squares showed him nothing. I have no idea what was on my face. "I don't know where Sheila is now. Hell, I don't really understand what happened."

"How long did she work for you?"

"Two years. Maybe three."

"And how did she get free?"

"Huh?"

"You don't seem like the sort of guy who lets employees branch out," Squares said. "So I'm asking what happened to her."

"She worked the streets, right. Started getting some regulars. She was good at what she did. And somewhere along the way, she hooked up with some bigger players. It happens. Not often. But it happens."

"What do you mean, bigger players?"

"Dealers. Big-time dealers, I think. She started muling and delivering, I think. And worse, she started getting clean. I was going to lean on her, like you said, but she had some heavy-duty friends."

"Like who?"

"You know Lenny Misler?"

Squares leaned back. "The attorney?"

"The mob attorney," Castman corrected him. "She got picked up carrying. He repped her."

Squares frowned. "Lenny Misler took on the case of a street-walker caught carrying?"

"You see my point? She comes out, I start sniffing around, you know. Find out what's she up to. A couple of major-league goons pay me a visit. They tell me to stay away. I'm not stupid. Plenty more tang where that came from."

"What happened next?"

"Never saw her again. Last I heard she was going to college. You believe that?"

"Do you know what college?"

"No. I'm not even sure it's true. Could have been just a rumor."

"Anything else?"

"Nope."

"No other rumors?"

Castman's eyes started moving, and I could see the desperation. He wanted to keep us there. But he had nothing else to tell us. I looked at Squares. He nodded and turned to leave. I followed.

"Wait!"

We ignored him.

"Please, man, I'm begging you. I told you everything, right? I cooperated. You can't just leave me here."

I saw his endless days and nights in the room, and I didn't care.

"Fucking assholes!" he shouted. "Hey, man, you. Lover boy. You enjoy my leftovers, you hear. And remember this: Everything she does to you, every time she gets you off—I taught her that. You hear me? You hear what I'm saying?"

My cheeks flushed, but I didn't turn around. Squares opened the door.

"Shit." Castman's voice was softer now. "It doesn't leave, you know."

I hesitated.

"She may look all nice and clean. But where she's been, you don't ever come back. You know what I'm saying?"

I tried to shut out his words. But they hammered their way in and bounced around my skull. I walked out and closed the door. Back in the dark. Tanya met us on the way out.

"Are you going to tell?" she asked, her words slurred.

I never hurt him. That was what she said. She never raised a hand to him. Too true.

Without another word, we hurried back outside, almost diving into the night air. We sucked down deep breaths, divers breaking the surface short on air, got back to the van, and drove away.

10

Grand Island, Nebraska

Sheila wanted to die alone.

Strangely enough, the pain was diminishing now. She wondered why. There was no light, though, no moment of stark clarity. There was no comfort in death. No angels surrounded her. No long-gone relatives—she thought of her grandmother, the woman who'd made her feel special, who'd called her "Treasure"—came and held her hand.

Alone. In the dark.

She opened her eyes. Was she dreaming right now? Hard to say. She'd been hallucinating earlier. She'd been slipping in and out of consciousness. She remembered seeing Carly's face and begging her to go away. Had that been real? Probably not. Probably an illusion.

When the pain got bad, really bad, the line between awake and sleep, between reality and dreams, blurred. She did not fight it anymore. It was the only way you could survive the agony. You try to block the pain. That doesn't work. You try to break the pain down into manageable time intervals. That doesn't work either. Finally, you find the only outlet available: your sanity.

You let go of your sanity.

But if you can recognize what's happening, are you really letting go?

Deep philosophical questions. They were for the living. In the

end, after all the hopes and dreams, after all the damage and re-
building, Sheila Rogers would end up dying young and in pain and
at the hands of another.

Poetic justice, she supposed.

Because now, as she felt something inside her cleave and tear
and pull away, there was indeed a clarity. A horrible, inescapable
one. The blinders were being lifted, and for once she could see the
truth.

Sheila Rogers wanted to die alone.

But he was in the room with her. She was sure of it. She could
feel his hand resting gently on her forehead now. It made her cold.
As she felt the life force slipping away, she made one last plea.

"Please," she said. "Go away."

11

Squares and I did not discuss what we'd seen. We also did not call the police. I pictured Louis Castman trapped in that room, unable to move, nothing to read, no TV or radio, nothing to look at except those old photographs. If I were a better person, I might have even cared.

I also thought about the Garden City man who'd shot Louis Castman and then turned his back, his rejection probably scarring Tanya worse than Castman ever could. I wondered if Mr. Garden City still thought about Tanya or if he'd just gone on as if she'd never existed. I wondered if her face haunted his dreams.

I doubted it.

I thought about all this because I was curious and horrified. But I also did it because it stopped me from thinking about Sheila, about what she'd been, about what Castman had done to her. I reminded myself that she was the victim here, kidnapped and raped and worse, and that nothing she had done had been her fault. I should not view her any differently. But this clearheaded and obvious rationale would not stick.

And I hated myself for that.

It was nearly four in the morning when the van pulled up to my building.

"What do you make of it so far?" I asked.

Squares stroked his stubble. "What Castman said at the end there. About it never leaving her. He's right, you know."

"You speaking from experience?"

"As a matter of fact, I am."

"So?"

"So my guess is that something from her past came back and got her."

"We're on the right track then."

"Probably," Squares said.

I grabbed the door handle and said, "Whatever she's done—whatever you've done—it may never leave you. But it doesn't condemn you either."

Squares stared out the window. I waited. He kept staring. I stepped out and he drove away.

A message on the phone knocked me back a step. I checked the time on the LCD. The message had been left at 11:47 P.M. Awfully late. I figured it had to be family. I was wrong.

I hit the play button and a young woman said, "Hi, Will."

I didn't recognize the voice.

"It's Katy. Katy Miller."

I stiffened.

"Long time, right? Look, I, uh, sorry I'm calling so late. You're probably asleep, I don't know. Listen, Will, could you give me a call as soon as you get this? I don't care what time it is. I just, well, I need to talk to you about something."

She left her number. I stood there, dumbstruck. Katy Miller. Julie's little sister. The last time I'd seen her . . . she'd been six years old or so. I smiled, remembering a time—sheesh, Katy couldn't have been more than four—when she had hidden behind her father's army trunk and jumped out at an inopportune time. I remember Julie and I covering ourselves with a blanket, no time to pull up our pants, trying not to laugh our asses off.

Little Katy Miller.

She'd be, what, seventeen or eighteen by now. Odd to think about. I knew the effect Julie's death had on my family, and I could pretty much surmise what it had done to Mr. and Mrs. Miller. But I'd never really considered the impact on little Katy. I thought again about that time Julie and I had pulled up the blanket giggling, and now I remembered that we'd been in the basement. We'd been messing around on the very couch where Julie would be found murdered.

Why, after all these years, was Katy calling me?

It could be just a condolence call, I reminded myself, though that seemed odd on several levels, not the least of which would be the hour of her call. I replayed the message, searching for a hidden meaning. I didn't find one. She had said to call anytime. But it was four in the A.M., and I was exhausted. Whatever it was, it could wait until morning.

I climbed into bed and remembered the last time I'd seen Katy Miller. My family had been asked to stay away from the funeral. We complied. But two days later, I went by myself to the graveyard off Route 22. I sat by Julie's tombstone. I said nothing. I did not cry. I did not feel comfort or closure or anything else. The Miller family pulled up in their white Oldsmobile Cierra, and I made myself scarce. But I'd met little Katy's eyes. There was a strange resignation in her face, a knowing that went beyond her years. I saw sadness and horror and maybe I saw pity too.

I left the graveyard then. I had not seen or spoken to her since.

12

Belmont, Nebraska

Sheriff Bertha Farrow had seen worse.

Murder scenes were bad, but for overall vomit-inducing, bone-crunching, head-splitting, blood-splattering grossness, it was hard to beat the metal-against-flesh effect of an old-fashioned automobile accident. A head-on collision. A truck crossing the divider. A tree that splits the car from the bumper to the backseat. A high-speed tumble over a guardrail.

Now, that did serious damage.

And yet this sight, this dead woman at this fairly bloodless scene, was somehow much worse. Bertha Farrow could see the woman's face—her features twisted in fear, uncomprehending, maybe desperate—and she could see that the woman had died in great pain. She could see the mangled fingers, the misshapen rib cage, the bruises, and she knew that the damage here had been done by a fellow human being, flesh against flesh. This was not the result of a patch of ice or someone changing radio stations at eighty miles an hour or a rush truck delivery or the ill effects of alcohol or speed.

This had been intentional.

"Who found her?" she asked her deputy George Volker.

"The Randolph boys."

"Which ones?"

"Jerry and Ron."

Bertha calculated. Jerry would be about sixteen. Ron fourteen.

"They were walking with Gypsy," the deputy added. Gypsy was the Randolphs' German shepherd. "He sniffed her out."

"Where are the boys now?"

"Dave took them home. They were kinda shook up. I got statements. They don't know nothing."

Bertha nodded. A station wagon came tearing up the highway. Clyde Smart, the county medical examiner, stopped his wagon with a screech. The door flew open, and Clyde sprinted toward them. Bertha cupped a hand over her eyes.

"No rush, Clyde. She ain't going anywhere."

George snickered.

Clyde Smart was used to this. He was closing in on fifty, about Bertha's age. The two had been in office for nearly two decades. Clyde ignored her joke and ran past them. He looked down at the body, and his face dropped.

"Sweet Jesus," the M.E. said.

Clyde squatted beside her. He gently pushed the hair back from the corpse's face. "Oh God," he said. "I mean—" He stopped, shook his head.

Bertha was used to him too. Clyde's reaction did not surprise her. Most M.E.s, she knew, stayed clinical and detached. Not Clyde. People were not tissue and messy chemicals to him. She'd seen Clyde cry over bodies plenty of times. He handled each DOA with incredible, almost ridiculous, respect. He performed autopsies as though he could make the person recover. He'd deliver bad news to families, and he'd genuinely share their grief.

"Can you give me an approximate time of death?" she asked.

"Not long," Clyde said softly. "The skin is still in early rigor mortis. I'd say no more than six hours. I'll get a liver temperature reading and—" He spotted the hand with the fingers that jutted out in unnatural directions. "Oh my God," he said again.

Bertha looked back at her deputy. "Any ID?"

"None."

"Possible robbery?"

"Too brutal," Clyde said. He looked up. "Someone wanted her to suffer."

There was a moment of silence. Bertha could see tears forming in Clyde's eyes.

"What else?" she asked.

Clyde quickly looked back down. "She's no vagrant," he said. "Well dressed and nourished." He checked her mouth. "Decent enough dental work."

"Any signs of rape?"

"She's dressed," Clyde said. "But my God, what wasn't done to her? Very little blood here, certainly not enough for this to be the murder scene. My guess is that someone drove by and dumped her here. I'll know more when I get her on the table."

"Okay then," Bertha said. "Let's check Missing Persons and run her prints."

Clyde nodded as Sheriff Bertha Farrow started walking away.

13

I didn't have to call Katy back.

The ring hit me like a cattle prod. My sleep had been so deep, so total and dreamless, there could be no slow swim to the surface. One moment I was drowning in the black. The next I jolted upright, heart racing. I checked the digital clock: 6:58 A.M.

I groaned and leaned over. The caller ID was blocked. A useless contraption. Everyone you'd want to avoid or who'd wanted to hide simply paid for the block.

My voice sounded too awake in my own ears as I chirped a merry "Hello?"

"Uh, Will Klein?"

"Yes?"

"It's Katy Miller." Then, as if an afterthought, "Julie's sister."

"Hi, Katy," I said.

"I left a message for you last night."

"I didn't get in until four in the morning."

"Oh. I guess I woke you up then."

"Don't worry about it," I said.

Her voice sounded sad and young and forced. I remembered when she was born. I did a little math. "You're, what, a senior now?"

"I start college in the fall."

"Where?"

"Bowdoin. It's a small college."

"In Maine," I said. "I know it. It's an excellent school. Congratulations."

"Thanks."

I sat up a little more, trying to think of a way to bridge the silence. I fell back on the classics: "It's been a long time."

"Will?"

"Yes?"

"I'd like to see you."

"Sure, that would be great."

"How about today?"

"Where are you?" I asked.

"I'm in Livingston," she said. Then added, "I saw you come by our house."

"I'm sorry about that."

"I can come to the city if you want."

"No need," I said. "I'll be out visiting my father today. How about we hook up before that?"

"Yeah, okay," she said. "But not here. You remember the basketball courts by the high school?"

"Sure," I said. "I'll meet you there at ten."

"Okay."

"Katy," I said, switching ears. "I don't mind telling you that this call is a little weird."

"I know."

"What do you want to see me about?"

"What do you think?" she replied.

I did not answer right away, but that did not matter. She was already off the line.

14

Will left his apartment. The Ghost watched.

The Ghost did not follow him. He knew where Will was going. But as he watched, his fingers flexed and tightened, flexed and tightened. His forearms bunched. His body quaked.

The Ghost remembered Julie Miller. He remembered her naked body in that basement. He remembered the feel of her skin, warm at first, for just a little while, and then slowly stiffening into something akin to wet marble. He remembered the purple-yellow of her face, the pinpoints of red in the bulging eyes, her features contorted in horror and surprise, shattered capillaries, the saliva frozen down the side of her face like a knife scar. He remembered the neck, the unnatural bend in death, the way the wire had actually slashed deep into her skin, slicing through the esophagus, nearly decapitating her.

All that blood.

Strangulation was his favorite method of execution. He had visited India to study the Thuggee, the so-called cult of silent assassins, who'd perfected the secret art of strangulation. Over the years, the Ghost had mastered guns and knives and the like, but when possible, he still preferred the cold efficiency, the final silence, the bold power, the personal touch of strangulation.

A careful breath.

Will disappeared from view.

The brother.

The Ghost thought about all those kung fu movies, the ones where one brother is murdered and the other lives to avenge the death. He thought about what would happen if he simply killed Will Klein.

No, this was not about that. This went way beyond revenge.

Still he wondered about Will. He was the key, after all. Had the years changed him? The Ghost hoped so. But he would find out soon enough.

Yes, it was almost time to meet with Will and catch up on old times.

The Ghost crossed the street toward Will's building.

Five minutes later, he was in the apartment.

I took the Community Bus Line out to the intersection of Livingston Avenue and Northfield. The hotbed of the great suburb of Livingston. An old elementary school had been converted into a poor man's strip mall with specialty stores that never seemed to do any business. I hopped off the bus along with several domestic workers heading out from the city. The bizarre symmetry of reverse commute. Those who lived in towns like Livingston head into the city in the morning; those who clean their houses and watch their children do the opposite. Balance.

I headed down Livingston Avenue toward Livingston High School, which was clustered together with the Livingston Public Library, the Livingston Municipal Court Building, and the Livingston police station. See a pattern here? All four edifices were made of brick and looked as though they were built at the same time, from the same architect, from the same supply of brick—as though one building had begot another.

I grew up here. As a child, I borrowed the classics by C. S. Lewis and Madeleine L'Engle from that library. I fought (and lost) a speeding ticket in that municipal building when I was eighteen. I spent my high school years, one of six hundred kids in my graduating class, in the cluster's biggest building.

I took the circle halfway around and veered to the right. I found the basketball courts and stood under a rusted rim. The town tennis courts were on my left. I played tennis in high school. I was actually pretty good too, though I never had the heart for sports. I lacked the competitive spirit to be great. I didn't want to lose, but I didn't fight hard enough to win.

"Will?"

I turned and when I saw her, I felt my blood turn to ice. The clothes were different—hip-hugging jeans, circa-seventies clogs, a too-tight too-short shirt that revealed a flat, albeit pierced, belly—but the face and the hair . . . It felt like I was falling. I looked away for a moment, in the direction of the soccer field, and I could have sworn I saw Julie out there.

"I know," Katy Miller said. "Like seeing a ghost, right?"

I turned back to her.

"My dad," she said, jamming her tiny hands into the tight jean pockets. "He still can't look at me straight on without crying."

I did not know what to say to that. She came closer to me. We both faced the high school. "You went here, right?" I asked.

"Graduated last month."

"Like it?"

She shrugged. "Glad to get out."

The sun shone, making the building a cold silhouette, and for a moment, it looked a bit like a prison. High school is like that. I was fairly popular in high school. I was vice president of the student council. I was co-captain of the tennis team. I had friends. But as I tried to dig up a pleasant memory, none came. They were all tainted with the insecurity that marks those years. In hindsight, high school—adolescence, if you will—feels a little like protracted combat. You just need to survive, get through it, come out of it okay. I wasn't happy in high school. I'm not sure you're supposed to be.

"I'm sorry about your mother," Katy said.

"Thank you."

She took a pack of cigarettes out of her back pocket and offered me one. I shook her off. I watched her light up and resisted the urge to lecture. Katy's eyes took in everything but me. "I was an accident, you know. I came late. Julie was already in high school. My parents were told they couldn't have more children. Then . . ." She shrugged again. "So they weren't expecting me."

"It's not like the rest of us are well planned," I said.

She laughed a little at that, and the sound echoed deep inside me. It was Julie's laugh, even the way it faded away.

"Sorry about my dad," Katy said. "He just freaked when he saw you."

"I shouldn't have done that."

She took too long a drag and tilted her head. "Why did you?"

I thought about the answer. "I don't know," I said.

"I saw you. From the moment you turned the corner. It was weird, you know. I remember as a little kid watching you walk from your house. My bedroom. I mean, I'm still in the same bedroom, so it's like I was watching the past or something. It felt weird."

I looked to my right. The drive was empty now, but during the school year, that was where the parents sat in cars and waited for their kids. Maybe my high school memories are not all good, but I remember my mom picking me up there in her old red Volkswagen. She'd be reading a magazine and the bell would ring and I'd walk toward her and when she'd spot me, when she first raised her head and sensed that I was coming near, her smile, that Sunny smile, would burst forth from deep in her heart, that blinding smile of unconditional love, and I realized now with a hard thud that nobody would ever smile at me that way again.

Too much, I thought. Being here. The visual echo of Julie on Katy's face. The memories. It was all too much.

"You hungry?" I asked her.

"Sure, I guess."

She had a car, an old Honda Civic. Trinkets, lots of them, hung from the rearview mirror. The car smelled of bubble gum and fruity shampoo. I didn't recognize the music blaring from the speakers, but I didn't mind it either.

We drove to a classic New Jersey diner on Route 10 without speaking. There were autographed photographs of local anchormen behind the counter. Each booth had a mini-jukebox. The menu was slightly longer than a Tom Clancy novel.

A man with a heavy beard and heavier deodorant asked us how many. We told him that we were two. Katy added that we wanted a smoking table. I didn't know smoking sections still existed, but apparently big diners are throwbacks. As soon as we sat, she pulled the ashtray toward her, almost as if for protection.

"After you came by the house," she said, "I went to the grave-yard."

The water boy filled our glasses. She inhaled on the cigarette and did that lean-back-and-up blowout. "I haven't gone in years. But after I saw you, I don't know, I felt like I should."

She still would not look at me. I find this a lot with the kids at the shelter. They avoid your eyes. I let them. It does not mean anything. I try to hold their gaze, but I've learned that eye contact is overrated.

"I barely remember Julie anymore. I see the pictures and I don't know if my memories are real or something I made up myself. I think, oh I remember when we went on the teacups at Great Adventure and then I'll see the picture and I won't know if I really remember it or if I just remember the picture. You know what I mean?"

"I think so, yes."

"And after you came by, I mean, I had to get out of the house. My dad was raging. My mom was crying. I just had to get out."

"I didn't mean to upset anyone," I said.

She waved my words away. "It's okay. It's good for them in a weird way. Most of the time we tiptoe around it, you know. It's creepy. Sometimes I wish . . . I wish I could just scream, 'She's dead.' " Katy leaned forward. "You want to hear something totally freaky?"

I gestured for her to go ahead.

"We haven't changed the basement. That old couch and TV. That ratty carpet. That old trunk I used to hide behind. They're all still there. Nobody uses them. But they're there. And our laundry room is still down there. We have to walk through that room to get to it. You understand what I'm saying? That's how we live. We tiptoe around upstairs, you know, like we're living on ice and we're afraid the floor is going to crack and we're all going to fall down into that basement."

She stopped and sucked on the cigarette as if it were an air hose. I sat back. Like I said before: I'd never really thought about Katy Miller, about what the murder of her sister had done to her. I thought about her parents, of course. I thought about the devastation. I often wondered why they'd stay in the house, but then again, I never really understood why my parents had not moved either. I mentioned before the link between comfort and self-inflicted pain, the desire to hold on because suffering was preferable to forgetting. Staying in that house had to be the ultimate example.

But I'd never really considered the case of Katy Miller, about what it must have been like growing up among those ruins, with your sister's look-alike specter forever at your side. I looked at Katy again, as if for the first time. Her eyes continued to dart about like scared birds. I could see tears there now. I reached out and took her hand, again so like her sister's. The past came at me so hard I nearly fell back.

"This is so weird," she said.

Truer words, I thought. "For me too."

"It needs to end, Will. My whole life . . . whatever really happened that night, it needs to end. Sometimes I hear on TV when they catch the bad guy someone says, 'It won't bring her back,' and I think, 'Duh.' But that's not the point. It ends. You catch the guy, it gives it some kind of finality. People need that."

I had no idea where she was going with this. I tried to pretend that she was one of the center's kids, that she'd come in needing my help and love. I sat and looked at her and tried to let her know that I was here to listen.

"You don't know how much I hated your brother—not just for what he did to Julie, but for what he did to the rest of us by running away. I prayed they'd find him. I had this dream where he'd be surrounded and he put up a fight and then the cops would smoke him. I know you don't want to hear this. But I need you to understand."

"You wanted closure," I said.

"Yeah," she said. "Except . . ."

"Except what?"

She looked up and for the first time our eyes locked. I grew cold again. I wanted to withdraw my hand, but I could not move. "I saw him," she said.

I thought that I heard wrong.

"Your brother. I saw him. At least I think it was him."

I found my voice enough to ask, "When?"

"Yesterday. At the graveyard."

The waitress came over then. She withdrew the pencil from her ear and asked what we wanted. For a moment neither of us spoke. The waitress cleared her throat. Katy ordered some sort of salad. The waitress looked at me. I asked for a cheese omelette. She asked what kind of cheese—American, Swiss, cheddar. I said cheddar would be fine. Did I want home fries or french fries with that? Home fries. White toast, rye toast, wheat toast. Rye. And nothing to drink, thank you.

The waitress finally left.

"Tell me," I said.

Katy stubbed out the cigarette. "It's like I said before. I went to the graveyard. Just to get out of the house. Anyway, you know where Julie's buried, right?"

I nodded.

"That's right. I saw you there. Couple of days after her funeral."

"Yes," I said.

She leaned forward. "Did you love her?"

"I don't know."

"But she broke your heart."

"Maybe," I said. "A long time ago."

Katy stared down at her hands.

"Tell me what happened," I said.

"He looked pretty different. Your brother, I mean. I don't remember him much. Just a little. And I've seen pictures." She stopped.

"Are you saying he was standing by Julie's grave?"

"By a willow tree."

"What?"

"There's a tree there. Maybe a hundred feet away. I didn't come in the front gate. I hopped a fence. So he wasn't expecting me. See, I came up from the back and I saw this guy standing under the willow tree and he's just staring in the direction of Julie's stone. He never heard me. He was just lost, you know. I tapped him on the shoulder. He jumped like a mile in the air and when he turned around and saw me . . . well, you see what I look like. He nearly screamed. He thought I was a ghost or something."

"And you were sure it was Ken?"

"Not sure, no. I mean, how could I be?" She took out another cigarette and then said, "Yeah. Yeah, I know it was him."

"But how could you be sure?"

"He told me he didn't do it."

My head spun. My hands fell to my sides and gripped the cushion. When I finally spoke, my words came out slowly. "What exactly did he say?"

"At first, just that. 'I didn't kill your sister.' "

"What did you do?"

"I told him he was a liar. I told him I was going to scream."

"Did you?"

"No."

"Why not?"

Katy still had not lit the new cigarette. She withdrew it from

95

her lips and put it on the tabletop. "Because I believed him," she said. "Something in his voice, I don't know. I'd hated him for so long. You have no idea how much. But now . . ."

"So what did you do?"

"I stepped back. I was still going to scream. But he came toward me. He took my face in his hands and looked me in the eye and said, 'I'm going to find the killer, I promise.' That was it. He looked at me a little more. Then he let go and ran off."

"Have you told—"

She shook her head. "No one. Sometimes I'm not even sure it happened. Like I imagined the whole thing. Dreamt it or made it up. Like my memories of Julie." She looked up at me. "Do you think he killed Julie?"

"No," I said.

"I've seen you on the news," she said. "You've always thought he was dead. Because they found some of his blood at the scene."

I nodded.

"Do you still believe that?"

"No," I said. "I don't believe that anymore."

"What made you change your mind?"

I didn't know how to reply to that. "I guess," I said, "I'm looking for him too."

"I want to help."

She'd said want. But I know she meant need.

"Please, Will. Let me help."

And I said okay.

15

Sheriff Bertha Farrow frowned over Deputy George Volker's shoulder. "Hate these things," she said.

"You shouldn't," Volker replied, fingers dancing on the keyboard. "Computers are our friends."

She frowned some more. "So what is our friend doing now?"

"Scanning Jane Doe's fingerprints."

"Scanning?"

"How to explain this to a total technophobe . . . ?" Volker looked up and rubbed his chin. "It's like a Xerox machine and fax machine in one. It makes a copy of the fingerprint and then it emails it over to the CJIS in West Virginia."

CJIS stood for Criminal Justice Information Services. Now that every police force was online—even those in the most hillbilly of Hicksville boonies like them—fingerprints could be sent over the Internet for identification. If the fingerprints were listed in the National Crime Information Center's enormous database, they'd have a match and a positive ID in no time.

"I thought the CJIS was in Washington," Bertha said.

"Not anymore. Senator Byrd got it moved."

"Good man to have as senator."

"Oh yeah."

Bertha hoisted her holster and headed down the corridor. Her police station shared space with Clyde's morgue, which was convenient if not sporadically pungent. The morgue had terrible ventilation, and every once in a while a heavy cloud of formaldehyde and decay floated out and hovered.

With only a moment's hesitation, Bertha Farrow opened the door to the morgue. There were no gleaming drawers or shiny instruments or any of the stuff that you see on TV. Clyde's morgue was pretty close to makeshift. The job was only part-time because, let's face it, there was not that much to do. Car accident victims were pretty much the extent out here. Last year, Don Taylor had gotten drunk and shot himself in the head by accident. His long-suffering wife liked to joke that ol' Don fired because he looked in the mirror and mistook himself for a moose. Marriage. But really, that was about it. The morgue—hell, the term was a generous description of this converted janitorial room—could only hold maybe two corpses at a time. If Clyde needed more storage, he used Wally's funeral home facilities.

Jane Doe's body was on the table. Clyde stood over her. He wore blue scrubs and pale surgical gloves. He was crying. Opera blared from the boom box, the wail of something appropriately tragic.

"Open her up yet?" Bertha asked, though the answer was obvious.

Clyde wiped his eyes with two fingers. "No."

"You waiting for her permission?"

He shot Bertha a red-eyed glare. "I'm still doing the external."

"How about a cause of death, Clyde?"

"Won't know for sure until I complete the autopsy."

Bertha moved closer to him. She put her hand on his shoulder, faking comfort and pretending to bond. "How about a preliminary guess, Clyde?"

"She was beaten pretty badly. See here?"

He pointed to where you might normally find a rib cage. There was little definition. The bones had caved in, crushed down like a boot on Styrofoam.

"Lots of bruising," Bertha said.

"Discoloration, yeah, but see here?" He put his finger on something poking up the skin near the stomach.

"Broken ribs?"

"Smashed ribs," he corrected her.

"How?"

Clyde shrugged. "Probably used a heavy ball peen hammer, something like that. My guess—and it's only a guess—is that one of the ribs splintered off and pierced a major organ. It might have punctured a lung or sliced through her belly. Or maybe she got lucky and it went straight through her heart."

Bertha shook her head. "She don't seem the lucky type to me."

Clyde turned away. He lowered his head and started crying again. His body heaved from the stifled sobs.

"These marks on her breasts," Bertha said.

Without looking he said, "Cigarette burns."

What she'd figured. Mangled fingers, cigarette burns. You did not have to be Sherlock Holmes to deduce that she was tortured.

"Do it all, Clyde. Blood samples, tox screen, everything."

He sniffled and finally turned back around. "Yeah, Bertha, sure, okay."

The door behind them opened. They both turned. It was Volker. "Got a hit," he said.

"Already?"

George nodded. "Top of the NCIC list."

"What do you mean, top of the list?"

Volker gestured toward the body on the table. "Our Jane Doe," he said. "She was wanted by none other than the FBI."

16

Katy dropped me off on Hickory Place, maybe three blocks from my parents' house. We did not want anybody to see us together. That was probably paranoia on our part, but I figured, what the hell.

"So what now?" Katy asked.

I had been wondering that myself. "I'm not sure. But if Ken didn't kill Julie—"

"Then someone else did."

"Man," I said, "we're good at this."

She smiled. "So I guess we look for suspects?"

It sounded ridiculous—who were we, the Mod Squad?—but I nodded.

"I'll start checking," she said.

"Checking what?"

She gave me a teenager shrug, using her whole body. "I don't know. Julie's past, I guess. Figure out who'd have wanted to kill her."

"The police did that."

"They only looked at your brother, Will."

She had a point. "Okay," I said, again feeling ridiculous.

"Let's hook up later tonight."

I nodded and slid out. Nancy Drew sped off without a good-bye. I stood there and soaked in the solitude. I was not all that eager to move.

The streets of suburbia were empty, but the well-paved drive-ways were full. The paneled station wagons of my youth had been replaced by a vast variety of quasi-off-road vehicles—minivans, fam-ily trucks (whatever that meant), SUVs. Most of the houses were in the classic split-level mode of the circa-1962 housing boom. Many were bloated with additions. Others had undergone extensive exte-rior renovations circa 1974 involving too-white, too-smooth stone; the look had aged about as well as the powder-blue tux I'd worn to the prom.

When I arrived at our house, there were no cars out front and no mourners inside. No surprise there. I called out to my father. No answer. I found him alone in the basement with a cutting razor in his hand. He was in the middle of the room, surrounded by old wardrobe boxes. The sealing tape had been sliced open. Dad stood perfectly still among the boxes. He did not turn around when he heard my footsteps.

"So much already packed away," he said softly.

The boxes had belonged to my mother. My father reached into one and plucked out a thin silver headband. He turned to me and held it up. "You remember this?"

We both smiled. Everyone, I guess, goes through fashion stages, but not like my mother. She set them, defined them, became them. There was her Headband Era, for example. She'd grown her hair out and worn a potpourri of the multihued bands like an Indian princess. For several months—I'd say the Headband Era lasted maybe six—you would never see her without one. When the head-bands were retired, the Suede-Fringe Period began in earnest. That was followed by the Purple Renaissance—not my favorite, I assure you, like living with a giant eggplant or Jimi Hendrix groupie—and then the Riding-Crop Age—this from a woman whose closest connection to a horse was seeing Elizabeth Taylor in *National Velvet*.

The fashion stages, like so many other things, ended with Julie Miller's murder. My mom—Sunny—packed the clothes away and stored them in the dingiest corner of the basement.

Dad flipped the headband back into the box. "We were going to move, you know."

I hadn't.

"Three years ago. We were going to get a condo in West Orange and maybe a winter place in Scottsdale, near Cousin Esther and

Harold. But when we found out your mother was sick, we put it all on hold." He looked at me. "You thirsty?"

"Not really."

"How about a Diet Coke? I know I could use one."

Dad hurried past me and toward the stairs. I looked at the old boxes, my mother's handwriting on the sides in thick marker. On the shelf in the back I could still see two of Ken's old tennis rackets. One was the first he'd ever used, when he was only three. Mom had saved it for him. I turned away and followed him. When we reached the kitchen, he opened the refrigerator door.

"You want to tell me what happened yesterday?" he began.

"I don't know what you mean."

"You and your sister." Dad pulled out a two-liter bottle of Diet Coke. "What was that all about?"

"Nothing," I said.

He nodded as he opened a cabinet. He took out two glasses, opened the freezer, filled them with ice. "Your mother used to eavesdrop on you and Melissa," he said.

"I know."

He smiled. "She wasn't very discreet. I'd tell her to cut it out, but she'd just tell me to hush, it was a mother's job."

"You said, me and Melissa."

"Yes."

"Why not Ken?"

"Maybe she didn't want to know." He poured the sodas. "Very curious about your brother lately."

"It's a natural enough question."

"Sure, natural. And after the funeral, you were asking me if I think he's still alive. And then the next day, you and Melissa have an argument about him. So I'll ask you one more time: What's going on?"

The photograph was still in my pocket. Don't ask me why. I'd made color copies with my scanner that morning. But I couldn't let go of it.

When the doorbell rang, we both jumped, startled. We looked at each other. Dad shrugged. I told him I'd get it. I took a quick sip of the Diet Coke and put it back on the counter. I trotted to the front door. When I opened it, when I saw who it was, I nearly toppled back.

Mrs. Miller. Julie's mom.

She held out a platter wrapped with aluminum foil. Her eyes were lowered as though she were making an offering on an altar. For a moment, I froze, unsure what to say. She glanced up. Our eyes met just as they had when I stood on her curb two days earlier. The pain I saw in them felt alive, electric. I wondered if she felt the same coming from mine.

"I just thought . . ." she began. "I mean, I just . . ."

"Please," I said. "Come in."

She tried to smile. "Thank you."

My father moved from the kitchen and said, "Who's there?"

I backed up. Mrs. Miller stepped into view, still holding up the platter as if for protection. My father's eyes widened, and I saw something behind them burst.

His voice was a rage-filled whisper. "What the hell are you doing here?"

"Dad," I said.

He ignored me. "I asked you a question, Lucille. What the hell do you want?"

Mrs. Miller lowered her head.

"Dad," I said more urgently.

But it was no use. His eyes had gone small and black. "I don't want you here," he said.

"Dad, she came to offer—"

"Get out."

"Dad!"

Mrs. Miller shrunk back. She pushed the platter into my hands. "I better go, Will."

"No," I said. "Don't."

"I shouldn't have come."

Dad shouted, "Damn right you shouldn't have come."

I shot him a glare, but his eyes stayed on her.

With her eyes still lowered, Mrs. Miller said, "I'm sorry for your loss."

But my father was not through. "She's dead, Lucille. It doesn't do any good now."

Mrs. Miller fled then. I stood holding the platter. I looked at my father in disbelief. He looked back and said, "Throw that crap away."

I was not sure what to do here. I wanted to follow her, to apologize, but she was halfway up the block and moving fast. My father had moved back into the kitchen. I followed, slamming the platter down on the counter.

"What the hell was that about?" I asked.

He picked up his drink. "I don't want her here."

"She came to pay her respects."

"She came to ease her guilt."

"What are you talking about?"

"Your mother is dead. There's nothing she can do for her now."

"That doesn't make any sense."

"Your mother called Lucille. Did you know that? Not long after the murder. She wanted to offer her condolences. Lucille told her to go to hell. She blamed us for raising a murderer. That's what she said. It was our fault. We raised a murderer."

"That was eleven years ago, Dad."

"Do you have any idea what that did to your mother?"

"Her daughter had just been murdered. She was in a lot of pain."

"So she waits until now to make it right? When it won't do any good?" He shook his head sternly. "I don't want to hear it. And your mother, well, she can't."

The front door opened then. Aunt Selma and Uncle Murray entered with their grieving smiles in place. Selma took over the kitchen. Murray busied himself with a loose wall plate he'd spotted yesterday.

And my father and I stopped talking.

17

Special Agent Claudia Fisher stiffened her spine and knocked on the door.

"Come in."

She turned the knob and entered the office of Assistant Director in Charge Joseph Pistillo. The ADIC—immaturely nicknamed, naturally enough, a-dick—ran the New York office. Outside of the director in Washington, an ADIC was the most senior and powerful agent in the FBI.

Pistillo looked up. He did not like what he saw. "What?"

"Sheila Rogers was found dead," Fisher reported.

Pistillo cursed. "How?"

"She was found on a roadside in Nebraska. No ID. They ran her prints through NCIC and got a hit."

"Damn."

Pistillo chewed on a cuticle. Claudia Fisher waited.

"I want a visual confirmation," he said.

"Done."

"What?"

"I took the liberty of emailing Sheriff Farrow the mug shots of Sheila Rogers. She and the M.E. confirmed it was the same woman. The height and weight match too."

Pistillo leaned back. He grabbed a pen, raised it to eye level, and studied it. Fisher stood at attention. He signaled for her to sit. She obeyed. "Sheila Rogers's parents live in Utah, right?"

"Idaho."

"Whatever. We need to contact them."

"I have the local police on standby. The chief knows the family personally."

Pistillo nodded. "Okay, good." He took the pen out of his mouth. "How was she killed?"

"Probably internal bleeding from a beating. The autopsy is still under way."

"Jesus."

"She was tortured. Her fingers had been snapped back and twisted, probably by a pair of pliers. There were cigarette burns on her torso."

"How long has she been dead?"

"She probably died sometime last night or early in the morning."

Pistillo looked at Fisher. He remembered how Will Klein, the lover, had sat in that very chair yesterday. "Fast," he said.

"Excuse me?"

"If, as we were led to believe, she ran away, they found her fast."

"Unless," Fisher said, "she ran to them."

Pistillo leaned back. "Or she never ran at all."

"I'm not following."

He studied the pen some more. "Our assumption has always been that Sheila Rogers fled because of her connection to the Albuquerque murders, right?"

Fisher tilted her head back and forth. "Yes and no. I mean, why come back to New York just to run away again?"

"Maybe she wanted to go to the mother's funeral, I don't know," he said. "Either way, I don't think that's the case anymore. Maybe she never knew we were on to her. Maybe—stay with me here, Claudia—maybe someone kidnapped her."

"How would that have worked?" Fisher asked.

Pistillo put down the pen. "According to Will Klein, she left the apartment at, what, six in the morning?"

"Five."

"Fine, five. So let's put this together using the accepted scenario. Sheila Rogers walks out at five. She goes into hiding. Some-

106

one finds her and tortures her and dumps her in the boonies of Nebraska. That sound about right?"

Fisher nodded slowly. "Like you said, fast."

"Too fast?"

"Maybe."

"Time-phase-wise," Pistillo said, "it's far more likely that someone grabbed her right away. As soon as she left the apartment."

"And flew her to Nebraska?"

"Or drove like a demon."

"Or . . . ?" Fisher began.

"Or?"

She looked at her boss. "I think," she said, "that we're both coming to the same conclusion. The time line is too close. She probably disappeared the night before."

"Which means?"

"Which means that Will Klein lied to us."

Pistillo grinned. "Exactly."

Fisher's words started coming fast now. "Okay, here's a more likely scenario: Will Klein and Sheila Rogers go to the funeral of Klein's mother. They return to his parents' house afterward. According to Klein, they drive back to their apartment that night. But we have no independent confirmation of that. So maybe"—she tried to slow down but that wasn't happening—"maybe they don't head home. Maybe he hands her over to an accomplice, who tortures and kills her and dumps the body. Will meanwhile drives back to his apartment. He goes to work in the morning. When Wilcox and I brace him at his office, he makes up this story about her leaving in the morning."

Pistillo nodded. "Interesting theory."

She stood at attention.

"Do you have a motive?" he asked.

"He needed to silence her."

"For?"

"Whatever happened in Albuquerque."

They both mulled it over in silence.

"I'm not convinced," Pistillo said.

"Neither am I."

"But we agree that Will Klein knows more than he's saying."

"For certain."

107

Pistillo let loose a long breath. "Either way, we need to give him the bad news about Ms. Rogers's demise."

"Yes."

"Call that local chief out in Utah."

"Idaho."

"Whatever. Have him inform the family. Then get them on a plane for official identification."

"What about Will Klein?"

Pistillo thought about that. "I'll reach out to Squares. Maybe he can help us deliver the blow."

18

My apartment door was ajar.

After Aunt Selma and Uncle Murray's arrival, my father and I carefully avoided each other. I love my father. I think I have made that pretty clear. But a small part of me irrationally blames him for my mother's death. I don't know why I feel that way, and it is very hard to admit this even to myself, but from the moment she first became ill, I looked at him differently. As though he hadn't done enough. Or perhaps I blamed him for not saving her after Julie Miller's murder. He hadn't been strong enough. He hadn't been a good enough husband. Couldn't true love have helped Mom recover, salved her spirit?

Like I said, irrational.

My door was only open a crack, but it made me pause. I always lock it—hey, I live in a doorman-free building in Manhattan—but then again I had not been thinking straight of late. Perhaps in my haste to meet Katy Miller I'd just forgotten. That would be natural enough. And the dead bolt gets stuck sometimes. Maybe I'd never fully closed the door in the first place.

I frowned. Not likely.

I put my hand on a door panel and pushed ever so slightly. I waited to hear the door creak. It did not. I heard something. Faint at first. I leaned my head through the opening and immediately felt my insides turn to ice.

Nothing I saw was out of the ordinary. The lights were out, as a matter of fact. The blinds were drawn, so there was not much illumination. No, nothing out of the ordinary—or again, nothing that I could see. I stayed in the corridor and leaned in a little more.

But I could hear music.

Again, that alone would not cause too much alarm. I do not make it a practice to leave music playing like some security-conscious New Yorkers, but I confess to a major streak of absent-mindedness. I could have left my CD player on. That alone would not chill me like this.

What did chill me, however, was the song selection.

That was what was getting to me. The song playing—I tried to remember when I last heard it—was "Don't Fear the Reaper." I shuddered.

Ken's favorite song.

By Blue Oyster Cult, a heavy metal band, though this song, their most famous, was more subdued, almost ethereal. Ken used to grab his tennis racket and fake-guitar the solos. And I know that I do not have a copy of that particular song on any of my CDs. No way, unh-unh. Too many memories.

What the hell was going on here?

I stepped into the room. As I said before, the lights were out. It was dark. I stopped and felt awfully stupid. Hmm. Why not just flick on the lights, numbnuts? Wouldn't that be a good idea?

As I reached for the switch, another inner voice said, Better yet, why not just run? That was what we always yell at the movie screens, right? The killer is hiding inside the house. The stupid teenager, after finding her best friend's decapitated corpse, decides that this would be the perfect time to stroll through the darkened house instead of, say, fleeing and screaming like a mad animal.

Gee, all I had to do was strip down to a bra and I could be playing the part.

The song faded down in a guitar solo. I waited for the silence. It was brief. The song started up again. The same song.

What the hell was going on?

Flee and scream. That was the ticket. I would do just that. Except for one thing. I had not stumbled across any headless corpse. So how would this play out here? What exactly would I do? Call the police? I could just see that. What seems to be the problem, sir?

Well, my stereo is playing my brother's favorite song so I decided to start running down the hall screaming. Can you rush over here with guns drawn? Uh-huh, sure, we're on our way.

How dorky would that sound?

And even if I assumed that someone had broken in, that there was indeed a prowler still in my apartment, someone who had brought his own CD with him . . .

. . . well, who was that most likely to be?

My heart picked up a beat as my eyes began to adjust to the dark. I decided to leave the lights off. If there was an intruder, there was no reason to let him know I was standing there, an easy target. Or would turning on the light scare him into view?

Christ, I'm not good at this.

I decided to leave the lights off.

Okay, fine, let's play it that way. Lights stay off. Now what?

The music. Follow the music. It was coming from my bedroom. I turned in that direction. The door was closed. I stepped toward it. Carefully. I was not going to be a total idiot. I opened the front door all the way and left it like that—in case I had to scream or make a run for it.

I moved forward in a sort of spastic slide, leading with the left foot but keeping the right toes firmly pointed toward the exit. It re-minded me of one of Squares's yoga stances. You spread your legs and you bend one way but both your weight and your "awareness" go in the opposite direction. The body moves one way, the mind an-other. This was what some yogis, not Squares thankfully, referred to as "spreading your consciousness."

I slid a yard. Then another. Blue Oyster Cult's Buck Dharma— the fact that I remembered not only that name, but that his real name was Donald Roeser said a lot about my childhood—sang how we can be like they are, like Romeo and Juliet.

In a word: dead.

I reached the bedroom door. I swallowed and pushed against the frame. No go. I'd have to turn the knob. My hand gripped the metal. I looked over my shoulder. The door was still wide open. My right foot stayed pointed in that direction, though I could no longer be sure of my "awareness." I turned the knob as silently as possible, but it still sounded like a gunshot in my ear.

I pushed just a little, just to clear the frame. I let go of the knob. The music was louder now. Crisp and clear. Probably playing on the Bose CD player Squares had gotten me for my birthday two years ago.

I stuck my head in, just for a quick look. And that was when someone grabbed me by the hair.

I barely had time to gasp. My head was tugged forward so hard, my feet left the ground. I flew across the room, my hands stretched out Superman style, and landed in a thudding belly flop.

The air left my lungs with a whoosh. I tried to roll over, but he—I assumed it was a he—was already on top of me. His legs straddled my back. An arm snaked around my throat. I tried to struggle, but his grip was impossibly strong. He pulled back and I gagged.

I couldn't move. Totally at his mercy, he lowered his head toward mine. I could feel his breath in my ear. He did something with his other arm, got a better angle or counterweight, and squeezed. My windpipe was being crushed.

My eyes bulged. I pawed at my throat. Useless. My fingernails tried to dig into his forearm, but it was like trying to penetrate mahogany. The pressure in my head was building, growing unbearable. I flailed. My attacker did not budge. My skull felt like it was about to explode. And then I heard the voice:

"Hey, Willie boy."

That voice.

I placed it instantly. I had not heard it in—Christ, I tried to remember—ten, fifteen years maybe? Since Julie's death anyway. But there are certain sounds, voices mostly, that get stored in a special section of the cortex, on the survival shelf if you will, and as soon as you hear them, your every fiber tenses, sensing danger.

He let go of my neck—suddenly and completely. I collapsed to the floor, thrashing, gagging, trying to dislodge something imaginary from my throat. He rolled off me and laughed. "You've gone soft on me, Willie boy."

I flipped over and scooted away in a back crawl. My eyes confirmed what my ears had already told me. I could not believe it. He had changed, but there was no mistake.

"John?" I said. "John Asselta?"

He smiled that smile that touched nothing. I felt myself drop back in time. The fear—the fear I hadn't experienced since adolescence—surfaced. The Ghost—that was what everyone called him,

112

though no one had the courage to say it to his face—had always had that effect on me. I don't think I was alone in that. He terrified pretty much everyone, though I had always been protected. I was Ken Klein's little brother. For the Ghost, that was enough.

I have always been a wimp. I have shied away from physical confrontations all my life. Some claim that makes me prudent and mature. But that was not it. The truth is, I am a coward. I am deathly afraid of violence. That might be normal—survival instinct and all—but it still shames me. My brother, who was, strangely enough, the Ghost's closest friend, had the enviable aggression that separated the wanna-bes from the greats. His tennis, for example, reminded some of a young John McEnroe in that take-on-the-world, pit-bull, won't-lose, borderline going-too-far competitiveness. Even as a child, he'd battle you to the death—and then stomp on the remains after you fell. I was never like that.

I scrambled to my feet. Asselta rose straight up, like a spirit from the grave. He spread his arms. "No hug for an old friend, Willie boy?"

He approached, and before I could react, he embraced me. He was pretty short, what with that strange long-torso, short-arms build. His cheek pressed my chest. "Been a long time," he said.

I was not sure what to say, where to start. "How did you get in?"

"What?" He released me. "Oh, the door was open. I'm sorry about sneaking up on you like that but . . ." He smiled, shrugged it away. "You haven't changed a bit, Willie boy. You look good."

"You shouldn't have just . . ."

He tilted his head, and I remembered the way he would simply lash out. John Asselta had been a classmate of Ken's, two years ahead of me at Livingston High School. He captained the wrestling team and was the Essex County lightweight champ two years running. He probably would have won the states, but he got disqualified for purposely dislocating a rival's shoulder. His third violation. I still remember the way his opponent screamed in pain. I remembered how some of the spectators got violently ill at the sight of the dangling appendage. I remembered Asselta's small smile as they carted his opponent away.

My father claimed that the Ghost had a Napoleon complex. That explanation seemed too simplistic to me. I don't know what it was, if the Ghost needed to prove himself or if he had an extra Y chromosome or if he was just the meanest son of a bitch in existence.

Whatever, he was definitely a psycho.

No way around it. He enjoyed hurting people. An aura of destruction surrounded his every step. Even the big jocks steered clear of him. You never met his eye, never got in his path, because you never knew what could provoke him. He would strike with no hesitation. He'd break your nose. He'd knee you in the balls. He'd gouge your eyes. He would hit you when your back was turned.

He gave Milt Saperstein a concussion during my sophomore year. Saperstein, a nerdy freshman complete with pocket protector against polyester print, had made the mistake of leaning up against the Ghost's locker. The Ghost smiled and let him go with a pat on the back. Later that day, Saperstein was walking between classes when, bam, the Ghost ran up behind him and smashed his forearm into Milt's head. Saperstein never saw him coming. He crumbled to the ground, and with a laugh, the Ghost stomped on his skull. Milt had to be taken to the emergency room at St. Barnabas.

No one saw a thing.

When he was fourteen—if legend was true—the Ghost killed a neighbor's dog by sticking firecrackers up his rectum. But worse than that, worse than pretty much anything, were the rumors that the Ghost, at the tender age of ten, stabbed a kid named Daniel Skinner with a kitchen knife. Supposedly Skinner, who was a couple of years older, picked on the Ghost, and the Ghost had responded with a knife strike straight to the heart. Rumor also had it that he spent some time in both juvie and therapy and that neither one had stuck. Ken claimed ignorance on the subject. I asked my father about it once, but he would neither confirm nor deny.

I tried to push the past away. "What do you want, John?"

I never understood my brother's friendship with him. My parents had not been happy about it either, though the Ghost could be charming with adults. His almost albino complexion—ergo the nickname—belied gentle features. He was almost pretty, with long lashes and a Dudley Do-Right cleft in the chin. I had heard that after graduation he had gone into the military. Supposedly he'd been enlisted in something clandestine involving Special Ops or Green Berets, something like that, but nobody could confirm that with any certainty.

The Ghost did the head-tilt again. "Where's Ken?" he asked in that silky, pre-strike voice.

I did not respond.

114

"I've been gone a long time, Willie boy. Overseas."

"Doing what?" I asked.

He flashed me the teeth again. "Now that I'm back, I thought I'd look up my old best bud."

I did not know what to say to that. But I suddenly flashed to when I stood on the veranda last night. The man staring at me from the end of the street. It had been the Ghost.

"So, Willie boy, where can I find him?"

"I don't know."

He put his hand up to his ear. "Excuse me?"

"I don't know where he is."

"But how can that be? You're his brother. He loved you so."

"What do you want here, John?"

"Say," he said, and he showed the teeth yet again, "whatever happened to your high school hottie Julie Miller? You two get hitched?"

I stared at him. He held the smile. He was putting me on, I knew that. He and Julie had, strangely enough, been close. I never understood that. Julie had claimed to see something there, something under the lashing-out psychosis. I once joked that she must have pulled a thorn from his paw. I wondered now how to play it. I actually considered running, but I knew that I would never make it. I also knew that I was no match for him.

This was creeping me out big-time.

"You've been gone a long time?" I asked.

"Years, Willie boy."

"So when was the last time you saw Ken?"

He feigned deep thought. "Oh, must have been, what, twelve years ago? I've been overseas since. Haven't kept up."

"Uh-huh."

He narrowed his eyes. "You sound like you're doubting me, Willie boy." He moved closer to me. I tried not to flinch. "You afraid of me?"

"No."

"Big bro's not here to protect you anymore, Willie boy."

"And we're not in high school either, John."

He looked up into my eyes. "You think the world's so different now?"

I tried to hold my ground.

"You look scared, Willie boy."

115

"Get out," I said.

His reply was sudden. He dropped to the floor and whipped out my legs from under me. I fell hard on my back. Before I could move, he had me wrapped up in an elbow lock. There was already tremendous pressure on the joint, but then he lifted up against my triceps. The elbow started bending the wrong way. A deep pain knifed down my arm.

I tried to move with it. Give way. Anything to relieve the pressure.

The Ghost spoke in the calmest voice I've ever heard. "You tell him no more hiding, Willie boy. You tell him other people could get hurt. Like you. Or your dad. Or your sister. Or maybe even that little Miller vixen you met with today. You tell him that."

His hand speed was unearthly. In one move, he released my arm and shot his fist straight into my face. My nose exploded. I fell back against the floor, my head swimming, only half conscious. Or maybe I passed out. I don't know anymore.

When I looked up again, the Ghost had vanished.

19

Squares handed me a freezer bag of ice. "Yeah, but I oughta see the other guy, right?"

"Right," I said, putting the bag on my rather tender nose. "He looks like a matinee idol."

Squares sat on the couch and threw his boots up on the coffee table. "Explain."

I did.

"Guy sounds like a prince," Squares said.

"Did I mention that he tortured animals?"

"Yep."

"Or that he had a skull collection in his bedroom?"

"Say, that must have impressed the ladies."

"I don't get it." I lowered the bag. My nose felt like it was jammed with crushed-up pennies. "Why would the Ghost be looking for my brother?"

"Hell of a question."

"You think I should call the cops?"

Squares shrugged. "Give me his full name again."

"John Asselta."

"I assume you don't have a current residence."

"No."

"But he grew up in Livingston?"

"Yes," I said. "On Woodland Terrace. Fifty-seven Woodland Terrace."

"You remember his address?"

Now it was my turn to shrug. That was the way Livingston was. You remembered stuff like that. "His mother, I don't know what her deal was. She ran away or something when he was very young. His dad lived in a bottle. Two brothers, both older. One—I think his name was Sean—was a Vietnam vet. He had this long hair and matted beard and all he'd do was walk around town talking to himself. Everyone figured he was crazy. Their yard was like a junkyard, always overgrown. People in Livingston didn't like that. The cops used to ticket them for it."

Squares wrote down the info. "Let me look into it."

My head ached. I tried to focus. "Did you have someone like that in your school?" I asked. "A psycho who'd just hurt people for the fun of it?"

"Yeah," Squares said. "Me."

I found it hard to believe. I knew abstractly Squares had been a punk of biblical proportions, but the idea that he'd been like the Ghost, that I'd have shuddered as he passed me in the halls, that he would crack a skull and laugh at the sound . . . it just would not compute.

I put the ice back on my nose, wincing when it touched down. Squares shook his head. "Baby."

"Pity you didn't consider a career in medicine."

"Your nose is probably broken," he said.

"I figured."

"You want to go to the hospital?"

"Nah, I'm a tough guy."

That made him snicker. "Nothing they could do anyway." Then he stopped, gnawed on the inside of his cheek, said, "Something's come up."

I did not like the tone of his voice.

"I got a call from our favorite fed, Joe Pistillo."

Again I lowered down the ice. "Did they find Sheila?"

"Don't know."

"What did he want?"

"Wouldn't say. He just asked me to bring you in."

"When?"

"Now. He said he was calling me as a courtesy."

118

"Courtesy for what?"

"Damned if I know."

"My name is Clyde Smart," the man said in the gentlest voice Edna Rogers had ever heard. "I'm the county medical examiner."

Edna Rogers watched her husband, Neil, shake the man's hand. She settled for just a nod in his direction. The woman sheriff was there. So was one of her deputies. They all, Edna Rogers thought, had properly solemn faces. The man named Clyde was trying to dispense some comforting words. Edna Rogers shut him out.

Clyde Smart finally moved to the table. Neil and Edna Rogers, married forty-two years, stood next to each other and waited. They did not touch. They did not gather strength from one another. Many years had passed since they had last leaned on each other.

Finally, the medical examiner stopped talking and pulled back the sheet.

When Neil Rogers saw Sheila's face, he reeled back like a wounded animal. He kept his eyes up now and let out a cry that reminded Edna of a coyote when a storm is brewing. She knew from her husband's anguish, even before looking herself, that there would be no reprieve, no last-minute miracle. She summoned the courage and gazed at her daughter. She reached out a hand—the maternal desire to comfort, even in death, never let up—but she made herself stop.

Edna continued to stare down until her vision blurred, until Edna could almost see Sheila's face transforming, the years running backward, peeling down, until her firstborn was her baby again, her whole life ahead of her, a second chance for her mother to do it right.

And then Edna Rogers started to cry.

20

"What happened to your nose?" Pistillo asked me.

We were back in his office. Squares stayed in the waiting room. I sat in the armchair in front of Pistillo's desk. His chair, I noticed this time, was set a little higher than mine, probably for reasons of intimidation. Claudia Fisher, the agent who'd visited me at Covenant House, stood behind me with her arms crossed.

"You should see the other guy," I said.

"You got into a fight?"

"I fell," I said.

Pistillo didn't believe me, but that was okay. He put both hands on his desk. "We'd like you to run through it again for us," he said.

"Through what?"

"How Sheila Rogers disappeared."

"Have you found her?"

"Just bear with us please." He coughed into his fist. "What time did Sheila Rogers leave your apartment?"

"Why?"

"Please, Mr. Klein, if you could just help us out here."

"I think she left around five in the morning."

"You're sure about that?"

"Think," I said. "I used the word *think*."

"Why aren't you sure?"

"I was asleep. I thought I heard her leave."

"At five?"

"Yes."

"You looked at the clock?"

"Are you for real? I don't know."

"How else would you know it was five?"

"I have a great internal clock, I don't know. Can we move on?"

He nodded and shifted in his seat. "Ms. Rogers left you a note, correct?"

"Yes."

"Where was the note?"

"You mean, where in the apartment?"

"Yes."

"What's the difference?"

He offered up his most patronizing smile. "Please."

"On the kitchen counter," I said. "It's made of Formica, if that helps."

"What did the note say exactly?"

"That's personal."

"Mr. Klein—"

I sighed. No reason to fight him. "She told me that she'd love me always."

"What else?"

"That was it."

"Just that she'd love you always?"

"Yep."

"Do you still have the note?"

"I do."

"May we see it?"

"May you tell me why I'm here?"

Pistillo sat back. "After leaving your father's house, did you and Ms. Rogers head straight back to your apartment?"

The change of subjects threw me. "What are you talking about?"

"You attended your mother's funeral, correct?"

"Yes."

"Then you and Sheila Rogers returned to your apartment. That was what you told us, no?"

"That's what I told you."

"And is it the truth?"

"Yes."

121

"Did you stop on the way home?"

"No."

"Can anyone verify that?"

"Verify that I didn't stop?"

"Verify that you two went back to your apartment and stayed there for the remainder of the evening."

"Why would anyone have to verify that?"

"Please, Mr. Klein."

"I don't know if anyone can verify it or not."

"Did you talk with anyone?"

"No."

"Did a neighbor see you?"

"I don't know." I looked over my shoulder at Claudia Fisher. "Why don't you canvass the neighborhood? Isn't that what you guys are famous for?"

"Why was Sheila Rogers in New Mexico?"

I turned back around. "I don't know that she was."

"She never told you that she was going?"

"I know nothing about it."

"How about you, Mr. Klein?"

"How about me what?"

"Do you know anyone in New Mexico?"

"I don't even know the way to Santa Fe."

"San Jose," Pistillo corrected him, smiling at the lame joke. "We have a list of your recent incoming calls."

"How nice for you."

He sort of shrugged. "Modern technology."

"And that's legal? You having my phone records?"

"We got a warrant."

"I bet you did. So what do you want to know?"

Claudia Fisher moved for the first time. She handed me a sheet of paper. I glanced down at what appeared to be a photocopy of a phone bill. One number—an unfamiliar one—was highlighted in yellow.

"Your residence received a phone call from a pay phone in Paradise Hills, New Mexico, the night before your mother's funeral." He leaned in a little closer. "Who was that call from?"

I studied the number, totally confused yet again. The call had come in at six-fifteen in the evening. It'd lasted eight minutes. I did not know what it meant, but I didn't like the whole tone of this conversation. I looked up.

"Should I have a lawyer?"

That slowed Pistillo down. He and Claudia Fisher exchanged another glance. "You can always have a lawyer," he said a little too carefully.

"I want Squares in here."

"He's not a lawyer."

"Still. I don't know what the hell is going on, but I don't like these questions. I came down because I thought you had information for me. Instead, I'm being interrogated."

"Interrogated?" Pistillo spread his hands. "We're just chatting."

A phone trilled behind me. Claudia Fisher snapped up her cell phone à la Wyatt Earp. She put it to her ear and said, "Fisher." After listening for about a minute, she hung up without saying good-bye. Then she nodded some kind of confirmation at Pistillo.

I stood up. "I've had enough of this."

"Sit down, Mr. Klein."

"I'm tired of your bullshit, Pistillo. I'm tired of—"

"That call," he interjected.

"What about it?"

"Sit down, Will."

He'd used my first name. I did not like the sound of it. I stood where I was and waited.

"We were just waiting for visual confirmation," he said.

"Of what?"

He did not reply to my query. "So we flew Sheila Rogers's parents in from Idaho. They made it official, though the fingerprints had already told us what we needed to know."

His face grew soft. My knees buckled, but I managed to stay upright. He looked at me now with heavy eyes. I started to shake my head, but I knew there was no way to duck the blow.

"I'm sorry, Will," Pistillo said. "Sheila Rogers is dead."

21

Denial is an amazing thing.

Even as I felt my stomach twist and drop, even as I felt the ice spread out and chill me from the center, even as I felt the tears push hard against my eyes, I somehow managed to detach. I nodded while concentrating on the few details that Pistillo was willing to give me. She'd been dumped on the side of a road in Nebraska, he said. I nodded. She'd been murdered in—to use Pistillo's words—"a rather brutal fashion." I nodded some more. She had been found with no ID on her, but the fingerprints had matched and then Sheila's parents had flown in and identified the body for official purposes. I nodded again.

I did not sit. I did not cry. I stood perfectly still. I felt something inside me harden and grow. It pressed against my rib cage, made it almost impossible to breathe. I heard his words as though from afar, as though through a filter or from underwater. I flashed to a simple moment: Sheila reading on our couch, her legs tucked under her, the sleeves of her sweater stretched too long. I saw the focus on her face, the way she prepared her finger for the next page turn, the way her eyes narrowed during certain passages, the way she looked up and smiled when she realized that I was staring.

Sheila was dead.

I was still back there, with Sheila, back in our apartment, grasping smoke, trying to hold on to what was already gone, when Pistillo's words cut through the haze.

"You should have cooperated with us, Will."

I surfaced as if from a sleep. "What?"

"If you'd told us the truth, maybe we could have saved her."

Next thing I remember, I was out in the van.

Squares alternated between pounding on the steering wheel and swearing vengeance. I had never seen him so agitated. My reaction had been just the opposite. It was like someone had pulled out my plug. I stared out the window. Denial was still holding, but I could feel reality start hammering against the walls. I wondered how long before the walls collapsed under the onslaught.

"We'll get him," Squares said yet again.

For the moment, I did not much care.

We double-parked in front of the apartment building. Squares jumped out.

"I'll be fine," I said.

"I'll walk you up anyway," he said. "I want to show you something."

I nodded numbly.

When we entered, Squares reached into his pocket and pulled out a gun. He swept through the apartment, gun drawn. No one. He handed me the weapon.

"Lock the door. If that creepy asshole comes back, blow him away."

"I don't need this," I said.

"Blow him away," he repeated.

I kept my eyes on the gun.

"You want me to stay?" he asked.

"I think I'm better off alone."

"Yeah, okay, but you need me, I got the cell. Twenty-four, seven."

"Right. Thanks."

He left without another word. I put the gun on the table. Then I stood and looked at our apartment. Nothing of Sheila was here anymore. Her smell had faded. The air felt thinner, less substantial. I wanted to close all the windows and doors, batten them down, try to preserve something of her.

Someone had murdered the woman I love.

For the second time?

No. Julie's murder had not felt like this. Not even close. Denial was, yep, still there, but a voice was whispering through the cracks: Nothing would be the same ever again. I knew that. And I knew that I would not recover this time. There are blows you can take and get back up from—like what happened with Ken and Julie. This was not like that. Lots of feelings ricocheted through me. But the most dominant was despair.

I would never be with Sheila again. Someone had murdered the woman I love.

I concentrated on the second part. Murdered. I thought about her past, about the hell she had gone through. I thought about how valiantly she'd struggled, and I thought about how someone—probably someone from her past—had sneaked up behind her and snatched it all away.

Anger began to seep in too.

I moved over to the desk, bent down, and reached into the back of the bottom drawer. I pulled out the velour box, took a deep breath, and opened it.

The ring's diamond was one-point-three carats, with G color, VI rating, round cut. The platinum band was simple with two rectangle baguettes. I'd bought it from a booth in the diamond district on 47th Street two weeks ago. I'd only shown it to my mother, and I had planned on proposing, so she could see. But Mom had no good days after that. I waited. Still, it gave me comfort that she'd known that I had found someone and that she more than approved. I had just been waiting for the right time, what with my mother dying and all, to give it to Sheila.

Sheila and I had loved each other. I would have proposed in some corny, awkward, quasi-original way and her eyes would have misted over and then she would have said yes and thrown her arms around me. We would have gotten married and been life partners. It would have been great.

Someone had taken all that away.

The wall of denial began to buckle and crack. Grief spread over me, ripping the breath from my lungs. I collapsed into a chair and hugged my knees against my chest. I rocked back and forth and started to cry, really cry, gut-wrenching, soul-tearing cries.

I don't know how long I sobbed. But after a while, I forced my-self to stop. That was when I decided to fight back against the grief. Grief paralyzes. But not anger. And the anger was there too, linger-ing, looking for an opening.

So I let it in.

22

When Katy Miller heard her father raise his voice, she stopped in the doorway.

"Why would you go over there?" he shouted.

Her mother and father stood in the den. The room, like so much of the house, had a hotel-chain feel to it. The furniture was functional, shiny, sturdy, and totally lacking in warmth. The oils on the wall were inconsequential images of sailing ships and still lifes. There were no figurines, no vacation souvenirs, no collections, no family photographs.

"I went to pay my respects," her mother said.

"Why the hell would you do that?"

"I thought it was the right thing to do."

"The right thing? Her son murdered our daughter."

"Her son," Lucille Miller repeated. "Not her."

"Don't give me that crap. She raised him."

"That doesn't make her responsible."

"You never believed that before."

Her mother kept her spine stiff. "I've believed it for a long time," she said. "I just haven't said anything."

Warren Miller turned away and began to pace. "And that jackass threw you out?"

"He's in pain. He just lashed out."

"I don't want you to go back," he said, waving an impotent finger. "You hear me? For all you know, she helped that murdering son of a bitch hide."

"So?"

Katy stifled a gasp. Mr. Miller's head snapped around. "What?"

"She was his mother. Would we have done differently?"

"What are you talking about?"

"If it was the other way around. If Julie had killed Ken and needed to hide. What would you have done?"

"You're talking nonsense."

"No, Warren, I'm not. I want to know. I want to know if the roles were reversed, what would we have done? Would we have turned Julie in? Or would we have tried to save her?"

As her father turned away, he spotted Katy in the doorway. Their eyes met and for the umpteenth time in her life, he could not hold his daughter's gaze. Without another word Warren Miller stormed upstairs. He made his way into the new "computer room" and closed the door. The "computer room" was Julie's old bedroom. For nine years it had remained exactly the same as the day Julie died. Then one day, without warning, her father had gone into the room and packed up everything and stored it away. He painted the walls white and bought a new computer desk at Ikea. Now it was the computer room. Some took this as a sign of closure or, at least, moving on. The truth was just the opposite. The whole act was forced, a dying man showing he can get out of bed when all it really did was make him sicker. Katy never went in there. Now that the room had no tangible signs of Julie, her spirit seemed somehow more aggressive. You relied on your mind now instead of your eyes. You conjured up what you were never meant to see.

Lucille Miller headed into the kitchen. Katy followed in silence. Her mother began to wash dishes. Katy watched, wishing— also for the umpteenth time—that she could say something that would not wound her mother deeper. Her parents never talked to her about Julie. Never. Over the years, she had caught them discussing the murder maybe half a dozen times. It always ended like this. In silence and tears.

"Mom?"

"It's okay, honey."

Katy stepped closer. Her mother scrubbed harder. Katy noticed that her mother's hair had more streaks of white. Her back was a little more bent, her complexion grayer.

"Would you have?" Katy asked.

Her mother said nothing.

"Would you have helped Julie run?"

Lucille Miller kept scrubbing. She loaded the dishwasher. She poured in the detergent and turned it on. Katy waited a few more moments. But her mother would not speak.

Katy tiptoed upstairs. She heard her father's anguished sobs emanating from the computer room. The sound was muffled by the door but not nearly enough. Katy stopped and rested her palm on the wood. She thought that maybe she could feel the vibrations. Her father's sobs were always so total, so full-body. His choked voice begged, "Please, no more" over and over, as if imploring some unseen tormenter to put a bullet in his brain. Katy stood there and listened, but the sound did not let up.

After a while she had to turn away. She continued to her own room. Then she packed her clothes in a knapsack and prepared herself to end this once and for all.

I was still sitting in the dark with my knees up against my chest.

It was near midnight. I screened calls. Normally I would have turned off the phone, but the denial was still potent enough to make me hope that maybe Pistillo would call and tell me it was all a big mistake. The mind does that. It tries to find a way out. It makes deals with God. It makes promises. It tries to convince itself that maybe there is a reprieve, that this could all be a dream, the most vicious of nightmares, and that somehow you can find your way back.

I had picked up the phone only once and that was for Squares. He told me that the kids at Covenant House wanted to have a memorial service for Sheila tomorrow. Would that be all right? I told him that I thought Sheila would have really liked that.

I looked out the window. The van circled the block again. Yep, Squares. Protecting me. He had been circling all night. I knew that he would not stray far. He probably hoped that trouble arose just so he could unload on someone. I thought about Squares's comment that he had not been all that different from the Ghost. I thought about the power of the past and what Squares had gone through and what Sheila had gone through and marveled at how they'd found the strength to swim against the riptide.

The phone rang again.

I looked down into my beer. I was not one for drinking away my problems. I sort of wished that I were. I wanted to be numb right now, but the opposite was happening. My skin was being ripped off so that I could feel everything. My arms and legs grew impossibly heavy. It felt as though I were sinking under, drowning, that I would always be just inches from the surface, my legs held by invisible hands, unable to break free.

I waited for the answering machine to pick up. After the third ring, I heard a click and then my voice said to leave a message at the beep. When the beep sounded I heard a semi-familiar voice.

"Mr. Klein?"

I sat up. The woman on the answering machine tried to stifle a sob.

"This is Edna Rogers. Sheila's mother."

My hand shot out and snatched the receiver. "I'm here," I said.

Her answer was to cry. I started crying too.

"I didn't think it would hurt so much," she said after some time had passed.

Alone in what had been our apartment, I started rocking back and forth.

"I cut her out of my life so long ago," Mrs. Rogers continued. "She wasn't my daughter anymore. I had other children. She was gone. For good. That's not what I wanted. It was just the way it was. Even when the chief came to my house, even when he told me she was dead, I didn't react. I just nodded and stiffened my back, you know?"

I didn't know. I said nothing. I just listened.

"And then they flew me out here. To Nebraska. They said they had her fingerprints already, but they needed a family member to identify her. So Neil and me, we drove to the airport in Boise and flew here. They took us to this little station. On TV they always do it behind glass. You know what I mean? They stand outside and they wheel in the body and it's behind glass. But not here. They brought me into this office and there was this . . . this lump covered with a sheet. She wasn't even on a stretcher. She was on a table. And then this man pulled back the sheet and I saw her face. For the first time in fourteen years, I saw Sheila's face. . . ."

She lost it then. She started crying and for a long time there was no letup. I held the receiver to my ear and waited.

"Mr. Klein," she began.

131

"Please call me Will."

"You loved her, Will, didn't you?"

"Very much."

"And you made her happy?"

I thought about the diamond ring. "I hope so."

"I'm staying overnight in Lincoln. I want to fly to New York to-morrow morning."

"That would be nice," I said. I told her about the memorial service.

"Will there be time for us to talk afterward?" she asked.

"Of course."

"There are some things I need to know," she said. "And there are some things—some hard things—I have to tell you."

"I'm not sure I understand."

"I'll see you tomorrow, Will. We'll talk then."

I had one visitor that night.

At one in the morning, the doorbell rang. I figured it was Squares. I managed to get to my feet and shuffle across the floor. Then I remembered the Ghost. I glanced back. The gun was still on the table. I stopped.

The bell sounded again.

I shook my head. No. I was not that far gone. Not yet anyhow. I moved toward the door and looked through the peephole. But it wasn't Squares or the Ghost.

It was my father.

I opened the door. We stood and looked at each other as if from a great distance. He was out of breath. His eyes were swollen and tinged with red. I stood there, unmoving, feeling everything inside me collapse away. He nodded and held out his arms and beckoned me forward. I stepped into his embrace. I pressed my cheek against the scratchy wool of his sweater. It smelled wet and old. I started to sob. He shushed me and stroked my hair and pulled me closer. I felt my legs give way. But I did not slide down. My father held me up. He held me up for a very long time.

23

Las Vegas

Morty Meyer split the tens. He signaled the dealer to hit both. The first came up a nine, the second an ace. Nineteen on the first hand. And blackjack.

He was on a roll. Eight straight hands had gone his way, twelve of the last thirteen—up a solid eleven grand. Morty was in the zone. The ever-elusive winner's high tingled down his arms and legs. It felt delicious. Nothing like it. Gambling, Morty had learned, was the ultimate temptress. You come after her, she scorns you, rejects you, makes you miserable, and then, when you're ready to give her up, she smiles at you, puts her warm hand on your face, gently caresses you, and it feels so good, so damn good. . . .

The dealer busted. Oh yes, another winner. The dealer, a hausfrau with overtreated haylike hair, swept up the cards and gave him his chips. Morty was winning. And yes, despite what those bozos at Gamblers Anonymous tried to peddle, you could indeed win at a casino. Someone had to win, didn't they? Look at the odds, for chrissake. The house can't beat everyone. Hell, with dice you can actually play on the house's side. So, of course, some people won. Some people went home with money. Had to be. Impossible any other way. To say no one won was just part of the overreaching GA crap that left the organization with no credibility. If they start off lying to you, how can you trust them to help?

Morty played in Las Vegas, Las Vegas— the real Las Vegas, the city itself, no strip-strolling tourist trade in pseudo-suede and sneakers, no whistling and hollering or squeals of joy, no faux Statue of Liberty or Eiffel Tower, no Cirque du Soleil, no roller coasters, no 3-D movie rides or gladiator costumes or dancing water fountains or bogus volcanoes or kid-appeal arcades. This was downtown Las Vegas. This was where grimy men with barely a mouth of teeth per table, the dust from their pickups still coming off them with each shoulder slump, lost their meager paychecks. The players here were bleary-eyed, exhausted, their faces lined, their hard times baked on by the sun. A man came here after slaving at a job that he hated because he did not want to go home to his trailer or equivalent, his abode with the broken TV, the screaming babies, the let-herself-go wife who used to stroke him in the back of that pickup and now eyed him with naked repulsion. He came here with the closest thing that he would ever know to hope, with that wispy belief that he was one score away from changing his life. But the hope never lasted. Morty was not even sure it was ever really there. Deep down, the players knew it was never meant to be. They would always be on the toe end of the kick. They were destined for a lifetime of disappointment, for slouching with their faces forever pressed against the glass.

The table changed dealers. Morty leaned back. He stared at his winnings and the old shadow crossed over him again: He missed Leah. Some days he still woke up and turned to her, and when he remembered, the sorrow consumed him. He would not be able to get out of bed. He looked now at the grimy men in this casino. When he was younger, Morty would have called them losers. But they had an excuse for being here. They may as well have been born with the loser L branded into their behinds. Morty's parents, immigrants from a shtetl in Poland, had sacrificed for him. They had sneaked into this country, faced terrible poverty an ocean away from everything familiar, fought and clawed—all so their son would have a better life. They had worked themselves to an early-ish grave, hanging on just long enough to see Morty graduate medical school, to see that their struggle had meant something, had steered the genealogical trajectory for the better now and forever. They died in peace.

Morty was dealt a six up, seven down. He hit and got a ten. Busted. He lost the next hand too. Damn. He needed this money. Locani, a classic leg-breaking bookie, wanted his cash. Morty, a

134

loser's loser when you really think about it, had stalled him by offering up information. He had told Locani about the masked man and injured woman. At first, Locani did not seem to care, but the word spread and all of a sudden someone wanted details.

Morty told them *almost* everything.

He did not, would not, tell them about the passenger in the backseat. He did not have a clue what was going on, but there were some things even he would not do. Low as he had sunk, Morty would not tell them about that.

He was dealt two aces. He split them. A man sat next to him. Morty felt rather than saw him. He felt him in his old bones, as though the man were an incoming weather front. He did not turn his head, afraid, as irrational as this sounded, even to look.

The dealer hit both hands. A king and a jack. Morty had just gotten two blackjacks.

The man leaned close and whispered, "Quit while you're ahead, Morty."

Morty slowly turned and saw a man with eyes of washed-out gray and skin that went beyond white, too translucent really, so that you felt as though you could see his every vein. The man smiled.

"It might be time," the silvery whisper continued, "to cash in your chips."

Morty tried not to shudder. "Who are you? What do you want?"

"We need to chat," the man said.

"About what?"

"About a certain patient who recently visited your esteemed practice."

Morty swallowed. Why had he opened his mouth to Locani? He should have stalled with something else, anything else. "I already told them everything I know."

The pale man cocked his head. "Did you, Morty?"

"Yes."

Those washed-out eyes fell on him hard. Neither man spoke or moved. Morty felt his face redden. He tried to stiffen his back, but he could feel himself wither under the gaze.

"I don't think you have, Morty. I think you're holding back."

Morty said nothing.

"Who else was in the car that night?"

He stared at his chips and tried not to shudder. "What are you talking about?"

135

"There was someone else, wasn't there, Morty?"

"Hey, leave me alone, will you? I'm on a roll here."

Rising from his seat, the Ghost shook his head. "No, Morty," he said, touching him gently on the arm. "I would say that your luck is about to take a turn for the worse."

24

The memorial service was held in the Covenant House auditorium.

Squares and Wanda sat on my right, my father on my left. Dad kept his arm behind me, sometimes rubbing my back. It felt nice. The room was packed, mostly with the kids. They hugged me and cried and told me how much they'd miss Sheila. The service lasted almost two hours. Terrell, a fourteen-year-old who'd been selling himself for ten dollars a pop, played a song on the trumpet that he'd composed in her memory. It was the saddest, sweetest sound I'd ever heard. Lisa, who was seventeen years old and diagnosed bipolar, spoke of how Sheila had been the only one she could talk to when she learned that she was pregnant. Sammy told a funny story about how Sheila tried to teach him how to dance to that "crappy white-girl" music. Sixteen-year-old Jim told the mourners that he had given up on himself, that he'd been ready to commit suicide, and when Sheila smiled at him, he realized that there was indeed good in this world. Sheila convinced him to stay another day. And then another.

I pushed away the pain and listened closely because these kids deserved that. This place meant so much to me. To us. And when we had doubts about our success, about how much we were helping, we always remembered that it was all about the kids. They were not cuddly. Most were unattractive and hard to love. Most would live terrible lives and end up in jail or on the streets or dead. But that did not mean you gave up. It meant just the opposite, in fact. It meant we had to love them all the more. Unconditionally. Without a flinch. Sheila had known that. It had mattered to her.

Sheila's mother—at least, I assumed it was Mrs. Rogers—came in about twenty minutes into the ceremony. She was a tall woman. Her face had the dry, brittle look of something left too long in the sun. Our eyes met. She looked a question at me, and I nodded a yes. As the service continued, I turned and glanced at her every once in a while. She sat perfectly still, listening to the words about her daughter with something approaching awe.

At one point, when we rose as a congregation, I saw something that surprised me. I'd been gazing over the sea of familiar faces, when I spotted a familiar figure with a scarf covering most of her face.

Tanya.

The scarred woman who took "care" of that scum Louis Castman. Again I assumed that it was Tanya. I was fairly certain. Same hair, same height and build, and even though most of her face was covered, I could still see something familiar in the eyes. I had not really thought about it before, but of course there was a chance that she and Sheila had known each other from their days on the street.

We sat back down.

Squares spoke last. He was eloquent and funny and brought Sheila to life in a way I knew I never could. He told the kids how Sheila had been "one of you," a struggling runaway who'd fought her own demons. He remembered her first day here. He remembered watching Sheila bloom. And mostly, he said, he remembered watching her fall in love with me.

I felt hollow. My insides had been scooped out, and again I was struck with the realization that this pain would be permanent, that I could stall, that I could run around and investigate and dig for some inner truth, but in the end, it would change nothing. My grief would forever be by my side, my constant companion in lieu of Sheila.

When the ceremony ended, no one knew exactly what to do. We all sat for an awkward moment, no one moving, until Terrell started playing his trumpet again. People rose. They cried and hugged me all over again. I don't know how long I stood there and took it all in. I was thankful for the outpouring, but it made me miss

Sheila all the more. The numb slid back up because this was all too raw. Without the numb, I wouldn't get through it.

I looked for Tanya, but she was gone.

Someone announced that there was food in the cafeteria. The mourners slowly milled toward it. I spotted Sheila's mother standing in a corner, both hands clutching a small purse. She looked drained, as if the vitality had leaked out from a still-open wound. I made my way toward her.

"You're Will?" she said.

"Yes."

"I'm Edna Rogers."

We did not hug or kiss cheeks or even shake hands.

"Where can we talk?" she asked.

I led her down the corridor toward the stairs. Squares picked up that we wanted to be alone and diverted foot traffic. We passed the new medical facility, the psychiatric offices, the drug treatment areas. Many of our runaways are new or expectant mothers. We try to treat them. Many others have serious mental problems. We try to help them too. And of course, a whole slew of them have a potpourri of drug problems. We do our best there too.

We found an empty dorm room and stepped inside. I closed the door. Mrs. Rogers showed me her back. "It was a beautiful service," she said.

I nodded.

"What Sheila became—" She stopped, shook her head. "I had no idea. I wish I could have seen that. I wish that she'd called and told me."

I did not know what to say to that.

"Sheila never gave me a moment of pride when she was alive." Edna Rogers tugged a handkerchief out of her bag as though someone inside were putting up a fight. She gave her nose a quick, decisive swipe, and then tucked it away again. "I know that sounds unkind. She was a beautiful baby. And she was fine in elementary school. But somewhere along the way"—she looked away, shrugged—"she changed. She became surly. Always complaining. Always unhappy. She stole money from my purse. She ran away time after time. She had no friends. The boys bored her. She hated

139

school. She hated living in Mason. Then one day she dropped out of school and ran away. Except this time she never came back."

She looked at me as if expecting a response.

"You never saw her again?" I asked.

"Never."

"I don't understand," I said. "What happened?"

"You mean what made her finally run away?"

"Yes."

"You think there was some big event, right?" Her voice was louder now, challenging. "Her father must have abused her. Or maybe I beat her. Something that explains it all. That's the way it works. Nice and tidy. Cause and effect. But there was nothing like that. Her father and I, we weren't perfect. Far from it. But it wasn't our fault either."

"I didn't mean to imply—"

"I know what you were implying."

Her eyes ignited. She pursed her lips and looked a dare at me. I wanted off this subject.

"Did Sheila ever call you?" I said.

"Yes." ·

"How often?"

"The last time was three years ago."

She stopped, waiting for me to continue.

I asked, "Where was she when she called?"

"She wouldn't tell me."

"What did she say?"

This time it took her a long while to respond. Edna Rogers began to circle the room and look at the beds and the dressers. She fluffed a pillow and tucked in a sheet corner. "Once every six months or so, Sheila would call home. She was usually stoned or drunk or high, whatever. She'd get all emotional. She'd cry and I'd cry and she'd say horrible things to me."

"Like what?"

She shook her head. "Downstairs. What that man with the tattoo on his forehead said. About you two meeting here and falling in love. That true?"

"Yes."

She stood upright and looked at me. Her lips curled into what might pass for a smile. "So," she said, and I heard something creep into her voice, "Sheila was sleeping with her boss."

Edna Rogers curled the smile some more, and it was like looking at a different person.

"She was a volunteer," I said.

"Uh-huh. And what exactly was she volunteering to do for you, Will?"

I felt a shiver skitter down my back.

"Still want to judge me?" she asked.

"I think you should leave."

"Can't take the truth, is that it? You think I'm some kind of monster. That I gave up on my kid for no good reason."

"It's not my place to say."

"Sheila was a miserable kid. She lied. She stole—"

"Maybe I'm beginning to understand," I said.

"Understand what?"

"Why she ran away."

She blinked and then glared at me. "You didn't know her. You still don't."

"Didn't you hear a thing that was said down there?"

"I heard." Her voice grew softer. "But I never knew that Sheila. She'd never let me. The Sheila I knew—"

"In all due deference, I'm really not in the mood to hear you trash her any further."

Edna Rogers stopped. She closed her eyes and sat on the edge of a bed. The room grew very still. "That's not why I came here."

"Why did you come?"

"I wanted to hear something good, for one thing."

"You got that," I said.

She nodded. "That I did."

"What else do you want?"

Edna Rogers stood. She stepped toward me, and I fought off the desire to move away. She looked me straight in the eye. "I'm here about Carly."

I waited. When she did not elaborate, I said, "You mentioned that name on the phone."

"Yes."

"I didn't know any Carly then, and I don't know any now."

She showed me the cruel, curled smile again. "You wouldn't be lying to me, would you, Will?"

I felt a fresh shiver. "No."

"Sheila never mentioned the name Carly?"

"No."

"You're sure about that?"

"Yes. Who is she?"

"Carly is Sheila's daughter."

I was struck dumb. Edna Rogers saw my reaction. She seemed to enjoy it.

"Your lovely volunteer never mentioned that she had a daughter, did she?"

I said nothing.

"Carly is twelve years old now. And no, I don't know who the father is. I don't think Sheila did either."

"I don't understand," I said.

She reached into her purse and took out a picture. She handed it to me. It was one of those newborn hospital shots. A baby wrapped in a blanket, new eyes blinking out, unseeing. I flipped it over. The handwriting said "Carly." The date of birth was written under it.

My head began to spin.

"The last time Sheila called me was on Carly's ninth birthday," she said. "And I spoke to her myself. Carly, that is."

"So where is she now?"

"I don't know," Edna Rogers said. "That's why I'm here, Will. I want to find my granddaughter."

25

When I stumbled back home, Katy Miller was sitting by my apartment door, her knapsack between her splayed legs.

She scrambled to her feet. "I called but . . ."

I nodded.

"My parents," Katy told me. "I just can't stay in that house another day. I thought maybe I could crash on your couch."

"It's not a good time," I said.

"Oh."

I put the key in the door.

"It's just that I've been trying to put it together, you know. Like we said. Who could have killed Julie. And I started wondering. How much do you know about Julie's life after you two broke up?"

We both stepped inside the apartment. "I don't know if now is a good time."

She finally saw my face. "Why? What happened?"

"Someone very close to me died."

"You mean your mother?"

I shook my head. "Someone else close to me. She was murdered."

Katy gasped and dropped the knapsack. "How close?"

"Very."

"A girlfriend?"

"Yes."

"Someone you loved?"

"Very much."

She looked at me.

"What?" I said.

"I don't know, Will. It's like someone murders the women you love."

The same thought I'd earlier pushed away. Vocalized, it sounded even more ridiculous. "Julie and I broke up more than a year before her murder."

"So you were over her?"

I did not want to travel that route again. I said, "What about Julie's life after we broke up?"

Katy fell onto the couch the way teenagers do, as if she had no bones. Her right leg was draped over the arm, her head back with the chin tilted up. She wore ripped jeans again and another top that was so tight it looked like the bra was on the outside. Her hair was tied back in a ponytail. A few of the strands fell loose and onto her face.

"I started thinking," she said, "if Ken didn't kill her, someone else did, right?"

"Right."

"So I started looking into her life at the time. You know, calling old friends, trying to remember what was going on with her, that kind of thing."

"And what did you find?"

"That she was pretty messed up."

I tried to focus on what she was saying. "How so?"

She dropped both legs to the floor and sat up. "What do you remember?"

"She was a senior at Haverton."

"No."

"No?"

"Julie dropped out."

That surprised me. "You're sure?"

"Senior year," she said. Then she asked, "When did you last see her, Will?"

I thought about it. It had indeed been a while. I told her so.

"So when you broke up?"

I shook my head. "She ended it on the phone."

"For real?"

144

"Yes."

"Cold," Katy said. "And you just accepted that?"

"I tried to see her. But she wouldn't let me."

Katy looked at me as though I'd just spouted the lamest excuse in the history of mankind. Looking back on it, I guess maybe she was right. Why hadn't I gone to Haverton? Why hadn't I demanded to meet face-to-face?

"I think," Katy said, "Julie ended up doing something bad."

"What do you mean?"

"I don't know. Maybe that's going too far. I don't remember much, but I remember she seemed happy before she died. I hadn't seen her that happy in a long time. I think maybe she was getting better, I don't know."

The doorbell rang. My shoulders slumped at the sound. I was not much in the mood for more company. Katy, reading me, jumped up and said, "I'll get it."

It was a deliveryman with a fruit basket. Katy took the basket and brought it back into the room. She dropped it on the table. "There's a card," she said.

"Open it."

She plucked it out of the tiny envelope. "It's a condolence basket from some of the kids at Covenant House." She pulled something from an envelope. "A mass card too."

Katy kept staring at the card.

"What's the matter?"

Katy read it again. Then she looked up at me. "Sheila Rogers?"

"Yes."

"Your girlfriend's name was Sheila Rogers?"

"Yeah, why?"

Katy shook her head and put down the card.

"What is it?"

"Nothing," she said.

"Don't give me that. Did you know her?"

"No."

"Then what is it?"

"Nothing." Katy's voice was firmer this time. "Just drop it, okay?"

The phone rang. I waited for the machine. Through the speaker I heard Squares say, "Pick it up."

I did.

Without preamble, Squares said, "You believe the mother? About Sheila having a daughter?"

"Yes."

"So what are we going to do about it?"

I had been thinking about it since I first heard the news. "I have a theory," I said.

"I'm a-listening."

"Maybe Sheila's running away had something to do with her daughter."

"How?"

"Maybe she was trying to find Carly or bring her back. Maybe she learned that Carly was in trouble. I don't know. But something."

"Sounds semi-logical."

"And if we can trace Sheila's steps," I said, "maybe we can find Carly."

"And maybe we'll end up like Sheila."

"A risk," I agreed.

There was a hesitation. I looked over at Katy. She was staring off, plucking her lower lip.

"So you want to continue," Squares said.

"Yes, but I don't want to put you in danger."

"So this is the part where you tell me I can step away at any time?"

"Right, and then this is the part where you say you'll stick with me to the end."

"Cue the violins," Squares said. "Now that we're past all that, Roscoe via Raquel just called me. He may have come up with a serious lead on how Sheila ran. You game for a night ride?"

"Pick me up," I said.

146

26

Philip McGuane saw his old nemesis on the security camera. His receptionist buzzed him.

"Mr. McGuane?"

"Send him in," he said.

"Yes, Mr. McGuane. He's with—"

"Her too."

McGuane stood. He had a corner office overlooking the Hudson River near the isle of Manhattan's southwestern tip. In the warmer months, the new mega-cruise ships with their neon decor and atrium lobbies glide by, some climbing as high as his window. Today nary a stir. McGuane kept flicking the remote on the security camera, keeping up with his federal antagonist Joe Pistillo and the female underling he had in tow.

McGuane spent a lot on security. It was worth it. His system employed eighty-three cameras. Every person who entered his private elevator was digitally recorded from several angles, but what really made the system stand out was that the camera angles were designed to shoot in such a way that anyone entering could be made to look as though they were also leaving. Both the corridor and elevator were painted spearmint green. That might not seem like much—it was, in effect, rather hideous—but to those who understood special effects and digital manipulation, it was key. An image on the green background could be plucked out and placed on another background.

His enemies felt comfortable coming here. This was, after all, his office. No one, they surmised, would be brazen enough to kill someone on his own turf. That was where they were wrong. The brazen nature, the very fact that the authorities would think the same thing—and the fact that he could offer up evidence that the victim had left the facility unharmed—made it the ideal spot to strike.

McGuane pulled out an old photograph from his top drawer. He had learned early that you never underestimate a person or a situation. He also realized that by making opponents underestimate him, he could finagle the advantage. He looked now at the picture of the three seventeen-year-old boys—Ken Klein, John "the Ghost" Asselta, and McGuane. They'd grown up in the suburb of Livingston, New Jersey, though McGuane had lived on the opposite side of town from Ken and the Ghost. They hooked up in high school, drawn to each other, noticing—or perhaps this was giving them all too much credit—a kinship in the eyes.

Ken Klein had been the fiery tennis player, John Asselta the psycho wrestler, McGuane the wow-'em charmer and student council president. He looked at the faces in the photograph. You would never see it. All you saw were three popular high school kids. Nothing beyond that facade. When those kids shot up Columbine a few years back, McGuane had watched the media reaction with fascination. The world looked for comfortable excuses. The boys were outsiders. The boys were teased and bullied. The boys had absent parents and played video games. But McGuane knew that none of that mattered. It may have been a slightly different era, but that could have been them—Ken, John, and McGuane—because the truth is, it does not matter if you are financially comfortable or loved by your parents or if you keep to yourself or fight to stay afloat in the mainstream.

Some people have that rage.

The office door opened. Joseph Pistillo and his young protégé entered. McGuane smiled and put away the photograph.

"Ah, Javert," he said to Pistillo. "Do you still hunt me when all I did was steal some bread?"

"Yeah," Pistillo said. "Yeah, that's you, McGuane. The innocent man hounded."

McGuane turned his attention to the female agent. "Tell me, Joe, why do you always have such a lovely colleague with you?"

"This is Special Agent Claudia Fisher."

"Charmed," McGuane said. "Please have a seat."

"We'd rather stand."

McGuane shrugged a suit-yourself and dropped into his chair. "So what can I do for you today?"

"You're having a tough time, McGuane."

"Am I?"

"Indeed."

"And you're here to help? How special."

Pistillo snorted. "Been after you a long time."

"Yes, I know, but I'm fickle. Suggestion: Send a bouquet of roses next time. Hold the door for me. Use candlelight. A man wants to be romanced."

Pistillo put two fists on the desk. "Part of me wants to sit back and watch you get eaten alive." He swallowed, tried to hold something deep inside him in check. "But a bigger part of me wants to see you rot in jail for what you've done."

McGuane turned to Claudia Fisher. "He's very sexy when he talks tough, don't you think?"

"Guess who we just found, McGuane?"

"Hoffa? About time too."

"Fred Tanner."

"Who?"

Pistillo smirked. "Don't play that with me. Big thug. Works for you."

"I believe he's in my security department."

"We found him."

"I didn't know he was lost."

"Funny."

"I thought he was on vacation, Agent Pistillo."

"Permanently. We found him in the Passaic River."

McGuane frowned. "How unsanitary."

"Especially with two bullet holes in the head. We also found a guy named Peter Appel. Strangled. He was an ex-army sharp-shooter."

"Be all that you can be."

Only one strangled, McGuane thought. The Ghost must have been disappointed that he'd had to shoot the other.

"Yeah, well, let's see," Pistillo went on. "We have these two men dead. Plus we have the two guys in New Mexico. That's four."

"And you didn't use your fingers. They're not paying you enough, Agent Pistillo."

"You want to tell me about it?"

"Very much," McGuane said. "I admit it. I killed them all. Happy?"

Pistillo leaned over the desk so that their faces were inches apart. "You're about to go down, McGuane."

"And you had onion soup for lunch."

"Are you aware," Pistillo said, not backing off, "that Sheila Rogers is dead too?"

"Who?"

Pistillo stood back up. "Right. You don't know her either. She doesn't work for you."

"Many people work for me. I'm a businessman."

Pistillo looked over at Fisher. "Let's go," he said.

"Leaving so soon?"

"I've waited a long time for this," Pistillo said. "What do they say? Revenge is a dish best served cold."

"Like vichyssoise."

Another smirk from Pistillo. "Have a nice day, McGuane."

They left. McGuane sat there and did not move for ten minutes. What had been the purpose of that visit? Simple. To shake him up. More underestimation. He hit line three, the safe phone, the one checked daily for listening devices. He hesitated. Dialing the number. Would that show panic?

He weighed the pros and cons and decided to risk it.

The Ghost answered on the first ring with a drawn-out "Hello?"

"Where are you?"

"Just off the plane from Vegas."

"Learn anything?"

"Oh yes."

"I'm listening."

"There was a third person in the car with them," the Ghost said.

McGuane shifted in his seat. "Who?"

"A little girl," the Ghost said. "No more than eleven or twelve years old."

27

Katy and I were on the street when Squares pulled up. She leaned over and kissed me on the cheek. Squares arched an eyebrow in my direction. I frowned at him.

"I thought you were staying on my couch," I said to her.

Katy had been distracted since the fruit basket's arrival. "I'll be back tomorrow."

"And you don't want to tell me what's going on?"

She stuck her hands deep in her pockets and shrugged. "I just need to do a little research."

"On?"

She shook her head. I did not press it. She gave me a quick grin before taking off. I got in the van.

Squares said, "And she is?"

I explained as we headed uptown. There were dozens of sandwiches and blankets packed in the bag. Squares handed them out to the kids. The sandwiches and blankets, in the same vein as his rap about the missing Angie, made excellent icebreakers, and even if they didn't, at least the kids would have something to eat and something to keep them warm. I had seen Squares work wonders with those items. The first night, a kid would most likely refuse any help at all. He or she might even curse or become hostile. Squares would take no offense. He'd just keep coming at him. Squares believed that consistency was the key. Show the kid you're there all

the time. Show the kid you're not leaving. Show the kid it's unconditional.

A few nights later, that kid will take the sandwich. Another, he'll
want a blanket. After a while, he'll start looking for you and the van.

I reached back and lifted a sandwich into view. "You're working
again tonight?"

He lowered his head and looked at me above his sunglasses.
"No," he said dryly, "I'm just really hungry."

He drove some more.

"How long are you going to avoid her, Squares?"

Squares flipped on the radio. Carly Simon's "You're So Vain."
Squares sang along. Then he said, "Remember this song?"

I nodded.

"That rumor that it was about Warren Beatty. Was that true?"

"Don't know," I said.

We drove some more.

"Let me ask you something, Will."

He kept his eyes on the road. I waited.

"How surprised were you to learn that Sheila had a kid?"

"Very."

"And," he went on, "how surprised would you be to learn I had
one too?"

I looked at him.

"You don't understand the situation, Will."

"I'd like to."

"Let's concentrate on one thing at a time."

The traffic was miraculously light this evening. Carly Simon
faded away and then the Chairman of the Board begged his woman
to give him just a little more time and their love would surely grow.
Such desperation in that simple plea. I love this song.

We cut across town and took the Harlem River Drive north.
When we passed a group of kids huddled under an overpass,
Squares pulled over and shifted into park.

"Quick work stop," he said.

"You want help?"

Squares shook his head. "It won't take long."

"You going to use the sandwiches?"

Squares examined his potential help-ees and considered. "Nah.
Got something better."

152

"What?"

"Phone cards." He handed me one. "I got TeleReach to donate over a thousand of them. The kids go nuts for them."

They did too. As soon as they saw them, the kids flocked to him. Count on Squares. I watched the faces, tried to separate the smeared mass into individuals with wants and dreams and hopes. Kids do not survive long out here. Forget the incredible physical dangers. They can often get past that. It is the soul, the sense of self, that erodes out here. Once the erosion reaches a certain level, well, that's the ball game.

Sheila had been saved before reaching that level.

Then someone had killed her.

I shook it off. No time for that now. Focus on the task at hand. Keep moving. Action kept the grief at bay. Let it fuel you, not slow you down.

Do it—corny as it might sound—for her.

Squares returned a few minutes later. "Let's rock and roll."

"You haven't told me where we're going."

"Corner of 128th Street and Second Avenue. Raquel will meet us there."

"And what's there?"

He grinned. "A possible clue."

We exited the highway and passed a sprawl of housing projects. From two blocks away, I spotted Raquel. This was not difficult. Raquel was the size of a small principality and dressed like an explosion at the Liberace museum. Squares slowed the van next to him and frowned.

"What?" Raquel said.

"Pink pumps with a green dress?"

"It's coral and turquoise," Raquel said. "Plus the magenta purse pulls it all together."

Squares shrugged and parked in front of a storefront with a faded sign that read GOLDBERG PHARMACY. When I stepped out, Raquel wrapped me in an embrace that felt like wet foam rubber. He reeked of Aqua Velva, and my mind couldn't help but think that in this case, indeed, there was something about an Aqua Velva man.

"I'm so sorry," he whispered.

"Thank you."

He released me, and I was able to breathe again. He was crying.

153

His tears grabbed hold of his mascara and ran it down his face. The colors mixed and got diverted in the rough of his beard, so that his face started looking like a candle in the back of Spencer's Gifts.

"Abe and Sadie are inside," Raquel said. "They're expecting you."

Squares nodded and headed into the pharmacy. I followed. A ding-dong sounded when we entered. The smell reminded me of a cherry tree–shaped freshener dangling from a rearview window. The store shelves were high and packed and tight. I saw bandages and deodorants and shampoos and cough medicines, all laid out with seemingly little organization.

An old man with half-moon reading glasses on a chain appeared. He wore a sweater-vest over a white shirt. His hair was high and thick and white and looked like a powdered wig from Bailey's. His eyebrows were extra bushy, giving him the look of an owl.

"Look! It's Mr. Squares!"

The two men hugged, the old man giving Squares's back a few hard pats. "You look good," the old man said.

"You too, Abe."

"Sadie," he shouted. "Sadie, Mr. Squares is here."

"Who?"

"The yoga guy. With that tattoo."

"The one on his forehead?"

"That's him."

I shook my head and leaned toward Squares. "Is there anyone you don't know?"

He shrugged. "I've lived a charmed life."

Sadie, an older woman who would never see five feet even in Raquel's highest pumps, stepped down from behind the pharmacy stand. She frowned at Squares and said, "You look skinny."

"Leave him alone," Abe said.

"Shush you. You eating enough?"

"Sure," Squares said.

"You're bones. Pure bones."

"Sadie, can you leave the man alone?"

"Shush you." She smiled conspiratorially. "I got kugel. You want some?"

"Maybe later, thanks."

"I'll put some in the Tupperware."

"That would be nice, thank you." Squares turned to me. "This is my friend, Will Klein."

The two old people showed me sad eyes. "He's the boyfriend?"

"Yes."

They inspected me. Then they looked at each other.

"I don't know," Abe said.

"You can trust him," Squares said.

"Maybe we can, maybe we can't. But we're like priests here. We don't talk. You know that. And she was particularly adamant. We were to say nothing, no matter what."

"I know that."

"We talk, what good are we?"

"I understand."

"We talk, we could be killed."

"No one will know. I give you my word."

The old couple looked at each other some more. "Raquel," Abe said. "He's a good boy. Or girl. I don't know, I get so confused sometimes."

Squares stepped toward them. "We need your help."

Sadie took her husband's hand in a gesture so intimate I almost turned away. "She was such a beautiful girl, Abe."

"And so nice," he added. Abe sighed and looked at me. The door opened and the ding-dong chimed again. A disheveled black man walked in and said, "Tyrone sent me."

Sadie moved toward him. "I'll take care of you over here," she said.

Abe kept staring at me. I looked at Squares. I didn't understand any of this.

Squares took off his sunglasses. "Please, Abe," he said. "It's important."

Abe held up a hand. "Okay, okay, just stop with the face, please." He waved us forward. "Come this way."

We walked to the back of the store. He lifted the counter flap, and we walked under. We passed the pills, the bottles, the bags of filled prescriptions, the mortars and pestles. Abe opened a door. We headed down into the basement. Abe flicked on the light.

"This," he announced, "is where it all happens."

I saw very little. There was a computer, a printer, and a digital camera. That was about it. I looked at Abe and then at Squares.

"Does someone want to clue me in?"

"Our business is simple," Abe said. "We keep no records. If the police want to take this computer, fine, go ahead. They'll learn

155

nothing. All the records are located up here." He tapped his fore-head with his finger. "And hey, lots of those records are getting lost every day, am I right, Squares?"

Squares smiled at him.

Abe spotted my confusion. "You still don't get it?"

"I still don't get it."

"Fake IDs," Abe said.

"Oh."

"I'm not talking about the ones underage kids use to drink."

"Right, okay."

He lowered his voice. "You know anything about them?"

"Not much."

"I'm talking here about the ones people need to disappear. To run away. To start again. You're in trouble? Poof, I'll make you disap-pear. Like a magician, no? You need to go away, really go away, you don't go to a travel agent. You come to me."

"I see," I said. "And there's a big need for your"—I wasn't sure of the term—"services?"

"You'd be surprised. Oh, it's not usually very glamorous. Lots of times it's just parole jumpers. Or bail jumpers. Or someone the authorities are looking to arrest. We service a lot of illegal immi-grants too. They want to stay in the country, so we make them citi-zens." He smiled at me. "And every once in a while we get someone nicer."

"Like Sheila," I said.

"Exactly. You want to know how it works?"

Before I could answer, Abe had started up again. "It's not like on the TV," he said. "On the TV they always make it so complicated, am I right? They look for a kid who died and then they send away for his birth certificate or something like that. They make up all these complicated forgeries."

"That's not how it's done?"

"That's not how it's done." He sat at the computer terminal and started typing. "First of all, that would take too long. Second, with the Net and the Web and all that nonsense, dead people quickly be-come dead. They don't stay alive anymore. You die, so does your so-cial security number. Otherwise I could just use the social security numbers of old people who die, right? Or people who die in middle age? You understand?"

"I think so," I said. "So how do you create a fake identity?"

"Ah, I don't create them," Abe said with a big smile. "I use real ones."

"I don't follow."

Abe frowned at Squares. "I thought you said he worked the street."

"A long time ago," Squares said.

"Yeah, okay, let's see." Abe Goldberg turned back to me. "You saw that man upstairs. The one who came in after you."

"Yes."

"He looks unemployed, no? Probably homeless."

"I wouldn't know."

"Don't play politically correct with me. He looked like a vagrant, am I right?"

"I guess."

"But he's a person, see. He has a name. He had a mother. He was born in this country. And"—he smiled and waved his hands theatrically—"he has a social security number. He might even have a driver's license, maybe an expired one. No matter. As long as he has a social security number, he exists. He has an identity. You follow?"

"I follow."

"So let's say he needs a little money. For what, I don't want to know. But he needs money. What he doesn't need is an identity. He's out on the street, so what good is it doing him? It's not like he has a credit rating or owns land. So we run his name through this little computer here." He patted the top of the monitor. "We see if he has any outstanding warrants against him. If he doesn't—and most don't—then we buy his ID. Let's say his name is John Smith. And let's say you, Will, need to be able to check into hotels or whatever under a name other than your own."

I saw where he was heading. "You sell me his social security number and I become John Smith."

Abe snapped his fingers. "Bingo."

"But suppose we don't look alike."

"There's no physical descriptions associated with your social security number. Once you have it, you call up any bureau and you can get whatever paperwork you need. If you're in a rush, I have the equipment here to give you an Ohio driver's license. But it won't hold up under tough scrutiny. But the thing is, the identity will."

"Suppose our John Smith gets rousted and needs an ID."

"He can use it too. Heck, five people can use it at the same time. Who's going to know? Simple, am I right?"

"Simple," I agreed. "So Sheila came to you?"

"Yes."

"When?"

"What, two, three days ago. Like I said before, she wasn't our usual customer. Such a nice girl. So beautiful too."

"Did she tell you where she was going?"

Abe smiled and touched my arm. "Does this look like an ask-a-lot-of-questions business? They don't want to say—and I don't want to know. You see, we never talk. Not a word. Sadie and I have our reputation, and like I said upstairs, loose lips can get you killed. You understand?"

"Yes."

"In fact, when Raquel first put out feelers, we didn't say boo. Discretion. That's what this business is about. We love Raquel. But we still said nothing. Zip, not a word."

"So what made you change your mind?"

Abe looked hurt. He turned to Squares, then back to me. "What, you think we're animals? You think we don't feel anything?"

"I didn't mean—"

"The murder," he interrupted. "We heard what happened to that poor, lovely girl. It isn't right." He threw up his hands. "But what can I do? I can't go to the police, am I right? Thing is, I trust Raquel and Mr. Squares here. They're good men. They dwell in the dark but they shine a light. Like my Sadie and me, see?"

The door above us opened, and Sadie came down. "I've closed up," she said.

"Good."

"So where were you?" she asked him.

"I was telling him why we may be willing to talk."

"Okay."

Sadie Goldberg slowly felt her way down the stairs. Abe turned his owl eyes on me again and said, "Mr. Squares tells us that there is a little girl involved here."

"Her daughter," I said. "She's probably about twelve years old."

Sadie clucked a tsk-tsk. "You don't know where she is."

"That's right."

Abe shook his head. Sadie moved next to him, their bodies

touching, somehow fitting together. I wondered how long they'd been married, if they had children, where they'd come from, how they came to these shores, how they ended up in this business.

"You want to know something?" Sadie said to me.

I nodded.

"Your Sheila. She had"—she raised two fists in the air—"a special something. A spirit about her. She was beautiful, of course, but there was something more. The fact that she's gone . . . we feel lessened. She came in and she looked so scared. And maybe the identity we gave her didn't hold up. Maybe that's why she's dead."

"So," Abe said, "we want to help." He wrote something down on a piece of paper and handed it to me. "The name we gave her was Donna White. That's the social security number. I don't know if it'll help you or not."

"And the real Donna White?"

"A homeless crack addict."

I stared down at the scrap of paper.

Sadie moved toward me and put a hand on my cheek. "You look like a nice man."

I looked up at her.

"Find that little girl," she said.

I nodded once and then again. Then I promised that I would.

28

Katy Miller was still shaking when she arrived at her house.

This can't be, she thought. It's a mistake. I got the name wrong.

"Katy?" her mother called out.

"Yeah."

"I'm in the kitchen."

"I'll be there in a little while, Mom."

Katy headed for the basement door. When her hand reached the knob, she stopped.

The basement. She hated to go down there.

You would think that after so many years, she'd be desensitized to the threadbare couch and water-stained carpet and so-old-it's-not-even-cable-ready television. She wasn't. For all her senses knew, her sister's body was still down there, bloated and decayed, the stench of death so thick it made it hard to swallow.

Her parents understood. Katy never had to do laundry. Her father never asked her to fetch his toolbox or get a fresh bulb from the storage room. If a task required a trip into these bowels, her mother and father tried to take it on for her.

But not this time. This time, she was on her own.

At the top of the stairs she flicked the light switch. One naked bulb—the glass fixture had broken during the murder—came to life. She crept down the stairs. She kept her line of vision up and over the couch and carpet and TV.

Why did they still live here?

It made little sense to her. When JonBenét was murdered, the Ramseys had moved across the country. But then again, everyone thought that they killed her. The Ramseys were probably running away from the stares of neighbors as much as the memory of their daughter's demise. That, of course, was not the case here.

But still, there was something about this town. Her parents had stayed. And so had the Kleins. Neither had been willing to surrender.

What did that mean?

She found Julie's trunk in the corner. Her father had put some kind of wooden crate under it in case of a flood. Katy flashed back and saw her sister packing for college. She remembered crawling into the trunk as Julie packed, pretending at first that the trunk was a protective fort and then, after that, pretending that Julie might pack her up too, so that they could go to college together.

There were boxes piled on the top. Katy removed them and put them in a corner. She examined the trunk's lock. There was no key, but all she needed was a flat edge. She found an old butter knife with the stored silver. She stuck it into the opening and turned. The lock fell open. She unsnapped the two clasps and slowly, like Van Helsing opening Dracula's coffin, she lifted the lid.

"What are you doing?"

Her mother's voice startled her. She leapt back.

Lucille Miller moved closer. "Isn't that Julie's trunk?"

"Jesus, Mom, you scared the hell out of me."

Her mother came closer. "What are you doing with Julie's trunk?"

"I'm . . . I'm just looking."

"At what?"

Katy straightened up. "She was my sister."

"I know that, honey."

"Don't I have a right to miss her too?"

Her mother looked at her for a long time. "And that's why you're down here?"

Katy nodded.

"Is everything else okay?" her mother asked.

"Fine."

"You've never been one for reminiscing, Katy."

"You've never let me," she said.

Her mother considered that. "I guess that's true."

161

"Mom?"

"Yes?"

"Why did you stay?"

For a moment, her mother seemed ready to give Katy the usual rebuff about not wanting to talk about it. But—what with Will's surprise visit to the curb and her working up the courage to pay her respects to the Klein family—this was turning into a rather bizarre week. Her mother sat on one of the boxes. She smoothed out her skirt.

"When a tragedy hits you," her mother began. "I mean, when it first hits you, it's the end of the world. It's like being dumped in the ocean during a storm. The water tosses you and thrashes you and there is nothing you can do but try to stay afloat. Part of you—maybe even most of you—doesn't even want to keep your head above water. You want to stop fighting and just sink away. But you can't. The survival instinct won't let you—or maybe, in my case, it was because I had another child to raise. I don't know. But either way, like it or not, you stay afloat."

Her mother wiped the corner of her eye with one finger. She sat up a little and forced a smile. "My analogy isn't holding," she said.

Katy took her mother's hand. "It sounds pretty good to me."

"Maybe," Mrs. Miller allowed, "but you see, after a while, the storm part is over. And that's when it gets even worse. I guess you can say you're washed up onshore. But all that thrashing and tossing has caused irreparable harm. You are in tremendous pain. And that's still not the end of it. Because now you're left with an awful alternative."

Katy waited, still holding her mother's hand.

"You can try to move past the pain. You can try to forget and get on with your life. But for your father and me"—Lucille Miller closed her eyes and shook her head firmly—"forgetting would be too obscene. We couldn't betray your sister like that. The pain may be enormous, but how could we go on if we abandoned Julie? She existed. She was real. I know that doesn't make sense."

But, Katy thought, maybe it did.

They sat in silence. Eventually Lucille Miller let go of Katy's hand. She slapped her thighs and stood. "I'll leave you alone now."

Katy listened to her footsteps. Then she turned back to the trunk. She dug through the contents. It took her nearly half an hour, but she found it.

And it changed everything.

29

When we were back in the van, I asked Squares what we should do next.

"I have a source," he said, a true understatement if ever I've heard one. "We'll run the name Donna White through the airline computers, see if we can figure out when she flew out or where she stayed, something."

We lapsed into silence.

"Someone has to say it," Squares began.

I stared down at my hands. "Go ahead, then."

"What are you trying to do here, Will?"

"Find Carly," I said too quickly.

"And then what? Raise her as your own?"

"I don't know."

"You realize, of course, that you're using this to block."

"So are you."

I looked out the car window. The neighborhood was full of rubble. We drove past housing projects that housed mostly misery. I looked for something good. I didn't see any.

"I was going to propose," I said.

Squares kept driving, but I saw something in his posture give way.

"I bought a ring. I showed it to my mother. I was just waiting for some time to pass. You know, after my mom's death and all."

We stopped at a red light. Squares would not turn and look at me.

"I have to keep searching," I said, "because I'm not sure what I'll do if I don't. I'm not suicidal or anything, but if I stop running"—I stopped, tried to think how to say this, settled for the simple—"it'll catch up to me."

"It's going to catch you eventually, no matter what," Squares said.

"I know. But by then, maybe I'll have done something good. Maybe I'll have saved her daughter. Maybe, even though she's dead, I'll have helped her."

"Or," Squares countered, "you might find out that she was not the woman you believed her to be. That she fooled us all and worse."

"Then so be it," I said. "You still with me?"

"To the end, Kemosabi."

"Good, because I think I have an idea."

His leather face cracked into that smile. "Rock and roll, dude. Lay it on me."

"We've been forgetting something."

"What?"

"New Mexico. Sheila's fingerprints were found at a murder scene in New Mexico."

He nodded. "You think that murder has something to do with Carly?"

"Could be."

He nodded. "But we don't even know who was killed in New Mexico. Hell, we don't even know where the murder scene is exactly."

"That's where my plan comes into action," I said. "Drop me off at home. I think I need to do a little Web surfing."

Yes, I had a plan.

It stood to reason that the FBI were not the ones to discover the bodies. Probably a local cop did. Or maybe a neighbor. Or a relative. And since this murder had taken place in a town not already anesthetized to such sudden violence, the crime had probably been reported in the local paper.

I surfed to refdesk.com and clicked on national newspapers. They had thirty-three listings for New Mexico. I tried the ones in the Albuquerque area. I sat back and let the page load. Found one. Okay, good. I clicked on to the archives and started searching. I typed "murder" in. Too many hits. I tried "double murder." That didn't work either. I tried another paper. Then another.

It took almost an hour, but I finally nailed it:

TWO MEN FOUND MURDERED
Small community shocked
by Yvonne Sterno

Late last night, the gated Albuquerque suburb of Stonepointe was reeling from news that two men were both shot in the head, probably in broad daylight, and found in one of the community's homes. "I didn't hear a thing," said Fred Davison, a neighbor. "I just can't believe something like this could happen in our community." The two men remain unidentified. Police had no comment other than to say that they were investigating. "This is an ongoing investigation. We're following several leads." The homeowner is listed as Owen Enfield. An autopsy is scheduled for this morning.

That was about it. I searched the next day. Nothing. I searched the day after. Still nothing. I searched for all the stories written by Yvonne Sterno. There were pieces on local weddings and charity events. Nothing, not another word, about the murders.

I sat back.

Why weren't there more stories?

One way to find out. I picked up the phone and began to dial the number for the *New Mexico Star-Beacon*. Maybe I'd get lucky and reach Yvonne Sterno. And maybe she'd tell me something.

The switchboard was one of those machines that ask you to spell your party's last name. I had dialed the S-T-E-R when the machine cut in and told me to hit the pound key if I was trying to reach Yvonne Sterno. I followed orders. Two rings later a machine picked up.

"This is Yvonne Sterno at the *Star-Beacon*. I'm either on the phone or away from my desk."

I hung up. I was still online so I brought up switchboard.com. I typed in Sterno's name and tried the Albuquerque area. Bingo. A "Y and M Sterno" was listed as living at 25 Canterbury Drive in Albuquerque. I dialed the number. A woman answered.

"Hello?" Then she shouted, "Quiet back there, Mommy's on the phone."

The squeal of young children did not let up.

165

"Yvonne Sterno?"

"You selling something?"

"No."

"Then yes, speaking."

"My name is Will Klein—"

"Sure sounds like you're selling something."

"I'm not," I said. "Are you the same Yvonne Sterno that writes for the *Star-Beacon*?"

"What did you say your name was?" Before I could reply, she shouted, "Hey, I told you two to knock if off. Tommy, give him the Game Boy. No, now!" Back to me. "Hello?"

"My name is Will Klein. I wanted to talk to you about that double murder you wrote about recently."

"Uh-huh. And what's your interest in the case?"

"I just have a few questions."

"I'm not a library, Mr. Klein."

"Please, call me Will. And bear with me for just a moment. How often do murders occur in places like Stonepointe?"

"Rarely."

"And double murders where the victims are found like this?"

"This would be the first that I'm aware of."

"So," I said, "why didn't it get more coverage?"

The kids erupted again. So did Yvonne Sterno. "That's it! Tommy, get up to your room. Right, right, save it for the judge, bud, let's move. And you, give me that Game Boy. Hand it over before I stick it down the disposal." I heard the phone being picked up again. "And again I will ask you: What's your interest in the case?"

I knew enough reporters to know that the way to their hearts is through their byline. "I may have pertinent information on the case."

"Pertinent," she repeated. "That's a good word there, Will."

"I think you'll find what I say interesting."

"Where you calling from anyway?"

"New York City," I said.

There was a pause. "A long way from the murder scene."

"Yes."

"So I'm listening. What, pray tell, will I find both pertinent and interesting?"

"First I need to know a few basics."

"That's not how I work, Will."

166

"I looked up your other pieces, Mrs. Sterno."

"It's miz. And since we're all buddy-buddy, just call me Yvonne."

"Fine," I said. "You mostly do features, Yvonne. You cover weddings. You cover society dinners."

"They have great eats, Will, and I look fabulous in a black dress. What's your point?"

"A story like this doesn't fall in your lap every day."

"Okay, you're getting me all hot and bothered here. Your point?"

"My point is, take a chance. Just answer a few questions. What's the harm? And who knows, maybe I'm legit."

When she did not respond, I pushed ahead.

"You land a big murder story like this. But the article doesn't list victims or suspects or any real details."

"I didn't know any," she said. "The report came in over the scanner late at night. We barely made it in time for the morning edition."

"So why no follow-up? This had to be a huge event. Why was there only that one piece?"

Silence.

"Hello?"

"Give me a second. The kids are acting up again."

Only I wasn't hearing any noise this time.

"I was closed down," she said softly.

"Meaning?"

"Meaning we were lucky to get even that much into the paper. By the next morning there were feds all over the place. The local SAC—"

"SAC?"

"Special Agent in Charge. The head fed in the area. He got my boss to shut the story down. I tried a little on my own, but all I got was a bunch of no-comments."

"Is that odd?"

"I don't know, Will. I haven't covered a murder before. But yeah, I'd say it sounds pretty odd."

"What do you take it to mean?"

"From the way my boss has been acting?" Yvonne took a deep breath. "It's big. Very big. Bigger than a double murder. Your turn, Will."

I wondered how far I should go. "Are you aware of any fingerprints found at the scene?"

167

"No."

"There was one set belonging to a woman."

"Go on."

"That woman was found dead yesterday."

"Whoa, Nelly. Murdered?"

"Yes."

"Where?"

"A small town in Nebraska."

"Her name?"

I leaned back. "Tell me about the homeowner, Owen Enfield."

"Oh I see. Back and forth. I give, you give."

"Something like that. Was Enfield one of the victims?"

"I don't know."

"What do you know about him?"

"He's lived there three months."

"Alone?"

"According to neighbors, he moved in alone. A woman and child have been hanging around a lot the last few weeks."

Child.

A tremor started in my heart. I sat up. "How old was the child?"

"I don't know. School age."

"Like maybe twelve."

"Yeah maybe."

"Boy or girl."

"Girl."

I froze.

"Yo, Will, you there?"

"Got a name on the girl?"

"No. No one really knew anything about them."

"Where are they now?"

"I don't know."

"How can that be?"

"One of the great mysteries of life, I guess. I haven't been able to track them down. But like I said, I'm off the case. I haven't been trying all that hard."

"Can you find out where they are?"

"I can try."

"Is there anything else? Have you heard the name of a suspect or one of the victims, anything?"

"Like I said, it's been quiet. I only work at the paper part-time.

As you might have been able to discern, I'm a full-time mother. I just caught the story because I was the only one in when it came over the band. But I have a few good sources."

"We need to find Enfield," I said. "Or at least the woman and girl."

"Seems like a good place to start," she agreed. "You want to tell me your interest in all this?"

I thought about that. "You up for rattling cages, Yvonne?"

"Yeah, Will. Yeah, I am."

"Are you any good?"

"Want a demonstration?"

"Sure."

"You may be calling me from New York City, but you're actually from New Jersey. In fact—though there must certainly be more than one Will Klein out there—my bet is you're the brother of an infamous murderer."

"An alleged infamous murderer," I corrected her. "How did you know?"

"I have Lexis-Nexis on my home computer. I plugged in your name and that's what came up. One of the articles mentioned that you now live in Manhattan."

"My brother had nothing to do with any of this."

"Sure, and he was innocent of killing your neighbor too, right?"

"That's not what I mean. Your double murder has nothing to do with him."

"Then what's your connection?"

I let loose a breath. "Someone else who was very close to me."

"Who?"

"My girlfriend. Her fingerprints were the ones found at the scene."

I heard the kids act up again. It sounded like they were running through the room making siren noises. Yvonne Sterno did not yell at them this time. "So it was your girlfriend who was found dead in Nebraska?"

"Yes."

"And that's your interest in this?"

"Part of it."

"What's the other part?"

I was not prepared yet to tell her about Carly. "Find Enfield," I said.

169

"What was her name, Will? Your girlfriend."

"Just find him."

"Hey, you want us to work together? You don't hold out on me. I can find out in five seconds by looking it up anyway. Just tell me."

"Rogers," I said. "Her name was Sheila Rogers."

I heard her typing some more. "I'll do my best, Will," she said. "Hang tight, I'll call you soon."

30

I had a strange quasi-dream.

I say "quasi" because I was not fully asleep. I floated in that groove between slumber and consciousness, that state where you sometimes stumble and plummet and need to grab the sides of the bed. I lay in the dark, my hands behind my head, my eyes closed.

I mentioned earlier how Sheila had loved to dance. She even made me join a dance club at the Jewish Community Center in West Orange, New Jersey. The JCC was close to both my mother's hospital and the house in Livingston. We'd go out every Wednesday to visit my mother and then at six-thirty head for our meeting with our fellow dancers.

We were the youngest couple in the club by—and this is just a rough estimate—seventy-five years, but man, the older folks knew how to move. I'd try to keep up, but there was simply no way. I felt self-conscious in their company. Sheila did not. Sometimes, in the middle of a dance, she would let go of my hands and sway away from me. Her eyes would close. There would be a sheen on her face as she totally disappeared in the bliss.

There was one older couple in particular, the Segals, who'd been dancing together since a USO gathering in the forties. They were a handsome, graceful couple. Mr. Segal always wore a white ascot. Mrs. Segal wore something blue and a pearl choker. On the floor, they were pure magic. They moved like lovers. They moved like one. During the breaks, they were outgoing and friendly to the rest of us. But when the music played, they saw only each other.

On a snowy night last February—we thought that the club would probably be canceled, but it wasn't—Mr. Segal showed up by himself. He still wore the white ascot. His suit was impeccable. But one look at the tightness in his face and we knew. Sheila gripped my hand. I could see a tear escape from her eye. When the music started, Mr. Segal stood, stepped without hesitation onto the dance floor, and danced by himself. He put out his arms and moved as though his wife were still there. He guided her across the floor, cradling her ghost so gently that none of us dared disturb him.

The next week Mr. Segal did not show at all. We heard from some of the others that Mrs. Segal had lost a longtime battle with cancer. But she danced until the end. The music started up then. We all found our partners and took to the floor. And as I held Sheila close, impossibly close, I realized that, sad as the Segal story was, they'd had it better than anyone I had ever known.

Here was where I entered the quasi-dream, though from the beginning I recognized that it was just that. I was back at the JCC Dance Club. Mr. Segal was there. So were a bunch of people I had never seen before, all without partners. When the music started, we all danced by ourselves. I looked around. My father was there, doing a clumsy solo fox-trot. He nodded at me.

I watched the others dance. They all clearly felt the presence of their dearly departed. They looked into their partners' ghostly eyes. I tried to follow suit, but something was wrong. I saw nothing. I was dancing alone. Sheila would not come to me.

Far away, I heard the phone ring. A deep voice on the answering machine penetrated my dream. "This is Lieutenant Daniels of the Livingston Police Department. I am trying to reach Will Klein."

In the background, behind Lieutenant Daniels, I heard the muffled laugh of a young woman. My eyes flew open, and the JCC Dance Club disappeared. As I reached for the phone, I heard the young woman whoop another laugh.

It sounded like Katy Miller.

"Perhaps I should call your parents," Lieutenant Daniels was saying to whoever was laughing.

"No." It was Katy. "I'm eighteen. You can't make me—"

I picked up the phone. "This is Will Klein."

172

Lieutenant Daniels said, "Hi, Will. This is Tim Daniels. We went to school together, remember?"

Tim Daniels. He'd worked at the local Hess station. He used to wear his oil-smeared uniform to school, complete with his name embroidered on the pocket. I guessed that he still liked uniforms.

"Sure," I said, totally confused now. "How's it going?"

"Good, thanks."

"You're on the force now?" Nothing gets by me.

"Yep. And I still live in town. Married Betty Jo Stetson. We have two daughters."

I tried to conjure up Betty Jo, but nothing came. "Wow, congrats."

"Thanks, Will." His voice grew grave. "I, uh, read about your mother in the *Tribune*. I'm sorry."

"I appreciate that, thanks," I said.

Katy Miller started laughing again.

"Look, the reason I'm calling is, well, I guess you know Katy Miller?"

"Yes."

There was a moment of silence. He probably remembered that I'd dated her older sister and what fate had befallen her. "She asked me to call you."

"What's the problem?"

"I found Katy on the Mount Pleasant playground with a half-empty bottle of Absolut. She's totally blitzed. I was going to call her parents—"

"Forget that!" Katy shouted again. "I'm eighteen!"

"Right, whatever. Anyway, she asked me to call you instead. Hey, I remember when we were kids. We weren't perfect either, you know what I mean?"

"I do," I said.

And that was when Katy yelled something, and my body went rigid. I hoped that I'd heard wrong. But her words, and the almost mocking way she shouted them, worked like a cold hand pressed against the back of my neck.

"Idaho!" she yelled. "Am I right, Will? Idaho!"

I gripped the receiver, sure I heard wrong. "What is she saying?"

"I don't know. She keeps yelling out something about Idaho, but she's still pretty wasted."

Katy again: "Friggin' Idaho! Potato! Idaho! I'm right, aren't I?"

My breath had gone shallow.

"Look, Will, I know it's late, but can you come down and get her?"

I found my voice enough to say, "I'm on my way."

31

Squares crept up the stairs rather than risk the noise from the elevator waking Wanda.

The Yoga Squared Corporation owned the building. He and Wanda lived on the two floors above the yoga studio. It was three in the morning. Squares slid open the door. The lights were out. He stepped into the room. The streetlights provided harsh slivers of illumination.

Wanda sat on the couch in the dark. Her arms and legs were crossed.

"Hey," he said very softly, as if afraid of waking someone up, though there was no one else in the building.

"Do you want me to get rid of it?" she said.

Squares wished that he had kept his sunglasses on. "I'm really tired, Wanda. Just let me grab a few hours of sleep."

"No."

"What do you want me to say here?"

"I'm still in the first trimester. All I'd have to do is swallow a pill. So I want to know. Do you want to get rid of it?"

"So all of a sudden it's up to me?"

"I'm waiting."

"I thought you were the great feminist, Wanda. What about a woman's right to choose?"

"Don't hand me that crap."

Squares jammed his hands in his pockets. "What do you want to do?"

Wanda turned her head to the side. He could see the profile, the long neck, the proud bearing. He loved her. He had never loved anyone before, and no one had ever loved him either. When he was very small, his mother liked to burn him with her curling iron. She finally stopped when he was two years old—on the very day, coincidentally, that his father beat her to death and hung himself in a closet.

"You wear your past on your forehead," Wanda said. "We don't all have that luxury."

"I don't know what you mean."

Neither of them had turned on the light. Their eyes were adjusting, but everything was a murky haze and maybe that made it easier.

Wanda said, "I was valedictorian of my high school class."

"I know."

She closed her eyes. "Let me just say this, okay?"

Squares nodded for her to proceed.

"I grew up in a wealthy suburb. There were very few black families. I was the only black girl in my class of three hundred. And I was ranked first. I had my pick of colleges. I chose Princeton."

He knew all this already, but he said nothing.

"When I got there, I started to feel like I didn't measure up. I won't go into the whole diagnosis, about my lack of self-worth and all that. But I stopped eating. I lost weight. I became anorexic. I wouldn't eat anything I couldn't get rid of. I would do sit-ups all day. I dropped under ninety pounds and I would still look at myself in the mirror and hate the fatty who stared back at me."

Squares moved closer to her. He wanted to take her hand. But idiot that he was, he did not.

"I starved myself to the point where I had to be hospitalized. I damaged my organs. My liver, my heart, the doctors still are not sure how much. I never went into cardiac arrest, but for a while, I think I was pretty close. I eventually recovered—I won't go into that either—but the doctors told me that I'd probably never get pregnant. And if I did, I'd most likely not be able to carry to term."

Squares stood over her. "And what does your doctor say now?" he asked.

"She makes no promises." Wanda looked at him. "I've never been so scared in my life."

He felt his heart crumble in his chest. He wanted to sit next to her and put his arms around her. But again something held him back and he hated himself for it. "If going through with this is a risk to your health—" he began.

"Then it's my risk," she said.

He tried to smile. "The great feminist returns."

"When I said I was scared, I wasn't just talking about my health."

He knew that.

"Squares?"

"Yeah."

Her voice was nearly a plea. "Don't shut me out, okay?"

He did not know what to say, so he settled for the obvious. "It's a big step."

"I know."

"I don't think," he said slowly, "that I'm equipped to handle it."

"I love you."

"I love you too."

"You're the strongest man I've ever known."

Squares shook his head. Some drunk on the street started scream-singing that love grows where his Rosemary goes and nobody knows but him. Wanda uncrossed her arms and waited.

"Maybe," Squares began, "we shouldn't go through with this. For the sake of your health, if nothing else."

Wanda watched him step back and away. Before she could reply, he was gone.

I rented a car at a twenty-four-hour place on 37th Street and drove out to the Livingston police station. I had not been in these hallowed halls since the Burnet Hill Elementary School class trip when I was in first grade. On that sunny morning, we were not allowed to see the station's holding cell where I now found Katy because, like tonight, someone had been in it. The idea of that—that maybe a big-time criminal was locked up just yards from where we stood—was about as cool an idea as a first-grader can wrap his brain around.

Detective Tim Daniels greeted me with too firm a handshake. I noticed that he hoisted his belt a lot. He jangled—or his keys or cuffs or whatever did—whenever he walked. His build was beefier than in his youth, but his face remained smooth and unblemished.

I filled out some paperwork and Katy was released into my custody. She had sobered up in the hour it took me to get out there. There was no laugh in her now. Her head hung low. Her face had taken on a classic teenage-sullen posture.

I thanked Tim again. Katy did not even attempt a smile or wave. We started for the car, but when we were out in the night air, she grabbed my arm.

"Let's take a walk," Katy said.

"It's four in the morning. I'm tired."

"I'll throw up if I sit in a car."

I stopped. "Why were you yelling about Idaho on the phone?"

But Katy was already crossing Livingston Avenue. I started after her. She picked up speed as she reached the town circle. I caught up.

"Your parents are going to be worried," I said.

"I told them I was staying with a friend. It's okay."

"You want to tell me why you were drinking alone."

Katy kept walking. Her breathing grew deeper. "I was thirsty."

"Uh-huh. And why were you yelling about Idaho?"

She looked at me but didn't break stride. "I think you know."

I grabbed her arm. "What kind of game are you playing here?"

"I'm not the one playing games here, Will."

"What are you talking about?"

"Idaho, Will. Your Sheila Rogers was from Idaho, right?"

Again her words hit me like a body blow. "How did you know that?"

"I read it."

"In the paper?"

She chuckled. "You really don't know?"

I took hold of her shoulders. "What are you talking about?"

"Where did your Sheila go to college?" she asked.

"I don't know."

"I thought you two were madly in love."

"It's complicated."

"I bet it is."

"I still don't understand, Katy."

"Sheila Rogers went to Haverton, Will. With Julie. They were in the same sorority."

I stood, stunned. "That's not possible."

"I can't believe you don't know. Sheila never told you?"

I shook my head. "Are you sure?"

"Sheila Rogers of Mason, Idaho. Majored in communications. It's all in the sorority booklet. I found it in an old trunk in the basement."

"I don't get it. You remembered her name after all these years?"

"Yeah."

"How come? I mean, do you remember the name of everyone in Julie's sorority?"

"No."

"So why would you remember Sheila Rogers?"

"Because," Katy said, "Sheila and Julie were roommates."

32

Squares arrived at my apartment with bagels and spreads from a place cleverly christened La Bagel on 15th and First. It was ten A.M., and Katy was sleeping on the couch. Squares lit up a cigarette. I noticed that he was still wearing the same clothes from last night. This was not easy to discern—it was not as though Squares was a leading figure in the haut monde community—but this morning he looked extra disheveled. We sat at the stools by the kitchen counter.

"Hey," I said, "I know you want to blend in with the street people but . . ."

He took a plate out of a cabinet. "You going to keep wowing me with the funny lines, or are you going to tell me what happened?"

"Is there a reason I can't do both?"

He lowered his head and again looked at me over the sunglasses. "That bad?"

"Worse," I said.

Katy stirred on the couch. I heard her say "Ouch." I had the extra-strength Tylenol at the ready. I handed her two with a glass of water. She downed them and stumbled toward the shower. I returned to the stool.

"How does your nose feel?" Squares asked.

"Like my heart moved up there and is trying to thump its way out."

He nodded and took a bite out of a bagel with lox spread. He chewed slowly. His shoulders drooped. I knew that he had not stayed home that night. I knew that something had happened between him and Wanda. And mostly, I knew that he did not want me to ask about it.

"You were saying about worse?" he prompted.

"Sheila lied to me," I said.

"We knew that already."

"Not like this."

He kept chewing.

"She knew Julie Miller. They were sorority sisters in college. Roommates even."

He stopped chewing. "Come again?"

I told him what I'd learned. The shower stayed on the whole time. I imagined that Katy would ache from the alcohol aftereffects for some time yet. Then again, the young recuperate faster than the rest of us.

When I finished filling him in, Squares leaned back, crossed his arms, and grinned. "Styling," he said.

"Yeah. Yeah, that's the word that came to my mind too."

"I don't get it, man." He started spreading another bagel. "Your old girlfriend, who was murdered eleven years ago, was college roommates with your most recent girlfriend, who was also murdered."

"Yes."

"And your brother was blamed for the first murder."

"Yes again."

"Okay, yeah." Squares nodded confidently. Then: "I still don't get it."

"It had to be a setup somehow," I said.

"What was a setup?"

"Sheila and me." I tried to shrug. "It must have all been a setup. A lie."

He made a yes-and-no gesture with his head. His long hair fell onto his face. He pushed it back. "To what end?"

"I don't know."

"Think about it."

"I have," I said. "All night."

"Okay, suppose you're right. Suppose Sheila did lie to you or, I don't know, set you up somehow. You with me?"

"With you."

He raised both palms. "To what end?"

"Again I don't know."

"Then let's go through the possibilities," Squares said. He raised his finger. "One, it could be a giant coincidence."

I just looked at him.

"Hold up, you dated Julie Miller, what, more than twelve years ago?"

"Yes."

"So maybe Sheila didn't remember. I mean, do you remember the name of every friend's ex? Maybe Julie never talked about you. Or maybe Sheila just forgot your name. And then years later you two meet . . ."

I just looked at him some more.

"Yeah, okay, that's pretty begging," he agreed. "Let's forget that. Possibility two"—Squares raised another finger, paused, looked up in the air—"hell, I'm lost here."

"Right."

We ate. He mulled it over some more. "Okay, let's assume that Sheila knew exactly who you were from the beginning."

"Let's."

"I still don't get it, man. What are we left with here?"

"Styling," I replied.

The shower stopped. I picked up a poppy-seed bagel. The seeds stuck to my hand.

"I've been thinking about it all night," I said.

"And?"

"And I keep coming back to New Mexico."

"How so?"

"The FBI wanted to question Sheila about an unsolved double murder in Albuquerque."

"So?"

"Years earlier, Julie Miller was also murdered."

"Also unsolved," Squares said, "though they suspect your brother."

"Yes."

"You see a connection between the two," Squares said.

"There has to be."

Squares nodded. "Okay, I see point A and I see point B. But I don't see how you get from one to the other."

"Neither," I said, "do I."

We grew silent. Katy peeked her head through the doorway. Her face had that morning-after pallor. She groaned and said, "I just up-chucked again."

"Appreciate the update," I said.

"Where's my clothes?"

"The bedroom closet," I said.

She gestured an in-pain thank-you and closed the door. I looked at the right side of the couch, the spot where Sheila liked to read. How could this be happening? The old adage "Better to have loved and lost than to never have loved at all" came to me. I wondered about that. But more than that, I wondered what was worse— to lose the love of a lifetime or to realize that maybe she never loved you at all.

Some choice.

The phone rang. This time I did not wait for the machine. I lifted the receiver and said hello.

"Will?"

"Yes?"

"It's Yvonne Sterno," she said. "Albuquerque's answer to Jimmy Olsen."

"What have you got?"

"I've been up all night working on this."

"And?"

"And it keeps getting weirder."

"I'm listening."

"Okay, I got my contact to go through the deeds and tax records. Now understand that my contact is a government employee, and I got her to go in during her off hours. You usually have a better chance of turning water into wine or having my uncle pick up a check than getting a government employee to show up—"

"Yvonne?" I interrupted.

"Yeah?"

"Assume that I'm already impressed by your resourcefulness. Tell me what you got."

"Yeah, okay, you're right," she said. I heard papers being shuf-fled. "The murder-scene house was leased by a corporation called Cripco."

"And they are?"

"Untraceable. It's a shell. They don't seem to do anything."

I thought about that.

"Owen Enfield also had a car. A gray Honda Accord. Also leased by the fine folks at Cripco."

"Maybe he worked for them."

"Maybe. I'm trying to check that now."

"Where's the car now?"

"That's another interesting thing," Yvonne said. "The police found it abandoned in a mall in Lacida. That's about two hundred miles east of here."

"So where is Owen Enfield?"

"My guess? He's dead. For all we know, he was one of the victims."

"And the woman and little girl? Where are they?"

"No clue. Hell, I don't even know who they are."

"Did you talk to the neighbors?"

"Yes. It's like I said before: No one knew much about them."

"How about a physical description?"

"Ah."

"Ah what?"

"That's what I wanted to talk to you about."

Squares kept eating, but I could tell he was listening. Katy was still in my room, either dressing or making another offering to the porcelain gods.

"The descriptions were pretty vague," Yvonne continued. "The woman was in her mid-thirties, attractive, and a brunette. That's about as much as any of the neighbors could tell me. No one knew the little girl's name. She was around eleven or twelve with sandy-brown hair. One neighbor described her as cute as a button, but what kid that age isn't? Mr. Enfield was described as six feet with a gray crew cut and goatee. Forty years old, more or less."

"Then he wasn't one of the victims," I said.

"How do you know?"

"I saw a photo of the crime scene."

"When?"

"When I was questioned by the FBI about my girlfriend's whereabouts."

"You could see the victims?"

"Not clearly, but enough to know that neither had a crew cut."

"Hmm. Then the whole family has up and vanished."

"Yes."

"There's one other thing, Will."

"What's that?"

"Stonepointe is a new community. Everything is fairly self-contained."

"Meaning?"

"Are you familiar with QuickGo, the convenience store chain?"

"Sure," I said. "We have QuickGos out here too."

Squares took off his sunglasses and looked a question at me. I shrugged and he moved toward me.

"Well, there's a big QuickGo at the edge of the complex," Yvonne said. "Almost all the residents use it."

"So?"

"One of the neighbors swore she saw Owen Enfield there at three o'clock on the day of the murders."

"I'm not following you, Yvonne."

"Well," she said, "the thing is, all the QuickGos have security cameras." She paused. "You following me now?"

"Yeah, I think so."

"I already checked," she went on. "They keep them for a month before they tape over them."

"So if we can get that tape," I began, "we might be able to get a good view of Mr. Enfield."

"Big if, though. The store manager was firm. There was no way he was going to turn anything over to me."

"There has to be a way," I said.

"I'm open to ideas, Will."

Squares put his hand on my shoulder. "What?"

I covered the mouthpiece and filled him in. "You know anybody connected to QuickGo?" I said.

"Incredible as this might sound, the answer is nope."

Damn. We mulled it over for a bit. Yvonne started humming the QuickGo jingle, one of those torturous tunes that enters through the ear canal and proceeds to ricochet around the skull in search of an escape route it will never find. I remembered the new commercial campaign, the one where they updated the old jingle by adding an electric guitar and a synthesizer and bass, and fronting the band with a big-time pop star simply known as Sonay.

Hold the phone. Sonay.

Squares looked at me. "What?"

"I think you may be able to help after all," I said.

185

33

Sheila and Julie had been members of Chi Gamma sorority. I still had the rent-a-car from my late-night sojourn to Livingston, so Katy and I decided to take the two-hour drive up to Haverton College in Connecticut and see what we could learn.

Earlier in the day, I called the Haverton registrar's office to do a little fact-checking. I'd learned that the sorority's housemother back then had been one Rose Baker. Ms. Baker had retired three years ago and moved into a campus house directly across the street. She was to be the main target of our pseudo-investigation.

We pulled in front of the Chi Gamma house. I remembered it from my too-infrequent visits during my Amherst College days. You could tell right off that it was a sorority house. It had that antebellum, faux Greco-Roman-columns-thing going on, all in white, and with soft ruffled edges that gave the whole edifice a feminine feel. Something about it reminded me of a wedding cake.

Rose Baker's residence was, to speak kindly, more modest. The house had started life as a small Cape Cod, but somewhere along the way the lines had been ironed flat. The one-time red color was now a dull clay. The window lace looked cat-shredded. Shingles had flaked off as if the house had an acute case of seborrhea.

Under normal circumstances, I would have made an appointment of some kind. On TV, they never do that. The detective shows up and the person is always home. I always found that both unreal-istic and unwieldy, yet perhaps now I understood a little better. First off, the chatty lady in the registrar's office informed me that Rose Baker rarely left home, and when she did, she rarely strayed far. Second—and I think, more important—if I called Rose Baker and she asked me why I wanted to see her, what would I say? Hi, let's talk murder? No, better just to show up with Katy and see where that got us. If she was not in, we could always explore the archives in the library or visit the sorority house. I had no idea what good any of this would do, but hey, we were just flying blind here.

As we approached Rose Baker's door, I could not help but feel a pang of envy for the knapsack-laden students I saw walking to and fro. I'd loved college. I loved everything about it. I loved hanging out with sloppy slacker friends. I loved living on my own, doing laundry too rarely, eating pepperoni pizza at midnight. I loved chatting with the accessible, hippielike professors. I loved debating lofty issues and harsh realities that never, ever, penetrated the green of our campus.

When we reached the overly cheerful welcome mat, I heard a familiar song wafting through the wooden portal. I made a face and listened closer. The sound was muffled, but it sounded like Elton John—more specifically, his song "Candle in the Wind" from the classic *Goodbye Yellow Brick Road* double album. I knocked on the door.

A woman's voice chimed, "Just a minute."

A few seconds later, the door opened. Rose Baker was probably in her seventies and dressed, I was surprised to see, for a funeral. Her wardrobe, from the big-brimmed hat with matching veil to the sensible shoes, was black. Her rouge looked as if it'd been liberally applied via an aerosol can. Her mouth formed a nearly perfect "O" and her eyes were big red saucers, as if her face had frozen immedi-ately after being startled.

"Mrs. Baker?" I said.

She lifted the veil. "Yes?"

"My name is Will Klein. This is Katy Miller."

The saucer eyes swiveled toward Katy and locked into position.

"Is this a bad time?" I asked.

She seemed surprised by the question. "Not at all."

I said, "We'd like to speak with you, if that's okay."

"Katy Miller," she repeated, her eyes still on her.

"Yes, ma'am," I said.

"Julie's sister."

It was not a question, but Katy nodded anyway. Rose Baker pushed open the screen door. "Please come in."

We followed her into the living room. Katy and I stopped short, taken aback by what we saw.

It was Princess Di.

She was everywhere. The entire room was sheathed, blanketed, overrun with Princess Di paraphernalia. There were photographs, of course, but also tea sets, commemorative plates, embroidered pillows, lamps, figurines, books, thimbles, shot glasses (how respectful), a toothbrush (eeuw!), a night-light, sunglasses, salt-'n-pepper shakers, you name it. I realized that the song I was hearing was not the original Elton John–Bernie Taupin classic, but the more recent Princess Di tribute version, the lyrics now offering a good-bye to our "English rose." I had read somewhere that the Di-tribute version was the biggest-selling single in world history. That said something, though I was not sure I wanted to know what.

Rose Baker said, "Do you remember when Princess Diana died?"

I looked at Katy. She looked at me. We both nodded yes.

"Do you remember the way the world mourned?"

She looked at us some more. And we nodded again.

"For most people, the grief, the mourning, it was just a fad. They did it for a few days, maybe a week or two. And then"—she snapped her fingers, magician style, her saucer eyes bigger than ever—"it was over for them. Like she never existed at all."

She looked at us and waited for clucks of agreement. I tried not to make a face.

"But for some of us, Diana, Princess of Wales, well, she really was an angel. Too good for this world maybe. We won't ever forget her. We keep the light burning."

She dabbed her eye. A sarcastic rejoinder came to my lips, but I bit it back.

"Please," she said. "Have a seat. Would you care for some tea?"

Katy and I both politely declined.

"A biscuit, then?"

She produced a plate with cookies in the shape of, yup,

188

Princess Diana's profile. Sprinkles formed the crown. We begged off, neither of us much in the mood to nibble on dead Di. I decided to start right in.

"Mrs. Baker," I said, "you remember Katy's sister, Julie?"

"Yes, of course." She put down the plate of cookies. "I remember all of the girls. My husband, Frank—he taught English here—died in 1969. We had no children. My family had all passed away. That sorority house, those girls, for twenty-six years they were my life."

"I see," I said.

"And Julie, well, late at night, when I lay in bed in the dark, her face comes to me more than most. Not just because she was a special child—oh, and she was—but of course, because of what happened to her."

"You mean her murder?" It was a dumb thing to say, but I was new at this. I just wanted to keep her talking.

"Yes." Rose Baker reached out and took Katy's hand. "Such a tragedy. I'm so sorry for your loss."

Katy said, "Thank you."

Uncharitable as this might sound, my mind could not help but think: Tragedy, yes, but where was Julie's image—or the image of Rose Baker's husband or family, for that matter—in this swirling potpourri of royal grief?

"Mrs. Baker, do you remember another sorority sister named Sheila Rogers?" I asked.

Her face pinched up and her voice was short. "Yes." She shifted primly. "Yes, I do."

From her reaction, it was pretty obvious that she had not heard about the murder. I decided not to tell her yet. She clearly had a problem with Sheila, and I wanted to know what it was. We needed honesty here. If I were to tell her that Sheila was dead now, she might sugarcoat her answers. Before I could follow up, Mrs. Baker held up her hand. "May I ask you a question?"

"Of course."

"Why are you asking me all this now?" She looked at Katy. "It all happened so long ago."

Katy took that one. "I'm trying to find the truth."

"The truth about what?"

"My sister changed while she was here."

189

Rose Baker closed her eyes. "You don't need to hear this, child."

"Yes," Katy said, and the desperation in her voice was palpable enough to knock out a window. "Please. We need to know."

Rose Baker kept her eyes closed for another moment or two. Then she nodded to herself and opened them. She folded her hands and put them in her lap. "How old are you?"

"Eighteen."

"About the age Julie was when she first came here." Rose Baker smiled. "You look like her."

"So I've been told."

"It's a compliment. Julie lit up a room. In many ways she reminds me of Diana herself. Both of them were beautiful. Both of them were special—almost divine." She smiled and wagged a finger. "Ah, and both had a wild streak. Both were inordinately stubborn. Julie was a good person. Kind, smart as a whip. She was an excellent student."

"Yet," I said, "she dropped out."

"Yes."

"Why?"

She turned her eyes on me. "Princess Di tried to be firm. But no one can control the winds of fate. They blow as they may."

Katy said, "I'm not following you."

A Princess Di clock chimed the hour, the sound a hollow imitation of Big Ben. Rose Baker waited for it to grow silent again. Then she said, "College changes people. Your first time away, your first time on your own . . ." She drifted off, and for a moment I thought I'd have to nudge her into continuing. "I'm not saying this right. Julie was fine at first, but then she, well, she started to withdraw. From all of us. She cut classes. She broke up with her hometown boyfriend. Not that that was unusual. Almost all the girls do first year. But in her case, it came so late. Junior year, I think. I thought she really loved him."

I swallowed, kept still.

"Earlier," Rose Baker said, "you asked me about Sheila Rogers."

Katy said, "Yes."

"She was a bad influence."

"How so?"

"When Sheila joined us that same year"—Rose put a finger to her chin and tilted her head as if a new idea had just forced its way in—"well, maybe she was the winds of fate. Like the paparazzi that

190

made Diana's limousine speed up. Or that awful driver, Henri Paul. Did you know that his blood alcohol level was three times the legal limit?"

"Sheila and Julie became friends?" I tried.

"Yes."

"Roommates, right?"

"For a time, yes." Her eyes were moist now. "I don't want to sound melodramatic, but Sheila Rogers brought something bad to Chi Gamma. I should have thrown her out. I know that now. But I had no proof of wrongdoing."

"What did she do?"

She shook her head again.

I thought about it for a moment. Junior year, Julie had visited me at Amherst. I, on the other hand, had been discouraged from coming down to Haverton, which was a little strange. I flashed back to the last time Julie and I had been together. She had set up a quiet getaway at a bed and breakfast in Mystic instead of having us stay on campus. At the time, I'd thought it romantic. Now, of course, I knew better.

Three weeks later, Julie called and broke it off with me. But looking back on it now, I remembered that she had been acting both lethargic and strange during that visit. We were in Mystic only one night and even as we made love, I could feel her fading away from me. She blamed it on her studies, said that she'd been cramming big-time. I bought it because, in hindsight, I wanted to.

When I now added it all together, the solution was fairly obvious. Sheila had come here straight from the abuse of Louis Castman and drugs and the streets. That life is not so easy to leave behind. My guess was, she dragged some of that decay with her. It does not take much to poison the well. Sheila arrives at the start of Julie's junior year, Julie begins to act erratically.

It made sense.

I tried another tack. "Did Sheila Rogers graduate?"

"No, she dropped out too."

"The same time as Julie?"

"I'm not even sure either of them officially dropped out. Julie just stopped going to class toward the end of the year. She stayed in her room a lot. She slept past noon. When I confronted her"—her voice caught—"she moved out."

"Where did she move to?"

"An apartment off campus. Sheila stayed there too."

"So when exactly did Sheila Rogers drop out?"

Rose Baker pretended to think about it. I say pretend, because I could see that she knew the answer right away and that this act was somehow for our benefit. "I think Sheila left after Julie died."

"How long after?" I asked.

She kept her eyes down. "I don't remember ever seeing her after the murder."

I looked at Katy. Her eyes, too, were on the floor. Rose Baker put a trembling hand to her mouth.

"Do you know where Sheila went?" I asked.

"No. She was gone. That was all that mattered."

She would not look at us anymore. I found that troubling.

"Mrs. Baker?"

She still would not face me.

"Mrs. Baker, what else happened?"

"Why are you here?" she asked.

"We told you. We wanted to know—"

"Yes, but why now?"

Katy and I looked at each other. She nodded. I turned to Rose Baker and said, "Yesterday, Sheila Rogers was found dead. She was murdered."

I thought that maybe she had not heard me. Rose Baker kept her gaze locked on a black-velvet Diana, a grotesque and frightening reproduction. Diana's teeth were blue, and her skin looked like a bad bottle-tan. Rose stared at the image and I started thinking again about the fact that there were no pictures of her husband or her family or her sorority girls—only this dead stranger from overseas. And I wondered about how I was dealing with all this death, how I kept chasing shadows to divert the pain, and I wondered if maybe there was something like that going on here too.

"Mrs. Baker?"

"Was she strangled like the others?"

"No," I said. And then I stopped. I turned to Katy. She had heard it too. "Did you say others?"

"Yes."

"What others?"

"Julie was strangled," she said.

"Right."

Her shoulders slumped. The wrinkles on her face seemed more pronounced now, the crevices sinking deeper into the flesh. Our visit had unleashed demons she had stuffed in boxes or maybe buried beneath the Di accoutrements. "You don't know about Laura Emerson, do you?"

Katy and I exchanged another glance. "No," I said.

Rose Baker's eyes started darting across the walls again. "Are you sure you won't have some tea?"

"Please, Mrs. Baker. Who is Laura Emerson?"

She stood and hobbled over to the fireplace mantel. Her fingers reached out and gently touched down on a ceramic bust of Di. "Another sorority sister," she said. "Laura was a year behind Julie."

"What happened to her?" I asked.

She found a piece of dirt stuck on the ceramic bust. She used her nail to scratch it off. "Laura was found dead near her home in North Dakota eight months before Julie. She'd been strangled too."

Icy hands were grabbing at my legs, pulling me back under. Katy's face was white. She shrugged at me, letting me know that this was new to her too.

"Did they ever find her killer?" I asked.

"No," Rose Baker said. "Never."

I tried to sift through it, process this new data, get a grip on what this all meant. "Mrs. Baker, did the police question you after Julie's murder?"

"Not the police," she said.

"But someone did?"

She nodded. "Two men from the FBI."

"Do you remember their names?"

"No."

"Did they ask you about Laura Emerson?"

"No. But I told them anyway."

"What did you say?"

"I reminded them that another girl had been strangled."

"How did they react to that?"

"They told me that I should keep that to myself. That saying something could compromise the investigation."

Too fast, I thought. This was all coming at me too fast. It would not compute. Three young women were dead. Three women from the same sorority house. That was a pattern if ever I saw one. A pattern meant that Julie's murder was not the random, solo act of violence that the FBI had led us—and the world—to believe.

And worst of all, the FBI knew it. They had lied to us all these years.

The question now was, why.

34

Man, I had a good head of steam going. I wanted to explode into Pistillo's office. I wanted to burst in and grab him by the lapels and demand answers. But real life does not work that way. Route 95 was littered with construction delays. We hit terrible traffic on the Cross Bronx Expressway. The Harlem River Drive crawled like a wounded soldier. I leaned on the horn and swerved in and out of lanes, but in New York, that just raises you to average.

Katy used her cell phone to call her friend Ronnie, who she said was good with computers. Ronnie checked out Laura Emerson on the Internet, pretty much confirming what we already knew. She'd been strangled eight months before Julie. Her body had been found at the Court Manor Motor Lodge in Fessenden, North Dakota. The murder received extensive though vague local coverage for two weeks before fading off the front page and into stardust. There was no mention of sexual assault.

I veered hard off the exit, drove through a red light, found the Kinney parking lot near Federal Plaza, pulled in. We hurried toward the building. I kept my head high and my feet in motion, but alas, there was a security checkpoint. We had to walk through a metal detector. My keys set it off. I emptied my pockets. Now it was my belt. The guard ran a wand that looked like a vibrator over my persons. Okay, we were cleared.

When we reached Pistillo's office, I demanded to see him in my firmest voice. His secretary appeared unintimidated. She smiled with the genuineness of a politician's wife and sweetly asked us to have a seat. Katy looked at me and shrugged. I would not sit. I paced like a caged lion, but I could feel my fury ebbing.

Fifteen minutes later, the secretary told us that Assistant Director in Charge Joseph Pistillo—that was exactly how she said it, with the full title—would see us now. She opened the door. I blasted into the office.

Pistillo was already standing and at the ready. He gestured at Katy. "Who is this?"

"Katy Miller," I said.

He looked stunned. He said to her, "What are you doing with him?"

But I was not about to be sidetracked. "Why didn't you ever say anything about Laura Emerson?"

He turned back to me. "Who?"

"Don't insult me, Pistillo."

Pistillo waited a beat. Then he said, "Why don't we all sit?"

"Answer my question."

He lowered himself into his seat, his eyes never leaving me. His desk looked shiny and sticky. The smell of lemon Pledge clawed at the air.

"You're in no position to make demands," he said.

"Laura Emerson was strangled eight months before Julie."

"So?"

"Both of them were from the same sorority house."

Pistillo steepled his fingers. He played the wait game and won.

I said, "Are you going to tell me you didn't know about it?"

"Oh, I knew."

"And you don't see a connection?"

"That's correct."

His eyes were steady, but he was practiced at this.

"You can't be serious," I said.

He let his gaze wander the walls now. There was not much to look at it. There was a photograph of President Bush and an American flag and a few diplomas. That was pretty much it. "We looked into it at the time, of course. I think the local media picked up on it too. They might have even run something—I don't remember anymore. But in the end none of them saw a true connection."

"You have to be kidding."

196

"Laura Emerson was strangled in another state at another time. There were no signs of rape or sexual assault. She was found in a motel. Julie"—he turned to Katy—"your sister was found in her home."

"And the fact that they both belonged to the same sorority?"

"A coincidence."

"You're lying," I said.

He did not like that, and his face reddened a shade. "Watch it," he said, pointing a beefy finger in my direction. "You have no standing here."

"Are you telling us that you saw no link between the murders?"

"That's right."

"And what about now, Pistillo?"

"What about now?"

The rage was building back up again. "Sheila Rogers was a member of that sorority too. Is that another coincidence?"

That caught him off guard. He leaned back, trying to get some distance. Was it because he didn't know or because he didn't think I'd find out about it? "I'm not going to talk to you about an ongoing investigation."

"You knew," I said slowly. "And you knew that my brother was innocent."

He shook his head, but there was nothing behind it. "I knew—correction: know—nothing of the sort."

But I did not believe him. He had been lying from the start. Of that I was now certain. He stiffened as though bracing for my next outburst. But to my surprise, my voice grew suddenly soft.

"Do you realize what you've done?" I said, barely a whisper. "The damage to my family. My father, my mother . . . ?"

"This doesn't involve you, Will."

"Like hell it doesn't."

"Please," he said. "Both of you. Stay out of this."

I stared at him. "No."

"For your own sakes. You're not going to believe this, but I'm trying to protect you."

"From?"

He did not reply.

"From?" I repeated.

He slapped the arms of his chair and stood. "This conversation is over."

197

"What do you really want with my brother, Pistillo?"

"I'm not going to comment any further on an ongoing investigation." He moved toward the door. I tried to block his path. He gave me his hardest look and walked around me. "You stay away from my investigation, or I'll arrest you for hindering."

"Why are you trying to frame him?"

Pistillo stopped and turned around. I saw something change his demeanor. A straightening of the spine maybe. A quick flicker in the eyes. "You want to get into truths, Will?"

I did not like his change of tone. I suddenly wasn't sure of the answer. "Yes."

"Then," he said slowly, "let's start with you."

"What about me?"

"You've always been so convinced your brother was innocent," he continued, his posture more aggressive now. "How come?"

"Because I know him."

"Really? So how close were you and Ken near the end?"

"We were always close."

"Saw him often, did you?"

I shuffled my feet. "You don't have to see someone a lot to be close."

"Is that a fact? So tell us, Will: Who do you think killed Julie Miller?"

"I don't know."

"Well then, let's examine what you think happened, shall we?" Pistillo strode toward me. Somewhere along the way, I had lost the upper hand. There was fire in his belly now, and I had no idea why. He stopped just close enough to start invading my space. "Your dear brother, the one you were so close to, had sexual relations with your old girlfriend the night of the murder. Isn't that your theory, Will?"

I might have squirmed. "Yes."

"Your ex-girlfriend and your brother doing the nasty." He made a tsk-tsk noise. "That must have infuriated you."

"What are you babbling about?"

"The truth, Will. We want to deal in truths, right? So come on, let's all put our cards on the table." His eyes stayed on me, level and cool. "Your brother comes home for the first time in, what, two years. And what does he do? He strolls down the block and has intercourse with the girl you loved."

198

"We'd broken up," I said, though even I could hear the whiny weakness in my own voice.

He gave a small smirk. "Sure, that always ends it, doesn't it? Open season on her after that—especially for a beloved brother." Pistillo stayed in my face. "You claim that you saw someone that night. Someone mysteriously lurking around the Miller house."

"That's right."

"How exactly did you see him?"

"What do you mean?" I asked. But I knew.

"You said you saw someone by the Miller house, correct?"

"Yes."

Pistillo smiled and spread his hands. "But you see, you never told us what *you* were doing there that night, Will." He said it in a casual, almost singsong voice. "You, Will. Outside the Miller house. Alone. Late at night. With your brother and your ex alone inside . . ."

Katy turned and looked at me.

"I was taking a walk," I said quickly.

Pistillo paced, pressing his advantage. "Uh-huh, sure, okay, so let's see if we got this straight. Your brother is having sex with the girl you still loved. You happen to be taking a walk by her house that night. She ends up dead. We find your brother's blood at the scene. And you, Will, *know* that your brother didn't do it."

He stopped and gave me the grin again. "So if you were the investigating officer, who would you suspect?"

A large stone was crushing my chest. I could not speak.

"If you're suggesting . . ."

"I'm suggesting you go home," Pistillo said. "That's all. Go home, both of you, and stay the hell out of this."

35

Pistillo offered to find Katy a ride home. She declined and said that she would stay with me. He didn't like that, but what could he do?

We drove back to the apartment in silence. Once inside, I showed her my impressive collection of take-out menus. She ordered Chinese. I ran downstairs and picked it up. We spread the white boxes out on the table. I sat in my usual seat. Katy sat in Sheila's. I flashed back to Chinese with Sheila—her hair tied back, fresh out of the shower and smelling sweet, in that terry-cloth robe, the freckles on her chest . . .

It was odd what you would always remember.

The grief roared back at me in high, crippling waves. Whenever I stopped moving, it hit me hard and deep. Grief wears you down. If you don't guard against it, it will exhaust you past the point of caring.

I dumped some fried rice on my plate and followed it up with a dash of lobster sauce. "Are you sure you still want to stay tonight?"

Katy nodded.

"I'll give you the bedroom," I said.

"I'd rather sleep on the couch."

"You sure?"

"Positive."

We pretended to eat.

"I didn't kill Julie," I said.

"I know."

We pretended to eat some more.

She finally asked, "Why were you there that night?"

I tried to smile. "You don't buy that I was taking a walk?"

"No."

I put down the chopsticks as if they could shatter. I wondered how to explain this, here in my apartment, talking to the sister of the woman I once loved, sitting in the chair of the woman I'd wanted to marry. Both murdered. Both connected to me. I looked up and said, "I guess that maybe I wasn't really over Julie."

"You wanted to see her?"

"Yes."

"And?"

"I rang the bell," I said. "But nobody answered."

Katy thought about it. She looked down at her plate and tried to sound casual. "Your timing was strange."

I picked up the chopsticks.

"Will?"

I kept my head down.

"Did you know your brother was there?"

I moved the food around the plate. She lifted her head and watched me. I heard my neighbor open and close his door. A horn honked. Someone on the street was shouting in what might have been Russian.

"You knew," Katy said. "You knew Ken was at our house. With Julie."

"I didn't kill your sister."

"What happened, Will?"

I folded my arms across my chest. I leaned back, closed my eyes, tilted my head all the way back. I did not want to go back there, but what choice did I have? Katy wanted to know. She deserved to know.

"It was such a strange weekend," I began. "Julie and I had been broken up over a year. I hadn't seen her in all that time. I'd tried to bump into her on school breaks, but she never seemed to be around."

"She hadn't been home in a long while," Katy said.

I nodded. "The same with Ken. That was what made it all so bizarre. All of a sudden, all three of us are back in Livingston at the same time. I can't remember the last time that happened. Ken was acting strangely too. He was looking out the window all the time. He wouldn't leave the house. He was up to something. I don't know what. Anyway, he asked me if I was still hung up on Julie. I told him no. That we were history."

"You lied to him."

"It was like . . ." I tried to figure out how to explain this. "My brother was like a god to me. He was strong and brave and . . ." I shook my head. I was not saying this right. I started again. "When I was sixteen, my parents took the family on a trip to Spain. The Costa del Sol. The whole place was one big party scene. It was sort of like Florida spring break for the Europeans. Ken and I hung out at this one disco near our hotel. On our fourth night there, a guy bumped me on the dance floor. I looked over at him. He laughed at me. I went back to dancing. Then another guy bumped me. I tried to ignore him too. Then the first guy, he ran up to me and just pushed me down." I stopped, tried to blink away the memory as if it were sand in my eye. I looked at her. "Do you know what I did?"

She shook her head.

"I yelled for Ken. I didn't jump up. I didn't push the guy back. I yelled for my big brother and scrambled away."

"You were scared."

"Always," I said.

"That's natural."

I didn't think so.

"So did he come?" she asked.

"Of course."

"And?"

"A fight broke out. There was a big group of them from some Scandinavian country. Ken got the hell beat out of him."

"And you?"

"I never so much as threw a punch. I hung back and tried to reason with them, convince them to stop." The shame flushed my cheeks yet again. My brother, who had been in more than his share of fights, was right. A beating hurts for a little while. The shame of cowardice never leaves. "Ken broke his arm during the scuffle. His right arm. He was an incredible tennis player. Nationally ranked. Stanford was interested in him. His serve was never the same after that. He ended up not going to college."

"That's not your fault."

How wrong she was. "The point is, Ken always defended me. Sure, we fought the way brothers do. He'd tease me mercilessly. But he'd step in the way of a freight train to protect me. And me, I never had the courage to reciprocate."

Katy put her hand to her chin.

"What?" I said.

"It's odd, that's all."

"What is?"

"That your brother would be insensitive enough to sleep with Julie."

"It wasn't his fault. He asked me if I was over her. I told him I was."

"You gave him the green light," she said.

"Yes."

"But then you ended up following him."

"You don't understand," I said.

"No, I do," Katy said. "We all do stuff like that."

36

I fell into such a deep sleep that I never heard him sneak up on me.

I had found fresh sheets and blankets for Katy, made sure she was comfortable on the couch, taken a shower, tried to read. The words swam by in a murky haze. I'd go back and reread and reforget the same paragraph over and over again. I signed on to the Internet and surfed. I did a few push-ups, sit-ups, yoga stretches Squares had taught me. I did not want to lie down. I did not want to stop, to let the grief catch me again unawares.

I was a worthy adversary, but eventually sleep managed to corner and take me down. I was out, falling in a totally dreamless pit, when I felt a jerk on my hand and heard the click. Still asleep, I tried to pull my hand back to my side, but it would not move.

Something metallic dug into my wrist.

My eyelids were fluttering open when he leapt on top of me. He landed hard, knocking the wind out of my lungs. I gulped as whoever he was straddled my chest. His knees pinned down my shoulders. Before I could mount any sort of serious struggle, my attacker yanked my free hand to the side above my head. I didn't hear the click this time, but I felt the cold metal close around my skin.

Both of my hands were cuffed to the bed.

My veins flooded with ice. For a moment I simply shut down, just as I always had during physical altercations. I opened my mouth, about to scream or at least say something. My attacker grabbed the back of my head and pulled me forward. Without hesitation, he ripped off a piece of duct tape and covered my mouth. Then, for good measure, he started winding a fresh band of tape around the back of my skull and over my mouth, ten maybe fifteen times, as if he were shrink-wrapping my head.

I could no longer speak or cry out. Breathing was a chore—I had to suck the air through my broken nose. It hurt like hell. My shoulders ached from the cuffs and his body weight. I struggled, which was totally futile. I tried to buck him off me. More futile. I wanted to ask him what he wanted, what he planned to do now that I was helpless.

And that was when I thought about Katy alone in the other room.

The bedroom was dark. My assailant was no more than a shadow to me. He wore a mask of some kind, something dark, but I could not see what, if anything, was on it. Breathing was becoming nearly impossible. I snorted through the pain.

Whoever he was, he finished taping my mouth. He hesitated for only a second before bouncing off me. And then, as I watched in helpless horror, he headed for the bedroom door, opened it, stepped into the room where Katy was sleeping, and closed the door behind him.

My eyes bulged. I tried to scream, but the tape muffled any sound. I bucked like a bronco. I kicked and flailed. No progress.

Then I stopped and listened. For a moment there was nothing. Pure silence.

And then Katy screamed.

Oh Christ. I bucked some more. Her scream had been brief, cut off midway, as though someone had turned off a switch. Panic took full flight now. Full, red-alert panic. I jerked hard on both cuffs. I twisted my head back and forth. Nothing.

Katy screamed again.

The sound was fainter this time—the gasp of a wounded animal. No way anyone would hear it, and even if they did, nobody would react. Not in New York. Not at this time of night. And even if they did—even if someone called the police or rushed to her rescue—it would be too late.

I freaked out then.

My sanity felt as though it were being torn in two. I went nuts.

I thrashed around, seizure style. My nose hurt like hell. I swallowed some of the fibers from the duct tape. I struggled some more.

But I made no progress.

Oh God. Okay, calm down. Be cool. Think a second.

I turned my head toward my right cuff. It did not feel that tight. There was give there. Okay, maybe, if I went a little slower, I could pull my hand out. That was it. Calm down. Try to narrow your hand, squeeze it through.

So I tried. I tried to will my hand into something thinner. I rounded my palm by forcing the bottom of my thumb toward the bottom of my pinky. Then I pulled down, slowly at first, then with more force. No go. The skin bunched around the metal ring and then started ripping. I did not care. I kept pulling.

It wasn't working.

The other room had gone quiet.

I strained my ears for a sound. Any sound at all. Nothing. I tried to curl up my body, tried to lift myself off the bed so hard that, I don't know, maybe the bed would lift up too. Just an inch or two and then maybe it'd break on the way down. I bucked some more. The bed did indeed slide a few inches out. But it was not doing any good.

I was still trapped.

I heard Katy scream again. And in a scared, panic-filled voice, she shouted, "John—"

And then she was cut off again.

John, I thought. She'd said John.

Asselta?

The Ghost . . .

Oh no, please, oh God, no. I heard something muffled. Voices. A groan maybe. Like something being smothered by a pillow. My heart beat wildly against my rib cage. The fear struck at me from every angle. I flung my head from side to side, looked for something, anything.

The phone.

Could I . . . ? My legs were still free. Maybe I could swing them up, grab the phone with my feet, drop the receiver into my hand. From there I could, I don't know, maybe dial 911 or 0. My feet were already on the rise. I contracted the muscles in my abdomen, lifted my legs, swung them to the right. But I was still in hysteria mode. My weight teetered to the side. I lost control of my legs. I pulled back up, trying to regain balance, and when I did, my foot hit the phone.

The receiver clattered to the floor.

Damn.

Now what? My mind snapped—I mean, I totally lost it. I thought of animals caught in those claw traps, the ones who gnaw off a limb to escape. I thrashed to exhaustion, at my wit's end and about to give up, when I remembered something Squares had taught me.

Plow pose.

That's what it was called. In Hindu: Halāsana. You usually do it from a shoulder stand. You lie on your back and flip your legs all the way over your head as you lift your hips. Your toes would touch the floor behind your head. I did not know if I could go that far, but it didn't matter. I crunched my stomach and swung my legs up as hard as I could. I threw them back behind me. The balls of my feet thudded against the wall. My chest was up against my chin, making it harder than ever to breathe.

I pushed against the wall with my legs. The adrenaline kicked in. The bed slid away from the wall. I pushed some more, got enough room. Okay, good. Now for the hard part. If the cuffs were too tight, if they did not allow my wrists to turn within them, I would either not be able to make it or dislocate both shoulders. No matter.

Silence, dead silence, from the other room.

I let my legs fall toward the floor. I was doing, in effect, a back somersault off the bed. The weight of my legs gave me the momentum and—in a stroke of luck—my wrists turned in the cuffs. My feet landed hard. I went with it, scraping the front of my thighs and abdomen on the low headboard.

When I finished, I was standing up behind the bed.

My hands were still cuffed. My mouth was still taped. But I was standing. I felt another surge of adrenaline.

Okay, now what?

No time. I bent my knees. I lowered my shoulder to the back of the headboard and I drove the bed toward the door as if I were an offensive lineman and the bed was a tackle sled. My legs moved like pistons. I did not hesitate. I did not let up.

The bed crashed into the door.

The collision was jarring. Pain knifed down my shoulder, my

arms, my spine. Something popped and hot pain flooded my joints. Ignoring it, I pulled back and rammed the door again. Then again. The tape made my scream audible only in my own ears. The third time, I pulled extra hard on both cuffs at the precise moment the bed made contact with the wall.

The bed rails gave way.

I was free.

I pushed the bed away from the door. I tried unwrapping the tape from my mouth, but it was taking too long. I grabbed the knob and turned it. I flung open the door and leapt into the darkness.

Katy was on the floor.

Her eyes were closed. Her body was limp. The man was straddling her chest. He had his hands on her throat.

He was choking her.

Without hesitation, I launched myself at him, rocketlike. It seemed to take me a long time to reach him, as if I were leaping through syrup. He saw me coming—had plenty of time to prepare—but it still meant that he would have to release her throat. He turned and faced me. I still couldn't see anything but a black outline. He grabbed hold of my shoulders, put his foot into my stomach, and using my own momentum, he simply rolled back.

I flew across the room. My arms windmilled in the air. But I lucked out again. Or so I thought. I landed on the soft reading chair. It wobbled for a second. Then it toppled over from my weight. My head bounced hard against the side table before banging to the floor.

I fought off the dizziness and tried to get to my knees. When I started rising for a second offensive, I saw something that terrified me like nothing before ever had.

The black-clad assailant was up too. He had a knife now. And he was heading toward Katy with it.

Everything slowed down. What happened next took no more than a second or two. But in my mind's eye, it happened in some alternate time warp. Time does that. It is indeed relative. Moments fly by. And moments freeze-frame.

I was too far away to reach him. I knew that. Even through the dizziness, through the blow from hitting my head on the table . . .

The table.

Where I'd placed Squares's gun.

Was there time to reach it and turn and fire? My eyes were still on Katy and her assailant. No. Not enough time. I knew that immediately.

The man bent over and grabbed Katy by the hair.

As I went for the gun, I pawed at the tape on my mouth. The tape shifted enough for me to shout, "Freeze or I'll shoot!"

His head turned in the dark. I was already scrambling on the floor. I moved flat on my stomach, crawling commando style. He saw that I was unarmed and turned back to finish what he had started. My hand found the gun. No time to aim. I pulled the trigger.

The man startled back from the sound.

That bought me time. I swung around with the gun, already pulling the trigger again. The man rolled back like a gymnast. I could still barely make him out, just a shadow. I started moving the gun toward the black mass, still firing. How many bullets did this thing hold? How many had I fired?

He jerked back, but kept on moving. Had I hit him?

The man jumped toward the door. I yelled for him to stop. He didn't. I considered firing into his back, but something, perhaps a fly-through of humanity, made me stop. He was already out the door. And I had bigger worries.

I looked down at Katy. She was not moving.

37

Another officer—the fifth, by my count—came to hear my story.

"I want to know how she is first," I said.

The doctor had stopped working on me. In the movies, the doctor always defends his patients. He tells the cop that they cannot question him right now, that he needs his rest. My doctor, an emergency room intern from, I think, Pakistan, had no such hang-up. He popped back my shoulder while they began their grilling. He poured iodine on my wrist wounds. He toyed with my nose. He took out a hacksaw—what a hospital was doing with a hacksaw I don't want to know—and cut off my handcuffs, all while I got grilled. I was still wearing my sleeping boxers and pajama top. The hospital had covered my bare feet with paper sandals.

"Just answer my question," the cop said.

This had been going on for two hours now. The adrenaline had died down, and the ache was starting to gnaw on my bones. I'd had enough.

"Yeah, okay, you got me," I said. "First, I put cuffs on both my hands. Then I broke up some furniture, fired several bullets into the walls, choked her nearly to death in my own apartment, and then called the police on myself. You got me."

"Could have worked that way," the officer said. He was a big man with a waxy mustache that made me think of a barbershop quartet. He had given me his name, but I stopped caring three cops ago.

"Excuse me?"

"A ruse maybe."

"I dislocated my shoulder and cut up my hands and broke my bed to divert suspicion?"

He gave a classic cop-shrug. "Hey, I had a guy one time, he cut off his dick so we wouldn't think he killed his girl. Said a bunch of black guys attacked them. Thing is, he only meant to cut it a little but he ended up slicing all the way through."

"That's a great story," I said.

"Could be the same thing here."

"My penis is fine, thanks for caring."

"You tell us about some guy breaking in. Neighbors heard the shots."

"Yes."

He gave me the skeptical eyes. "So how come none of your neighbors saw him running out?"

"Because—and this is just a wild stab in the dark—it was two in the morning?"

I was still sitting up on the examining table. My legs hung off. They were starting to go to sleep from the angle. I hopped down.

"Where do you think you're going?" the cop asked.

"I want to see Katy."

"I don't think so." The cop twitched the mustache. "Her parents are with her right now."

He studied my face for a reaction. I tried not to give him one.

The mustache twitched. "Her father has some pretty strong opinions about you," he said.

"I bet he does."

"He thinks you did this."

"For what purpose?"

"You mean what motive?"

"No, I mean purpose, intent. Do you think I was trying to kill her?"

He crossed his arms and shrugged. "Sounds reasonable to me."

"Then why did I call you while she was still alive?" I asked. "I went through this big ruse, right? So why didn't I finish her off?"

"Strangling someone isn't that easy," he said. "Maybe you thought she was dead."

"You realize, of course, how idiotic that sounds."

The door behind him opened, and Pistillo entered. He gave me a look as heavy as the ages. I closed my eyes and massaged the bridge of my nose with my forefinger and thumb. Pistillo was with one of the cops who had questioned me earlier. The cop signaled to his mustached compadre. The mustached cop looked annoyed by the interruption, but he followed the other one out the door. I was alone now with Pistillo.

He did not say anything at first. Pistillo circled the room, studying the glass jar of cotton balls, the tongue depressors, the hazardous-waste disposal can. Hospital rooms normally smell of antiseptic, but this one reeked of male-flight-attendant cologne. I did not know if it was from a doctor or cop, but I could see Pistillo's nose twitch in disgust. I was already used to it.

"Tell me what happened," he said.

"Didn't your friends with the NYPD fill you in?"

"I told them I wanted to hear it from you," Pistillo said. "Before they throw your ass in jail."

"I want to know how Katy is."

He weighed my request for a second or two. "Her neck and vocal cords will be sore, but she'll be fine."

I closed my eyes and let the relief flow over me.

"Start talking," Pistillo said.

I told him what happened. He stayed quiet until I got to the part about her shouting out the name "John."

"Any idea who John is?" he asked.

"Maybe."

"I'm listening."

"A guy I know when I was growing up. His name is John Asselta."

Pistillo's face dropped.

"You know him?" I asked.

He ignored my question. "What makes you think she was talking about Asselta?"

"He's the one who broke my nose."

I filled him in on the Ghost's break-in and assault. Pistillo did not look happy.

"Asselta was looking for your brother?"

"That's what he said."

212

His face reddened. "Why the hell didn't you tell me this before?"

"Yeah, it's weird," I said. "You've always been the guy I could turn to, the friend I could trust with anything."

He stayed angry. "Do you know anything about John Asselta?"

"We grew up in the same town. We used to call him the Ghost."

"He's one of the most dangerous wackos out there," Pistillo said. He stopped, shook his head. "It couldn't have been him."

"What makes you say that?"

"Because you're both alive."

Silence.

"He's a stone-cold killer."

"So why isn't he in jail?" I asked.

"Don't be naïve. He's good at what he does."

"Killing people?"

"Yes. He lives overseas, no one knows where exactly. He's worked for government death squads in Central America. He helped despots in Africa." Pistillo shook his head. "No, if Asselta wanted her dead, we'd be tying a toe tag on her right about now."

"Maybe she meant another John," I said. "Or maybe I just heard wrong."

"Maybe." He thought about that. "One other thing I don't get. If the Ghost or anyone else wanted to kill Katy Miller, why not just do it? Why go to the trouble of cuffing you down?"

That had troubled me too, but I had come up with one possibility. "Maybe it was a setup."

He frowned. "How do you figure?"

"The killer cuffs me to the bed. He chokes Katy to death. Then"—I could feel a tingle on my scalp—"maybe he'd set it up to make it look like I did it." I looked up at him.

Pistillo frowned. "You're not going to say 'Like my brother,' are you?"

"Yeah," I said. "Yeah, I think I am."

"That's horseshit."

"Think about it, Pistillo. One thing you guys could never explain: Why was my brother's blood at the scene?"

"Julie Miller fought him off."

"You know better. There was too much blood for that." I moved closer to him. "Ken was framed eleven years ago, and maybe tonight someone wanted history to repeat itself."

He scoffed. "Don't be melodramatic. And let me tell you something. The cops aren't buying your Houdini-cuff-escape story. They think you tried to kill her."

"What do you think?" I asked him.

"Katy's father is here. He's riled up as all hell."

"That's hardly surprising."

"It makes you wonder, though."

"You know I didn't do it, Pistillo. And despite your theatrics yesterday, you know I didn't kill Julie."

"I warned you to stay away."

"And I chose not to heed your warning."

Pistillo let loose a long breath and nodded. "Exactly, tough guy, so here's how we're going to play it." He stepped closer and tried to stare me down. I did not blink. "You're going to jail."

I sighed. "I think I've already surpassed my minimum daily requirement of threats today."

"No threat, Will. You're going to be shipped off to jail this very night."

"Fine, I want a lawyer."

He looked at his watch. "Too late for that. You'll spend the night in lockup. Tomorrow you'll get arraigned. The charges will be attempted murder and assault two. The D.A.'s office will claim that you're a flight risk—case in point: your brother—and they'll ask for the judge to deny bail. My guess is, the judge will grant it."

I started to speak but he held up a hand. "Save your breath because—and you're not going to like this—I don't care if you did it or not. I'm going to find enough evidence to convict you. And if I can't find it, I'll create it. Go ahead, tell your lawyer about this chat. I'll just deny it. You're a murder suspect who's helped hide his killer-brother for eleven years. I'm one of the country's most respected law enforcement agents. Who do you think they'll believe?"

I looked at him. "Why are you doing this?"

"I told you to stay away."

"What would you have done if you were in my place? If it was your brother?"

"That's not the point. You didn't listen. And now your girlfriend is dead and Katy Miller just barely escaped with her life."

"I never hurt either one of them."

"Yeah, you did. You caused it. If you'd listened to me, you think they'd be where they are now?"

214

His words hit home, but I pushed on. "And what about you, Pistillo? What about your burying Laura Emerson's connection—"

"Hey, I'm not here to play point-counterpoint with you. You're going to jail tonight. And make no mistake, I'll get you convicted."

He headed for the door.

"Pistillo?" When he turned around, I said, "What are you really after here?"

He stopped and leaned so that his lips were only inches from my ear. He whispered, "Ask your brother," and then he was gone.

38

I spent the night in the precinct holding pen at Midtown South on West 35th Street. The cell reeked of urine and vomit and that sour-vodka smell when a drunk sweats. It was still a step up from the aroma of flight-attendant cologne. I had two cellmates. One was a cross-dressing hooker who cried a lot and seemed confused about sitting or standing when using the metal toilet. My other cellmate was a black man who slept the whole time. I have no jail stories about being beaten or robbed or raped. The night was totally uneventful.

Whoever was working the night shift spun a CD of Bruce Springsteen's "Born to Run." Talk about comfort food. Like every good Jersey boy, I had the lyrics memorized. This may sound strange, but I always thought of Ken when I listened to the Boss's power ballads. We were not blue collar or suffering hard times, and neither of us had been into fast cars or hanging out on the shore (in Jersey, it's always "the shore," never "the beach")—then again, judging by what I've seen at recent E Street Band concerts, that was probably true of most of his listeners—but there was something in the stories of struggle, the spirit of a man in chains trying to break free, of wanting something more and finding the courage to run away, that not only resonated with me but made me think of my brother, even before the murder.

But tonight, when Bruce sang that she was so pretty he got lost in the stars, I thought about Sheila. And I ached all over again.

My one call had been to Squares. I woke him up. When I told him what happened, he said, "Bummer." Then he promised to find me a good lawyer and see what he could learn about Katy's condition.

"Oh, the security tapes from that QuickGo," Squares said.

"What about them?"

"Your idea worked. We'll be able to see them tomorrow."

"If they let me out of here."

"Yeah, I guess," Squares said. Then he added, "If they don't give you bail, man, that would suck."

In the morning, the cops escorted me down to central booking at 100 Centre Street. The corrections department took over from there. I was held in a pen located in the basement. If you no longer believe that America is a melting pot, you should spend some time with the potpourri of (in)humanity that inhabits this mini–United Nations. I heard at least ten different languages. There were shades of skin color that could inspire the people at Crayola. There were baseball caps and turbans and toupees and even a fez. Everyone talked at the same time. And when I could understand them—hey, even when I couldn't—they were all claiming innocence.

Squares was there when I stood before the judge. So was my new attorney, a woman named Hester Crimstein. I recognized her from some famous case, but I could not put my finger on which one. She introduced herself to me and never looked my way again. She turned and stared at the young D.A. as though he were a bleeding boar and she was a panther with an industrial-sized case of piles.

"We request that Mr. Klein be held over without bail," the young D.A. said. "We believe that he is a very serious flight risk."

"Why's that?" the judge, who seemed to be perspiring boredom from every pore, asked.

"His brother, a murder suspect, has been on the run for the past eleven years. Not only that, your honor, but his brother's victim was this victim's sister."

That got the judge's attention. "Come again?"

"The defendant, Mr. Klein, is accused of trying to murder one Katherine Miller. Mr. Klein's brother, Kenneth, is a suspect in the eleven-year-old murder of Julie Miller, the victim's older sister."

The judge, who'd been rubbing his face, stopped abruptly. "Oh, wait, I remember the case."

217

The young D.A. smiled as if he'd been given a gold star.

The judge turned to Hester Crimstein. "Ms. Crimstein?"

"Your honor, we believe that all charges against Mr. Klein should be dropped immediately," she said.

The judge started rubbing his face again. "Label me shocked, Ms. Crimstein."

"Short of that, we believe that Mr. Klein should be released on his own recognizance. Mr. Klein has no criminal record at all. He has a job working with the poor in this city. He has roots in the community. As for that ridiculous comparison to his brother, that's guilt by association at its worst."

"You don't think the people have a valid concern, Ms. Crimstein?"

"Not at all, your honor. I understand that Mr. Klein's sister recently got her hair permed. Does that make it more likely that he will do the same?"

There was laughter.

The young D.A. was feeling his oats. "Your honor, with all due deference to my colleague's silly analogy—"

"What's silly about it?" Crimstein snapped.

"Our point is that Mr. Klein certainly has the resources to flee."

"That's ludicrous. He has no more means than anyone else. The reason they're making this claim is because they believe his brother fled—and no one is even sure about that. He may be dead. But either way, your honor, the assistant district attorney is leaving out one crucial element in all this."

Hester Crimstein turned to the young D.A. and smiled.

"Mr. Thomson?" the judge said.

Thomson, the young D.A., kept his head down.

Hester Crimstein waited another beat and then dove in. "The victim of this heinous crime, one Katherine Miller, claimed this morning that Mr. Klein was innocent."

The judge did not like that. "Mr. Thomson?"

"That's not exactly true, your honor."

"Not exactly?"

"Ms. Miller claimed that she did not see her assailant. It was dark. He wore a mask."

"And," Hester Crimstein finished for him, "she said that it wasn't my client."

"She said she did not *believe* it was Mr. Klein," Thomson countered. "But, your honor, she's injured and confused. She didn't see the attacker, so she really couldn't rule him out—"

"We're not trying the case here, counselor," the judge interrupted. "But your request for no bail is denied. Bail is set at thirty thousand dollars."

The judge banged the gavel. And I was free.

39

I wanted to head up to the hospital and see Katy. Squares shook his head and told me that would be a bad idea. Her father was there. He refused to leave her side. He had hired an armed guard to stand outside her door. I understood. Mr. Miller had failed to protect one daughter. He would never let himself do that again.

I called the hospital on Squares's cell phone, but the switchboard operator said that no calls were allowed. I dialed a local florist and sent her a get-well bouquet. It seemed pretty simplistic and dumb—Katy gets nearly strangled to death in my apartment and I send a basket with flowers, a teddy bear, and a mini-Mylar balloon on a stick—but it was the only way I could come up with to let her know that I was thinking of her.

Squares drove his own car, a 1968 venetian-blue Coupe de Ville that was about as inconspicuous as our cross-dressing friend Raquel/Roscoe at a Daughters of the American Revolution gathering, through the Lincoln Tunnel. Tough going, the tunnel, as always. People claimed that the traffic was getting worse. I'm not so sure. As a kid, our family car—in those days, one of those paneled station wagons—used to creep through that tunnel every other Sunday. I remember how sluggish that trek would be, in the dark, those stupid yellow warning lights hanging batlike from the tunnel's ceiling as if we really need to be told to go slow, that little glass booth with the worker in it, the soot painting the tunnel tiles a urine-hued ivory, all of us peering anxiously ahead for the breaking light of day, and then, finally, with those metal-looking rubber dividers rising in greeting, we would ascend into the world of high-rises, an alternate reality, as if we'd traveled through a transporter. We'd go to the Ringling Bros. and Barnum & Bailey circus and twirl those little lights on a string, or maybe Radio City Music Hall for some show that dazzled for about ten minutes and then bored, or stand in line for half-priced tickets at the TKTS booth, or browse the books at the big Barnes & Noble (I think there was only one back then), or hit the Museum of Natural History, or a street fair—my mom's favorite was September's New York Is Book Country on Fifth Avenue.

My father would grumble about the traffic and the parking and the all-purpose "filth," but my mother loved New York. She longed for the theater, the arts, the razz and jangle of the city. Sunny had managed to shrink herself enough to fit into the suburban world of carpools and tennis sneakers, but her dreams, those long-ago suppressed longings, were right there, right beneath the surface. She loved us, I know that, but sometimes, when I sat behind her in that station wagon and watched her looking out the car window, I wondered if she would have been happier without us.

"Smart thinking," Squares said.

"What?"

"Remembering that Sonay was a devout practioner of Yoga Squared."

"So how did it work?"

"I called Sonay and told her our problem. She told me that QuickGo was run by two brothers, Ian and Noah Muller. She called them, told them what she wanted, and . . ." Squares shrugged.

I shook my head. "You are amazing."

"Yes. Yes, I am."

QuickGo's offices were housed in a warehouse off Route 3 in the heart of northern New Jersey's swamps. New Jersey gets goofed on a lot, mostly because our most-traveled byroads cut through the butt-ugliest sections of the so-called Garden State. I am one of those who staunchly defend my home state. Most of New Jersey is surprisingly gorgeous, but our critics do score points on two fronts. One, our cities are beyond decay. Trenton, Newark, Atlantic City, take your pick. They get and deserve little respect. Take Newark as a case in point. I have friends who grew up in Quincy, Massachusetts. They always say they are from Boston. I have friends who grew up

221

in Bryn Mawr. They always say they are from Philadelphia. I grew up less than nine miles from the heart of Newark. I have never once said or heard anyone I know say that they were from Newark.

Two—and I don't care what others say—there is an odor in the North Jersey marshlands. It is often faint but nonetheless unmistakable. It is not pleasant. It does not smell like nature. It smells like smoke and chemicals and a leaking septic tank. That was the odor that greeted us as we stepped out of the car at the QuickGo warehouse.

Squares said, "Did you fart?"

I looked at him.

"Hey, just trying to break the tension."

We headed into the warehouse. The Muller brothers were worth close to a hundred million dollars each, yet they shared a small office that sat in the middle of a hangarlike room. Their desks, which looked like something bought at an elementary school close-out, were pushed together facing each other. Their chairs were pre-ergonomics shellacked-wood. There were no computers or fax machines or photocopiers, just the desks, tall metal filing cabinets, and two phones. All four walls were glassed. The brothers liked to look out at the cargo boxes and forklifts. They did not much care who looked in.

The brothers looked alike and were dressed the same. They wore what my father called "charcoal slacks" with white button-downs over V-neck Ts. The shirts were buttoned low enough that their gray chest hair jutted out like steel wool. The brothers rose and aimed their widest smiles at Squares.

"You must be Ms. Sonay's guru," one said. "Yogi Squares."

Squares replied with a serene, wise-man head nod.

They both rushed over and shook his hand. I half expected them to take a knee.

"We had them overnight the tapes," the taller of the brothers said, clearly looking for approval. Squares deigned another nod at him. They led us across the cement floor. I heard the beep-beep of vehicles in reverse. Garagelike doors were opened and trucks were loaded. The brothers greeted every worker, and the workers responded.

We entered a windowless room with a Mr. Coffee on the counter. A TV with a coat-hanger antenna and VCR sat on one of those metal carts I had not seen since the days when the A-V kid would wheel them into my elementary school class.

The taller brother turned on the TV. Pure static blew forth. He stuck a tape in the VCR. "This tape covers twelve hours," he said. "You told me the guy was in the store around three o'clock, right?"

"That's what we were told," Squares said.

"I have it set at two forty-five. The tape moves pretty quickly since it only captures an image every three seconds. Oh, and the fast forward doesn't work, sorry. We don't have a remote control either, so just press the Play button right here whenever you're ready. We figured you'd want privacy so we'll leave. Take your time."

"We may need to keep the tape," Squares said.

"Not a problem. We can make copies."

"Thank you."

One brother shook Squares's hand again. The other—I'm not making this up—bowed. Then we were left alone. I approached the VCR and pressed Play. The static disappeared. So did the sound. I played with the volume button on the TV, but, of course, there was no sound.

The images were in black and white. There was a clock on the bottom of the screen. The camera pointed at the cash register from above. A young woman with long blond hair worked it. Her moving in jerky, every-three-second clips made me dizzy.

"How are we going to know this Owen Enfield?" Squares asked.

"We look for a forty-year-old guy with a crew cut, I guess."

Watching now, I realized that this task might be easier than I'd first thought. The customers were all elderly and in golf-club garb. I wondered if Stonepointe catered mostly to retirees. I made a mental note to ask Yvonne Sterno.

At 3:08.15, we spotted him. His back anyway. He wore shorts and a collared shortsleeve shirt. We could not see his face, but he had a crew cut. He headed past the register and down the last aisle. We waited. At 3:09.24, our potential Owen Enfield turned the corner, heading back toward the long-haired blonde at the cash register. He carried a half-gallon of what looked like milk and a loaf of bread. I put my hand near the pause button so I could stop it and get a better look.

But there was no need.

The Vandyke beard might throw you off. So, too, the close-cropped gray hair. If I had casually stumbled across this tape, or if I had walked past him on a busy street, I might not have noticed. But I was anything but casual right now. I was concentrating. And I knew. I hit the pause button anyway: 3:09.51.

Any doubts were erased. I stood there, unmoving. I did not know if I should celebrate or cry. I turned toward Squares. His eyes were on me instead of the screen. I nodded at him, confirming what he already suspected.

Owen Enfield was my brother, Ken.

40

The intercom buzzed.

"Mr. McGuane?" the receptionist, part of his security force, asked.

"Yes."

"Joshua Ford and Raymond Cromwell are here."

Joshua Ford was the senior partner at Stanford, Cummings, and Ford, a firm that employed more than three hundred attorneys. Raymond Cromwell would thus be the note-taking, extra-hour-billing underling. Philip watched them both on the monitor. Ford was a big guy, six-four, two-twenty. He had a reputation for being tough, aggressive, nasty, and fitting that profile, he worked his face and mouth as though he were chomping on either a cigar or human leg. Cromwell, in contrast, was young, soft, manicured, and waxy-smooth.

McGuane looked over at the Ghost. The Ghost smiled, and McGuane felt another cold gust. Again he wondered about the intelligence of bringing Asselta in on this. In the end, he had decided that it would be okay. The Ghost had a stake in this too.

Besides, the Ghost was good at this.

Still keeping his eyes on that skin-crawling smile, McGuane said, "Please send in Mr. Ford alone. Make sure that Mr. Cromwell is comfortable in the waiting room."

"Yes, Mr. McGuane."

McGuane had debated how to play this. He did not care for violence for violence's sake, but he never shrank from it either. It was a means to an end. The Ghost was right about that atheist-in-foxhole crap. The truth is, we are mere animals, organisms even, slightly more complex than your basic paramecium. You die, you're gone. It was pure megalomania to think we humans are somehow above death, that we, unlike any other creature, have the ability to transcend it. In life, sure, we are special, dominant, because we are the strongest and most ruthless. We rule. But in death, to believe that we are somehow special in God's eyes, that we can worm our way into his good graces by kissing his ass, well, and not to sound like a Communist here, but that's the sort of thinking that the rich have used to keep the poor in place since the beginning of man's rule.

The Ghost moved toward the door.

You take the edge any way you can get it. McGuane often treaded along byways others considered taboo. You were never supposed to kill, for example, a fed or a D.A. or a cop. McGuane had killed all three. You were never supposed to attack, to use another example, powerful people who could make trouble and draw attention.

McGuane did not buy that one either.

When Joshua Ford opened the door, the Ghost had the iron baton ready. It was the approximate length of a baseball bat, with a powerful spring that helped it snap with the force of a blackjack. If you were to hit someone on the head with any kind of force, it would crush the skull like an eggshell.

Joshua Ford entered with a rich-man's swagger. He smiled at McGuane. "Mr. McGuane."

McGuane smiled back. "Mr. Ford."

Sensing someone to his right, Ford turned toward the Ghost, his hand outstretched for a customary shake. The Ghost had his eyes elsewhere. He aimed the metal bar for the shin and hit it flush. Ford cried out and dropped to the floor like a marionette with its strings cut. The Ghost hit him again, this time in the right shoulder. Ford felt his arm go dead. The Ghost smashed the baton against the rib cage. There was a cracking sound. Ford tried to roll into a ball.

From across the room, McGuane asked, "Where is he?"

Joshua Ford swallowed and croaked, "Who?"

Big mistake. The Ghost snapped the weapon down on the

man's ankle. Ford howled. McGuane looked behind him at the security monitor. Cromwell was comfortably ensconced in the waiting room. He would hear nothing. Neither would anybody else.

The Ghost hit the lawyer again, finding the same spot on the ankle. There was a crunching sound like a truck tire over a beer bottle. Ford put up a hand, pleading for mercy.

Over the years, McGuane had learned that it was best to strike before you interrogate. Most people, when presented with the threat of pain, will try to talk their way out of it. That goes double for men who are accustomed to using their mouths. They'll search for angles, for half-truths, for credible lies. They are rational, the assumption goes, and thus their opponents must be the same. Words can be used to defuse.

You need to strip them of that delusion.

The pain and fear that accompany a sudden physical assault are devastating to the psyche. Your cognitive reasoning—your intelligentsia, if you will, your evolved man—fades away, caves in. You are left with the Neanderthal, the primitive true-you who knows only to escape pain.

The Ghost looked over at McGuane. McGuane nodded. The Ghost stepped back and let McGuane move closer.

"He stopped in Vegas," McGuane explained. "That was his big mistake. He visited a doctor there. We checked the nearby pay phones for out-of-state calls made an hour before and an hour after his visit. There was only one call of interest. To you, Mr. Ford. He called you. And just to make sure, I had a man watch your office. The feds paid you a visit yesterday. So you see, it all adds up. Ken had to have a lawyer. He'd want someone tough and independent and not connected in any way to me. That would be you."

Joshua Ford said, "But—"

McGuane held up his hand to stop him. Ford obeyed and closed his mouth. McGuane stepped back, looked at the Ghost, and said, "John."

The Ghost advanced and without hesitating, he whacked Ford on the side of the arm above the elbow. The elbow bent back the wrong way. Ford's face lost whatever color was left.

"If you deny or pretend you don't know what I'm talking about," McGuane said, "my friend here will stop the love taps and start to hurt you. Do you understand?"

Ford took a few seconds. When he finally looked up, McGuane

was surprised by the steadiness of the man's gaze. Ford looked at the Ghost, then at McGuane. "Go to hell," Ford spat out.

The Ghost looked at McGuane. He arched an eyebrow, smiled, and said, "Brave."

"John . . ."

But the Ghost ignored him. He whipped the iron bar across Ford's face. There was a wet ripping sound as his head snapped to the side. Blood squirted across the room. Ford fell back and did not move. The Ghost lined up for another blow to the knee.

McGuane said, "Is he still conscious?"

That made the Ghost pause. He bent down. "Conscious," the Ghost reported, "but his breathing is sporadic." He stood back up. "Another blow and Mr. Ford might go nighty-night."

McGuane thought about that. "Mr. Ford?"

Ford looked up.

"Where is he?" McGuane asked again.

This time Ford shook his head.

McGuane walked over to the monitor. He swiveled it so that Joshua Ford could see the screen. Cromwell was sitting cross-legged, sipping coffee.

The Ghost pointed at the monitor. "He wears nice shoes. Are they Allen-Edmonds?"

Ford tried to sit up. He got his hands underneath him, tried to push, fell back.

"How old is he?" McGuane asked.

Ford did not reply.

The Ghost lifted the bar. "He asked you—"

"Twenty-nine."

"Married?"

Ford nodded.

"Kiddies?"

"Two boys."

McGuane studied the monitor some more. "You're right, John. Those are nice shoes." He turned to Ford. "Tell me where Ken is, or he dies."

The Ghost carefully put down the metal bar. He reached into his pocket and pulled out a Thuggee strangulation stick. The handle portion was made of mahogany. It was eight inches long and two inches in diameter. The surface was octagonal. Deep grooves were

228

cut into it, making it easier to grip. There was a braided rope attached to either end. The rope was made of horsehair.

"He's got nothing to do with this," Ford said.

"Listen to me closely," McGuane said. "I'm only going to say this once."

Ford waited.

"We never bluff," McGuane said.

The Ghost smiled. McGuane waited a beat, his eyes on Ford. Then he hit the intercom button. The security receptionist responded.

"Yes, Mr. McGuane."

"Bring Mr. Cromwell here."

"Yes, sir."

They both watched the monitor as a beefy security guard came to the door and waved toward Cromwell. Cromwell uncrossed his legs, put down his coffee, rose, straightened out his jacket. He followed the security guard out the door. Ford turned to McGuane. Their eyes met and locked.

"You're a stupid man," McGuane said.

The Ghost regripped the wooden handle and waited.

The security guard opened the door. Raymond Cromwell entered with his smile at the ready. When he saw the blood and his boss crumbled on the floor, his face dropped like someone had short-circuited the muscles. "What the—?"

The Ghost stepped behind Cromwell and kicked the back of both legs. Cromwell let out a cry and dropped to his knees. The Ghost's moves were practiced, effortlessly graceful, like a grotesque ballet.

The rope dropped over the younger man's head. When it fully circled his neck, the Ghost jerked back violently while simultaneously putting his knee against Cromwell's spine. The rope tightened hard against Cromwell's waxy-smooth skin. The Ghost twisted the handle, effectively cutting off blood flow to the brain. Cromwell's eyes bulged. His hands pawed at the rope. The Ghost held on.

"Stop!" Ford shouted. "I'll talk!"

But there was no reply.

The Ghost kept his gaze on his victim. Cromwell's face was a horrid shade of purple.

"I said—" Ford quickly turned to McGuane. McGuane stood at

ease with his arms folded. The two men locked eyes. The quiet sounds, the awful gurgling struggle coming from Cromwell, echoed in the stillness.

Ford whispered, "Please."

But McGuane shook his head and repeated his earlier statement: "We never bluff."

The Ghost turned the handle one more time and held on.

41

I had to tell my father about the security tape.

Squares dropped me off at a bus stop near the Meadowlands. I had no idea what to do about what I'd just seen. Somewhere along the New Jersey Turnpike, while staring out at the decaying industrial plants, my brain slipped on the autopilot. It was the only way to keep moving.

Ken was indeed alive.

I had seen the proof. He had been living in New Mexico and using the name Owen Enfield. Part of me was ecstatic. There was a chance at redemption, a chance to be with my brother again, a chance—dare I even think of it?—to make this all right.

But then I thought about Sheila.

Her fingerprints had been found in my brother's house, along with two dead bodies. How did Sheila fit into all this? I had no idea—or maybe I just didn't want to face the obvious. She had betrayed me—when my mind would function, the only scenarios I could come up with involved betrayal of one form or another—and if I dwelled on that for too long, if I really allowed myself to sink into the simple memories—the way she tucked her feet under her when we talked on the couch, the way she pulled her hair back as though she were standing under a waterfall, the way she smelled in that terry-cloth robe when she came out of the shower, the way she wore my oversize sweatshirts on fall nights, the way she hummed in my ear when we danced, the way she could stop my breath with a look from across the room—that it had all been some sort of elaborate lie . . .

Autopilot.

So I plodded on with one thought in mind: closure. My brother and my lover had both left me without warning, gone before goodbye. I knew that I could never put any of this behind me until I knew the truth. Squares had warned me about this in the beginning, about maybe not liking what I found, but maybe in the end, this was all necessary. Maybe now, finally, it was my turn to be brave. Maybe now I would save Ken instead of the other way around.

So that was what I'd focus on: Ken was alive. He was innocent—if I had been subconsciously harboring any doubts before, Pistillo had erased them. I could see and be with him again. I could—I don't know—avenge the past, let my mother rest in peace, something.

On this, the last day of our official mourning, my father was not at the house. Aunt Selma was in the kitchen. She told me that he'd taken a walk. Aunt Selma wore an apron. I wondered where she had gotten it. We did not have one, I was certain of that. Had Selma brought it with her? She seemed always to be wearing an apron, even when she wasn't, if you know what I mean. I watched her cleaning out the sink. Selma, Sunny's quiet sister, labored quietly. I had always taken her for granted. I think most people did. Selma was just . . . there. She was one of those people who lived life below the radar, as though she were afraid of drawing the attention of the fates. She and Uncle Murray had no children. I did not know why, though I'd once overheard my parents talking about a stillborn. I stood and looked at her, as if for the first time, just looking at yet another human being struggling every day to do right.

"Thank you," I said to her.

Selma nodded.

I wanted to tell her that I loved her and appreciated her and wanted us, especially now that Mom was gone, to be closer, that I know Mom would have wanted that. But I couldn't. I hugged her instead. Selma stiffened at first, startled by my aberrant display of affection, but then she relaxed.

"It'll be okay," she told me.

I knew my father's favorite walking route. I crossed Coddington

Terrace, carefully avoiding the Miller house. My father, I knew, did that too. He had changed the route years ago. I cut through both the Jarats' and Arnays' yards, and then took the path that crossed the Meadowbrook to the town's Little League fields. The fields were empty, the season over, and my father sat alone on the top row of the metal bleachers. I remembered how much he loved coaching, that white T-shirt with the three-quarter-length green sleeves, the word *Senators* across the front, the green cap with the S sitting too high on his head. He loved the dugout, hanging his arms casually off the dusty rafters, the sweat forming in the pits. He'd put his right foot on the first cinder step, the left on the concrete, and in one fluid smooth motion he'd take the cap off, do the forearm swipe of the brow, put the cap neatly back in place. His face glowed on those late-spring nights, especially when Ken played. He coached with Mr. Bertillo and Mr. Horowitz, his two best friends, beer buddies, both dead of heart attacks before sixty, and I know that as I sat next to him now, he could still hear those clapping hands and that repetitive banter and smell that sweet Little League clay-dirt.

He looked at me and smiled. "Remember the year your mom umped?"

"A little, I guess. What was I, four?"

"Yeah, something like that." He shook his head, still smiling, lost in the memory. "This was during the height of your mother's women's lib stage. She wore these slogan T-shirts that said A WOMAN'S PLACE IS IN THE HOUSE AND SENATE, stuff like that. Keep in mind that this was a few years before girls were allowed to play Little League, okay? So somewhere along the way, your mom learned that there were no female umpires. She checked the rule book and saw that there was nothing forbidding that."

"So she signed up?"

"Yep."

"And?"

"Well, the elder statesmen threw a fit, but the rules were the rules. So they let her ump. But there were a couple of problems."

"Like?"

"Like she was the worst umpire in the world." Dad smiled again, a smile I rarely saw anymore, a smile so firmly rooted in the past that it made me ache. "She barely knew the rules. Her eyesight, as you know, was terrible. I remember in her first game she stuck up her thumb and yelled 'Safe.' Whenever she made a call,

233

she'd go through all these gyrations. Like something Bob Fosse choreographed."

We both chuckled and I could almost see him watching her, waving off her theatrics, half embarrassed, half thrilled.

"Didn't the coaches go nuts?"

"Sure, but you know what the league did?"

I shook my head.

"They teamed her up with Harvey Newhouse. You remember him?"

"His son was in my class. He played pro football, right?"

"For the Rams, yeah. Offensive tackle. Harvey must have been three hundred pounds. So he took behind the plate and your mom took the field and whenever a coach would get out of hand, Harvey would just glare at him and the coach sat back down."

We chuckled again and then fell gently into silence, both of us wondering how a spirit like that could be smothered away, even before the onset of the disease. He finally turned and looked at me. His eyes widened when he noticed the bruises.

"What the hell happened to you?"

"It's okay," I said.

"Did you get in a fight?"

"I'm fine, really. I need to talk to you about something."

He was quiet. I wondered how to approach this, but Dad took care of that.

"Show me," he said.

I looked at him.

"Your sister called this morning. She told me about the picture."

I still had it with me. I pulled it out. He took it in his palm, as though afraid that he might crush it. He looked down and said, "My God." His eyes began to glisten.

"You didn't know?" I said.

"No." He looked at the photograph again. "Your mother never said anything until, you know." I saw something cross his face. His wife, his life partner, had kept this from him, and it hurt.

"There's something else," I said.

He turned to me.

"Ken's been living in New Mexico." I gave him a thumbnail sketch of what I'd learned. Dad took it in quietly and steadily, as if he'd found his sea legs.

When I'd finished, Dad said, "How long had he been living out there?"

"Just a few months. Why?"

"Your mother said he was coming back. She said he'd be back when he proved his innocence."

We sat in silence. I let my mind wander. Suppose, I thought, it went something like this: Eleven years ago, Ken was framed. He ran off and lived overseas—in hiding or something, just like the news report. Years pass. He comes back home.

Why?

Was it, like my mother had said, to prove his innocence? That made sense, I guess, but why now? I didn't know, but whatever the reason, Ken did indeed return—and it backfired on him. Someone found out.

Who?

The answer seemed obvious: whoever murdered Julie. That person, be it a he or she, would need to silence Ken. And then what? No idea. There were still pieces missing.

"Dad?"

"Yes."

"Did you ever suspect Ken was alive?"

He took his time. "It was easier to think he was dead."

"That's not an answer."

He let his gaze roam again. "Ken loved you so much, Will."

I let that hang in the air.

"But he wasn't all good."

"I know that," I said.

He let that settle in. "When Julie was murdered," my father said, "Ken was already in trouble."

"What do you mean?"

"He came home to hide."

"From what?"

"I don't know."

I thought about it. I again remembered that he had not been home in at least two years and that he'd seemed on edge, even as he asked me about Julie. I just didn't know what that all meant.

Dad said, "Do you remember Phil McGuane?"

I nodded. Ken's old friend from high school, the "class leader" who was now reputed to be "connected." "I heard he moved into the Bonannos' old place."

"Yes."

During my childhood, the Bonannos, famed old-time mafiosi, had lived in Livingston's biggest estate, the one with the big iron gate and the driveway guarded by two stone lions. Rumor had it—as you may have surmised, suburbia is rife with rumors—that there were bodies buried on the property and that the fence could electrocute and if a kid tried to sneak through the woods out back, he'd get shot in the head. I doubt any of those stories were true, but the police finally arrested Old Man Bonanno when he was ninety-one.

"What about him?" I asked.

"Ken was mixed up with McGuane."

"How?"

"That's all I know."

I thought about the Ghost. "Was John Asselta involved too?"

My father went rigid. I saw fear in his eyes. "Why would you ask me that?"

"The three of them were all friends in high school," I began—and then I decided to go the rest of the way. "I saw him recently."

"Asselta?"

"Yes."

His voice was soft. "He's back?"

I nodded.

Dad closed his eyes.

"What is it?"

"He's dangerous," my father said.

"I know that."

He pointed at my face. "Did he do that?"

Good question, I thought. "In part, at least."

"In part?"

"It's a long story, Dad."

He closed his eyes again. When he opened them, he put his hands on his thighs and stood. "Let's go home," he said.

I wanted to ask him more, but I knew that now was not the time. I followed him. Dad had a hard time getting down the rickety bleacher steps. I offered him a hand. He refused it. When we both reached the gravel, we turned toward the path. And there, smiling patiently with his hands in his pockets, stood the Ghost.

For a moment I thought it was my imagination, as if our thinking about him had conjured up this horrific mirage. But I heard the

236

sharp intake of air coming from my father. And then I heard that voice.

"Ah, isn't this touching?" the Ghost said.

My father stepped in front of me as though trying to shield me. "What do you want?" he shouted.

But the Ghost laughed. " 'Gee, son, when I struck out in the big game,' " he said, mocking, " 'it took a whole roll of Life Savers to make me feel better.' "

We stayed rooted to the spot. The Ghost looked up at the sky, closed his eyes, took a great big sniff of air. "Ah, Little League." He lowered his gaze to my father. "Do you remember that time my old man showed up at a game, Mr. Klein?"

My father set his jaw.

"It was a great moment, Will. Really. A classic. My dear ol' dad was so wasted, he took a leak right on the side of the snack bar. Can you imagine? I thought Mrs. Tansmore was going to have a stroke." He laughed heartily, the sound clawing at me as it echoed. When it died down, he added, "Good times, eh?"

"What do you want?" my father said again.

But the Ghost was on his own track now. He would not be derailed. "Say, Mr. Klein, do you remember coaching that all-star team in the state finals?"

My father said, "I do."

"Ken and I were in, what, fourth grade, was it?"

Nothing from my father this time.

The Ghost snapped, "Oh wait." The smile slid off his face. "I almost forgot. I missed that year, didn't I? And the next year too. Jail time, don't you know."

"You never went to jail," my father said.

"True, true, you're absolutely right, Mr. Klein. I was"—the Ghost made quote marks with his skinny fingers—"hospitalized. You know what that means, Willie boy? They lock up a child with the most depraved whack-jobs that ever cursed this wretched planet, so as to make him all better. My first roommate, his name was Timmy, was a pyromaniac. At the tender age of thirteen, Timmy killed his parents by setting them on fire. One night he stole a book of matches from a drunk orderly and lit up my bed. I got to go to the medical wing for three weeks. I almost set myself on fire so I wouldn't have to go back."

237

A car drove down Meadowbrook Road. I could see a little boy in the back, perched high by a safety seat of some kind. There was no wind. The trees stood too still.

"That was a long time ago," my father said softly.

The Ghost's eyes narrowed as if he were giving my father's words very special attention. Finally he nodded and said, "Yes, yes, it was. You're right about that too, Mr. Klein. And it wasn't like I had a great home life to begin with. I mean, what were my prospects anyway? You could almost look at what happened to me as a blessing: I could get therapy instead of living with a father who beat me."

I realized then that he was talking about the killing of Daniel Skinner, the bully who'd been stabbed with the kitchen knife. But what struck me then, what gave me pause, was how his story sounded like the kids we help at Covenant House—abusive home life, early crime, some form of psychosis. I tried to look at the Ghost like that, as if he were just one of my kids. But the picture would not hold. He was not a kid anymore. I don't know when they cross over, at what age they go from being a kid who needs help to a degenerate who should be locked up, or even if that was fair.

"Hey, Willie boy?"

The Ghost tried to meet my eye then, but my father leaned in the way of even his gaze. I put a hand on his shoulder as if to tell him I could handle it.

"What?" I said.

"You do know I was"—again with the finger quotes—"hospitalized again, don't you?"

"Yes," I said.

"I was a senior. You were a sophomore."

"I remember."

"I had only one visitor the whole time I was there. Do you know who it was?"

I nodded. The answer was Julie.

"Ironic, don't you think?"

"Did you kill her?" I asked.

"Only one of us here is to blame."

My father stepped back in the way. "That's enough," he said.

I slid to the side. "What do you mean?"

"You, Willie boy. I mean you."

I was confused. "What?"

"That's enough," my father said again.

238

"You were supposed to fight for her," the Ghost went on. "You were supposed to protect her."

The words, even coming from this lunatic, pierced my chest like an ice pick.

"Why are you here?" my father demanded.

"The truth, Mr. Klein? I'm not exactly sure."

"Leave my family alone. You want someone, you take me."

"No, sir, I don't want you." He considered my father, and I felt something cold coil in the pit of my belly. "I think I prefer you this way."

The Ghost gave a little wave good-bye then and stepped into the wooded area. We watched him move deeper into the brush, fading away until, like his nickname, he vanished. We stood there for another minute or two. I could hear my father's breathing, hollow and tinny, as if coming up from a deep cavern.

"Dad?"

But he had already started toward the path. "Let's go home, Will."

42

My father would not talk.

When we got back to the house, he headed up to his bedroom, the one he had shared with my mother for nearly forty years, and closed the door. There was so much coming at me now. I tried to sort through it, but it was too much. My brain threatened to shut down. And still I didn't know enough. Not yet anyway. I needed to learn more.

Sheila.

There was one more person who might be able to shed some light on the enigma that had been the love of my life. So I made my excuses, said my good-byes, and headed back into the city. I hopped on a subway and headed up to the Bronx. The skies had started to darken and the neighborhood was bad, but for once in my life, I was beyond being scared.

Before I even knocked, the door opened a crack, the chain in place. Tanya said, "He's asleep."

"I want to talk to you," I said.

"I have nothing to say."

"I saw you at the memorial service."

"Go away."

"Please," I said. "It's important."

Tanya sighed and took off the chain. I slipped inside. The dim lamp was on in the far corner, casting the faintest of glows. As I let my eyes wander over this most depressing place, I wondered if Tanya was not as much a prisoner here as Louis Castman. I faced her. She shrunk back as if my gaze had the ability to scald.

"How long do you plan on keeping him here?" I asked.

"I don't make plans," she replied.

Tanya did not offer me a seat. We both just stood there, facing each other. She crossed her arms and waited.

"Why did you come to the service?" I asked.

"I wanted to pay my respects."

"You knew Sheila?"

"Yes."

"You were friends?"

Tanya may have smiled. Her face was so mangled, the scars running jagged lines with her mouth, I couldn't be sure. "Not even close."

"Why did you come then?"

She cocked her head to the side. "You want to hear something weird?"

I was not sure how to respond, so I settled for a nod.

"That was the first time I've been out of this apartment in sixteen months."

I was not sure how to respond to that either, so I tried, "I'm glad you came."

Tanya looked at me skeptically. The room was silent save for her breathing. I don't know what was physically wrong with her, if it was connected to the brutal slashing or not, but every breath sounded as though her throat were a narrow straw with a few drops of liquid stuck inside.

I said, "Please tell me why you came."

"It's like I told you. I wanted to pay my respects." She paused. "And I thought I could help."

"Help?"

She looked at the door to Louis Castman's bedroom. I followed her gaze. "He told me why you came here. I thought maybe I could fill in some more of the pieces."

"What did he say?"

"That you were in love with Sheila." Tanya moved closer to the lamp. It was hard not to look away. She finally sat and gestured for me to do likewise. "Is that true?"

"Yes."

"Did you murder her?" Tanya asked.

The question startled me. "No."

She did not seem convinced.

"I don't understand," I said. "You came to help?"

"Yes."

"Then why did you run off?"

"You haven't figured that out?"

I shook my head.

She sat—more like collapsed—onto a chair. Her hands fell into her lap, and her body started rocking back and forth.

"Tanya?"

"I heard your name," she said.

"Pardon?"

"You asked why I ran off." She stopped rocking. "It was because I heard your name."

"I don't understand."

She looked at the door again. "Louis didn't know who you were. Neither did I—not until I heard your name at the service, when Squares eulogized her. You're Will Klein."

"Yes."

"And"—her voice grew soft now, so soft I had to lean forward to hear it—"you're Ken's brother."

Silence.

"You knew my brother?"

"We met. A long time ago."

"How?"

"Through Sheila." She straightened her back and looked at me. It was odd. They say that the eyes are the windows to the soul. That's nonsense. Tanya's eyes were normal. I saw no scars there, no hint of defect, no shade of her history or her torments. "Louis told you about a big-time gangster who got involved with Sheila."

"Yes."

"That was your brother."

I shook my head. I was about to protest further, but I held it back when I saw that she had more to say.

"Sheila never fit into this lifestyle. She was too ambitious. She and Ken found each other. He helped set her up at a fancy college in Connecticut, but that was more to sell drugs than anything else. Out here, you see guys slicing up each other's intestines for a spot

242

on a street corner. But a fancy rich-kid school, if you could move in and control that, you could score an easy mint."

"And you're saying that my brother set this up?"

She started rocking again. "Are you seriously telling me you didn't know?"

"Yes."

"I thought—" She stopped.

"What?"

She shook her head. "I don't know what I thought."

"Please," I said.

"It's just weird. First Sheila's with your brother. Now she pops up again with you. And you act like you don't know anything about it."

Again, I did not know how to respond. "So what happened to Sheila?"

"You'd know better than me."

"No, I mean back then. When she was up at this college."

"I never saw her after she left the life. I got a couple of calls, that's all. But those stopped too. But Ken was bad news. You and Squares, you seemed nice. Like maybe she found some good. But then when I heard your name . . ." She shrugged the thought away.

"Does the name Carly mean anything to you?" I asked.

"No. Should it?"

"Did you know that Sheila had a daughter?"

That got Tanya rocking again. Her voice was pained. "Oh God."

"You knew?"

She shook her head hard. "No."

I followed right up. "Do you know a Philip McGuane?"

Still shaking her head. "No."

"How about John Asselta? Or Julie Miller?"

"No," she said quickly. "I don't know any of these people." She stood now and spun away from me. "I had hoped she escaped," she said.

"She did," I said. "For a time."

I saw her shoulders slump. Her breathing seemed even more labored. "It should have ended better for her."

Tanya started toward the door then. I did not follow. I looked back to Louis Castman's room. Again I thought that there were two prisoners here. Tanya stopped. I could feel her eyes on me. I turned to her.

"There are surgeries," I said to her. "Squares knows people. We can help."

"No, thank you."

"You can't live on vengeance forever."

She tried a smile. "You think that's what this is about?" She pointed to her mutilated face. "You think I keep him here because of this?"

I was confused again.

Tanya shook her head. "He told you how he recruited Sheila?"

I nodded.

"He gives himself all the credit. He talks about his natty clothes and smooth lines. But most of the girls, even the ones fresh off the bus, they're afraid to go with a guy alone. So you see, what really made the difference was that Louis had a partner. A woman. To help close the sale. To lull the girls into feeling safe."

She waited. Her eyes were dry. A tremor began deep inside me and spread out. Tanya moved to the door. She opened it for me. I left and never went back.

43

There were two phone messages on my voice mail. The first was from Sheila's mother, Edna Rogers. Her tone was stiff and impersonal. The funeral would be in two days, she stated, at a chapel in Mason, Idaho. Mrs. Rogers gave me times and addresses and directions from Boise. I saved the message.

The second was from Yvonne Sterno. She said it was urgent that I call her right away. Her tone was one of barely restrained excitement. That made me uneasy. I wondered if she'd learned the true identity of Owen Enfield—and if she had, would that be a positive or negative thing?

Yvonne answered on the first ring.

"What's up?" I asked.

"Got something big here, Will."

"I'm listening."

"We should have realized it earlier."

"What's that?"

"Put the pieces together. A guy with a pseudonym. The FBI's strong interest. All the secrecy. A small community in a quiet area. You with me?"

"Not really, no."

"Cripco was the key," she went on. "As I said, it's a dummy corporation. So I checked with a few sources. Truth is, they don't try to hide them that hard. The cover isn't that deep. The way they figure it, if someone spots the guy, they know or they don't know. They aren't going to do a big background check."

"Yvonne?" I said.

"What?"

"I don't have a clue what you're talking about."

"Cripco, the company who leased the house and the car, traces back to the United States marshal's office."

Once again I felt my head teeter and spin. I let it go and a bright hope surfaced in the dark, murky blur. "Wait a second," I said. "Are you saying that Owen Enfield is an undercover agent?"

"No, I don't think so. I mean, what would he be investigating at Stonepointe—someone cheating at gin rummy?"

"What then?"

"The U.S. marshal—not the FBI—runs the witness protection program."

More confusion. "So you're saying that Owen Enfield . . . ?"

"That the government was hiding him here, yeah. They gave him a new identity. The key, like I said before, is that they don't take the background that deep. A lot of people don't know that. Hell, sometimes they're even dumb about it. My source at the paper was telling me about this black drug dealer from Baltimore who they stuck in a lily-white suburb outside Chicago. A total screwup. That wasn't the case here, but if, say, Gotti were searching for Sammy the Bull, they'd either recognize him or not. They wouldn't bother checking his background to make sure. You know what I mean?"

"I think so."

"So the way I figure it, this Owen Enfield was bad news. Most of the guys in witness protection are. So he's in the program and for some reason he murders these two guys and runs off. The FBI doesn't want that out. Think how embarrassing it would be—the government cuts a deal with a guy and then he goes on a murder spree? Bad press all the way around, you know what I mean?"

I didn't say anything.

"Will?"

"Yeah."

There was a pause. "You're holding out on me, aren't you?"

I thought about what to do.

"Come on," she said. "Back and forth, remember? I give, you give."

I don't know what I would have said—if I would have told her that my brother and Owen Enfield were one and the same, if I would have concluded that publicizing this was better than keeping it in the dark—but the decision was taken from me. I heard a click and then the phone went dead.

There was a sharp knock on the door.

"Federal officers. Open up now."

I recognized the voice. It belonged to Claudia Fisher. I reached for the knob, twisted it, and was nearly knocked over. Fisher burst in with a gun drawn. She told me to put my hands up. Her partner, Darryl Wilcox, was with her. They both looked pale, weary, and maybe even frightened.

"What the hell is this?" I said.

"Hands up now!"

I did as she asked. She took out her cuffs, and then, as though thinking better of it, she stopped. Her voice was suddenly soft. "You'll come without a hassle?" she asked.

I nodded.

"Then come on, let's go."

44

I did not argue. I did not call their bluff or demand a phone call or any of that. I did not even ask them where we were going. Such protestations at this delicate juncture would, I knew, be either superfluous or harmful.

Pistillo had warned me to stay away. He had gone so far as to have me arrested for a crime I did not commit. He'd promised to frame me if need be. And still I had not backed down. I wondered where I'd unearthed this newfound bravery and I realized that it was simply a matter of having nothing more to lose. Maybe that was what bravery always is—being past the point of giving a rat's ass. Sheila and my mother were dead. My brother had been lost to me. You corner a man, even one as weak as this one, and you see the animal emerge.

We pulled up to a row of houses in Fair Lawn, New Jersey. Everywhere I looked I saw the same thing: tidy lawns, overdone flower beds, rusted once-white furniture, hoses snaking through the grass attached to sprinklers that vacillated in a lazy haze. We approached a house no different from any other. Fisher tried the knob. It was unlocked. They led me through a room with a pink sofa and console TV. Photographs of two boys ran along the top of the console. The photos were in age order, starting with two infants. In the last one, the boys, both teenagers now, were formally dressed, each bussing a cheek of a woman I assumed was their mother.

The kitchen had a swing door. Pistillo sat at the Formica table with an iced tea. The woman in the photograph, the probable mother, stood by the sink. Fisher and Wilcox made themselves scarce. I stayed standing.

"You have my phone tapped," I said.

Pistillo shook his head. "A tap just tells you where a call originated. What we're using here are listening devices. And just so we're clear, they were court ordered."

"What do you want from me?" I asked him.

"The same thing I've wanted for eleven years," he said. "Your brother."

The woman at the sink turned on the faucet. She rinsed out a glass. More photos, some with the woman, some with Pistillo and other youngsters but again mostly the same two boys, had been hung on the refrigerator by magnets. These were more recent and casual shots—at the shore, in the yard, that kind of thing.

Pistillo said, "Maria?"

The woman shut off the water and turned toward him.

"Maria, this is Will Klein. Will, Maria."

The woman—I assumed that this was Pistillo's wife—dried her hands on a dish towel. Her grip was firm.

"Nice to meet you," she said a little too formally.

I mumbled and nodded, and when Pistillo signaled, I sat on a metal chair with vinyl padding.

"Would you like something to drink, Mr. Klein?" Maria asked me.

"No, thank you."

Pistillo raised his glass of iced tea. "Dynamite stuff. You should have a glass."

Maria kept hovering. I finally accepted the iced tea just so we could move on. She took her time pouring and putting the glass in front of me. I thanked her and tried a smile. She tried one back, but it flickered even weaker than mine.

She said, "I'll wait in the other room, Joe."

"Thanks, Maria."

She pushed through the swinging door.

"That's my sister," he said, still looking at the door she'd just gone through. He pointed to the snapshots on the refrigerator. "Those are her two boys. Vic Junior is eighteen now. Jack is sixteen."

"Uh-huh." I folded my hands and rested them on the table. "You've been listening in on my calls."

"Yes."

"Then you already know that I don't have a clue where my brother is."

He took a sip of the iced tea. "That I do." He was still staring at the refrigerator; he head-gestured for me to do likewise. "You notice anything missing from those pictures?"

"I'm really not in the mood for games, Pistillo."

"No, me neither. But take a longer look. What's missing?"

I did not bother to look because I already knew. "The father."

He snapped his fingers and pointed at me like a game show host. "Got it on the first try," he said. "Impressive."

"What the hell is this?"

"My sister lost her husband twelve years ago. The boys, well, you can do the math on your own. They were six and four. Maria raised them on her own. I pitched in where I could, but an uncle isn't a father, you know what I mean?"

I said nothing.

"His name was Victor Dober. That name mean anything to you?"

"No."

"Vic was murdered. Shot twice in the head execution-style." He drained his iced tea and then added, "Your brother was there."

My heart lurched inside my chest. Pistillo stood, not waiting for a reaction. "I know my bladder is going to regret this, Will, but I'm going to have another glass. You want anything while I'm up?"

I tried to work through the shock. "What do you mean, my brother was there?"

But Pistillo was taking his time now. He opened the freezer, took out an ice tray, broke it open in the sink. The cubes clattered against the ceramic. He fished some out with his hand and filled his glass. "Before we begin, I want you to make a promise."

"What?"

"It involves Katy Miller."

"What about her?"

"She's just a kid."

"I know that."

"This is a dangerous situation. You don't have to be a genius to figure that out. I don't want her getting hurt again."

"Neither do I."

"So we agree then," he said. "Promise me, Will. Promise me you won't involve her anymore."

I looked at him and I knew that point was not negotiable. "Okay," I said. "She's out."

He checked my face, looking for the lie, but on this point he was right. Katy had already paid a huge price. I'm not sure I could stand it if she was forced to pay a higher one.

"Tell me about my brother," I said.

He finished pouring the iced tea and settled back into his chair. He looked at the table and then raised his eyes. "You read in the paper about the big busts," Pistillo began. "You read about how the Fulton Fish Market's been cleaned up. You see the parade of old men doing the perp walk on the news, and you think, those days are over. The mob is gone. The cops have won."

He finished pouring the iced tea and sat back down. My own throat suddenly felt parched, sandy, as if it might close up altogether. I took a deep sip from my glass. The tea was too sweet.

"Do you know anything about Darwin?" he asked.

I thought the question was rhetorical, but he waited for an answer. I said, "Survival of the strongest, all that."

"Not the strongest," he said. "That's the modern interpretation, and it's wrong. The key for Darwin was not that the strongest survive—the most adaptable do. See the difference?"

I nodded.

"So the smarter bad guys, they adapted. They moved their business out of Manhattan. They sold drugs, for example, in the less competitive burbs. For your basic corruption, they started feeding on the Jersey cities. Camden, for example. Three of the last five mayors have been convicted of crimes. Atlantic City, I mean, c'mon, you don't cross the street without graft. Newark and all that revitalization bullshit. Revitalization means money. Money means kickbacks and graft."

I shifted in my chair. "Is there a point to this, Pistillo?"

"Yeah, asshole, there's a big point." His face reddened. His features remained steady, though not without great effort. "My brother-in-law—the father of those boys—tried to clean the streets of these scumbags. He worked undercover. Someone found out. And he and his partner ended up dead."

"And you think my brother was involved in that?"

"Yeah. Yeah, I do."

"You have proof?"

"Better than that." Pistillo smiled. "Your brother confessed."

251

I leaned back as if he'd taken a swing at me. I shook my head. Calm down. He would say and do anything, I reminded myself. Hadn't he been willing to frame me just last night?

"But we're getting ahead of ourselves, Will. And I don't want you to get the wrong idea. We don't think your brother killed anyone."

Another whiplash. "But you just said—"

He held up a hand. "Hear me out, okay?"

Pistillo rose again. He needed time. I could see that. His face was surprisingly matter-of-fact, composed even, but that was because he was jamming the rage back in the closet. I wondered if that closet door would hold. I wondered how often, when he looked at his sister, that door gave way and the rage was let loose.

"Your brother worked for Philip McGuane. I assume you know who he is."

I was giving him nothing. "Go on."

"McGuane is more dangerous than your pal Asselta, mostly because he's smarter. The OCID considers him one of the top guns on the East Coast."

"OCID?"

"Organized Crime Investigation Division," he said. "At a young age, McGuane saw the writing on the wall. Talk about adapting, this guy is the ultimate survivor. I won't go into detail about the current state of organized crime—the new Russians, the Triad, the Chinese, the old-world Italians. McGuane stayed two steps ahead of the competition. He was a boss by the time he was twenty-three. He works all the classics—drugs, prostitution, loan-sharking—but he specializes in graft and kickbacks and setting up his drug trade in less competitive spots away from the city."

I thought about what Tanya had said, about Sheila selling up at Haverton College.

"McGuane killed my brother-in-law and his partner, a guy named Curtis Angler. Your brother was involved. We arrested him but on lesser charges."

"When?"

"Six months before Julie Miller was murdered."

"How come I never heard anything about it?"

"Because Ken didn't tell you. And because we didn't want your brother. We wanted McGuane. So we flipped him."

"Flipped him?"

"We gave Ken immunity in exchange for his cooperation."

"You wanted him to testify against McGuane?"

"More than that. McGuane was careful. We didn't have enough to nail him on the murder indictment. We needed an informant. So we wired him up and sent him back in."

"You're saying that Ken worked undercover for you?"

Something flashed hard in Pistillo's eyes. "Don't glamorize it," he snapped. "Your low-life brother wasn't a law enforcement officer. He was just a scumbag trying to save his own skin."

I nodded, reminding myself yet again that this could all be a lie. "Go on," I said again.

He reached back and grabbed a cookie from the counter. He chewed slowly and washed it down with the iced tea. "We don't know what happened exactly. I can only give you our working theory."

"Okay."

"McGuane found out. You have to understand. McGuane is a brutal son of a bitch. Killing someone is always an option for him, you know, like deciding to take the Lincoln or Holland Tunnel. A matter of convenience, nothing more. He feels nothing."

I saw now where he was heading with this. "So if McGuane knew that Ken had become an informant—"

"Dead meat," he finished for me. "Your brother understood the risk. We were keeping tabs, but one night he just ran off."

"Because McGuane found out?"

"That's what we think, yes. He ended up at your house. We don't know why. Our theory is that he thought it was a safe place to hide, mostly because McGuane would never suspect he'd put his family in danger."

"And then?"

"By now you must have guessed that Asselta was working for McGuane too."

"If you say so," I said.

He ignored that. "Asselta had a lot to lose here too. You mentioned Laura Emerson, the other sorority sister who was killed. Your brother told us that Asselta murdered her. She was strangled, which is Asselta's favorite method of execution. According to Ken, Laura Emerson had found out about the drug trade at Haverton and was set to report it."

I made a face. "And they killed her for that?"

"Yeah, they killed her for that. What do you think they'd do, buy

253

her an ice cream? These are monsters, Will. Get that through your thick head."

I remembered Phil McGuane coming over and playing Risk. He always won. He was quiet and observant, the sort of kid who makes you wonder about still waters and all that. He was class president, I think. I was impressed by him. The Ghost had been openly psychotic. I could see him doing anything. But McGuane?

"Somehow they learned where your brother was hiding. Maybe the Ghost followed Julie home from college, we don't know. Either way, he catches up to your brother at the Miller house. Our theory is that he tried to kill them both. You said you saw someone that night. We believe you. We also believe that the man you saw was probably Asselta. His fingerprints were found at the scene. Ken was wounded in the assault—that explains the blood—but somehow he got away. The Ghost was left with the body of Julie Miller. So what would be the natural thing to do? Make it look like Ken did it. What better way to discredit him or even scare him away?"

He stopped and started nibbling on another cookie. He would not look at me. I knew that he could be lying, but his words had the ring of truth. I tried to calm myself, let what he was telling me sink in. I kept my eyes on him. He kept his gaze on the cookie. Now it was my turn to fight back the rage.

"So all this time"—I stopped, swallowed, tried again—"so all this time, you knew that Ken didn't kill Julie."

"No, not at all."

"But you just said—"

"A theory, Will. It was just a theory. It's just as likely that he killed her."

"You don't believe that."

"Don't tell me what I believe."

"What could possibly be Ken's motive for killing Julie?"

"Your brother was a bad guy. Make no mistake about that."

"That's not a motive." I shook my head. "Why? If you knew Ken probably didn't kill her, why did you always insist he had?"

He chose not to reply. But maybe he didn't have to. The answer was suddenly obvious. I glanced at the snapshots on the refrigerator. They explained so much.

"Because you wanted Ken back at any cost," I said, answering my own question. "Ken was the only one who could give you McGuane. If he was hiding as a material witness, the world wouldn't really care. There would be no press coverage. There would be no major manhunt. But if Ken murdered a young woman in her family basement—the story of suburbia gone wrong—the media attention would be massive. And those headlines, you figured, would make it harder for him to hide."

He kept studying his hands.

"I'm right, aren't I?"

Pistillo slowly looked at me. "Your brother made a deal with us," he said coldly. "When he ran, he broke that deal."

"So that made it okay to lie?"

"It made it okay to track him down by any means necessary."

I was actually shaking. "And his family be damned?"

"Don't put that on me."

"Do you know what you did to us?"

"You know something, Will? I don't give a damn. You think you suffered? Look in my sister's eyes. Look at her sons'."

"That doesn't make it right—"

He slammed his hand on the table. "Don't tell me about right and wrong. My sister was an innocent victim."

"So was my mother."

"No!" He pounded the table, this time with his fist, and pointed a finger at me. "There's a big difference between them, so get it straight. Vic was a murdered cop. He didn't have a choice. He couldn't stop his family's suffering. Your brother, on the other hand, chose to run. That was his decision. If that somehow hurt your family, blame him."

"But you made him run," I said. "Someone was trying to kill him—and you top that off by making him think he'll be arrested for murder. You forced his hand. You pushed him farther underground."

"That was his doing, not mine."

"You wanted to help your family, and in the process you sacrificed mine."

Pistillo snapped then, knocking the glass across the table. The iced tea splashed on me. The glass fell to the floor and shattered. He rose and looked down at me. "Don't you dare compare what your family went through with what my sister went through. Don't you dare."

I met his eye. Arguing with him would be useless—and I still did not know if he was telling the truth or twisting it for his own purposes. Either way, I wanted to learn more. Antagonizing him would do me no good. There was more to this story. He was not done yet. There was still too much unanswered.

The door opened. Claudia Fisher leaned her head in to check on the commotion. Pistillo put up a hand to tell her it was fine. He settled back into his chair. Fisher waited a beat and then left us alone.

Pistillo was still breathing heavily.

"So what happened next?" I asked him.

He looked up. "You haven't guessed?"

"No."

"It was a stroke of luck actually. One of our agents was vacationing in Stockholm. A fluke thing."

"What are you talking about?"

"Our agent," he said. "He spotted your brother on the street."

I blinked. "Wait a second. When was this?"

Pistillo did a quick calculation in his head. "Four months ago."

I was still confused. "And Ken got away?"

"Hell no. The agent didn't take any chances. He tackled your brother right then and there."

Pistillo folded his hands and leaned toward me. "We caught him," he said, his voice barely a whisper. "We caught your brother and brought him back."

45

Philip McGuane poured the brandy.

The body of the young lawyer Cromwell was gone now. Joshua Ford lay out like a bear rug. He was alive and even conscious, but he was not moving.

McGuane handed the Ghost a snifter. The two men sat together. McGuane took a deep sip. The Ghost cupped his glass and smiled.

"What?" McGuane asked.

"Fine brandy."

"Yes."

The Ghost stared at the liquor. "I was just remembering how we used to hang out in the woods behind Riker Hill and drink the cheapest beer we could find. Do you remember that, Philip?"

"Schlitz and Old Milwaukee," McGuane said.

"Yeah."

"Ken had that friend at Economy Wine and Liquor. He never ID'ed him."

"Good times," the Ghost said.

"This"—McGuane raised his glass—"is better."

"You think so?" The Ghost took a sip. He closed his eyes and swallowed. "Are you familiar with the philosophy that every choice you make splits the world into alternate universes?"

"I am."

"I often wonder if there are ones where we turn out differently—or, conversely, were we destined to be here no matter what?"

McGuane smirked. "You're not growing soft on me, are you, John?

"Not likely," the Ghost said. "But in moments of candor, I cannot help but wonder if it had to be this way."

"You like hurting people, John."

"I do."

"You've always enjoyed it."

The Ghost thought about that. "No, not always. But of course, the larger question is why?"

"Why do you like hurting people?"

"Not just hurting them. I enjoy killing them painfully. I choose strangulation because it is a horrible way to die. No quick bullet. No sudden knife slash. You literally gasp for your last breath. You feel the life-nourishing oxygen being denied you. I do that to them, up close, watching them struggle for a breath that never comes."

"My, my." McGuane put down his snifter. "You must be a barrel of laughs at parties, John."

"Oh indeed," he agreed. Then growing serious again, the Ghost said, "But why, Philip, do I get a rush from that? What happened to me, to my moral compass, that I feel my most alive while snuffing out someone's breath?"

"You're not going to blame your daddy, are you, John?"

"No, that would be too pat." He put down his drink and faced McGuane. "Would you have killed me, Philip? If I hadn't taken out the two men at the cemetery, would you have killed me?"

McGuane opted for the truth. "I don't know," he said. "Probably."

"And you're my best friend," the Ghost said.

"You're probably mine."

The Ghost smiled. "We were something, weren't we, Philip?"

McGuane did not reply.

"I met Ken when I was four," the Ghost continued. "All the kids in the neighborhood were warned to stay away from our house. The Asseltas were a bad influence—that's what they were told. You know the deal."

"I do," McGuane said.

"But for Ken, that was a draw. He used to love to explore our house. I remember when we found my old man's gun. We were six, I think. I remember holding it. The feeling of power. It mesmerized us. We used the gun to terrify Richard Werner—I don't think you know him, he moved away in the third grade. We kidnapped him once and tied him up. He cried and wet his pants."

"And you loved it."

The Ghost nodded slowly. "Perhaps."

"I have a question," McGuane said.

"I'm listening."

"If your father owned a gun, why use a kitchen knife on Daniel Skinner?"

The Ghost shook his head. "I don't want to talk about that."

"You never have."

"That's right."

"Why?"

He did not answer the question directly. "My old man found out about us playing with the gun," he said. "He beat me pretty good."

"He did that a lot."

"Yes."

"Have you ever sought revenge on him?" McGuane asked.

"On my father? No. He was too pitiful to hate. He never got over my mother walking out on us. He always thought she'd come back. He used to prepare for it. When he drank, he'd sit alone on the couch and talk to her and laugh with her and then he'd start sobbing. She broke his heart. I've hurt men, Philip. I've seen men beg to die. But I don't think I ever heard anything as pitiful as my father sobbing for my mother."

From the floor, Joshua Ford made a low groan. They both ignored him.

"Where is your father now?" McGuane asked.

"Cheyenne, Wyoming. He dried out. He found a good woman. He's a religious nut now. Traded alcohol for God—one addiction for another."

"You ever talk to him?

The Ghost's voice was soft. "No."

They drank in silence.

"What about you, Philip? You weren't poor. Your parents weren't abusive."

"Just parents," McGuane agreed.

"I know your uncle was mobbed up. He got you into the business. But you could have gone straight. Why didn't you?"

259

McGuane chuckled.

"What?"

"We're more different than I thought."

"How's that?"

"You regret it," McGuane said. "You do it, you get a thrill from it, you're good at it. But you see yourself as evil." He sat up suddenly. "My God."

"What?"

"You're more dangerous than I thought, John."

"How so?"

"You're not back for Ken," McGuane said. And then, his voice dropping: "You're back for that little girl, aren't you?"

The Ghost took a deep sip. He chose not to answer.

"Those choices and alternate universes you were talking about," McGuane went on. "You think if Ken died that night, it would all be different."

"It would indeed be an alternate universe," the Ghost said.

"But maybe not a better one," McGuane countered. Then he added, "So what now?"

"We'll need Will's cooperation. He's the only one who can draw Ken out."

"He won't help."

The Ghost frowned. "You, of all people, know better."

"His father?" McGuane asked.

"No."

"His sister?"

"She's too far away," the Ghost said.

"But you have an idea?"

"Think," the Ghost said.

McGuane did. And when he saw it, his face broke into a smile. "Katy Miller."

46

Pistillo kept his eyes on me, waiting for my reaction to his bombshell. But I recovered fast. Maybe this was beginning to make sense.

"You captured my brother?"

"Yes."

"And you extradited him back to the United States?"

"Yes."

"So how come it wasn't in the papers?" I asked.

"We kept it under wraps," Pistillo said.

"Because you were afraid McGuane would find out?"

"For the most part."

"What else?"

He shook his head.

"You still wanted McGuane," I said.

"Yes."

"And my brother could still deliver."

"He could help."

"So you cut another deal with him."

"We pretty much reinstated the old one."

I saw a clearing in the haze. "And you put him in the witness protection program?"

Pistillo nodded. "Originally we kept him in a hotel under protective custody. But by then a lot of what your brother had was old.

He would still be a key witness—probably the most important we'd have—but we needed more time. We couldn't keep him in a hotel forever, and he didn't want to stay. Ken hired a big-time lawyer, and we worked out a deal. We found him a place in New Mexico. He had to report to one of our agents on a daily basis. We would call him to testify when we needed him. Any break in that deal, and the charges, including the murder charge from Julie Miller, could be reinstated."

"So what went wrong?"

"McGuane found out about it."

"How?"

"We don't know. A leak maybe. Whatever, McGuane sent out two goons to kill your brother."

"The two dead men at the house," I said.

"Yes."

"Who killed them?"

"We think your brother. They underestimated him. He killed them and ran again."

"And now you want Ken back again."

His gaze wandered over to the photographs on the refrigerator door. "Yes."

"But I don't know where he is."

"I know that now. Look, maybe we screwed up here. I don't know. But Ken needs to come in. We'll protect him, around-the-clock surveillance, a safe house, whatever he wants. That's the carrot. The stick is that his prison sentence is subject to his cooperation."

"So what do you want from me?"

"He'll reach out to you eventually."

"What makes you so sure?"

He sighed and stared at the glass.

"What makes you so sure?" I asked again.

"Because," Pistillo said, "Ken called you already."

A block of lead formed in my chest.

"There were two calls placed from a pay phone near your brother's house in Albuquerque to your apartment," he went on. "One was made about a week before the two goons were killed. The other, right after."

I should have been shocked, but I wasn't. Maybe it finally fit, only I didn't like how.

262

"You didn't know about the calls, did you, Will?"

I swallowed and thought about who, besides me, might answer the phone if Ken had indeed called.

Sheila.

"No," I said. "I didn't know about them."

He nodded. "We didn't know that when we first approached you. It was natural to figure you were the one who answered the phone."

I looked at him. "How does Sheila Rogers fit into this?"

"Her fingerprints were found at the murder scene."

"I know that."

"So let me ask you, Will. We knew your brother had called you. We knew your girlfriend had visited Ken's house in New Mexico. If you were us, what would you have concluded?"

"That I was somehow involved."

"Right. We figured that Sheila was your go-between or something, that you'd been helping your brother out. And when Ken ran off, we figured you two knew where he was."

"But now you know better."

"That's correct."

"So what do you suspect now?"

"The same thing you do, Will." His voice was soft, and—damn him—I heard pity in it. "That Sheila Rogers used you. That she worked for McGuane. That she's the one who tipped him off about your brother. And that when the hit went wrong, McGuane had her killed."

Sheila. Her betrayal pierced me deep, struck bone. To defend her now, to think I had been anything more to her than a dupe, would be to turn a blind eye in the worst way. You would have to be naïve beyond Pollyanna, to have rose-tinted glasses melded onto your face, to not be able to see the truth.

"I'm telling you all this, Will, because I was afraid you were about to do something stupid."

"Like talk to the press," I said.

"Yes—and because I want you to understand. Your brother had two choices. Either McGuane and the Ghost find him and kill him, or we find him and protect him."

"Right," I said. "And you guys have done a bang-up job of that so far."

"We're still his best option," he countered. "And don't think

263

McGuane will stop with your brother. Do you really think that attack on Katy Miller was a coincidence? For all your sakes, we need your cooperation."

I said nothing. I could not trust him. I knew that. I could not trust anyone. That was all I had learned here. But Pistillo was especially dangerous. He had spent eleven years looking into his sister's shattered face. That kind of thing twists you. I knew about stuff like that, about wanting to the point of distortion. Pistillo had made it clear that he would stop at nothing to get McGuane. He would sacrifice my brother. He had jailed me. And most of all, he had destroyed my family. I thought about my sister running off to Seattle. I thought about my mom, the Sunny smile, and realized that the man sitting in front of me, this man who claimed to be my brother's salvation, had smothered it away. He had killed my mother—no one could convince me that the cancer was not somehow connected to what she went through, that her immune system had not been another victim of that horrible night—and now he wanted me to help him.

I did not know how much of this was a lie. But I decided to lie right back. "I'll help," I said.

"Good," he said. "I'll make sure the charges against you are dropped right away."

I did not say thank you.

"We'll drive you back if you'd like."

I wanted to refuse, but I did not want to raise any warning flags. He wanted to deceive, well, I could try that too. So I said that would be fine. When I rose, he said, "I understand that Sheila's funeral is coming up."

"Yes."

"Now that there are no charges against you, you're free to travel."

I said nothing.

"Are you going to attend?" he asked.

This time I told the truth. "I don't know."

47

I couldn't stay at home waiting for I-don't-know-what, so in the morning, I went to work. It was a funny thing. I expected to be fairly worthless, but that wasn't the case at all. Entering Covenant House—I can only compare the experience to an athlete strapping on his "game face" when he enters the arena. These kids, I reminded myself, deserve nothing less than my best. Cliché, sure, but I convinced myself and faded contently into my work.

Sure, people came up to me and offered their condolences. And yes, Sheila's spirit was everywhere. There were few spots in this dwelling that did not hold a memory of her. But I was able to play through it. This is not to say I forgot about it or no longer wanted to pursue where my brother was or who killed Sheila or the fate of her daughter, Carly. That was all still there. But today there was not much I could do. I had called Katy's hospital room, but the blockade was still in place. Squares had a detective agency running Sheila's Donna White pseudonym through the airline computers and thus far, they had not gotten a hit. So I waited.

I volunteered to work the outreach van that night. Squares joined me—I had already filled him in on everything—and together we disappeared into the dark. The children of the street were lit up in the blue of the night. Their faces were flat, no lines, sleek. You see an adult vagrant, a bag lady, a man with a shopping cart, someone lying in a box, someone begging for change with a diner paper coffee cup, and you know that they are homeless. But the thing about adolescents, about the fifteen- and sixteen-year-olds who run away from abuse, who embrace addiction or prostitution or insanity, is that they blend in better. With adolescents you cannot tell if they are homeless or just wandering.

Despite what you hear, it is not that easy to ignore the plight of the adult homeless. It is too in-your-face. You may divert your eyes and keep walking and remind yourself that if you gave in, if you tossed them a dollar or some quarters, they'd just buy booze or drugs or whatever rationale sails your boat, but what you did, the fact that you just hurried by a human being in need, still registers, still causes a pang. Our kids, however, are truly invisible. They are seamlessly sewn into the night. You can neglect and there are no aftereffects.

Music blared, something with a heavy Latin beat. Squares handed me a stack of phone cards to hand out. We hit a dive on Avenue A known for its heroin and started our familiar rap. We talked and cajoled and listened. I saw the gaunt eyes. I saw the way they scratched away at the imaginary bugs under their skin. I saw the needle marks and the sunken veins.

At four in the morning, Squares and I were back in the van. We had not spoken to each other much in the last few hours. He looked out the window. The children were still out there. More seemed to come out as though the bricks bled them.

"We should go to the funeral," Squares said.

I did not trust my voice.

"You ever see her out here?" he asked. "Her face when she worked with these kids?"

I had. And I knew what he meant.

"You don't fake that, Will."

"I wish I could believe that," I said.

"How did Sheila make you feel?"

"Like I was the luckiest man in the world," I said.

He nodded. "You don't fake that either," he said.

"So how do you explain it all?"

"I don't." Squares shifted into drive and pulled into the street. "But we're doing so much with our heads. Maybe we just need to remember the heart too."

I frowned. "That sounds good, Squares, but I'm not sure it makes any sense."

"How about this then: We go to pay our respects to the Sheila we knew."

"Even if that was just a lie?"

"Even if. But maybe we also go to learn. To understand what happened here."

"Weren't you the one who said we might not like what we find?"

"Hey, that's right." Squares wriggled his eyebrows. "Damn, I'm good."

I smiled.

"We owe it to her, Will. To her memory."

He had a point. It came back to closure. I needed answers. Maybe someone at the funeral could supply some—and maybe the funeral in and of itself, the act of burying my faux beloved, would help the healing process. I couldn't imagine it, but I was willing to give anything a shot.

"And there's still Carly to consider." Squares pointed out the window. "Saving kids. That's what we're all about, isn't it?"

I turned to him. "Yeah," I said. And then: "And speaking of children."

I waited. I could not see his eyes—he often, like the old Corey Hart song, wore his sunglasses at night—but his grip on the steering wheel tightened.

"Squares?"

His tone was clipped. "We're talking about you and Sheila here."

"That's the past. Whatever we learn, it won't change that."

"Let's concentrate on one thing at a time, okay?"

"Not okay," I said. "This friendship thing. It's supposed to be a two-way street."

He shook his head. He started the van and drove. We fell into silence. I kept my eyes on his pockmarked, unshaven face. The tattoo seemed to darken. He was biting his lower lip.

After some time he said, "I never told Wanda."

"About having a child?"

"A son," Squares said softly.

"Where is he now?"

He took one hand off the wheel and scratched at something on his face. The hand, I noticed, had a quake to it. "He was six feet under before he was four years old."

I closed my eyes.

"His name was Michael. I wanted nothing to do with him. I only saw him twice. I left him alone with his mother, a seventeen-year-old drug addict you wouldn't trust to watch a dog. When he was three years old, she got stoned and drove straight into a semi. Killed them both. I still don't know if it was suicide or not."

"I'm so sorry," I said weakly.

"Michael would be twenty-one now."

I fumbled for something to say. Nothing was working, but I tried anyway. "That was a long time ago," I said. "You were just a kid."

"Don't try to rationalize, Will."

"I'm not. I just mean"—I had no idea how to put it—"if I had a child, I'd ask you to be the godfather. I'd make you the guardian if anything happened to me. I wouldn't do that out of friendship or loyalty. I'd do that to be selfish. For the sake of my kid."

He kept driving. "There are some things you can never forgive."

"You didn't kill him, Squares."

"Sure, right, I'm totally blameless."

We hit a red light. He flipped on the radio. Talk station. One of those radio infomercials selling a miracle diet drug. He snapped it off. He leaned forward and rested his forearms on the top of the steering wheel.

"I see the kids out here. I try to rescue them. I keep thinking that if I save enough, I don't know, maybe it will change things for Michael. Maybe I can somehow save him." The sunglasses came off. His voice grew harder. "But what I know is—what I've always known—is that no matter what I do, I'm not worth saving."

I shook my head. I tried to think of something comforting or enlightening or at least distracting, but nothing broke through the filter. Every line I came up with sounded hackneyed and canned. Like most tragedies, it explained so much and yet told you nothing about the man.

In the end, all I said was "You're wrong."

He put the sunglasses back on and faced the road. I could see him shutting down.

I decided to push it. "You talk about going to this funeral because we owe Sheila something. But what about Wanda?"

"Will?"

"Yeah."

"I don't think I want to talk about this anymore."

48

The early morning flight to Boise was uneventful. We took off from LaGuardia, which could be a lousier airport but not without a serious act of God. I got my customary seat in economy class, the one behind a tiny old lady who insists on reclining her seat against my knees for the duration of the flight. Studying her gray follicles and pallid scalp—her head was practically in my lap—helped distract me.

Squares sat on my right. He was reading an article on himself in *Yoga Journal*. Every once in a while he would nod at something he read about himself and say, "True, too true, I am that." He did that to annoy me. That was why he was my best friend.

I was able to keep the block up until we saw the WELCOME TO MASON, IDAHO sign. Squares had rented a Buick Skylark. We got lost twice on the trip. Even here, out in the supposed sticks, the strip malls dominated. There were all the customary mega-stores—the Chef Central, the Home Depot, the Old Navy—the country uniting in bloated monotony.

The chapel was small and white and totally unspectacular. I spotted Edna Rogers. She stood outside by herself, smoking a cigarette. Squares pulled to a stop. I felt my stomach tighten. I stepped out of the car. The grass was burnt brown. Edna Rogers looked our way. With her eyes still on me, she let loose a long breath of smoke.

I started toward her. Squares stayed by my side. I felt hollow, far away. Sheila's funeral. We were here to bury Sheila. The thought spun like the horizontal on an old TV set.

Edna Rogers kept puffing on the cigarette, her eyes hard and dry. "I didn't know if you'd make it," she said to me.

"I'm here."

"Have you learned anything about Carly?"

"No," I said, which was not really true. "How about you?"

She shook her head. "The police aren't looking too hard. They say there is no record of Sheila having a child. I don't even think they believe she exists."

The rest was a fast-forward blur. Squares interrupted and offered his condolences. Other mourners approached. They were mostly men in business suits. Listening in, I realized that most worked with Sheila's father at a plant that made garage-door openers. That struck me as odd, but at the time I didn't know why. I shook more hands and forgot every name. Sheila's father was a tall, handsome man. He greeted me with a bear hug and moved toward his co-workers. Sheila had a brother and a sister, both younger, both surly and distracted.

We all stayed outside, almost as though we were afraid to begin the ceremony. People broke down into groups. The younger folks stayed with Sheila's brother and sister. Sheila's father stood in a semi-circle with the suited men, all nodding, with fat ties and hands in their pockets. The women clustered nearest the door.

Squares drew stares, but he was used to that. He still had on the dust-ridden jeans, but he also wore a blue blazer and gray tie. He would have worn a suit, he said with a smile, but then Sheila would have never recognized him.

Eventually the mourners started to filter into the small chapel. I was surprised by the large turnout, but everyone I'd met was there for the family, not Sheila. She had left them a long time ago. Edna Rogers slid next to me and put her arm through mine. She looked up and forced a brave smile. I still did not know what to make of her.

We entered the chapel last. There were whispers about how "good" Sheila looked, how "lifelike," a comment I always found creepy in the extreme. I am not a religious fellow, but I like the way we of the Hebrew faith handle our dead—that is, we get them in the ground fast. We do not have open caskets.

I don't like open caskets.

I don't like them for all the obvious reasons. Looking at a dead body, one that has been drained of both life force and fluids, embalmed, dressed nicely, painted up, looking either like something from Madame Tussaud's wax museum or worse, so "lifelike" you almost expect it to breathe or suddenly sit up, yeah, you bet that gives me the creeps. But more than that, what kind of lasting image did a corpse laid out like a lox leave on the bereaved? Did I want my final memory of Sheila to be here, lying with her eyes closed in a well-cushioned—why were caskets always so well-cushioned?—hermetically sealed box of fine mahogany? As I got on at the end of the line with Edna Rogers—we actually stood on line to view this hollow vessel—these thoughts became heavy, weighing me down.

But there was no way out either. Edna gripped my arm a little too tightly. As we got closer, her knees buckled. I helped her stay upright. She smiled at me again, and this time, there seemed to be genuine sweetness in it.

"I loved her," she whispered. "A mother never stops loving her child."

I nodded, afraid to speak. We took another step, the process not so different from boarding that damn airplane. I almost expected a voice-over to say "Mourners in rows twenty-five and higher may now view the body." Stupid thought, but I let my mind dodge and veer. Anything to get away from this.

Squares stood behind us, last in line. I kept my eyes diverted, but as we moved forward, there was that unreasonable hope again knocking at my chest. I don't think this is unusual. It happened even at my mother's funeral, the idea that it was all somehow a mistake, a cosmic blunder, that I would look down at the casket and it would be empty or it wouldn't be Sheila. Maybe that was why some people liked open caskets. Finality. You see, you accept. I was with my mother when she died. I watched her last breath. Yet I was still tempted to check the casket that day, just to make sure, just in case maybe God changed his mind.

Many bereaved, I think, go through something like that. Denial is part of the process. So you hope against hope. I was doing that now. I was making deals with an entity I don't really believe in, praying for a miracle—that somehow the fingerprints and the FBI and Mr. and Mrs. Rogers's ID and all these friends and family members, that somehow they were all wrong, that Sheila was alive, that she had not been murdered and dumped on the side of the road.

271

But that, of course, did not happen.

Not exactly anyway.

When Edna Rogers and I arrived at the casket, I made myself look down. And when I did, the floor beneath me fell away. I started plummeting.

"They did a nice job, don't you think?" Mrs. Rogers whispered.

She gripped my arm and started to cry. But that was somewhere else, somewhere far away. I was not with her. I was looking down. And that was when the truth dawned on me.

Sheila Rogers was indeed dead. No doubt about that.

But the woman I loved, the woman I'd lived with and held and wanted to marry, was not Sheila Rogers.

49

I did not black out, but I came close.

The room did indeed spin. My vision did one of those in-and-out, closer-and-farther things. I stumbled toward, almost landing in the casket with Sheila Rogers—a woman I had never seen before but knew too intimately. A hand shot out and gripped my forearm. Squares. I looked at him. His face was set. His color gone. Our eyes met and he gave me the slightest of nods.

It hadn't been my imagination or a mirage. Squares had seen it too.

We stayed for the funeral. What else really could we do? I sat there, unable to take my eyes off the stranger's corpse, unable to speak. I was overcome, my body quaking, but nobody paid any attention. I was, after all, at a funeral.

After the casket was lowered into the ground, Edna Rogers wanted us to come back to the house. We begged off, blaming the airlines for the tight flight schedule. We slipped into the rental car. Squares started it up. We waited until we were out of sight. Then Squares pulled over and let me lose it.

"Let me see if we're on the same page here," Squares said.

I nodded, quasi-composed now. Again I had to block, this time muffling the possible euphoria. I did not keep my eye on the prize or the big picture or any of that. I concentrated on the details, on the minutiae. I focused on one tree because there was no way I could handle seeing the whole forest.

"All that stuff we learned about Sheila," he said, "her running away, her years on the streets, her selling drugs, her rooming with your old girlfriend, her fingerprints at your brother's place—all that—"

"Applied to that stranger we just buried," I finished for him.

"So our Sheila, I mean, the lady we both thought of as Sheila—"

"Did none of those things. And she was none of those things."

Squares considered that. "Styling," he said.

I managed a smile. "Most definitely."

On the airplane, Squares said, "If our Sheila is not dead, then she's alive."

I looked at him.

"Hey," he said, "people pay big bucks to soak in this kind of wisdom."

"And to think I get it for free."

"So what do we do now?"

I crossed my arms. "Donna White."

"The pseudonym she bought from the Goldbergs?"

"Right. Your people only ran an airline check?"

He nodded. "We were trying to figure out how she got out west."

"Can you get the agency to widen their search now?"

"Sure, I guess."

The flight attendant gave us our "snack." My brain kept whirring. This flight was doing me a ton of good. It gave me time to think. Unfortunately, it was also giving me time to shift realities, to see the repercussions. I fought that off. I didn't want hope clouding my thinking. Not yet. Not when I still knew so little. But still.

"It explains a lot," I said.

"Like?"

"Her secrecy. Her not wanting her picture taken. Her having so few possessions. Her not wanting to talk about her past."

Squares nodded.

"One time, Sheila"—I stopped because that was probably not

274

her name—"she slipped and mentioned growing up on a farm. But the real Sheila Rogers's father worked for a company that made garage-door openers. She was also terrified at the very idea of calling her parents—because, put simply, they weren't her parents. I took it all to mean a terribly abusive past."

"But it could just have easily have been someone in hiding."

"Right."

"So the real Sheila Rogers," Squares went on, his eyes looking up, "I mean, the one we just buried back there, she dated your brother?"

"So it seems."

"And her fingerprints were at the murder scene."

"Right."

"And your Sheila?"

I shrugged.

"Okay," Squares said, "So we assume the woman with Ken in New Mexico, the one the neighbors saw, that was the dead Sheila Rogers?"

"Yes."

"And they had a little girl with them," he went on.

Silence.

Squares looked at me. "Are you thinking the same thing I am?"

I nodded. "That the little girl was Carly. And that Ken might very well be her father."

"Yeah."

I sat back and closed my eyes. Squares opened his snack, checked the contents, cursed them.

"Will?"

"Yeah."

"The woman you loved. Any idea who she is?"

With my eyes still closed, I said, "None."

50

Squares went home. He promised to call me the moment they got anything on the Donna White pseudonym. I headed home, bleeding exhaustion. When I reached my apartment door, I put the key in the lock. A hand touched down on my shoulder. I jumped back, startled.

"It's okay," she said.

Katy Miller.

Her voice was hoarse. She wore a neck brace. Her face was swollen. Her eyes were bloodshot. Where the brace stopped under the chin, I could see the deep purple and yellow of bruising.

"Are you okay?" I asked.

She nodded.

I hugged her gingerly, too gingerly, using just my arms, keeping my distance for fear of hurting her further.

"I won't break," she said.

"When did you get out?" I asked.

"A few hours ago. I can't stay long. If my father knew where I was—"

I held up a hand. "Say no more."

We pushed open the door and stepped inside. She grimaced in pain as she moved. We made our way to the couch. I asked her if she wanted a drink or something to eat. She said no.

"Are you sure you should be out of the hospital?"

"They said it's okay, but I need to rest."

"How did you get away from your father?"

She tried a smile. "I'm headstrong."

"I see."

"And I lied."

"No doubt."

She looked off with just her eyes—she could not move her head—and her eyes welled up. "Thank you, Will."

I shook my head. "I can't help but feel it was my fault."

"That's crap," she said.

I shifted in my seat. "During the attack, you yelled out the name John. At least, I think that's what you said."

"The police told me."

"You don't remember?"

She shook her head.

"What do you remember?"

"The hands on my throat." She looked off. "I was sleeping. And then someone was squeezing my neck. I remember gasping for air." Her voice fell away.

"Do you know who John Asselta is?" I asked.

"Yeah. He was friends with Julie."

"Could you have meant him?"

"You mean when I yelled John?" She considered that. "I don't know, Will. Why?"

"I think"—I remembered my promise to Pistillo about keeping her out of it—"I think he may have had something to do with Julie's murder."

She took that without blinking. "When you say have something to do with—"

"That's all I can say right now."

"You sound like a cop."

"It's been a weird week," I said.

"So tell me what you got."

"I know you're curious, but I think you should listen to the doctors."

She looked at me hard. "What's that supposed to mean?"

"I think you need to rest."

"You want me to stay out of this?"

"Yes."

"You're afraid I'll get hurt again."

277

"Very much so, yes."

Her eyes caught fire. "I can take care of myself."

"No doubt. But we're on very dangerous ground right now."

"And what have we been on up to now?"

Touché. "Look, I need you to trust me here."

"Will?"

"Yeah."

"You're not getting rid of me that easy."

"I don't want to get rid of you," I said. "But I do need to protect you."

"You can't," she said softly. "You know that."

I said nothing.

Katy slid closer to me. "I need to see this through. You, more than anyone, should understand."

"I do."

"Then?"

"I promised I wouldn't say anything."

"Promised who?"

I shook my head. "Just trust me, okay?"

She stood up. "Not okay."

"I'm trying—"

"And if I told you to butt out, would you listen to me?"

I kept my head down. "I can't say anything."

She headed for the door.

"Wait a second," I said.

"I don't have time for this now," she said shortly. "My father will be wondering where I am."

I stood. "Call me, okay?" I gave her the cell phone number. I'd already memorized hers.

She slammed the door on her way out.

Katy Miller reached the street. Her neck hurt like hell. She was pushing too hard, she knew that, but that could not be helped. She was fuming. Had they gotten to Will? It hadn't seemed possible, but maybe he was just as bad as all the rest. Or maybe not. Maybe he really believed he was protecting her.

She would have to be even more careful now.

Her throat was dry. She craved a drink, but swallowing was still a painful chore. She wondered when this would all be over. Soon, she hoped. But she would see this through to the end. She had promised herself that. There was no going back, no end, not until Julie's murderer had been brought to justice one way or the other.

She headed south to 18th Street and then headed west into the meat-packing district. It was quiet now, in that lull between the daylight unloading and the perverse past-midnight nightlife. The city was like that, a theater that put on two different shows daily, changing props and sets and even actors. But day or night or even dusk, this street always had that rotted-meat smell. You could not get it out. Human or animal, Katy was not sure which.

The panic was back.

She stopped and tried to push it away. The feel of those hands clamped on her throat, toying with her, opening and closing her windpipe at will. Such power against such helplessness. He had stopped her breath. Think about that. He had squeezed her neck until she stopped breathing, until her life force began to ebb away.

Just like with Julie.

She was so lost in the horrible memory that she did not know he was there until he grabbed her elbow. She spun around. "What the—?"

The Ghost did not loosen his grip. "I understand you were calling for me," he said in that purr voice. Then smiling, he added, "Well, here I am."

51

I sat there. Katy had every right to be mad. But I could live with her anger. It was far preferable to another funeral. I rubbed my eyes. I put my feet up. I think I might have fallen asleep—I can't say for sure—but when the phone rang, I was surprised to see it was morning. I checked the caller ID. It was Squares. I fumbled for the receiver and put it to my ear.

"Hey," I said.

He skipped the pleasantries. "I think we found our Sheila."

Half an hour later, I entered the lobby of the Regina Hotel.

It was less than a mile from our apartment. We had thought she had run across the country, but Sheila . . . what else was I supposed to call her? . . . had stayed that close.

The detective agency Squares liked to use had little trouble tracking her down, especially since she'd gotten careless since her namesake's death. She had deposited money in First National and taken out a debit Visa card. You cannot stay in this city—hell, most anyplace—without a credit card. The days of signing into motels with a false name and paying cash are pretty much over. There are a few dives, dwellings not truly fit for human habitation, that might still look the other way, but almost everyplace else wants to, at the very least, take a credit card impression—in case you steal something or seriously damage your room. The transaction doesn't necessarily go through the system—like I said, they might just make an impression—but you still need the card.

She probably assumed that she was safe and that was understandable. The Goldbergs, a couple who survived by being discreet, had sold her an ID. No reason to believe that they would ever talk— the only reason they had was because of their friendship with Squares and Raquel, plus the fact that they in part blamed themselves for her theoretical murder. Add on to that the fact that now Sheila Rogers was "dead" and thus nobody would be tracking her down, well, it made sense that she would let down her guard just a bit.

The credit card had been used to withdraw funds from an ATM yesterday in Union Square. From there it was just a question of hitting the nearby hotels. Most detective work is done through sources and payoffs, which are really one and the same. The good detectives have paid sources at phone companies, the tax bureau, credit card companies, the DMV, whatever. If you think this is difficult—that it would be hard to find somebody who will provide confidential information for cash—you do not read the papers much.

But this was even easier. Just call the hotels and ask to speak with Donna White. You do that until one hotel says "Please hold" and connects you. And now, as I took the steps into the lobby of the Regina Hotel, I felt the jangle. She was alive. I couldn't let myself believe that—would not believe it—until I saw her with my own eyes. Hope does funny things to a brain. It can darken as well as lighten. Where before I had made myself believe that a miracle was possible, now I feared that it might all be taken away from me again, that this time, when I looked into that casket, my Sheila would be there.

Love you always.

That was what her note said. Always.

I approached the front desk. I'd told Squares that I wanted to handle this alone. He understood. The receptionist, a blond woman with a hesitant smile, was on the phone. She shot me the teeth and pointed to the phone to let me know that she would be off soon. I gave her a no-rush shrug and leaned against the desk, feigning relaxed.

A minute later, she replaced the receiver and gave me her undivided attention. "May I help you?"

"Yes," I said. My voice sounded unnatural, too modulated, as if I were hosting one of those lite-FM programs. "I'm here to see Donna White. Could you give me her room number?"

"I'm sorry, sir. We don't give out our guests' room numbers."

I almost slapped myself in the forehead. How stupid could I be? "Of course, my apologies. I'll call up first. Do you have a house phone?"

She pointed to the right. Three white phones, none with key-pads, lined the wall. I picked one up and listened to the ring. An operator came on. I asked her to connect me to the room of Donna White. She said—and I noticed that this is the new all-purpose, hotel-employee catch phrase—"A pleasure," and then I heard the phone ring.

My heart crawled up my windpipe.

Two rings. Then three. On the sixth ring, I was transferred into the hotel's voice mail system. A mechanical voice told me that the guest was not available at this time and what to do if I wanted to leave a message. I hung up.

Now what?

Wait, I guess. What else was there? I bought a newspaper at the stand and found a spot in the corner of the lobby where I could see the door. I kept the newspaper up over my face, *Spy vs. Spy* style, and felt like a total idiot. My insides churned. I never thought of myself as the type for an ulcer, but over the past few days, a burning acidity had started clawing at my stomach lining.

I tried to read the paper—a totally futile act, of course. I couldn't concentrate. I couldn't muster up the energy to care about current events. I couldn't keep my place while glancing at the door every three seconds. I turned the pages. I looked at the pictures. I tried to give a damn about the box scores. I flipped to the comics, but even Beetle Bailey was too taxing.

The blond receptionist would flick her gaze in my direction every once in a while. When our eyes met, she'd smile in a patroniz-ing way. Keeping her eye on me, no doubt. Or maybe that was more paranoid thinking. I was just a man reading a newspaper in the lobby. I had done nothing to arouse her suspicion.

An hour passed without incident. My cell phone rang. I put it to my ear.

"You see her yet?" Squares asked.

"She's not in her room. Or at least she's not answering the phone."

"Where are you now?"

"I'm staking out the lobby."

Squares made a sound.

"What?" I asked.

"Did you really say 'staking out'?"

"Give me a break, okay?"

"Look, why don't we just hire a couple of guys from the agency to do it right? They'll call us as soon as she gets in."

I considered that. "Not yet," I said.

And that was when she entered.

My eyes widened. My breathing started coming in deep swallows. My God. It was really my Sheila. She was alive. I fumbled the phone, almost dropping it.

"Will?"

"I have to go," I said.

"She there?"

"I'll call you back."

I clicked off the power. My Sheila—I'll call her that because I don't know how else to refer to her—had changed her hair. It was cut shorter, flipping up and under at the end of the swan neck. She had bangs now too. The color had been darkened to an Elvira black. But the effect . . . I saw her and it was like someone punched my chest with a giant fist.

Sheila kept moving. I started to rise. The dizziness made me pull up. She walked the way she always walked—no hesitation, head high, with purpose. The elevator door was already opened, and I realized that I might not make it in time.

She stepped inside. I was on my feet now. I hurried across the lobby without running. I did not want to make a scene. Whatever was happening here—whatever had made her vanish and change names and wear a disguise and Lord knows what else—needed to be somewhat finessed. I could not just yell out her name and sprint across the lobby.

My feet clacked on the marble. The sound echoed too loudly in my own ears. I was going to be late. I stopped and watched the elevator doors shut.

Damn.

I pressed the call button. Another elevator opened immediately. I started toward it but pulled up. Wait, what good would that do? I didn't even know what floor she was on. I checked the lights above my Sheila's elevator. They moved steadily. Floor five, then six.

Had Sheila been the only one in the elevator?

I thought so.

The elevator stopped on the ninth floor. Okay, fine. Now I pushed the call button. The same elevator was there. I hurried inside and pressed nine, hoping that I would get there before she entered her room. The door started closing. I leaned against the back. At the last second, a hand shot through. The doors banged against the hand and then opened. A sweaty man in a gray business suit sighed his way in, offering me a nod. He pressed eleven. The door closed again and we were on our way up.

"Hot out," he said to me.

"Yeah."

He sighed again. "Good hotel, don't you think?"

A tourist, I thought. I had been in a million New York City elevators before. New Yorkers understood the rules: You stare up at the flashing numbers. You do not engage anyone in conversation.

I told him that yes, it was nice, and as the doors opened, I dashed out. The corridor was long. I looked to my left. Nothing. I looked to my right and heard a door close. Like a hunting dog on point, I sprinted toward the sound. Right-hand side, I thought. End of the corridor.

I followed the audible scent, if you will, and deduced that the sound had come from either room 912 or 914. I looked at one door, then the other. I remembered an episode of *Batman* where Catwoman promises that one door will lead to her, the other to a live tiger. Batman chose wrong. Well, hell, this isn't *Batman*.

I knocked on both doors. I stood between them and waited.

Nothing.

I knocked again, harder this time. Movement. I was rewarded with some kind of movement emanating from room 912. I slid in front of the door. I adjusted my shirt collar. Now I could hear the security chain being slid to the side. I braced myself. The knob turned and the door began to swing open.

The man was burly and annoyed. He wore a V-neck undershirt and striped boxers. He barked, "What?"

"I'm sorry. I was looking for Donna White."

284

He put his fists on his hips. "Do I look like Donna White?"

Strange sounds emanated from the gruff man's room. I listened closer. Groans. Quasi-passionate groans of faux pleasure. The man met my eye, but he didn't look happy about it. I stepped back. Spectravision, I thought. In-room movies. The man was watching a skin flick. Porno interruptus.

"Uh, sorry," I said.

He slammed the door shut.

Okay, let's rule out room 912. At least, I hoped like hell I could. This was crazy. I raised my hand to knock on 914, when I heard a voice say, "Can I help you?"

I turned and at the end of the corridor, I saw a no-neck buzz cut wearing a blue blazer. The blazer had a small logo on his lapel and a patch on his upper arm. He puffed out his chest. Hotel security and proud of it.

"No, I'm fine," I said.

He frowned. "Are you a guest of the hotel?"

"Yes."

"What's your room number?"

"I don't have a room number."

"But you just said—"

I rapped the door hard. Buzz Cut hurried toward me. For a moment I thought he might make a diving tackle in order to protect the door, but at the last moment, he pulled up.

"Please come with me," he said.

I ignored him and knocked again. There was still no answer. Buzz Cut put his arm on mine. I shook it off, knocked again, and yelled, "I know you're not Sheila." That confused Buzz Cut. He frowned some more. We both stopped and watched the door. Nobody answered. Buzz Cut took my arm again, more gently this time. I did not put up a fight. He led me downstairs and through the lobby.

I was out on the sidewalk. I turned. Buzz Cut puffed his chest again and crossed his arms.

Now what?

Another New York City axiom: You cannot stand in one place on a sidewalk. Flow is essential. People hurry by and they don't expect to find something in their way. If they do, they may veer but they never stop.

I looked for a safe place. The secret was to stay as close to the actual building as possible—the shoulder of the sidewalk, if you will. I huddled near a plate glass window, took out the cell phone, called the hotel, and asked to be connected to Donna White's room. I got another "a pleasure" and was patched through.

There was no answer.

This time I left a simple message. I gave her my cell phone number and tried not to sound like I was begging when I asked her to call.

I slid the phone back into my pocket and again asked myself: Now what?

My Sheila was inside. The thought made me light-headed. Too much yearning. Too many possibilities and what-ifs. I made myself push it away.

Okay, fine, so what did that mean exactly? First off, was there another way out? A basement or back exit? Had she spotted me from behind those sunglasses? Was that why she hurried to the elevator? When I followed her, had I made a mistake about the room number? That could be. I knew that she was on the ninth floor. That was a start. Or did I? If she spotted me, could she have stopped at another floor as a decoy?

Do I stand out here?

I didn't know. I couldn't go home, that was for sure. I took a deep breath. I watched the pedestrians race by, so many of them, one bleary mass, separate entities making up a whole. And then, looking through the mass, I saw her.

My heart stopped.

She just stood there and stared at me. I was too overwhelmed to move. I felt something inside me give way. I put my hand to my mouth to stifle a cry. She moved toward me. Tears stung her eyes. I shook my head. She did not stop. She reached me and pulled me close.

"It's okay," she whispered.

I closed my eyes. For a long while we just held each other. We did not speak. We did not move. We just slipped away.

52

"My real name is Nora Spring."

We sat in the lower level of a Starbucks on Park Avenue South, in a corner near an emergency fire exit. No one else was down here. She kept her eyes on the stairs, worried I'd been followed. This Starbucks, like so many others, had earth tones, surreal swirling artwork, and large photographs of brown-skinned men too happily picking coffee beans. She held a venti iced latte between both hands. I went with the frappuccino.

The chairs were purple and oversize and just plush enough. We pushed them together. We held hands. I was confused, of course. I wanted answers. But beyond that, on a whole higher plane, the pure joy splashed through me. It was an amazing rush. It calmed me. I was happy. Whatever I was about to learn would not change that. The woman I loved was back. I would let nothing change that.

She sipped at the latte. "I'm sorry," she said.

I squeezed her hand.

"To run out like that. To let you think"—she stopped—"I can't even imagine what you must have thought." Her eyes found mine. "I never wanted to hurt you."

"I'm okay," I said.

"How did you learn I wasn't Sheila?"

"At her funeral. I saw the body."

"I wanted to tell you, especially after I heard she'd been murdered."

"Why didn't you?"

"Ken told me it might get you killed."

My brother's name jarred me. Nora turned away. I slid my hand up her arm and stopped at the shoulder. The tension had knotted her muscles. I gently kneaded them, a familiar moment for us. She closed her eyes and let my fingers work. For a long time neither of us spoke. I broke the silence. "How long have you known my brother?"

"Almost four years," she said.

I nodded through my shock, trying to encourage her to say more, but she still had her face turned away. I gently took hold of her chin and turned her to me. I kissed her lightly on the lips.

She said, "I love you so much."

I felt a soar that nearly lifted me off the chair. "I love you too."

"I'm scared, Will."

"I'll protect you," I said.

She held my gaze. "I've been lying to you. The whole time we've been together."

"I know."

"Do you really think we can survive that?"

"I lost you once," I said. "I'm not going to lose you again."

"You're that sure?"

"Love you," I said. "Always."

She studied my face. I don't know what she was looking for. "I'm married, Will."

I tried to keep my expression blank, but it was not easy. Her words wrapped around me and tightened, boa-constrictor-like. I almost pulled my hand away.

"Tell me," I said.

"Five years ago, I ran away from my husband, Cray. Cray was"—she closed her eyes—"incredibly abusive. I don't want to go into details. They're not important anyway. We lived in a town called Cramden. It's not far from Kansas City. One day, after Cray put me in the hospital, I ran away. That's all you need to know, okay?"

I nodded.

"I don't have any family. I had friends, but I really didn't want to get them involved. Cray is insane. He wouldn't let me go. He threatened . . ." Her voice trailed away. "Never mind what he threatened.

288

But I couldn't put anyone at risk. So I found a shelter that helps battered women. They took me in. I told them I wanted to start over. I wanted to get out of there. But I was afraid of Cray. You see, Cray is a town cop. You have no idea . . . you live in terror for so long, you start to think that a man is omnipotent. It's impossible to explain."

I scooted a little closer, still holding her hand. I had seen the effects of abuse. I understood.

"The shelter helped me escape to Europe. I lived in Stockholm. It was hard. I got a job as a waitress. I was lonely all the time. I wanted to come back, but I was still so afraid of my husband, I didn't dare. After six months, I thought I'd lose my mind. I still had nightmares about Cray finding me. . . ."

Her voice broke off. I had no idea what to do. I tried to scoot my chair closer to hers. The armrests were already touching, but I think she appreciated the gesture.

"Anyway, I finally met a woman. She was an American living in the area. We started cautiously, but there was something about her. I guess we both had that on-the-run look. We were also lonely as hell, though she at least had her husband and daughter. They were in deep hiding too. I didn't know why at first."

"This woman," I said. "It was Sheila Rogers?"

"Yes."

"And the husband." I stopped, swallowed. "That was my brother."

She nodded. "They have a daughter named Carly."

It was beginning to make sense.

"Sheila and I became close friends, and while it took him a little longer to trust me, I grew close to Ken too. I moved in with them, started helping them take care of Carly. Your niece is a wonderful child, Will. Smart and beautiful and, not to get metaphysical, but there is such an aura around her."

My niece. Ken had a daughter. I had a niece I had never seen.

"Your brother talked about you all the time, Will. He might mention your mother or your father or even Melissa, but you were his world. He followed your career. He knew all about your working at Covenant House. Here he had been in hiding for what, seven years? He was lonely too, I guess. So once he trusted me, he talked to me a lot. And what he talked about most was you."

I blinked and looked down at the table. I studied the Starbucks brown napkin. There was some stupid poem about aroma and a promise on it. Made from recycled paper. The color was brown because they did not use bleach.

"Are you okay?" she asked.

"I'm fine," I said. I looked up. "So what happened next?"

"I got in touch with a friend back home. She told me that Cray had hired a private detective and that he knew I was in the Stockholm area. I panicked, but at the same time, I was ready to move on. Like I said, I had lived with Cray in Missouri. I figured that if I moved to New York, maybe I'd be safe. But I needed a deeper ID, in case Cray kept hunting. Sheila was in the same boat. Her fake ID was all surface, just a name change. And that was when we came up with a simple plan."

I nodded. This one I knew. "You switched identities."

"Right. She became Nora Spring and I became Sheila Rogers. This way, if my husband came after me, he'd only find her. And if the people searching for them found Sheila Rogers, well, you see, it adds another layer."

I considered that, but something still did not add up. "Okay, so that's how you became Sheila Rogers. You switched identities."

"Yes."

"And you ended up in New York City."

"Yes."

"And"—here was the part I was having trouble with—"somehow we happened to meet."

Nora smiled. "You're wondering about us, aren't you?"

"I guess I am."

"You're thinking it's a hell of a coincidence that I volunteered at the very place you work."

"It would seem unlikely," I agreed.

"Well, you're right. It wasn't a coincidence." She sat back and sighed. "I'm not sure how to explain this, Will."

I just held her hand and waited.

"Okay, you have to understand. I was so lonely overseas. All I had was your brother and Sheila and, of course, Carly. I spent all that time hearing your brother rave about you, and it was like . . . it was like you were so different from any man I'd ever known. The truth is, I think I was half in love with you before we ever met. So I told myself when I came to New York that I'd just meet you, see

290

what you were really like. Maybe if it seemed okay, I'd even tell you that your brother was alive and that he was innocent, though Ken warned me repeatedly about the danger of that. It wasn't a plan or anything. I just came to New York and one day I walked into Covenant House, and call it destiny or fate or whatever, but the moment I saw you, I knew that I would love you forever."

I was scared and confused and smiling.

"What?" she said.

"I love you."

She put her head on my shoulder. We grew quiet now. There was more. It would come in time. For now, we just enjoyed the silence of being with one another. When Nora was ready, she started up again.

"A few weeks ago, I was sitting at the hospital with your mother. She was in such pain, Will. She couldn't take it anymore, she told me. She wanted to die. She was in such discomfort, well, you know."

I nodded.

"I loved your mother. I think you know that."

"I do," I said.

"I couldn't stand just sitting there doing nothing. So I broke my promise to your brother. Before she died, I wanted her to know the truth. She deserved that. I wanted her to know that her son was alive and that he loved her and that he hadn't hurt anybody."

"You told her about Ken?"

"Yes. But even in her haze, she was skeptical. She needed proof, I think."

I froze and turned to her. I saw it now. What had started it all. The visit to the bedroom after the funeral. The picture hidden behind the frame. "So you gave my mother that photograph of Ken."

Nora nodded.

"She never saw him. Just the photograph."

"That's right."

Which explained why we never knew about it. "But you told her he was coming back."

"Yes."

"Were you lying?"

She thought about that. "Maybe I was engaging in hyperbole, but no, I don't think it was an outright lie. You see, Sheila contacted me when they captured him. Ken had always been very careful. He had all sorts of provisions set up for Sheila and Carly. So when they caught him, Sheila and Carly ran off. The police never knew about them. Sheila stayed overseas until Ken thought it was safe. Then she sneaked back in."

"And she called you when she arrived?"

"Yes."

It was all adding up. "From a pay phone in New Mexico."

"Yes."

That would be the first call Pistillo was talking about—the one from New Mexico to my apartment. "So then what happened?"

"It all started going wrong," she said. "I got a call from Ken. He was in a frenzy. Someone had found them. He and Carly had been out of the house when two men broke in. They tortured Sheila to find out where he'd gone. Ken came home during the attack. He shot them both. But Sheila was seriously wounded. He called and told me that I had to run now. The police would find Sheila's finger-prints. McGuane and his people would also learn that Sheila Rogers had been with him."

"They'd all be looking for Sheila," I said.

"Yes."

"And that was you now. So you had to disappear."

"I wanted to tell you, but Ken was insistent. If you didn't know anything, you'd be safer. And then he reminded me that there was Carly to consider. These people tortured and killed her mother. I couldn't live with myself if anything happened to Carly."

"How old is Carly?"

"She'd be close to twelve by now."

"So she was born before Ken ran away."

"I think she was six months old."

Another sore point. Ken had a child and never told me about her. I asked, "Why did he keep her a secret?"

"I don't know."

So far, I had been able to follow the logic, but I could not see how Carly fit into this. I mulled it over. Six months before he van-ished. What had been going on in his life? It was right about the time the FBI had flipped him. Could it be connected to that? Was Ken afraid that his actions might put his infant daughter in danger? That made sense, I guess.

No, I was missing something.

I was about to ask a follow-up question, try to get more details, when my cell phone chirped. Squares probably. I glanced at the caller ID. Nope, not Squares. But I recognized the number instantly. Katy Miller. I pressed the answer button and put the phone to my ear.

"Katy?"

"Oooo, no, sorry, that's incorrect. Please try again."

The fear flooded back. Oh Christ. The Ghost. I closed my eyes. "If you hurt her, so help me—"

"Come, come, Will," the Ghost interrupted. "Impotent threats are beneath you."

"What do you want?"

"We need to chat, old boy."

"Where is she?"

"Who? Oh, you mean Katy? Why, she's right here."

"I want to talk to her."

"You don't believe me, Will? I'm wounded."

"I want to talk to her," I repeated.

"You want proof she's alive?"

"Something like that."

"How about this?" the Ghost began in his silkiest hush. "I can make her scream for you. Would that help?"

I closed my eyes again.

"Can't hear you, Will."

"No."

"You sure? It would be no problem. One piercing, nerve-shredding scream. What do you say?"

"Please don't hurt her," I said. "She has nothing to do with this."

"Where are you?"

"I'm on Park Avenue South."

"Be more specific."

I gave him a location two blocks away.

"I'll have a car there in five minutes. Get in it. Do you understand?"

"Yes."

"And, Will?"

"What?"

"Don't call anyone. Don't tell anyone. Katy Miller has a sore neck from a previous encounter. I can't tell you how tempting it would be to test it out." He stopped and whispered. "Still with me, old neighbor?"

"Yes."

"Hang tight then. This will all be over soon."

53

Claudia Fisher burst into the office of Joseph Pistillo.

Pistillo lifted his head. "What?"

"Raymond Cromwell didn't report in."

Cromwell was the undercover agent they'd assigned to Joshua Ford, Ken Klein's attorney. "I thought he was wired."

"They had an appointment at McGuane's. He couldn't wear a wire in there."

"And nobody's seen him since that appointment?"

Fisher nodded. "Same with Ford. Both are missing."

"Jesus Christ."

"So what do you want to do?"

Pistillo was already up and moving. "Get every available agent. We're raiding McGuane's office now."

To leave Nora alone like that—I had already gotten used to the name—was beyond heart-wrenching, but what choice did I have? The idea that Katy was alone with that sadistic psycho gnawed straight into my marrow. I remembered how it felt to be hand-cuffed to the bed, helpless while he attacked her. I closed my eyes and wished the image away.

Nora made an effort to stop me, but she understood. This was something I had to do. Our good-bye kiss was almost too tender. I pulled away. The tears were back in her eyes.

"Come back to me," she said.

I told her I would and hurried out.

The car was a black Ford Taurus with tinted windows. There was only the driver inside. I did not recognize him. He handed me an eyeshade, the kind they give out on airplanes, and told me to put it on and lie flat in the back. I did as he asked. He started up the car and pulled out. I used the time to think. I knew a lot now. Not all. Not enough. But a lot. And I was reasonably sure that the Ghost was right: It would all be over soon.

I ran it through in my mind and here was what I semi-concluded: Eleven years ago, Ken was involved in illegal activities with his old friends, McGuane and the Ghost. There was really no way around that anymore. Ken had done wrong. He might have been a hero to me, but my sister, Melissa, had pointed out that he was drawn to violence. I might amend that to say he craved action, the enticement of the edge. But that's just semantics.

Somewhere along the way, Ken was captured and agreed to help bring down McGuane. He risked his life. He went undercover. He wore a wire. Somehow McGuane and the Ghost found out. Ken ran. He came home, though I'm not sure why. I'm not sure how Julie fit in here either. By all accounts she had not been home in over a year. Was her return a coincidence? Was she there merely following Ken, perhaps as a lover, perhaps because he was her drug source? Did the Ghost follow her, knowing that she would eventually lead him to Ken?

I don't know any of that. Not yet anyhow.

Whatever, the Ghost found them, probably in a delicate moment. He attacked. Ken was injured, but he escaped. Julie was not so lucky. The Ghost wanted to put pressure on Ken, so he framed him for the murder. Terrified that he'd be killed or worse, Ken ran. He picked up his steady girlfriend, Sheila Rogers, and their infant daughter, Carly. The three of them disappeared.

My vision, even through my eyeshade, darkened. I heard a whooshing noise. We had entered a tunnel. Could be the Midtown, but my guess was that we were in the Lincoln, heading out toward New Jersey. I thought now about Pistillo and his role in all this. For him, it was the old ends-justify-means debate. Under certain circumstances, he might be a "means" guy, but this case was personal.

It was easy to see his point of view. Ken was a crook. He had made a deal and no matter what the reason, he had reneged on it by running. Open season on him. Make him a fugitive and let the world comb through the muck and find his man.

Years pass. Ken and Sheila stay together. Their daughter, Carly, grows. Then one day, Ken is captured. He is brought back to the States, convinced, I imagine, that they'll hang him for the murder of Julie Miller. But the authorities have always known the truth. They don't want him for that. They want the head of the beast. McGuane. And Ken can still help deliver him.

So they strike a deal. Ken hides out in New Mexico. Once they believe it's safe, Sheila and Carly come back from Sweden to stay with him. But McGuane is a powerful nemesis. He learned where they were. He sent two men. Ken wasn't home, but they tortured Sheila to find out where he was. Ken surprises them, kills them, packs his injured lover and daughter in the car, and then he runs again. He warns Nora, who is using Sheila's ID, that the authorities and McGuane are going to be on her tail. She is forced to run too.

That pretty much covered what I knew.

The Ford Taurus came to a stop. I heard the driver shut off the engine. Enough with the passive, I thought. If I had any hope of getting out of this alive, I would have to be more assertive. I pulled the eyeshade off and checked my watch. We had been driving for an hour. Then I sat up.

We were in the middle of thick woods. The ground was blanketed with pine needles. The trees were lush and heavy with green. There was a watchtower of sorts, a small aluminum structure that sat on a platform about ten feet off the ground. It looked like an oversize toolshed, built strictly for function. Something both neglected and industrial. Rust licked the corners and door.

The driver turned around. "Get out."

I did as he asked. My eyes stayed on the structure. I saw the door open, and the Ghost stepped out. He was dressed entirely in black, as though he were on his way to reading poetry in the Village. He waved to me.

"Hi, Will."

"Where is she?" I asked.

"Who?"

"Don't start that crap."

The Ghost folded his arms. "My, my," he said, "aren't we just the bravest little soldier?"

"Where is she?"

"You mean Katy Miller?"

"You know I do."

The Ghost nodded. He had something in his hand. A rope of some kind. A lasso maybe. I froze. "She looks so much like her sister, don't you think? How could I resist? I mean, that neck. That beautiful swan neck. Already bruised . . ."

I tried to keep the quake from my voice. "Where is she?"

He blinked. "She's dead, Will."

My heart sank.

"I grew bored waiting and—" He started laughing then. The sound echoed in the stillness, ripping through the air, clawing at the leaves. I stood there, unmoving. He pointed and shouted, "Gotcha! Oh, I'm only joshing, Willie boy. Having a little fun. Katy is just fine." He waved me forward. "Come on and see."

I hurried toward the platform, my heart firmly lodged in my throat. There was a rusted ladder. I climbed it. The Ghost was still laughing. I pushed past him and opened the door to the aluminum shack. I turned to my right.

Katy was there.

The Ghost's laugh was still ringing in my ears. I hurried over to her. Her eyes were open, though several strands of hair blocked them. The bruises on her neck had turned into a jaundiced yellow. Her arms were tied to a chair, but she looked uninjured.

I bent down and pushed the hair away. "Are you okay?" I asked.

"I'm fine."

I could feel the rage building. "Did he hurt you?"

Katy Miller shook her head. Her voice quaked. "What does he want with us?"

"Please let me answer that one."

We turned as the Ghost entered. He kept the door opened. The floor was littered with broken beer bottles. There was an old file cabinet in the corner. A laptop computer sat closed in one corner. Three metal folding chairs, the kind used for school assemblies, were out. Katy sat in one. The Ghost took the second and signaled for me to take the one on his immediate left. I remained standing. The Ghost sighed and stood back up.

"I need your help, Will." He turned toward Katy. "And I thought having Miss Miller here join us, well"—he gave me the skin-crawling grin—"I thought she might work as something of an incentive."

I squared up. "If you hurt her, if you so much as lay a hand—"

The Ghost did not wind up. He did not rear back. He merely snapped his hand from his side and caught me under the chin. He connected with a knife strike. A choking sound blew past my lips. It felt like I'd swallowed my own throat. I staggered and turned away. The Ghost took his time. He bent low and used an uppercut. His knuckles landed flush against my kidney. I dropped to my knees, nearly paralyzed by the blow.

He looked down at me. "Your posturing is getting on my nerves, Willie boy."

I felt close to throwing up.

"We need to contact your brother," he went on. "That's why you're here."

I looked up. "I don't know where he is."

The Ghost slid away from me. He moved behind Katy's chair. He gently, almost too gently, put his hands on her shoulders. She winced at his touch. He reached with both index fingers and stroked the bruises on her neck.

"I'm telling the truth," I said.

"Oh, I believe you," he said.

"So what do you want?"

"I know how to reach Ken."

I was confused. "What?"

"Have you ever seen one of those old movies where the fugitive leaves messages in classified ads?"

"I guess."

The Ghost smiled as though pleased with my response. "Ken is taking that one step further. He uses an Internet newsgroup. More specifically, he leaves and receives messages on something called rec.music.elvis. It is, as you might expect, a board for Elvis fans. So, for example, if his attorney needed to contact him, he would leave a date and time and post with a code name. Ken would then know when to IM said attorney."

"IM?"

"Instant message. I assume you've used it before. It's like a private chat room. Totally untraceable."

"How do you know all this?" I asked.

He smiled again and moved his hands closer to Katy's neck. "Information gathering," he said. "It's something of my forté."

His hands slid off Katy. I realized that I'd been holding my breath. He reached into his pocket and took out the rope lasso again.

"So what do you need me for?" I asked.

"Your brother would not agree to meet his attorney," the Ghost said. "I believe he suspected a trap. We set up another IM appointment, though. We are very much hoping that you can persuade him to meet with us."

"And if I can't?"

He held up the rope. There was a handle attached to the end. "Do you know what this is?"

I did not reply.

"It's a Punjab lasso," he said as if beginning a lecture. "The Thuggees used it. They were known as the silent assassins. From India. Some people think they were all wiped out in the nineteenth century. Others, well, others are not so sure." He looked at Katy and held the primitive weapon up high. "Need I go on here, Will?"

I shook my head. "He'll know it's a trap," he said.

"It's your job to convince him otherwise. If you fail"—he looked up, smiling—"well, on the positive side, you'll be able to see first-hand how Julie suffered all those years ago."

I could feel the blood leaving my extremities. "You'll kill him," I said.

"Oh, not necessarily."

I knew it was a lie, but his face was frighteningly sincere.

"Your brother made tapes, gathered incriminating information," he said. "But he has not shown any of it to the feds yet. He's kept it hidden all these years. That's a good thing. It shows cooperation, that he is still the Ken we know and love. And"—he stopped, thinking—"he has something I want."

"What?" I asked.

He shook me off. "Here's the deal: If he gives it all up and promises to disappear again, we can all go on."

A lie. I knew that. He'll kill Ken. And he'll kill us all. I had no doubt about that. "And if I don't believe you?"

He dropped the lasso around Katy's neck. She let out a small cry. The Ghost smiled and looked straight at me. "Does it really matter?"

I swallowed. "I guess not."

"Guess?"

"I'll cooperate."

He let go of the lasso; it hung from her neck like the most perverse necklace. "Don't touch it," he said. "We have an hour. Spend the time staring at her neck, Will. And imagine."

54

McGuane had been caught off guard.

He watched the FBI storm inside. He had not foreseen this. Yes, Joshua Ford was important. Yes, his disappearance would raise eyebrows, though they had made Ford call his wife and tell her he'd been called out of town on a "delicate matter." But this forceful a reaction? It seemed like overkill.

No matter. McGuane was always prepared. The blood had been cleaned with a newly developed peroxide agent, so that even a blue-light test would reveal nothing. The hairs and fibers had been taken care of, but even if a few were found, so what? He would not deny that Ford and Cromwell were here. He would happily admit it. He would also admit that they had departed. And he could offer proof: His security people had already replaced the real surveillance tape with the digitally altered one that would show both Ford and Cromwell departing the premises on their own accord.

McGuane pressed a button that automatically erased and reformatted the computer files. Nothing would be found. McGuane automatically backed up via email. Every hour, the computer sent an email to a secret account. The files thus stayed safely in cyberspace. Only McGuane knew the address. He could retrieve the backup whenever he wanted.

He rose and straightened his tie as Pistillo burst through the door with Claudia Fisher and two other agents. Pistillo pointed his weapon at McGuane.

McGuane spread his hands. No fear. Never show fear. "What a pleasant surprise."

"Where are they?" Pistillo shouted.

"Who?"

"Joshua Ford and Special Agent Raymond Cromwell."

McGuane did not blink. Ah, that explained it. "Are you saying that Mr. Cromwell is a federal agent?"

"I am," Pistillo barked. "Now, where is he?"

"I'd like to file a complaint then."

"What?"

"Agent Cromwell presented himself as an attorney," McGuane went on, his voice even as could be. "I trusted that representation. I confided in him, assuming that I was protected by attorney-client privilege. Now you tell me that he is an undercover agent. I want to make sure that nothing I said is used against me."

Pistillo's face was red. "Where is he, McGuane?"

"I don't have the slightest idea. He left with Mr. Ford."

"What was the nature of your business with them?"

McGuane smiled. "You know better than that, Pistillo. Our meeting would fall under attorney-client privilege."

Pistillo wanted so very much to pull the trigger. He aimed at the center of McGuane's face. McGuane still showed nothing. Pistillo lowered the weapon. "Search the place," he barked. "Box and tag everything. Place him under arrest."

McGuane let them cuff him. He would not tell them about the surveillance tape. Let them find it on their own. It would have that much more impact that way. Still, as the agents dragged him out, he knew that this was not good. He did not mind being brazen—as mentioned earlier, this was not the first federal agent he'd had killed—but he could not help but wonder if he had missed something, if he had left himself somehow exposed, if, at long last, he had made a crucial mistake that would cost him everything.

55

The Ghost stepped into the woods, leaving Katy and me alone. I sat in my chair and stared at the lasso around her neck. It was having the desired effect. I would cooperate. I would not risk having that rope tighten around the neck of that frightened girl.

Katy looked at me and said, "He's going to kill us."

It was not a question. It was true, of course, but I still denied it. I promised her that she would be okay, that I would find a way out, but I don't think I assuaged her worries. Little wonder. My throat was feeling better, but my kidney still ached from the punch. My eyes moved about the room.

Think, Will. And think fast.

I knew what was coming up. The Ghost would have me set up the meeting. Once Ken showed up, we were all dead. I thought about that. I would try to warn my brother. I would try to use some kind of code maybe. Our only hope was that Ken would smell a trap and surprise them. But I had to keep my options open. I had to look for a way out, any way out, even if it meant sacrificing myself to save Katy. There would be an opening, a mistake. I had to be ready to exploit it.

Katy whispered, "I know where we are."

I turned to her. "Where?"

"We're in the South Orange Water Reservation," she said. "We used to come here and drink. We're not far from Hobart Gap Road."

"How far?" I asked.

"A mile maybe."

"You know the way? I mean, if we make a run for it, would you be able to lead us out?"

"I think so," she said. Then, with a nod: "Yeah. Yeah, I could lead us out."

Okay, good. That was something. Not much maybe, but a start. I looked out the door. The driver leaned against the car. The Ghost stood with his hands behind his back. He bounced on his toes. His gaze was turned upward, as if bird-watching. The driver lit up a cigarette. The Ghost did not move.

I quickly scoured the floor and found what I was looking for—a big hunk of broken glass. I peeked out the door again. Neither man was looking. So I crept behind Katy's chair.

"What are you doing?" she whispered.

"I'm going to cut you loose."

"Are you out of your mind? If he sees you—"

"We have to try something," I said.

"But"—Katy stopped. "Even if you cut me free, then what?"

"I don't know," I admitted. "But be ready. There'll be a chance to escape somewhere down the line. We have to take advantage of it."

I pressed the broken edge against the rope and started sawing back and forth. The rope began to fray. The work was slow. I hurried the pace. The rope started giving way, strand by strand.

I was about halfway through the rope when I felt the platform shake. I stopped. Someone was on the ladder. Katy made a whimpering sound. I rolled away from her and made it back to my seat just as the Ghost entered. He looked at me.

"You're out of breath, Willie boy."

I slid the broken glass to the back of my seat, almost sitting on it. The Ghost frowned at me. I said nothing. My pulse raced. The Ghost looked toward Katy. She tried to stare back defiantly. She was so damn brave. But when I looked toward her, the terror struck me again.

The frayed rope was in plain sight.

The Ghost narrowed his eyes.

"Hey, let's get on with this," I said.

It was enough of a distraction. The Ghost turned to me. Katy adjusted her hands, giving the frayed rope some cover. Not much if

305

he looked closely. But maybe enough. The Ghost waited a beat and then he went for the laptop. For a second—for the briefest of seconds—he turned his back to me.

Now, I thought.

I would jump up, use the broken glass like a prison shiv, and jam it into the Ghost's neck. I calculated quickly. Was I too far away? Probably. And what about the driver? Was he armed? Did I dare—?

The Ghost spun back toward me. The moment, if there had ever been one, was over.

The computer was already on. The Ghost did some typing. He got online with a remote modem. He clacked some more keys and a textbox appeared. He smiled at me and said, "It's time to talk to Ken."

My stomach knotted. The Ghost hit the return button. On the screen, I saw what he had typed:

YOU THERE?

We waited. The answer came a moment later.

HERE.

The Ghost smiled. "Ah, Ken." He typed some more and hit the return.

IT'S WILL. I'M WITH FORD.

There was a long pause.

TELL ME THE NAME OF THE FIRST GIRL YOU MADE OUT WITH.

The Ghost turned to me. "As I expected, he wants proof it's really you."

I said nothing, but my mind raced.

"I know what you're thinking," he went on. "You want to warn him. You want to tell him an answer that's close to the truth." He moved over to Katy. He picked up the stick end of the lasso. He pulled just a little. The rope coiled against her neck.

"Here's the deal, Will. I want you to stand up. I want you to go over to the computer and type in the correct answer. I'll keep tightening the rope. If you play any games—if I even suspect you tried to play any sort of game—I won't stop until she's dead. Do you understand?"

I nodded.

He tightened the lasso a little more. Katy made a noise. "Go," he said.

306

I hurried to the screen. Fear numbed my brain. He was right. I had been trying to come up with a decent lie, something to warn him. But I couldn't. Not now. I put my fingers on the keys and typed:

CINDI SHAPIRO

The Ghost smiled. "For real? Man, she was a little hottie, Will. I'm impressed."

He let go of the lasso. Katy released a gasp. He moved back over to the keyboard. I looked back over at my chair. The broken glass was in plain view. I moved quickly back to my seat. We waited for the response.

GO HOME, WILL.

The Ghost rubbed his face. "Interesting response," he said. He thought about it. "Where did you make out with her?"

"What?"

"Cindi Shapiro. Were you at her house, your house, where?"

"Eric Frankel's bar mitzvah."

"Does Ken know that?"

"Yes."

The Ghost smiled. He typed again.

YOU TESTED ME. NOW IT'S YOUR TURN. WHERE DID I MAKE OUT WITH CINDI?

Another long pause. I was on the edge of my seat too. It was a smart move by the Ghost, turning the momentum around a bit. But more important, we really didn't know if this was Ken or not. This answer would prove it one way or another.

Thirty seconds passed. Then:

GO HOME, WILL.

The Ghost typed some more.

I NEED TO KNOW IT'S YOU.

A longer pause. And then finally:

FRANKEL'S BAR MITZVAH. GO HOME NOW.

Another jolt. It was Ken. . . .

I looked over at Katy. Her eyes met mine. The Ghost typed again.

WE NEED TO MEET.

The answer came fast: *NO CAN DO.*

PLEASE. IMPORTANT.

GO HOME, WILL. NOT SAFE.

WHERE R U?

307

HOW DID YOU FIND FORD?

"Hmm," the Ghost said. He thought about that and typed: PISTILLO.

There was another long pause.

I HEARD ABOUT MOM. WAS IT VERY BAD?

The Ghost did not consult me for this one. YES.

HOW'S DAD?

NOT GOOD. WE NEED TO SEE YOU.

Another pause: *NO CAN DO.*

WE CAN HELP YOU.

BETTER TO STAY AWAY.

The Ghost looked at me. "Should we try to tempt him with his favorite vice?"

I had no idea what he meant, but I watched him type and hit the return key:

WE CAN GET YOU MONEY. DO YOU NEED SOME?

I WILL. BUT WE CAN DO IT THRU OVERSEAS TRANS-FERS.

And then, as if reading my mind, the Ghost typed:

I REALLY NEED TO SEE YOU. PLEASE.

I LOVE YOU, WILL. GO HOME.

Again, as if he were inside my head, the Ghost typed:

WAIT.

SIGNING OFF NOW, BRO. DON'T WORRY.

The Ghost let out a deep breath. "This isn't working," he said out loud. He typed quickly.

SIGN OFF, KEN, AND YOUR BROTHER DIES.

A pause. Then: *WHO IS THIS?*

The Ghost smiled. ONE GUESS. HINT: CASPER THE FRIENDLY.

No pause this time.

LEAVE HIM ALONE, JOHN.

I THINK NOT.

HE HAS NOTHING TO DO WITH THIS.

YOU KNOW BETTER THAN TO PLAY WITH MY SYM-PATHIES. YOU SHOW UP, YOU GIVE ME WHAT I WANT, I DON'T KILL HIM.

LET HIM GO FIRST. THEN I'LL GIVE YOU WHAT YOU WANT.

The Ghost laughed and clacked the keys:

308

OH PLEASE. THE YARD, KEN. YOU REMEMBER THE YARD, DON'T YOU. I'LL GIVE YOU THREE HOURS TO GET THERE.

IMPOSSIBLE. I'M NOT EVEN ON THE EAST COAST.

The Ghost muttered, "Bull." Then he typed frantically:

THEN YOU BETTER HURRY. THREE HOURS. IF YOU'RE NOT THERE, I CUT OFF A FINGER. I CUT OFF ANOTHER EVERY HALF HOUR. THEN I GO TO THE TOES. THEN I GET CREATIVE. THE YARD, KEN. THREE HOURS.

The Ghost disconnected the line. He slammed the laptop closed and stood.

"Well," he said with the smile, "I think that went rather well, don't you?"

56

Nora called Squares on his cell phone. She gave him an abbreviated version of the events surrounding her disappearance. Squares listened without interruption, driving toward her all the way. They met up in front of the Metropolitan Life building on Park Avenue.

She hopped into the van and hugged him. It felt nice to be back in the outreach van.

"We can't call the police," Squares said.

She nodded. "Will was firm on that one."

"So what the hell can we do?"

"I don't know. But I'm scared, Squares. Will's brother told me about these people. They'll kill him, for sure."

Squares mulled it over. "How do you and Ken communicate?"

"Via a computer newsgroup."

"Let's get him a message. Maybe he'll have an idea."

The Ghost kept his distance.

Time was growing short. I stayed alert. If there was an opening, any opening, I was going to risk it. I palmed the broken bottle and studied his neck. I rehearsed in my mind how it might go. I tried to calculate what defensive move the Ghost might make and how I could counter it. Where, I wondered, were his arteries located? Where was he most vulnerable, his flesh the softest?

I glanced at Katy. She was holding up well. I thought again about what Pistillo had said, how adamant he had been that I leave Katy Miller out of this. He was right. This was my fault. When she first asked to help, I should have refused. I had put her at risk. The fact that I was indeed trying to help her, that I understood better than most how much she craved closure, did little to ease my guilt.

I had to find a way to save her.

I looked back at the Ghost. He stared at me. I did not blink.

"Let her go," I said.

He faked a yawn.

"Her sister was good to you."

"So?"

"There's no reason to hurt her."

The Ghost raised his palms and in that hushed-lisp, he said, "Who needs a reason?"

Katy closed her eyes. I stopped then. I was just making it worse. I checked the clock. Two hours to go. "The yard," a spot where pot smokers used to gather after a fun-filled day at Heritage Middle School, was no more than three miles from here. I knew why the Ghost had picked it. The site was easy to control. It was secluded, especially in the summer months. And once in, there would be little chance of getting out alive.

The Ghost's cell phone rang. He looked down at it as if he'd never heard the sound before. For the first time, I saw something that might have been confusion cross his face. I tensed, though I did not dare reach for the broken glass. Not yet. But I was ready.

He flicked on the cell and put it to his ear. "Go," he said.

He listened. I studied his colorless face. His expression remained calm, but something was happening here. He blinked more. He checked his watch. He did not speak for nearly two full minutes. Then he said, "I'm on my way."

He rose and walked toward me. He lowered his mouth toward my ear. "If you move from this chair," he said, "you'll beg me to kill her. Do you understand?"

I nodded.

The Ghost left, closing the door behind me. The room was

311

dark. The light was starting to fade, shafts breaking through the leaves. There were no windows in the front, so I had no way of knowing what they were doing.

"What's going on?" Katy whispered.

I put a finger to my lips and listened. An engine turned over. A car started up. I thought about his warning. Do not leave this seat. The Ghost was someone you wanted to obey, but then again, he was going to kill us anyway. I bent at the waist and dropped off the chair. It was not the smoothest move. Rather spastic, in fact.

I looked over at Katy. Our eyes met and again I signaled her to remain silent. She nodded.

I stayed as low as possible and crawled carefully toward the door. I would have gone to my belly and done it commando-style, but the small shards of glass would have ripped right through me. I moved slowly, trying not to cut myself.

When I reached the door, I put my head against the floorboard and peeked through the crack at the bottom. I saw the car drive off. I tried to get a better angle, but it was tough. I sat up and pressed my eye against the side crack. It was harder to see here. The opening was barely a slit. I rose a little and bang, there he was.

The driver.

But where was the Ghost?

I did the quick calculation. Two men, one car. One car drives off. I am not much with math, but that meant that only one man could be left. I turned to Katy. "He's gone," I whispered.

"What?"

"The driver is still here. The Ghost drove off."

I moved back toward my chair and picked up the large piece of broken glass. Stepping as gently as possible, fearing that even the slightest weight change could shake the structure, I made my way back behind Katy's chair. I sawed at the rope.

"What are we going to do?" she whispered.

"You know a way out of here," I said. "We'll make a run for it."

"It's getting dark."

"That's why we do it now."

"The other guy," she said. "He could be armed."

"He probably is, but would you rather wait for the Ghost to come back?"

She shook her head. "How do you know he's not coming back right now?"

"I don't." The rope cut through. She was free. She rubbed her wrists as I said, "You with me?"

She looked at me and I thought maybe it was the same way I used to look at Ken, that mixture of hope and awe and confidence. I tried to look brave, but I've never been the hero type. She nodded.

There was one window in the back. My plan, as it were, was to open it, climb out, and crawl through the woods. We would try to keep quiet as possible, but if he heard us, we would break into a run. I was counting on the fact that the driver was either unarmed or not supposed to wound us too seriously. They'd have to figure that Ken would be careful. They'd want to keep us alive—well, me anyway—to bait their trap.

Or maybe not.

The window was stuck. I pulled and pushed against the frame. Nothing. It had been painted over a million years ago. No chance of opening it.

"Now what?" she asked.

Cornered. The feeling of a cornered rat. I looked at Katy. I thought about what the Ghost had said, how I had somehow not protected Julie. I would not let that happen again. Not to Katy.

"Only one way out of here," I said. I looked at the door.

"He'll see us."

"Maybe not."

I pressed my eye against the crack. The sunlight was fading. The shadows had picked up strength. I saw the driver. He sat on a tree stump. I saw the ember from the end of his cigarette, a steady marker in the dark.

His back was turned.

I put the broken-glass shiv in my pocket. I signaled with a lowering palm for Katy to bend down. I reached for the knob. It turned easily. The door creaked when it opened. I stopped and looked out. The driver was still not looking. I had to risk it. I pushed the door open more. The squeak quieted. I stopped the door after only a foot. Enough to squeeze through.

Katy looked up at me. I nodded. She crawled through the door. I bent down and followed. We were both outside now. We lay flat on the platform. Totally exposed. I closed the door.

He still had not turned around.

Okay, next step: how to get off the platform. We couldn't use the ladder. It was too out in the open. I gestured for Katy to follow

313

me. We slid on our bellies toward the side. The platform was aluminum. That made it easier. No friction or splinters.

We reached the side of the shack. But when I turned the corner, I heard a noise not unlike a groan. And then something fell. I froze. A beam under the platform had given way. The whole structure swayed.

The driver said, "What the hell . . . ?"

We ducked low. I pulled Katy toward me, so that she was on the side of the shack too. He couldn't see us now. He'd heard the noise. He looked. He saw the door closed and the platform seemingly empty.

He shouted, "What the hell are you two doing in there?"

We both held our breath. I heard the crunch of leaves. I'd been prepared for this. I already had something of a plan in mind. I braced myself. And then he yelled again.

"What the hell are you two—?"

"Nothing," I shouted, pressing my mouth against the side of the shack, hoping my voice sounded muffled, as if it were coming from the inside. I had to risk this. If I didn't answer, he would definitely check it out. "This shack is a piece of crap," I said. "It keeps shifting on us."

Silence.

We both held our breaths. Katy pressed herself against me. I could feel her shivering. I patted her back. It would be all right. Sure, we were just fine. I strained my ears and tried to pick up the sound of his footsteps. But I heard nothing. I looked at her, urging her to crawl toward the back with my eyes. She hesitated but not for long.

My new plan, as it were, was to shimmy down the pole in the back corner. She would go first. If he heard her, a seemingly likely event, well, I had a plan of sorts for that too.

I pointed the way. She nodded, clear-eyed now, and moved toward the pole. She slid off and held on to the pole, firefighter-style. The platform lurched again. I stared helplessly as the platform wobbled some more. There was the groaning noise again, louder now. I saw a screw come loose.

"What the . . ."

But this time, the driver did not bother calling out. I could hear him moving toward us. Still holding on, Katy looked up at me.

"Jump down and run!" I shouted.

She let go and fell to the ground. The fall was not that far. After she landed, she looked back at me, waiting.

"Run!" I shouted again.

The man now: "Don't move or I'll shoot."

"Run, Katy!"

I threw my legs over the side and let go. My fall was somewhat longer. I landed hard. I remembered reading somewhere that you're supposed to land with knees bent and roll. I did that. I rolled into a tree. When I stood, I saw the man coming at us. He was maybe fifteen yards away. His face was twisted in rage.

"You don't stop, you're dead."

But he didn't have a gun in his hand.

"Run!" I shouted to Katy again.

"But—" she said.

"I'm right behind you! Go!"

She knew I was lying. I had accepted this as part of the plan. My job now was to slow down our adversary—slow him down enough so that Katy could escape. She hesitated, not liking the idea of my sacrifice.

He was almost on us.

"You can get help," I urged. "Go!"

She finally obeyed, leaping over the roots and high grass. I was already reaching into my pocket when the man leveled me with a tackle. The blow was bone-jarring, but I still managed to wrap my arms around him. We tumbled down together. This, too, I had learned someplace. Almost every fight ends up on the ground. In the movies, fighters punch and go down. In real life, people lower their heads and grab their opponents and end up in a grapple. I rolled with him, taking some hits, concentrating on the shiv in my hand.

I gave him a bear hug, squeezing him as tight as I could, though I knew I was not really hurting him. Didn't matter. It would slow him down. Every second counted. Katy would need the lead. I held on tight. He struggled. I would not let go.

That was when he landed the head butt.

He reared back and struck my face with his forehead. I have never been head-butted before, but it hurts like nothing else. It felt as though a wrecking ball had smashed into my face. My eyes watered up. My grip went slack. I fell away. He wound up for another blow, but something instinctive made me turn away, curl into a ball. He rose to his feet. He aimed a kick at my ribs.

But it was my turn now.

I prepared myself. I let the kick land and quickly trapped his foot against my stomach with one hand. With the other, I held the broken glass. I jammed it into the fat of his calf. He screamed as the glass sliced deep into his flesh. The sound echoed. Birds scattered. I pulled it out and stabbed again, this time in the hamstring area. I felt the warm gush of blood.

The man dropped and began to flail, fish-on-the-hook-style.

I was about to strike again when he said, "Please. Just go."

I looked at him. His leg hung useless. He would not be a threat to us. Not now anyway. I was not a killer. Not yet. And I was losing time. The Ghost might be back soon. We needed to get away before that.

So I turned and ran.

After twenty or thirty yards I looked behind me. The man was not pursuing me. He was struggling to a crawl. I started running again when I heard Katy's voice call, "Will, over here!"

I turned and spotted her.

"This way," she said.

We ran the rest of the way. Branches whipped our face. We stumbled on roots, but we never fell. Katy was good to her word. Fifteen minutes later, we headed out of the woods and onto Hobart Gap Road.

When Will and Katy emerged from the woods, the Ghost was there.

He watched from a distance. Then he smiled and stepped back into his car. He drove back and began the cleanup. There was blood. He had not expected that. Will Klein continued to surprise and, yes, impress him.

That was a good thing.

When he was done, the Ghost drove down South Livingston Avenue. There was no sign of Will or Katy. That was okay. He stopped at the mailbox on Northfield Avenue. He hesitated before dropping the package through the slot.

It was done.

The Ghost took Northfield Avenue to Route 280 and then the

Garden State Parkway north. It would not be long now. He thought about how this had all begun, and how it should end. He thought about McGuane and Will and Katy and Julie and Ken.

But most of all, he thought about his vow and why he had come back in the first place.

57

A lot happened in the next five days.

After our escape, Katy and I naturally contacted the authorities. We led them to the site where we'd been held. No one was there. The shack was empty. A search found traces of blood near where I'd stabbed the guy in the leg. But there were no prints or hairs. No clues at all. Then again, I had not expected there to be. And I was not sure it mattered.

It was nearly over.

Philip McGuane was arrested for the murder of an undercover federal officer named Raymond Cromwell and a prominent attorney named Joshua Ford. This time, however, he was held without bail. When I met with Pistillo, he had the satisfied gleam in the eye of a man who had finally conquered his own Everest, unearthed his own special chalice, conquered his toughest personal demon, however you want to put it.

"It's all falling apart," Pistillo said with a little too much glee. "We got McGuane nailed on a murder charge. The whole operation is ripping at the seams."

I asked him how they finally caught him. Pistillo, for once, was only too happy to share.

"McGuane made up this phony surveillance tape showing our agent leaving his office. This was supposed to be his alibi, and let me tell you, the tape was flawless. That's not hard to do with digital technology—at least, that's what the lab guy told me."

"So what happened?"

Pistillo smiled. "We got another tape in the mail. Postmarked from Livingston, New Jersey, if you can believe it. The real tape. It shows two guys dragging the body into the private elevator. Both men have already flipped and turned state's evidence. There was a note, too, telling us where we could find the bodies. And to top it off, the package also had the tapes and evidence your brother gathered all those years ago."

I tried to figure that one out, but nothing came to me. "Do you know who sent it?"

"Nope," Pistillo said, and he did not seem to care very much.

"So what happens to John Asselta?" I asked.

"We have an APB out on him."

"You've always had an APB out on him."

He shrugged. "What else can we do?"

"He killed Julie Miller."

"Under orders. The Ghost was just hired muscle."

That was hardly comforting. "You don't think you'll get him, do you?"

"Look, Will, I'd love to nail the Ghost, but I'll be honest with you. It won't be easy. Asselta is out of the country already. We have reports of him overseas. He'll get work with some despot who will protect him. But in the end—and it's important to remember this— the Ghost is just a weapon. I want the guys who pull the trigger."

I did not agree but I did not argue either. I asked him what this all meant for Ken. He took a while before answering.

"You and Katy Miller haven't told us everything, have you?"

I shifted in my seat. We had told them about the kidnapping, but we decided not to tell them about communicating with Ken. We kept that to ourselves. I said, "Yes, we did."

Pistillo held my gaze and then shrugged again. "The truth is, I don't know if we need Ken anymore. But he's safe now, Will." He leaned forward. "I know you haven't been in touch with him"—and I could see in his face that this time he did not believe that—"but if you somehow manage to reach him, tell him to come in from the cold. It's never been safer. And okay, yes, we could use him to verify that old evidence."

Like I said, an active five days.

Aside from my meeting with Pistillo, I spent that time with Nora. We talked about her past but not very much. The lingering shadows kept crossing her face. The fear of her ex-husband remained enormous. It enraged me, of course. We would have to deal with this Mr. Cray Spring of Cramden, Missouri. I didn't know how. Not yet. But I would not let Nora live in fear for the rest of her life. No way.

Nora told me about my brother, how he'd had money stashed away in Switzerland, how he spent his days hiking, how he seemed to seek peace out there and how peace seemed to elude him. Nora talked about Sheila Rogers too, the wounded bird I'd learned so much about, who found nourishment in both the international chase and her daughter. But mostly, Nora told me about my niece, Carly, and when she did, her face lit up. Carly loved to run down hills with her eyes closed. She was a voracious reader and loved to do cartwheels. She had the most infectious laugh. At first, Carly had been lonely and shy with Nora—her parents, for obvious reasons, did not let her socialize much—but Nora had patiently worked past that. Abandoning the child (abandoning was the word she used, though I thought it was too harsh), taking away the only friend Carly had been allowed to have—had been the hardest part for Nora.

Katy Miller kept her distance. She had gone away—she didn't tell me where and I didn't push it—but she called almost every day. She knew the truth now, but in the end, I don't think it helped much. With the Ghost still out there, there would be no closure. With the Ghost still out there, we both looked over our shoulders more than we should.

We were all living in fear, I guess.

But for me, closure was drawing near. I just needed to see my brother, maybe now more than ever. I thought about his lonely years. I thought about those long hikes of his. That was not Ken. Ken would never be happy like that. Ken was in your face. Ken was not one for hiding in shadows.

I wanted to see my brother again for all the old reasons. I wanted to go to a ball game with him. I wanted to play one-on-one. I wanted to stay up late and watch old movies with him. But, of course, now there were new reasons too.

I mentioned earlier that Katy and I kept our contact with Ken a secret. That was so Ken and I could keep our lines of communication open. What we eventually arranged was an Internet newsgroup switch. I told Ken not to let death scare him, hoping he'd pick up the clue. He did. Again it harks back to our childhood. Don't Fear Death aka Ken's favorite song, Blue Oyster Cult's "Don't Fear the Reaper." We found a board that posted information on the old heavy metal band. There were not many posts, but we managed to set up times to IM each other.

Ken was still being cautious, but he wanted this to end too. I still had Dad and Melissa, and I had spent the last eleven years with our mother. I missed Ken like mad, but I think that maybe he missed us more.

Anyway, it took some preparation, but eventually Ken and I set up a reunion.

When I was twelve and Ken was fourteen, we went to a summer camp in Marshfield, Massachusetts, named Camp Millstone. The camp was advertised as being "On Cape Cod!" which, if true, made the cape take up nearly half the state. The cabins were all named for colleges. Ken bunked in Yale. I bunked in Duke. We loved our summer there. We played basketball and softball and participated in blue-gray color wars. We ate crappy food and that appealingly dubbed camp succor "bug juice." Our counselors were both fun and sadistic. Knowing what I know now, I would never in a million years send a kid of my own to sleep-away camp. But I loved it.

Does that make sense?

I took Squares to see Camp Millstone four years ago. The camp was in foreclosure, so Squares bought the property and turned it into an upscale yoga retreat. He built himself a farmhouse on what had been Camp Millstone's soccer field. There was only one path in and out, and the farmhouse was in the middle of the field, so you could see anyone approaching.

We agreed that it would be the perfect reunion spot.

Melissa flew in from Seattle. Because we were extra-paranoid, we had her land in Philadelphia. She, my father, and I met at the Vince Lombardi Rest Stop on the New Jersey Turnpike. The three of us drove up together. No one else knew about the reunion, except

Nora, Katy, and Squares. The three of them were traveling up separately. They'd meet with us tomorrow because they, too, had an interest in closure.

But tonight, the first night, would be for the immediate family only.

I handled the driving duties. Dad sat in the passenger seat next to me. Melissa was in the back. No one did much talking. The tension pressed against our chests—mine, I think, most of all. I had learned not to assume anything. Until I saw Ken with my own eyes, until I hugged him and heard him speak, I would not let myself believe that it was finally okay.

I thought about Sheila and Nora. I thought about the Ghost and the high school class leader Philip McGuane and what he had become. It should have surprised me, but I'm not sure it did. We are always "shocked" when we hear about violence in the suburbs, as though a well-watered lawn, a split-level construction, Little League and soccer moms, piano lessons, Four Squares courts, and parent-teacher conferences, all worked as some sort of wolfsbane, warding off evil. If the Ghost and McGuane grew up just nine miles from Livingston—again, that was how far the heart of Newark was—no one would be "stunned" and "dismayed" by what they'd become.

I put in a CD of Springsteen's Summer 2000 concert in Madison Square Garden. It helped pass the time but not a lot. There was construction on Route 95—again, try to find a time when there isn't—and the ride took an agonizing five hours. We pulled up to the red farmhouse complete with fake silo. There were no other cars. That was to be expected. We were supposed to arrive first. Ken would follow.

Melissa got out of the car first. The sound of her door echoed across the field. When I stepped out, I could still visualize the old soccer field. The garage sat right where one goalpost used to be. The driveway ran across where the benches once were. I looked over at my father. He looked away.

For a moment, the three of us just stood there. I broke the spell, moving toward the farmhouse. Dad and Melissa trailed a few feet behind. We were all thinking about Mom. She should have been here. She should have had the chance to see her son one more time. That, we all realized, would have awakened the Sunny smile.

Nora had given comfort to my mother by giving her a photograph. I cannot tell you how much that will always mean to me.

Ken, I knew, would be coming alone. Carly was someplace safe. I did not know where. We rarely mentioned her during our communications. Ken might risk himself by attending this reunion. He would not risk his daughter. I, of course, understood.

We paced about the house. Nobody wanted anything to drink. There was a spinning wheel in one corner. The grandfather clock's tick-tocking was maddeningly loud in the still room. Dad finally sat. Melissa moved toward me. She looked up with her big-sister eyes and whispered, "Why doesn't it feel like the nightmare is about to end?"

I didn't even want to consider that.

Five minutes later, we heard an approaching car.

We all rushed to the window. I pushed back the curtain and peered out. It was dusk now. I could see just fine. The car was a gray Honda Accord, a totally inconspicuous pick. My heart picked up a step. I wanted to rush out, but I stayed where I was.

The Honda came to a stop. For several seconds—seconds kept by that damn grandfather clock—nothing happened. Then the driver's door opened. My hand gripped the curtain so hard it nearly ripped. I saw a foot hit the ground. And then someone slid out of the car and stood.

It was Ken.

He smiled at me, the Ken smile, that confident, let's-kick-life's-ass smile. That was all I needed. I let out a yelp of joy and broke for the door. I threw it open, but Ken was already sprinting toward me. He burst into the house and tackled me. The years melted away. Just like that. We were on the floor, rolling across the carpet. I giggled like I was seven. I heard him laugh too.

The rest of it was a wonderful blur. Dad jumped on. Then Melissa. I see it now in fuzzy snapshots. Ken hugging Dad; Dad grabbing Ken around the neck and kissing the top of his head, holding the kiss, his eyes squeezed shut, tears streaming down his cheeks; Ken spinning Melissa in the air; Melissa crying, patting her brother as if to make sure he was really there.

Eleven years.

I don't know how long we acted like that, how long we were that marvelous, delirious mess. Somewhere along the way, we calmed down enough to sit on a couch. Ken kept me close. On several occasions, he put me in a headlock and gave me "nuggies." I never knew being hit on the top of the head could feel so good.

"You took on the Ghost and survived," Ken said, my head in his armpit. "Guess you don't need me covering your back anymore."

And pulling away, I said in a desperate plea, "No, I do."

Darkness fell. We all went outside. The night air felt wonderful in my lungs. Ken and I walked ahead. Melissa and Dad stayed ten yards or so back, perhaps sensing that was what we wanted. Ken had his arm around my shoulders. I remember once during that year at camp I missed a key foul shot. My bunk lost the game because of that. My friends started picking on me. No big deal. It's camp. It happens to everyone. Ken took me for a walk that day. His arm was around me then too.

I felt that same kind of safe again.

He started telling me the story. It pretty much matched what I already knew. He had done some bad things. He had made a deal with the feds. McGuane and Asselta had found out.

He skittered around the question of why he had returned home that night, and more to the point, why he had been at Julie's house. But I wanted it all out in the open. There had been too much deception already. So I asked him flat out: "Why did you and Julie come home?"

Ken took out a pack of cigarettes.

"You smoke now?" I said.

"Yeah, but I'll give it up." He looked at me and said, "Julie and I thought it would be a good place to meet up."

I remembered what Katy said. Like Ken, Julie had not been home in more than a year. I waited for him to go on. He stared at the cigarette, still not lighting it.

"I'm sorry," he said.

"It's okay."

"I knew you were still hung up on her, Will. But I was taking drugs back then. I was a total shit. Or maybe none of that mattered. Maybe I was just being selfish, I don't know."

"It doesn't matter," I said. And that was true. It didn't. "But I still don't understand. How was Julie involved?"

"She was helping me."

"Helping you how?"

Ken lit the cigarette. I could see the lines on his face now. His features were chiseled but weathered now, making him almost more handsome. His eyes were still pure ice. "She and Sheila had an apartment near Haverton. They were friends." He stopped, shook his head. "Look, Julie got hooked on the stuff. It's my fault. When Sheila came up to Haverton, I introduced them. Julie fell into the life. She started working for McGuane too."

I had guessed that it was something like that. "She was selling drugs?"

He nodded. "But when I got caught, when I agreed to go back in, I needed a friend—an accomplice to help me take down McGuane. We were terrified at first, but then we all saw it as a way out. A way to find redemption, you know what I mean?"

"I guess."

"Anyway, they were watching me closely. But not Julie. There was no reason to suspect her of anything. She helped me smuggle out incriminating documents. When I made tapes, I'd pass them on to her. That was why we met up that night. We finally had enough information. We were going to give it to the feds and end this whole mess."

"I don't understand," I said. "Why would you guys keep the stuff yourself? Why not just turn everything over to the feds as you got it?"

Ken smiled. "You met Pistillo?"

I nodded.

"You have to understand, Will. I'm not saying all cops are corrupt or anything. But some are. I mean, one of them told McGuane I was in New Mexico. But more than that, some of them, like Pistillo, are too damn ambitious. I needed a bargaining chip. I couldn't leave myself that exposed. I had to turn it over on my own terms."

That, I thought, made sense. "But then the Ghost found out where you were."

"Yes."

"How?"

We reached a fence post. Ken put his foot up. I looked behind me. Melissa and Dad were keeping their distance. "I don't know, Will. Look, Julie and I were both so scared. Maybe that was part of it. Anyway, we were reaching the endgame. I thought we were home free. We were in the basement, on that couch, and we started kissing. . . ." He looked off again.

325

"And?"

"Suddenly there was a rope around my neck." Ken took a deep drag. "I was on top of her, and the Ghost had sneaked up on us. Next thing I knew, my air was gone. I was being strangled. John pulled back hard. I thought my neck would snap. I'm not even sure what happened next. Julie hit him, I think. That's how I got loose. He punched her in the face. I pulled away and started backing up. The Ghost took out a gun and fired. The first shot hit my shoulder." He closed his eyes.

"I ran then. God help me, I just ran."

We both soaked in the night. I could hear the crickets, but they played softly. Ken worked on his cigarette some more. I knew what he was thinking. Ran away. And then she died.

"He had a gun," I said. "It's not your fault."

"Yeah, sure." But Ken did not appear convinced. "You can probably guess what happened from there. I ran back to Sheila. We grabbed Carly. I had money stored away from my days working with McGuane. We took off, figuring that McGuane and Asselta would be close behind. It wasn't until a few days later, when the papers started listing me as a suspect in Julie's murder, that it hit me that I was not just running from McGuane but the whole world."

I asked the question that had been bothering me from the start. "Why didn't you tell me about Carly?"

His head snapped away as if I'd connected with a right on his jaw.

"Ken?"

He would not face me. "Can we skip that for now, Will?"

"I'd like to know."

"It's no big secret." His voice was strange now. I could hear the confidence start coming back, but it was somehow different, a shade off maybe. "I was in a dangerous spot. The feds captured me not long before her birth. I was afraid for her. So I didn't tell anybody she even existed. No one. I visited a lot, but I didn't even live with them. Carly stayed with her mother and Julie. I didn't want her connected to me in any way. You understand?"

"Yeah, sure," I said. I waited for him to say more. He smiled.

"What?"

"Just remembering camp," he said.

I smiled too.

"I loved it here," he said.

326

"Me too," I agreed. "Ken?"

"What?"

"How did you manage to hide for so long?"

He chuckled softly. Then he said, "Carly."

"Carly helped you hide?"

"My not telling anyone about her. I think it saved my life."

"How's that?"

"Everyone was looking for a fugitive on the run. That meant a single man. Or maybe a man who hooked up with a girl. What no one was looking for—and what could travel from spot to spot and remain invisible to law enforcement—was a family of three."

Again it made sense.

"The feds were lucky to catch me. I got careless. Or, I don't know, sometimes I think that maybe I wanted to be caught. Living like we were, always in fear, never putting down solid roots . . . it wears on you, Will. I missed you all so much. You most of all. Maybe I did let my guard down. Or maybe I needed it to end."

"So they extradited you?"

"Yeah."

"And you cut another deal."

"I thought they were going to pin Julie's murder on me for sure. But when I met up with Pistillo, well, he still wanted McGuane so badly. Julie was almost an afterthought. And they knew I hadn't done it. So . . ." He shrugged.

Ken talked then about New Mexico, about how he had never told the feds about Carly and Sheila, still protecting them. "I didn't want them to come back that early," he said, his voice softer now. "But Sheila wouldn't listen."

Ken told me about how he and Carly had been out of the house when the two men came by, how he came home and found them torturing his beloved, how he killed both men, and once again, how he ran. He told me how he stopped at the same pay phone and called Nora at my apartment—that would be the second call the FBI knew about. "I knew that they would come after her. Sheila's fingerprints were all over the house. If the feds didn't find her, McGuane might. So I told her she had to hide. Just until it was over."

It took a couple of days for Ken to find a discreet doctor in Las Vegas. The doctor had done what he could, but it was too late. Sheila Rogers, his eleven-year companion, died the next day. Carly

327

had been asleep in the back of the car when her mother drew her last breath. Not sure what else to do—and hoping it would take pressure off Nora—he put the body of his lover on the side of a road and drove away.

Melissa and Dad hovered closer now. We all let in a little silence.

"What then?" I asked softly.

"I dropped Carly off with a friend of Sheila's. A cousin actually. I knew she'd be safe there. Then I started making my way east."

And when he said that, when those words about making his way east left his mouth . . . that was when it all started to go wrong.

Have you ever had one of those moments? You are listening, you are nodding, you are paying attention. Everything seems to be making sense and following a logical course, and then you see something, something small, something seemingly irrelevant, something almost worth overlooking—and you realize with mounting dread that everything is terribly wrong.

"We buried Mom on a Tuesday," I said.

"What?"

"We buried Mom on Tuesday," I repeated.

"Right," Ken said.

"You were in Las Vegas that day, right?"

He thought about it. "That's right."

I played it over in my head.

"What is it?" Ken asked.

"I don't get something."

"What?"

"On the afternoon of the funeral"—I stopped, waited for him to face me, found his eyes—"you were at the other graveyard with Katy Miller."

Something flickered across his face. "What are you talking about?"

"Katy saw you at the cemetery. You were standing under a tree near Julie's tombstone. You told Katy you were innocent. You told her you were back to find the real killer. How did you do that if you were on the other side of the country?"

My brother did not respond then. We both stood there. I felt something inside me start shrinking even before I heard the voice that made my world teeter yet again.

"I lied about that."

328

We all turned as Katy Miller stepped out from behind the tree. I looked at her and said nothing. She moved closer.

Katy had a gun in her hand.

It was pointed at Ken's chest. My mouth dropped open. I heard Melissa gasp. I heard my father shout "No!" But that all seemed a light-year away. Katy looked directly at me, probing at me, trying to tell me something I could never understand.

I shook my head.

"I was only six years old," Katy said. "Easy enough to dismiss as a witness. What did I know anyway? Just a little kid, right? I saw your brother that night. But I saw John Asselta too. Maybe I mixed them up, the cops could say. How would a six-year-old know the difference between cries of passion and agony anyway? To a six-year-old, they're one and the same, aren't they? It was easy for Pistillo and his agents to finesse what I told them. They wanted McGuane. To them, my sister was just another suburban junkie."

"What are you talking about?" I said.

Her eyes turned to Ken. "I was there that night, Will. Hiding behind my father's old army trunk again. I saw everything." She looked at me again and I am not sure I ever saw such clear eyes.

"John Asselta didn't murder my sister," she said. "Ken did."

My support beams started giving way. I started shaking my head again. I looked at Melissa. Her face was white. I tried my father, but his head was down.

Ken said, "You saw us making love."

"No." Katy's voice was surprisingly steady. "You killed her, Ken. You chose strangulation because you wanted to pin it on the Ghost—the same way you strangled Laura Emerson because she threatened to report the drug selling at Haverton."

I stepped forward. Katy turned to me. I stopped.

"When McGuane failed to kill Ken in New Mexico, I got a call from Asselta," she began. Katy spoke as if she'd been rehearsing these lines for a long time, which, I suspect, she had. "He told me how they had already captured your brother in Sweden. I didn't believe him at first. I said, if they caught him, how come we didn't know about it? He told me how the FBI wanted to let Ken off because he could still deliver McGuane. I was in shock. After all this time, they were going to let Julie's murderer just walk away? I couldn't allow that. Not after what my family had been through. Asselta knew that, I guess. That was why he contacted me."

I was still shaking my head, but she pressed on.

"My job was to stay close because we figured that if Ken contacted anybody, it would be you. I made up that story about seeing him at the graveyard, so you would trust me."

I found my voice. "But you were attacked," I said. "In my apartment."

"Yes," she said.

"You even called out Asselta's name."

"Think about that, Will." Her voice was so even, so confident.

"Think about what?" I asked.

"Why were you cuffed to the bed like that?"

"Because he was going to set me up, the same way he set up—"

But now she was the one shaking her head. Katy gestured with the gun at Ken. "He cuffed you because he didn't want you to get hurt," she said.

I opened my mouth, but nothing came out.

"He needed to get me alone. He needed to find out what I'd told you—to see what I'd remembered—before he killed me. And yes, I called out John's name. Not because I thought it was him behind the mask. I called out to him for help. And you did save my life, Will. He would have killed me."

My eyes slowly slid toward my brother.

"She's lying," Ken said. "Why would I kill Julie? She was helping me."

"That's almost true," Katy said. "And you're right: Julie did see Ken's arrest as a chance for redemption, just like he told you. And yes, Julie had agreed to help bring McGuane down. But your brother took it a step too far."

"How?" I asked.

"Ken knew that he had to get rid of the Ghost too. No loose ends. And the way to do that was to frame Asselta for Laura Emerson. Ken figured that Julie would have no problem going along with that. But he was wrong. You remember how close Julie and John were?"

I managed a nod.

"There was a bond there. I don't pretend to know why. I don't think either of them could explain it either. But Julie cared about him. I think she was the only one who ever did. She would bring down McGuane. She would do that gladly. But she would never hurt John Asselta."

330

I couldn't speak.

"That's bull," Ken said. "Will?"

I did not look at him.

Katy continued. "When Julie found out what Ken was going to do, she called the Ghost to warn him. Ken came to our house to get the tapes and files. She tried to stall him. They had sex. Ken asked for the evidence, but Julie refused to give it to him. He grew livid. He demanded to know where she had hidden it. She wouldn't tell him. When he realized what was up, he snapped and strangled her. The Ghost arrived seconds too late. He shot Ken as he ran away. I think he would have gone after him, but when he saw Julie dead on the floor, he just lost it. He fell to the floor. He cradled her head and let out the most anguished, inhuman wail I've ever heard. It was like something inside of him broke that would never be fixed."

Katy closed the gap between us. She grabbed my gaze and would not let it go.

"Ken didn't run because he was afraid of McGuane or of being framed or any of that," she said. "He ran because he killed Julie."

I was tumbling down a deep shaft, reaching, trying to grab on to something. "But the Ghost," I said, flailing. "He kidnapped us. . . ."

"We set that up," she said. "He let us escape. What neither of us realized was that you'd be so willing and ready. That driver was only supposed to make it look good. We had no idea you'd hurt him so badly."

"But why?"

"Because the Ghost knew the truth."

"What truth?"

She again gestured toward Ken. "That your brother would never show just to save your life. He would never put himself in that danger. That something like this"—she lifted her free hand—"was the only way he'd ever agree to meet you."

I shook my head again.

"We had a man wait at the yard that night. Just in case. No one ever came."

I stumbled back. I looked at Melissa. I looked at my father. And I knew that it was all true. Every word that she said. It was true.

Ken had killed Julie.

"I never meant to hurt you," Katy said to me. "But my family needs closure. The FBI had set him free. I had no choice. I couldn't let him get away with what he did to my sister."

My father spoke for the first time. "So what are you going to do now, Katy? Are you just going to shoot him?"

Katy said, "Yes."

And that was when all hell broke loose again.

My father made the sacrifice. He let out a cry and dove toward Katy. She fired the gun. My father staggered and continued toward her. He knocked the weapon from her hands. He also went down, holding his leg.

But the distraction had been enough.

When I looked up, Ken had whipped out his own gun. His eyes—the ones I had described as pure ice—were focused on Katy. He was going to shoot her. There was no hesitation. He just had to aim and pull the trigger.

I jumped toward him. My hand hit his arm just as he pulled the trigger. The gun went off, but the shot was wild. I tackled my brother. We rolled on the ground again, but it was nothing like before. Not this time. He elbowed me in the stomach. It knocked the wind out of me. He rose. He pointed the gun at Katy.

"No," I said.

"I have to," Ken said.

I grabbed him. We wrestled. I told Katy to run. Ken quickly took the advantage. He flipped me over. Our eyes met.

"She's the last thread," he said.

"I won't let you kill her."

Ken put the barrel of the gun against my forehead. Our faces were no more than an inch apart. I heard Melissa scream. I told her to stay back. In the corner of my eye, I saw her take out a cell phone and start dialing.

"Go ahead," I said. "Pull the trigger."

"You think I won't?" he said.

"You're my brother."

"So?" And again I thought about evil, about the shapes it takes, how you are never truly safe from it. "Didn't you hear anything Katy said? Don't you understand what I'm capable of—how many people I've hurt and betrayed?"

"Not me," I said softly.

He laughed, his face still inches from mine, the gun still pressed against my forehead. "What did you say?"

"Not me," I repeated.

Ken threw his head back. His laugh grew, echoing in the still-

332

ness. The sound chilled me like no other. "Not you?" he said. He lowered his lips toward me.

"You," he whispered in my ear, "I've hurt and betrayed more than anyone."

His words hit me like cinder blocks. I looked up at him. His face tensed and I was sure he was going to pull the trigger. I closed my eyes and waited. There were shouts and commotion, but all of that seemed very far away. What I heard now—the only sound that really reached me—was Ken crying. I opened my eyes. The world faded away. There was just the two of us.

I can't say what happened exactly. Maybe it was the position I was in, on my back, helpless, and he, my brother, not my savior this time, not my protector, but looming over me, the cause of it all. Maybe Ken looked down and saw me vulnerable and something instinctive, something that had always needed to keep me safe, took over. Maybe that was what shook him. I don't know. But as our eyes met, his face began to soften, started shifting in degrees.

And then it all changed again.

I felt Ken's grip on me loosen, but he kept the gun against my forehead. "I want you to make me a promise, Will," he said.

"What?"

"It's about Carly."

"Your daughter."

Ken closed his eyes now, and I saw genuine anguish. "She loves Nora," he said. "I want you two to take care of her. You raise her. Promise me."

"But what about—?"

"Please," Ken said, his voice a desperate plea. "Please promise me."

"Okay, I promise."

"And promise me you'll never take her to see me."

"What?"

He was crying hard now. Tears ran down his cheeks, wetting both our faces. "Promise me, dammit. You never mention me to her. You raise her as your own. You never let her visit me in prison. Promise me that, Will. Promise me or I'll start firing."

"Give me the gun first," I said, "and I'll promise."

Ken looked down at me. He pushed the gun into my hand. And then he kissed me hard. I wrapped my arms around him. I held him, the murderer. I hugged him to me. He cried into my chest like a small child. We were like that for a long time, until we heard the sirens.

I tried to push him away. "Go," I whispered to him, pleading. "Please. Just run."

But Ken did not move. Not this time. I will never know why exactly. Maybe he had run enough. Maybe he was trying to reach through the evil. Maybe he just wanted to be held. I don't know. But Ken stayed in my arms. He held on to me until the police came over and pulled him away.

58

Four days later

Carly's plane was on time.

Squares dropped us off at the airport. He, Nora, and I headed toward Newark Airport's Terminal C together. Nora walked up ahead. She knew the child and was anxious and excited to see her again. Me, I was anxious and scared.

Squares said, "Wanda and I talked."

I looked at him.

"I told her everything."

"And?"

He stopped and shrugged. "Looks like we're both going to be fathers sooner than expected."

I hugged him, happy as hell for them both. I was not so sure about my own situation. I was about to raise a twelve-year-old girl I did not know. I would do my best, but despite what Squares had said, I could never be Carly's father. I had come to terms with a lot about Ken, including the possibility that he would probably spend the remainder of his life in prison, but his insistence on never seeing his daughter again gnawed at me. He wanted, I assume, to protect his child. He felt, again I assumed, that the girl was best off without him.

I say "assumed" because I could not ask him. Once in custody, Ken had refused to see me too. I did not know why, but his whispered words . . .

You I've hurt and betrayed more than anyone.

. . . kept echoing inside me, shredding with razor talons, inescapable.

Squares stayed outside. Nora and I rushed in. She was wearing the engagement ring. We were early, of course. We found the incoming gate and hurried down the corridor. Nora put her purse into the X-ray machine. I set the metal detector off, but it was just my watch. We rushed to the gate, though the plane was not due to touch down for another fifteen minutes.

We sat and held hands and waited. Melissa had decided to stay in town for a little while. She was nursing my father back to health. Yvonne Sterno had, as promised, gotten the exclusive story. I don't know what it will do for her career. I had not yet contacted Edna Rogers. I would soon, I guessed.

As for Katy, no charges had been filed following the shooting. I thought about how much she needed closure, and I wondered if that night had helped her or not. I think maybe it did.

Assistant Director in Charge Joe Pistillo had recently announced that he would retire at the end of the year. I now understood only too well why he was so eager for me to keep Katy Miller out of this—not just for her health but because of what she had seen. I don't know if Pistillo truly doubted the testimony of a six-year-old girl or if his sister's grieving face made him twist Katy's words to suit his purposes. I do know that the feds had kept Katy's old testimony under wraps, supposedly because they were trying to protect a little girl. But I have my doubts.

I had, of course, been crushed to learn the truth about my brother, and yet—this is going to sound odd—it was somehow okay. The ugliest truth, in the end, was still better than the prettiest of lies. My world was darker, but it was back on its axis.

Nora leaned over. "You okay?"

"Scared," I said.

"I love you," she said. "Carly will love you too."

We stared up at the arrivals monitor. It began to blink. The Continental Airlines gatekeeper picked up the microphone and announced that Flight 672 had landed. Carly's flight. I turned to Nora. She smiled and gave my hand another squeeze.

I let my eyes travel then. My gaze floated across the waiting passengers, the men in suits, the women with carry-ons, the families heading for vacation, the delayed, the frustrated, the worn. I casually swept over their faces and that was when I saw him looking at me. My heart stopped.

The Ghost.

A spasm ripped through me.

Nora said, "What?"

"Nothing."

The Ghost beckoned me toward him. I stood as though in a trance.

"Where are you going?"

"I'll be right back," I said.

"But she's going to be here."

"I just need to run to the bathroom."

I kissed the top of Nora's head gently. She looked concerned. She glanced across the gate, but the Ghost was no longer in sight. I knew better. If I walked, he would find me. Ignoring him would only make it worse. Running would be futile. He would ultimately find us.

I had to face him.

I started walking in the direction where he'd been. My legs felt rubbery, but I kept going. When I passed a long row of abandoned pay phones, I heard him.

"Will?"

I turned and he was there. He motioned for me to sit next to him. I did. We both faced the plate glass window rather than each other. The window magnified the rays. The heat was stifling. I squinted my eyes. So did he.

"I didn't come back for your brother," the Ghost said. "I came back for Carly."

His words turned me to stone. I said, "You can't have her."

He smiled. "You don't understand."

"Then tell me."

The Ghost shifted his body toward me. "You want people lined up, Will. You want the good guys on one side, the bad on the other. It doesn't work that way, does it? It is never that simple. Love, for example, leads to hate. I think that was what started it all. Primitive love."

"I don't know what you're talking about."

"Your father," he said. "He loved Ken too much. I look for the seed, Will. And that's where I find it. In your father's love."

"I still don't know what you're talking about."

337

"What I'm about to say," the Ghost continued, "I've only told one other person. Do you understand?"

I said that I did.

"You have to go back to when Ken and I were in the fourth grade," he said. "You see, I didn't stab Daniel Skinner. Ken did. But your father loved him so much that he protected him. He bought off my old man. Paid him five grand. Believe it or not, your father almost saw himself as charitable. My old man beat me all the time. Most people said I should be in foster care anyway. The way your father saw it, I would either get off on self-defense or end up getting therapy and three square meals a day."

I was stunned silent. I thought about our meeting up at the Little League field. My father's crippling fear, his icy silence when we got back, his telling Asselta, "You want someone, you take me." Once again it all made terrible sense.

"I only told one person the truth," he said. "Any guesses?"

Something else fell into place. "Julie," I said.

He nodded. The bond. It explained a lot about their strange bond.

"So why are you here?" I asked. "To take vengeance on Ken's daughter?"

"No," the Ghost said with a small laugh. "There is no easy way to tell you this, Will, but maybe science can help."

He handed me a folder. I looked down at it. "Open it," he said.

I did as he asked.

"It's the autopsy of the recently departed Sheila Rogers," he said.

I frowned. I didn't wonder how he got it. I was sure he had his sources. "What does this have to do with anything?"

"Look here." The Ghost pointed with a thin finger to an entry midway down. "You see down at the bottom? No scars on the pubic bone from the tears of the periosteum. No comments about pale striations over the breast and abdominal wall. Not unusual, of course. It wouldn't mean anything, unless you were looking for it."

"Looking for what?"

He closed the file. "Signs that the victim had given birth." He saw the look of confusion on my face and added, "Put simply, Sheila Rogers could not have been Carly's mother."

I was about to say something but the Ghost handed me another file. I looked at the name on it.

Julie Miller.

The cold spread inside me. He flipped it open and pointed to an entry and started reading, "Pubic scars, pale striations, changes in the microscopic architecture of the breast and uterine tissues," he said. "And the trauma was recent. See here? The scar from the episiotomy was still pronounced."

I stared at the words.

"Julie did not come home just to meet up with Ken. She was getting her act together after a very bad spell. She was finding herself again, Will. She wanted to tell you the truth."

"What truth?"

But he shook his head and continued. "She would have told you earlier, but she wasn't sure how you'd react. The way you so easily let her break up with you . . . that was what I meant when I said you were supposed to fight for her. You just let her go."

Our eyes locked.

"Julie had a baby six months before she died," the Ghost said. "She and the child, a girl, lived with Sheila Rogers in that apartment. I think Julie would have finally told you that night, but your brother took care of that. Sheila loved the child too. When Julie was murdered and your brother needed to escape, Sheila wanted to keep it as her own. And Ken, well, he saw how useful a baby could be to hide an international fugitive. He had no children. Neither did Sheila. It would be better than the best disguise."

Ken's whispered words came back to me. . . .

"Do you understand what I'm telling you, Will?"

You I've hurt and betrayed more than anyone.

The Ghost's voice cut through the haze. "You're not a substitute here. You're Carly's real father."

I don't think I was breathing anymore. I stared out at nothing. Hurt and betrayed. My brother. My brother had taken my child.

The Ghost stood. "I didn't come back for revenge or even justice," he continued. "But the truth is, Julie died protecting me. I failed her. I made a vow that I would save her child. It took me eleven years."

I stumbled to my feet. We stood side by side. Passengers were pouring off the plane. The Ghost jammed something in my pocket. A piece of paper. I ignored it.

"I sent that surveillance tape to Pistillo, so McGuane won't bother you. I found the evidence in the house that night and kept it all these years. You and Nora are safe now. I took care of every-thing."

More passengers disembarked. I stood and waited and listened.

"Remember that Katy is Carly's aunt, that the Millers are her grandparents. Let them be a part of her life. Do you hear me?"

I nodded, and that was when Carly came through the gate. Everything inside of me shut down. The girl walked out with such poise. Like . . . like her mother. Carly looked around and when she spotted Nora, her face broke into the most amazing smile. My heart broke. Right then and there, it shattered. The smile. That smile, you see, belonged to my mother. It was Sunny's smile, like an echo from the past, a sign that not all of my mother—nor all of Julie—had been extinguished.

I choked back a sob and felt a hand on my back.

"Go now," the Ghost whispered, gently pushing me toward my daughter.

I glanced back, but John Asselta was already gone. So I did the only thing I could. I made my way toward the woman I loved and my child.

EPILOGUE

Later that night, after I kissed Carly and helped her to bed, I found the piece of paper he'd jammed into my pocket. It was just the first few lines of a newspaper clipping:

KANSAS CITY HERALD

Man Found Dead in Car

Cramden, Mo.—Cray Spring, an off-duty police officer with the Cramden force, was found strangled in his car, apparently the victim of a robbery. His wallet was reportedly missing. Local police said his car was found in the parking lot behind a local bar. Police chief Evan Kraft said that there were no suspects at this time, and that the investigation was ongoing.

ACKNOWLEDGMENTS

The author wishes to thank the following for their technical expertise: Jim White, Executive Director, Covenant House Newark; Anne Armstrong-Coben, M.D., Medical Director, Covenant House Newark; Frank Gilliam, Outreach Manager, Covenant House Atlantic City; Mary Ann Daly, Director of Community Programs, Covenant House Atlantic City; Kim Sutton, Resident Manager, Covenant House Atlantic City; Steven Miller, M.D., Director of Pediatric Emergency Medicine, Children's Hospital of New York-Presbyterian, Columbia University; Douglas P. Lyle, M.D.; Richard Donnen (for the final push); Linda Fairstein, Manhattan Assistant District Attorney; Gene Riehl, FBI (retired); Jeffrey Bedford, FBI, Special Agent—all of whom provided the author with wonderful insights and now get to see him distort and dismiss them to suit his own purposes.

Covenant House is a real organization, though I took great liberties here. I made up a lot of stuff—that's why it's called fiction—but I tried to get the caring heart and soul of this important charity right. Those interested in helping or learning more should check out www.covenanthouse.org.

The author also wishes to thank his great team: Irwyn Applebaum, Nita Taublib, Danielle Perez, Barb Burg, Susan Corcoran, Cynthia Lasky, Betsy Hulsebosch, Jon Wood, Joel Gotler, Maggie Griffin, Lisa Erbach Vance, and Aaron Priest. You all mean a great deal to me.

To repeat: this is a work of fiction. That means I make stuff up.